Realm of Wind and Vines

BOOKS BY MARION BLACKWOOD

The Oncoming Storm

A Storm of Silver and Ash
A Storm of Shadows and Pearls
A Storm of Smoke and Flame
A Storm of Glass and Stars
A Storm of Mist and Thunder
A Storm of Blood and Swords
A Storm of Light and Darkness

***

Court of Elves

The Traitor Spy
The Wicked Betrayal
The Beautiful Liar
The Fire Soul
The Lethal Deception
The Desperate Gamble
The Last Stand

***

Ruthless Villains

Ruthless Villains
Wicked Villains
Heartless Villains
Vicious Villains
Merciless Villains

***

Ruthless Enemy

Ruthless Enemy
Wicked Enemy
Heartless Enemy

***

Flame and Thorns

Empire of Flame and Thorns
Throne of Ice and Blood
Court of Lies and Deceit
Realm of Wind and Vines

REALM OF WIND AND VINES

FLAME AND THORNS
BOOK FOUR

MARION BLACKWOOD

Copyright © 2025 by Marion Blackwood

All rights reserved. No part of this book may be reproduced in any form or by any electronic or mechanical means, including information storage and retrieval systems, without permission in writing from the publisher, except by reviewers, who may quote brief passages in a review. For more information, contact info@marionblackwood.com

ISBN 978-91-989043-8-3 (ebook)
ISBN 978-91-989043-9-0 (paperback)
ISBN 978-91-989044-0-6 (hardcover)
ISBN 978-91-989044-1-3 (special edition)

This is a work of fiction. Names, characters, places, and incidents either are the product of the author's imagination or are used fictitiously. Any resemblance to actual persons, living or dead, events, or locales is entirely coincidental.

www.marionblackwood.com

CONTENT WARNINGS

If you have specific triggers, you can find the full list of content warnings at: www.marionblackwood.com/content-warnings

For all of you who keep putting off doing what you really want while waiting for a perfect moment, because life is just too crazy right now.

There will never be a perfect moment.

Life is always crazy.

So start living it.

CHAPTER ONE

Winds tug at my hair, making it flutter behind me. The air tastes of salt and seaweed and freedom. Sunlight glitters like jewels in the endless water before me. I stare at it. The sea. It's breathtaking.

I have never seen the sea before. I didn't realize that it would be this massive. It's just water, spreading out completely uninterrupted. As far as the eye can see. An entire world of possibilities could be waiting there just on the other side of the horizon. The thought of it makes my heart flutter. When this is all over, I want to see it all. I want to see every inch of this world that I have been denied all my life while I was trapped in the Seelie Court.

My gaze flits to the west. Somewhere out there is the Western Isles. Draven's home. A mass of islands where the rest of the Black Dragon Clan are currently hiding. I wonder what it looks like.

A knife is pressed against my back.

I go still.

Even through my black fighting leathers, I can feel the tip of the blade firmly against my back, right by my left kidney.

"One small push is all it would take," a dark voice says from behind me.

My heart squeezes tight at the sound of Draven's voice. His dark and commanding voice that always makes my spine tingle. But now, ever since I forced a wildfire of hatred into his chest two weeks ago, every word he speaks to me is always laced with threats.

The overwhelming heartbreak inside me threatens to rise up again. A massive black wave, pressing in on me from all sides, suffocating me. But I know that if I let it crash over me, I am going to drown in it and never recover. So instead, I feed the rage and hatred burning in my own chest. It helps me block out the agonizing pain inside me and turns my heart into cold black ice.

"One small push," Draven repeats as he flexes his hand on the knife against my back, making it push a little harder against my fighting leathers. "And then this blade would puncture your kidney and you would fall over the edge of this cliff to drown in the sea below."

I resist the urge to look down at the sheer drop right before me. My toes are right at the edge of the cliff, and waves crash against the stones far below. Instead, I turn my head and meet Draven's gaze over my shoulder with a look full of challenge.

"If you really wanted me dead, you would've killed me already," I declare. "But you haven't. Because deep down, you know that you don't actually hate me."

Anger flits across his face, and he clenches his jaw. "Again with your desperate theories."

"It's not a theory. It's the truth. You love me. In order to save your life, I made you hate me by forcing a wildfire of hatred into your chest."

"No," he grinds out between gritted teeth.

We've had versions of this exact conversation several times in the past two weeks. I have tried to explain to him what really happened. I've tried to remind him of everything we have said and done for each other before this. I've tried to convince him with logic and truth. But every time, that unnatural flame of hatred that still burns fiercely in his chest finds excuses and explanations to justify itself. To condemn or even outright rewrite his past emotions to fit this newfound hatred.

"No," Draven repeats, more forcefully this time. The knife pushes harder against my back. "I hate you because I finally realized what you really are."

"And what's that?"

"Someone who ruins everything around you."

The words are a precision strike right through my heart. It's so violent that I almost gasp.

My mother's words echo through my mind. *You ruined us. You ruined everything.*

They're followed by the words of that Unseelie fae from the White Faction when she attacked me in that forest. *You ruined him! You ruined everything!*

Pain crackles through my chest like a vicious lightning bolt. I try to swallow it down, but I can't breathe. That oppressive wave of dark despair and crippling guilt inside me lurches in from all sides, wrapping around my chest like strangling vines. I try to draw in a breath, but no air makes it past my throat.

Panicked, I sweep my gaze over the area around us.

A short distance away, down on the sand beneath the cliffs, an old human man is fishing. Summoning my magic, I create a warm sparkling yellow flame of joy and shove it into his chest.

Pleasure floods my body.

Closing my eyes briefly, I inhale it like I'm starving. It's like floating on a perfect cloud. Like a warm sparkling hug. Like the perfect embrace telling me that everything will be okay. Every time I create emotions from nothing, I'm rewarded by this euphoric sensation. It's incredibly addictive, but it also helps smother the pain that flared up inside me, so I bask in that pleasure for another second before releasing my grip on my magic.

The connection to the old fisherman is broken, so the pleasure is gone, but I know that the unnatural flame of joy still remains inside him. Just like the hatred remains inside Draven.

Draven glances towards the fisherman, who has started to whistle now, but since Draven is standing behind me, he couldn't see that my eyes were glowing and therefore doesn't know what I just did. After presumably checking to make sure that the human isn't watching us, he focuses his attention back on me again.

"Do you know how much easier everyone's lives would be if you simply ceased to exist?" Draven snarls in my ear.

The pain tries to strangle me again, but with both the burning rage and hatred that now fills my soul as well as the lingering feeling of pleasure from when I created that emotion just now, it thankfully can't get through. So instead of feeling hurt, I let out a mocking scoff and arch an eyebrow at Draven over my shoulder.

"It's cute how you think that's going to hurt me." I give him a pointed look. "I grew up in a home where my parents told me that exact thing all the time, remember?"

A muscle flickers in his jaw, and he flexes his hand on the hilt of his blade again.

Just when I think he might actually follow through on his threat and ram that knife into my kidney, a voice echoes from the edge of the woods behind us.

"Oi!" Alistair bellows. "They're back. Let's go."

Draven remains looming behind me, his knife still at my back, for another second. Then he clicks his tongue in annoyance and spins on his heel before stalking back down the path. Turning around as well, I run a hand over my back where the knife used to be, but I can't feel any damage to the leather. Draven is already halfway to the trees.

I watch his powerful body as he expertly spins the blade in his hand and then slips it back into his thigh holster. Fire flickers through my veins. He is *mine*. And by all the gods and demons in hell, I will make sure he fucking remembers it.

Letting my hand drop back down again, I start down the path as well. Before I leave the edge of the cliff, I cast one last look at the old human fisherman. He is still whistling joyfully as he fishes down there on the beach below.

Deep down, I know that I should feel bad. Even though I gave him a positive emotion, I still changed his personality permanently. It's wrong. I know that. But I still can't bring myself to care. Because if I start to care about that, then I will start to care about everything else again too.

My gaze slides back to Draven as that world-ending pain tries to swallow me once more.

No. I can't care about the fisherman. Because then I will start to care about the way Draven looks at me now. And I will not survive that.

So I straighten my spine and leave behind the human whose life I permanently change without another thought as I instead follow Draven back to the tree line.

Alistair, who is also wearing the black fighting leathers that Jocasta gave us during the Great Games in the Unseelie Court, is leaning one shoulder against a tree trunk. His arms are crossed over his chest and there is a hint of impatience in his orange and green eyes as he watches us.

I'm thankful for it, because I hated the sympathy in everyone's eyes when they found out what happened to Draven. Alistair was one of the first to realize that, and he quickly started treating me and Draven as if nothing has changed. It honestly surprised me since I hadn't thought Alistair was that perceptive. But, as I've come to realize time and again, most of my preconceived notions about Alistair have turned out to be false.

"If you're done playing indecisive assassins, we've got a job to do," Alistair drawls as Draven and I reach him.

Draven cuts him a sidelong glance. "I could always practice my decisiveness on you, if you want."

"Uh-huh. You know, it's very difficult to stab someone with a blade that has been melted."

"Hard to melt a blade when it's already lodged in your back."

Alistair tips his head to the side, as if conceding the point. Pushing off from the tree trunk, he straightens and runs a hand through his curly blond hair before falling in beside us as we walk back into the woods towards where the rest of our companions are waiting.

When we come into view, Lyra and Galen immediately glance between me and Draven. They probably guessed what he was going to do when he left them to join me on the cliff, because a hint of relief flits across their faces when they see us.

Next to them, Isera watches us with that customary cold expression in her blue and silver eyes. She's one of the few who never gave me those awful sympathetic looks after she found out about what I had to do to Draven. She simply told me that I made the right choice and clapped me on the shoulder, and that was that. I don't think anything has ever made me like someone more than that simple act.

"It's clear," Isera declares while sweeping her long black hair off her shoulder. "No one from the Silver Clan is in the Seelie Court right now."

"We should still open the portal inside the thorn forest," Orion Nightbane adds, his black and silver eyes as sharp as ever. The spiky black crown on his head glints in the afternoon light as he cocks his head. The movement sends ripples through his long dark blue hair. "We just need an exact location."

"The opening where the river is pushed back up to the forest floor after being underground," I reply as we come to a halt in front of them.

Orion slides his gaze to the Unseelie fae with shoulder-length brown hair beside him. "You know it?"

Grey, the man with portal magic from the Unseelie Court, gives his king a nod. "Yes."

"Then let's get this over with."

A sparkling blue rectangle rises up from the ground as Grey summons a portal. My stomach twists and an unexpected pang of nausea rolls through me when the thorn forest around the Seelie Court becomes visible through that magical doorway.

Lyra claps her hands, startling everyone. But there is a bright smile on her lips as she strolls straight towards the portal. "Alright, let's go see the dryads."

Her genuine excitement dispels the heavy emotions that tried to settle over me. Straightening my spine, I draw in a deep breath.

Then I stride through the portal and back into the twisting thorn forest that has imprisoned me all my life.

CHAPTER TWO

Thorny vines cover the trees before me. They rustle in the warm wind, swaying like snakes waiting to strike, as I walk away from the portal to give the others room to move through as well. I suppress an involuntary shudder and turn away from the twisting forest to instead stare out at the city visible through the tree line.

A bright midday sun shines down over the grasslands that separate the forest from the lone city that currently makes up the entirety of the Seelie Court. From this distance, I can't see any of its inhabitants. But I know that they're there inside the city walls. Hungry and exhausted fae men and women who work their fingers to the bone in a once glorious city that is now nothing more than a backwater village.

After my visit to the capital of the Unseelie Court, the difference between their court and ours is glaringly obvious. I didn't realize it back when I lived here, because I had nothing to compare it to. But now that I've seen more of the world, I understand the true extent of what the Icehearts have done to us.

I suppress a bitter laugh. I felt like a child after I first left this court. I didn't know anything and I just believed the things that I had been told all my life. Finding out the truth was a harsh awakening, but one I desperately needed.

My gaze drifts towards the northern side of the city, where my parents live.

Another stab hits me straight to the chest. But this time, it's both pain and hope mixed together.

Back in the Unseelie Court, I not only found out the truth about our neighboring court, I also found out the truth about my own powers. A truth that my own mind has been blocking out and shielding me from almost my entire life.

That I can create emotions out of nothing. That doing so fills me with addictive pleasure. That the emotions I create are permanent.

And that I might have accidentally *made* my parents hate me with my magic.

That burst of pain and hope pulses in my chest as I stare at the pale stone walls of the city where my parents are waiting. All I need to do is to go down there and knock on their door. Then I can reach out with my magic and check. A few minutes. That's all I would need. And then I would know. Do my parents hate me of their own free will? Or has it been forced on them by my magic?

An embarrassingly large part of me wants to run down there right now and check, but I manage to suppress it. We have more pressing problems right now. But as soon as this is all over, I'm going to go back there and find out the truth. Whatever it may be.

"If you're just going to stand there and daydream like a useless piece of furniture, we'll leave you behind."

Tearing my gaze from the city before me, I turn around and meet Draven's harsh glare while arching an eyebrow in challenge. "Daydreaming? I was simply calculating how much space your scowl needs so that it doesn't cut anything down when you turn."

He blinks at me, looking stunned for a second, before drawing his eyebrows down and simply stalking away without another word. Lyra and Galen once more glance worriedly between the two of us. I pretend not to notice and instead start after Draven towards our entry point.

Alistair and Isera fall in beside me without a word. After giving Grey some instructions for when to return with the portal, Orion does the same. At last, Galen and Lyra exchange a glance and hurry to catch up as well.

The sound of rushing water fills the forest around us as we reach the spot where the River Andunir is pushed up through a hole in the ground before continuing to flow towards the lake beside the city. Draven has already stalked through and is making his way down the small hill below. I watch the way his muscular body moves while I follow him down into the underground forest where the dryads live.

I try to focus on why we're here. To recruit the dryads to our side so that we can hopefully win a war against two immortal dragon shifters who have ruled this continent for six millennia. But in this place, of all places, it's difficult to focus on anything other than my more personal problem. On *him*.

My heart beats erratically as we draw closer to the spot where the rock wall is located. The spot where I, for the first time, admitted to myself that I felt something for Draven. The spot where I finally acted on those burning emotions inside me.

Once we're almost there, I look more at Draven than my own two feet, and almost end up tripping over a root. Catching myself, I straighten again and then snap my gaze back to Draven. I wonder how he will react when we reach this spot. I know that he remembers. The unnatural hatred in his chest didn't wipe his memories. It's just forcing him to see his memories and his feelings through a manufactured lens of hatred. But maybe, just maybe, if we—

"This isn't a sprinting contest, you know," Orion snaps from somewhere behind.

"What's the matter, princeling? Can't keep up?" Draven replies without even turning to look.

"I find it quite amusing that you keep using the derogatory title *princeling* instead of my actual title. Could it be because you yourself are feeling insignificant now that your once prestigious Black Dragon Clan is hiding like rats and you're no longer the Commander of the Dread Legion?"

Draven comes to a halt right next to the rock wall. My heart leaps. Did the sight of it make him feel something other than hatred? I can barely remember to breathe as I close the distance to it as well.

But then Draven simply turns around and locks eyes with Orion instead, as if this place holds no special significance.

"Keep talking," Draven warns with a threatening smile. "See where that gets you."

Orion's eyes gleam, and he opens his mouth.

However, before he can say anything else, Isera cuts him off. "Enough." Then she turns to Draven and shoots him an impatient look. "Can't you see what he's doing, Ryat? Because he can't get out of this bargain himself, he's deliberately making himself as obnoxious as possible so that *you* will snap and send him back to the Unseelie Court instead."

A sly smile ghosts across Orion's lips, but it's gone by the time that Draven has finished shifting his gaze from Isera back to him. Draven arches an eyebrow at him. While still meandering slowly towards us, Orion lifts his toned shoulders in a lazy shrug in response to Draven's silent question. But his black and silver eyes are sharp when he gives Isera a sideways glance.

"Apparently, there is at least one person in this broken group of misfits who possesses some measure of intelligence." He clicks his tongue. "What a shame."

She scoffs. "Some measure?" Then a smile as sharp as a blade spreads across her lips. "Given that I outsmarted you and trapped you in this bargain, what does that say about you?"

Lightning flickers in his eyes.

While the two of them continue mocking and threatening each other while closing the final distance to us along with the rest of our companions, I shift my gaze back to Draven and once more search his face for any spark of recognition. There is nothing. He's just standing there, scowling at Orion.

Frustration and heartbreak rip through my soul, and that oppressive darkness presses in closer.

In a flash of stubborn defiance, I stalk the final two steps to the rock wall and lean against it. Then I pretend to stretch my arms above my head, mimicking the exact pose I was in when Draven pinned me to that rough stone surface and fucked me like I was his.

"Well," I drawl, leaning casually against the wall like that. "This brings back memories."

Draven turns towards me, already looking annoyed, with what is no doubt another angry curse on his lips. But then his gaze lands on me and he starts. Surprise flits across his face for a moment, and his gaze darts from me to the river where we bathed to get the green plant slime off, and then back to me.

Primal fire burns in his golden eyes for a second when he meets my gaze again.

And something *tugs* at my chest.

The feeling of it shocks me so much that I actually stumble, my arms dropping back down by my sides again. Draven gives his head a hard shake and then draws his eyebrows down in a scowl as he snaps his gaze back to the rest of our friends instead.

But I can barely concentrate on what's happening around me, because I'm still reeling from that tug.

Sucking in an unsteady breath, I stare down at my own chest.

Our mate bond is still broken. It still drifts there inside me like a violently snapped rope that ripples in the wind, seeking its other tether.

But that tug.

It was there. I felt it. It was real.

Tilting my head up, I stare at Draven while shock still rings inside my skull.

There was a tug on our mate bond. As if it tried to reattach itself. As if *he* tried to pull it back to himself.

I draw in another unsteady breath.

In the middle of that sea of dark despair and black rage that crowds my soul, a small spark of light suddenly blooms. Hope. That oppressive darkness inside me immediately tries to snuff it out, but it refuses to die. I lean into that small spark of hope with everything I have.

All is not yet lost. Draven is still in there. The real him is still fighting somewhere deep down underneath that massive flame of hatred that I forced into his chest. And if I can just figure out how to remove it, everything will be okay. The world will return to the way it should be. *He* will return.

I squeeze my hand into a fist as I cling to that tiny spark of light that now shines in the middle of the all-consuming darkness inside me.

There has to be a way to fix this.

There has to.

"Let's go," Draven declares once the others have caught up. "We're burning daylight."

"We're below ground," Alistair points out.

Draven turns his scowl on him.

"I also have fire magic," he continues with a helpful smile that seems specifically designed to annoy the scowling dragon shifter.

On his other side, Lyra presses her lips together to suppress a smile. When that doesn't work, she turns her whole head to hide her expression all together. Draven heaves a sigh and levels an exasperated look on Alistair. The snarky fire wielder just shrugs, that troublesome smile still on his lips.

However, they all pick up the pace a little as we start down the river again.

Once we reach the spot where Draven and I met up after we were ambushed by the dryads last time, we leave the river behind and start moving straight into the forest instead.

And then we walk.

Since the layers of thin tree trunks that make up the ceiling block out the view of the sun, I can't tell for certain how much time has passed, but I can feel the hours slipping away. Worry gnaws at my chest as I sweep my gaze over the endless forest before us while we make our way deeper into the woods.

Trees in all shapes and colors stare back at us impassively. Lyra jumps up gracefully and taps a thick branch above her as she passes it. It makes the branch shift slightly, rustling the beautiful pink leaves. A smile blows across Lyra's face as she watches it while she strolls past.

The sight of her easy smile dispels some of the tension in my chest. I'm glad she's here. I'm glad Draven has her friendship again. He needs it. In fact, I think we all need it. Between the seven of us, she might be the only one who actually contributes to the good mood at the moment.

"Enlighten me," Orion begins in a voice that somehow manages to sound both mocking and annoyed at the same time. "How did you find the dryads last time? Because it feels to me as if we're just wandering aimlessly through the forest."

Draven opens his mouth to reply, but given the irritation that flickers in his own eyes, I know that he's about to snap at the Unseelie King, which will just turn into another argument between the two of them.

So before he can get the first word out, I quickly reply, "We didn't. They kind of found us."

Orion shifts his gaze to me and arches a dark eyebrow. "So

what's the plan then? Just wander around hoping that they will find us again?"

"No, we know that they—"

Vines shoot out around me and wrap around my whole body.

I gasp as they snake around my wrists and ankles, quickly trapping me, but the sound is cut off as a thick vine slides between my teeth like a gag.

Then the world goes dark as another vine wraps around my head, blindfolding me as well.

CHAPTER THREE

A jolt shoots through my hip as I'm tossed to the ground. Vines are still wrapped around my body, keeping me immobile, gagged, and blindfolded. I let out a huff through the thick vine between my teeth while more thuds sound around me as my friends are no doubt deposited on the ground as well.

Abruptly, the vines pull back.

"Have I mentioned how much I fucking hate forests?" Alistair grumbles from somewhere on my left.

Pushing up to my knees, I blink against the sudden light.

My jaw drops open as I stare at the incredible scenery before me. Trees as thick as houses rise up like giants before us. From the glowing light that twinkles from holes in the massive trunks, there appears to be dwellings inside. Though there are no steps leading up to them. Only vines that ripple down along the bark. High above, vibrant green leaves rustle in the wind as the trees reach towards the heavens above.

I stare at the late afternoon sky, streaked with pink and gold. I have no idea where we were taken, but apparently, we are no longer underground.

"It was very foolish of you to come back here a second time," a familiar voice says.

Lowering my gaze back down from the imposing trees and the colorful sky above, I give my head a quick shake and blink at the source of the voice.

A woman made of the woods stands before me. Her dress is made of vines and leaves, with a few thin branches to add structure to it, and it pools around her like a green waterfall with specks of brown. It complements her pale green skin and deep brown eyes, making her truly look like an embodiment of the forest. The only other color she wears comes from the red flowers that grow around her head like a crown. Her long hair, made of fine vines and highlighted with beautiful leaves, ripples around her as if on a phantom wind.

It's her. The dryad leader, whose name I don't know, but who I have come to think of as the Dryad Queen.

I quickly scramble to my feet.

"We forgave your trespassing once because it was an accident," she says, her voice low and smooth but with a sharp edge of threat to it. "But now you have returned of your own free will."

I open my mouth to say something intelligent that I still haven't quite figured out, but before any words can make it out, we are all startled out of our stupor by what can only be classified as an excited squeal.

Everyone starts in surprise as Lyra jumps to her feet with another excited squeak. Her wavy brown hair flutters around her face with the sudden movement, but she just tosses it out of her face while grinning broadly. Her orange eyes practically sparkle in the golden afternoon sunlight when she meets the Dryad Queen's gaze.

"Hi!" Lyra blurts out.

The Dryad Queen blinks at her.

"Azaroth's flame, I'm so excited to meet you!" Lyra continues, the words spilling out of her mouth so fast that she almost trips over them. "When they told me they had actually met you last year, I was honestly a little skeptical because, like, no one has met a dryad. Well, no one I know, at least. Anyway, part of me was thinking that maybe they were just messing with me. But now here you are and here is your city and here we are and oh my god it's so exciting to meet you!"

To be honest, I didn't think that this wise and ancient dryad was even capable of looking shocked. Mabona's tits, was I wrong.

The Dryad Queen stares at Lyra with such a comically stunned expression on her face that I have to swallow down a very untimely burst of laughter. Her mouth is slightly open, and it looks like she had an entire speech planned that she can no longer remember because this grinning dragon shifter just threw the entire interaction off its logical course.

"Uhm, did you miss the part where she was in the middle of threatening us?" Alistair says, and arches an eyebrow at Lyra.

And that's when I notice that there is an entire circle of dryads surrounding us with drawn bows and arrows pointed at us. They, however, look equally stunned and keep glancing between Lyra and their queen.

"Oh, right!" Lyra slaps her forehead, as if she just realized that she interrupted a threatening monologue, and then waves her hand at the Dryad Queen. "Sorry. Go ahead and finish."

Galen lets out something between a sigh and a chuckle while Draven shakes his head and tries his best to suppress a smile.

In front of us, the Dryad Queen works her mouth a couple of times before she manages to recover. Drawing herself up to her full height, she fixes us with a wary stare.

"What is this?" she demands. "Why have you come?"

"We have come to ask you to help us fight," I reply, holding her suspicious stare.

She narrows her eyes. "Fight? What fight? I am not interested in helping you win your Atonement Trials."

"The Atonement Trials?" I blink at her. "What? No. Those happened months ago."

She just continues watching me with creased brows, which is when I realize that the dryads might have a very different perspective on time than we do. Compared to humans, we have very long lifespans, so they feel time more acutely than we do. But I'm starting to wonder if the difference between us and the dryads might be even bigger. Are they actually immortal?

Giving my head a quick shake, I clear my throat and try to push the conversation back on track. "Last time we spoke, you told me that you hate the Icehearts."

A hiss, like that of a furious viper about to strike, rips through the dryads around us. Isera snaps her gaze to them, ice forming in her palms. But none of them fire any arrows at us.

"We do," the Dryad Queen replies, her voice now cold and sharp.

"As I told you back then, we hate them too," I continue. "And now, we are fighting back. Both fae and dragon shifters." I motion between my friends before shifting my attention back to the Dryad Queen. "And we need your help. Will you fight with us?"

Dead silence falls across the grass. Behind us, trees of more normal sizes ripple faintly as another warm wind sweeps through the forest. It makes the twisting vines swing from the branches. Up ahead, shapes are moving inside the giant trees, as if the dryads who live in there are moving closer to peer out the windows.

The ring of archers around us remains motionless, but a few of them cast questioning glances at their queen. She, on the other hand, is watching me intently, as if she is trying to read my entire life history on my face.

I hold her gaze, barely daring to breathe.

"No."

The air is sucked out of my lungs as if she had punched me

instead of speaking one simple word. Dragging in a sharp breath, I blurt out, "What?"

"No," she repeats, her voice now devoid of emotion.

A snarl rips from Isera's throat, and her voice cuts through the air like a whip as she demands, "What do you mean *no?*"

"We will not fight with you."

"Why the hell not?"

Fury suddenly crackles like lightning in the Dryad Queen's eyes, but she doesn't reply to Isera's question. The sight of that raw fury makes ice skitter down my spine. But Isera doesn't back down.

"You're just going to hide in here?" she snaps. "While everyone else fights?"

The Dryad Queen seems to grow taller, and her voice gets deeper and more commanding as she declares, "We do not go to war. We are the guardians of this world. We cannot die of old age, but we can be killed. And it takes a thousand years for a new dryad to be birthed by this world. So we do not go to war." Rage flickers in her eyes again as she adds, "Without good cause."

"And this cause isn't good enough?" I press, shaking my head in confusion. "I thought you said that you hated the Icehearts."

Yet again, low snarls of raw hatred rip from some of the bow-wielding dryads around us.

"We do," the Dryad Queen once more confirms.

But she says nothing else. Gives no other explanation. I flex my hand as frustration bubbles through me, but before I can say anything, Galen speaks up.

"A *thousand* years? For one dryad?" Drawing a hand through his blond hair, he shakes his head and then sweeps stunned violet eyes over the dryads around us as if counting them. "So there have only been six dryads born since the war between fae and dragon shifters. Did you fight in that war? Is that why you're so cautious now?"

The Dryad Queen doesn't reply to either of his questions.

Instead, that raw fury and world-ending hatred flares in her eyes again as she says, "There have been no dryads born since the war."

"What?" Lyra says, looking genuinely sad. "Why?"

"That is why we cannot fight," the Dryad Queen says, once again ignoring the question. "Regardless of how much we hate the Icehearts. We cannot risk the extinction of our people."

The previous anger and frustration that seemed to bubble inside all of us fades like a regretful sigh on the wind. Even Isera doesn't argue with that reasoning. She simply crosses her arms and watches the dryads in cold silence. Orion, however, watches *her* with an expression that I can't read.

Next to me, Draven cocks his head while a considering look blows across his features. "What did the Icehearts do to you?"

The Dryad Queen shifts her gaze to him but says nothing. For a while, they just continue watching each other in tense silence. Draven, more than anyone, knows the cruelty that the Icehearts are capable of. But the Dryad Queen doesn't reply.

After a few more seconds of thick silence, she breaks his gaze and announces, "Since nightfall is almost here, we will allow you to stay this one night here in our home. At first light, you will be blindfolded and brought back to where you came from. Understood?"

Alistair, who hates forests, looks like he's about to once again point out that he has fire magic and therefore doesn't need daylight in order to find his way out of here, so I quickly nod and reply, "Yes, understood."

Alistair shoots me a scowl, confirming my theory, but doesn't argue further.

"Good." With a flick of her wrist, the Dryad Queen at last orders the archers to stand down. "Then follow me."

The leaves and vines that make up her hair and dress ripple as she spins around and starts towards the lights that twinkle from an opening in one of the massive trees. After exchanging a quick glance, we follow her.

Another question suddenly hits me, and I jog to catch up with the Dryad Queen. Even if they won't fight with us, they might be able to help us.

"Can I ask you a question?" I ask once I've caught up with her.

She glances at me from the corner of her eye but doesn't respond.

However, since she didn't say no either, I press on. "We've heard that there used to exist a partnership between Seelie fae and dragon shifters. Is that true?"

"Yes."

Anticipation surges through me. "How does it work?"

"I don't know."

"Do any of your people know?"

"No."

I try not to let the wave of disappointment crush me. "Is there really nothing, nothing at all, that you can tell me about it?"

"No. I know that it exists, but what it does and how it works was a secret between your two races."

A frustrated sigh slips from my lips. Goddess fucking damn it. I really thought that the dryads would know. But now, it looks like the only ones who do are the Icehearts. But how are we going to get that secret out of them?

My mind churns as the Dryad Queen leads us into the massive tree trunk.

I wonder if Lavendera knows. She seems to be pretty high up in their circle of trust. Could we turn her? Make her change sides? She might work for them, but ultimately, she's a fae from the Seelie Court. She's one of us.

Tapping my fingers against my thigh, I make a mental note to bring that up with the others later.

Lavendera is likely sitting on a mountain of information that even Draven doesn't know. Getting her on our side might just be the secret weapon we need in order to take on the Icehearts.

CHAPTER FOUR

Apparently, dryads don't eat. It shouldn't have surprised me, given that they're half plant. Or fully plant? To be fair, I'm not quite sure of the exact genetic composition of a dryad's body. The end result remains the same, though. They don't eat food.

They did, however, figure out that *we* need to eat. Which is why the table in front of us is filled with eclectic pieces of vaguely edible... things. Or at least, I hope they're edible.

I glance down at the chopped-up pieces of pale yellow matter on the thin board before me. It kind of looks like potatoes, so I hope I'm right. Since the dryads don't eat, they didn't have any plates, so they've served the food on a variety of flat objects whose normal use remain a mystery to me.

A wide smile spreads across Lyra's face when the dryad who is helping to feed us sets down a cob of corn in front of her. To her left, Alistair winces when he receives a carrot instead. I note with surprise that his carrot looks to have been grilled over a fire. As opposed to the dubious-looking pile of diced potatoes in front of me, which I have a sneaking suspicion might be raw.

But that is not the most awkward part of this whole situation. No, the worst part is that the entire room is filled with dryads who are sitting silently on sculpted wooden chairs and watching us with rapt interest. As if eating dinner is a spectator sport.

I sweep an uncertain glance over them all. Galen and Alistair do the same. Lyra is too excited about receiving the most obviously edible food item to notice the dryads' fascinated stares, and I already know that Isera could easily murder someone in front of an audience without even paying them any mind, so eating dinner like this should be a piece of cake. Apparently, both Orion and Draven have also perfected the not-so-subtle art of being so powerful and important that they can do whatever they want without worrying about what people will think, so they're ignoring our intrigued spectators like proper royalty.

Galen, Alistair, and I exchange a glance. However, before we can say anything, Lyra abruptly picks up Alistair's makeshift plate and switches it with hers.

He starts in surprise and turns to look at her. And so do the rest of us.

"Why are you taking Alistair's carrot?" Galen asks with a confused frown.

"I'm not taking it," Lyra answers, a smile still on her face. "I'm swapping it with my corn. Big difference."

Galen lets out a long-suffering sigh. "Fine, yes, you're swapping it. The question still remains the same."

"Alistair doesn't like carrots."

The fire wielder in question draws back slightly and blinks at her in surprise. "How did you know that?"

"We lived together for weeks in the Unseelie Court, remember?" she replies with a quick shake of her head, as if that should've been obvious.

"Well, yeah, but no one else picked up on that. I didn't memorize anyone else's eating habits either."

"Huh." She looks thoughtful for a second, and then just lifts her shoulders in a casual shrug. "Well, when I'm interested in someone, I tend to notice things."

Red flushes Alistair's cheeks in a heartbeat.

Across the table, Draven lets out a low chuckle and shakes his head at Lyra. "Go easy on him, will you? Or he might burst into flames and take us all out with him."

Alistair splutters something that sounds like the beginning of a curse at him, but Lyra just looks up from her dubiously grilled carrot and asks, "What?"

Her tone, and the expression on her face, is filled with innocence, but there is a mischievous gleam in her orange eyes that she can't quite hide. Draven just shakes his head again while suppressing a smile.

I stare at him from across the table, drinking in the sight of that faint smile. He has spent far too little time smiling in his life. He deserves a life full of joy. A life full of adventure and freedom. Full of love. And by his god and mine, I will make sure he gets it. I will make sure he gets everything. That *we* get fucking everything.

With that innocent grin on her mouth and the devilish glint in her eyes, Lyra casually picks up the carrot and takes a firm bite. Alistair, his cheeks still red, quickly grabs the cob of corn with both hands and starts eating.

The sudden start to the feast seems to snap all the dryads out of their silent trance, because a ripple goes through the room. Conversations start up at their tables for the first time as they focus on something other than our ongoing food consumption, but they still sneak glances at us every few seconds. As if to catalogue how we eat the food.

Isera slides a cool gaze over the ones who study us, making them quickly snap their attention back to their own companions.

"It's like ice."

We all turn towards Orion, but the Unseelie King has his gaze locked on Isera.

"Your face," he continues. "It really is like ice."

Isera shifts her gaze to him, and a mocking and highly

dangerous expression descends on her features. "Let me guess, I should smile more?"

"No. Why change something that is already perfect?" His black and silver eyes remain locked on her face, as if he is searing it into his mind. "It's like watching a shard of ice glinting in a harsh sun on a ruthlessly cold winter day. Lethal. Sharp. Unyielding." He cocks his head, making his long dark blue hair slide over his tailored tunic. "I've never seen anything quite like it before. I keep wondering if you truly are royalty or if you just played me with that sharp mind and tongue of yours, but it's at times like this when I can't deny that it must be true."

Our entire table stares at him in stunned silence.

"Wow," Draven begins, his voiced laced with mocking amusement. "Who knew the little prince was such a poet?"

Shock, and what looks an awful lot like panic, pulses across Orion's face for a fraction of a second. As if he can't believe that he just said all of that out loud. Then he quickly hides it behind a mask of dangerous threats. Tearing his gaze from Isera, he shifts his now dark eyes to Draven.

"Watch your mouth," he warns.

"Or what?" Draven flashes him a smirk full of challenge. "You'll compose *me* a poem as well?"

Indignant fury flashes across Orion's face, and his eyes begin to glow as he starts channeling magic. Draven just sits there and holds his gaze, daring him to do it. For a few seconds, it looks like he actually will. But then the glow fades from his eyes as he releases his grip on his magic instead.

Draven snickers. "Thought so."

"Oh I wouldn't relax yet, if I were you." Orion flashes him a sharp smile. "I simply prefer to strike when my victims least expect it. Better sleep with one eye open, you brooding beast."

Draven stretches his muscular arms above his head and yawns, the epitome of lazy confidence. "Once you've worked up the courage, you know where to find me."

Lightning flashes in Orion's eyes, but before he can retort, Galen quickly changes the subject.

"Uhm, is anyone else's food raw?" he asks, poking at the suspicious-looking pile in front of him with the point of his knife.

"Yes," I reply. "I'm pretty sure my potatoes are raw as well."

"I could fry them for you," Alistair offers with a shrug.

All of us turn to stare at him. Well, everyone except Isera, who is still watching Orion with an unreadable expression on her face.

"What?" Alistair asks with a frown. "I have fire magic, remember?"

"Hmm," Lyra mumbles through a mouthful of carrot. "Technically, we have fire too."

"Well, yeah, but to use it, you need to turn into a dragon." He waves a hand at the hollowed out tree trunk that we're currently occupying. "Let me know how that goes for you."

Draven chuckles.

I watch him while trying to memorize that wonderful sound.

As if noticing my stare, his gaze shifts to me. And that smile is immediately wiped off his face. Instead, hatred flares up in his eyes and he clenches his jaw.

That dark wave inside me threatens to crash over me, but I cling to that small spark of hope as I hold his gaze. He felt something other than hatred when we passed by that rock wall. I know it. He knows it. And if he felt it once, he can feel it again.

Draven flexes his hand.

Then he abruptly stands up from the beautifully sculpted table and shoves his chair back. "I need some air."

Without waiting for a reply, he stalks towards the door.

The others stare at him in surprise. But before Galen can follow him, I leap up from my seat and start after him.

"We'll be right back," I promise before hurrying after Draven.

Warm evening winds wash over me as I step out of the

massive tree trunk and back onto the grass outside. The sun has almost slipped behind the horizon now, and only a few streams of light hit the mass of normal trees and vines that surround the dryad's massive tree homes.

Turning my head from side to side, I scan the area for Draven and quickly find him pacing the ground on my left. A few dryads are moving between the tree trunks a short distance away, but as opposed to the ones inside, they don't pay us any mind. Straightening my spine, I stride over to Draven.

"You felt something back there at the rock wall," I declare.

It's not a question, but he tries to deny it anyway. Stopping his pacing, he turns to scowl at me. "No."

"There is no point in lying about it. I know you felt something." I lock hard eyes on him. "Because I could feel it too. Through our mate bond."

Alarm flits across his handsome face for a second before he doubles down on the scowl. "You're imagining things."

"Admit it. You felt something. You can feel something in your gut when you look at me."

"Yes, it's called disgust."

A frustrated snarl rips from my throat. "Goddess damn it, Draven. Stop insulting both of our intelligence and just admit it."

He flexes his hand again and then jerks his chin towards the door. "I don't want you here. Go back inside."

"I'm not going anywhere until you admit that you felt something."

Opening his mouth, he looks like he's about to snap at me again. But then he just forces out a long, calming breath and instead glances towards the tangle of trees across the grass.

"Fine," he grinds out. "Come with me. I don't want to talk about this here where people can hear."

Hope surges inside me. It's so intense that I have to scramble to catch up with him as he starts stalking towards the mass of trees and vines on the other side.

The last golden rays of the fading sun barely manage to pierce the woods, painting most of it in shadows. I follow Draven a short distance in. Far enough away that no one will be able to see or hear us. Then he stops right next to a large tree that is covered in vines.

"Alright, fine," he grinds out again. "I might have felt something when you leaned against the rock wall like that. But it was gone so quickly that I'm not even sure what I felt."

My heart starts thumping in my chest. "Okay. That's good. Can you remember anything about what it felt like? Anything at all?"

"No. I don't know." He glances at the tree next to us and then clears his throat. "Maybe you could… recreate it?"

That treacherous heart in my chest is pounding so hard that I'm sure Draven can hear it. Licking my lips, I try to stop the surge of hope inside me from burning out of control as I move over to the tree trunk. Draven watches me intently as I lean my back against it and then raise my hands above my head.

My heart skips a beat as that fire flickers in Draven's eyes for a second.

It's working.

I drag in an unsteady breath as he moves closer until he's standing right in front of me. His gaze sears through my skin as he rakes it over my body. A small gasp escapes my lips when he suddenly reaches up and starts undoing my black fighting leathers. Each brush of his fingers is like a bolt of lightning through my veins.

When he has gotten the jacket open, I slowly lower my arms so that he can slide it off my shoulders. His strong hands move confidently across my collarbones.

Then the black leather slips off my shoulders and lands with a thud on the ground behind my feet, leaving me in only a thin white undershirt.

Draven rakes his gaze over my body again. "Arms above your head."

I obey and raise my arms again before crossing my wrists above my head in the same way that I did back at that rock wall.

"This does bring back memories," Draven says slowly.

A warm shudder rolls through my body as he draws his hands up along my arms. Tilting my head back, I watch as he grabs a few of the vines that hang down from the tree.

"Draven?" I ask, uncertain.

"It was usually handcuffs, I remember," he says while moving the vines towards my crossed wrists. There is a devilish glint in his eyes. "But I suppose these will have to do."

Fire washes through me as he ties my hands firmly above my head and then slides his palms down my arms again. I arch my back as he reaches my chest and traces soft fingers over my collarbones.

Bracing his knee against the tree between my legs, he leans closer while he pushes the collar of my white shirt aside, exposing more of my chest. His mouth is so close to mine that I can feel his hot breath on my skin.

"Is this what you want?" he murmurs against my lips. "For me to tie you up and fuck you like you're mine?"

My heart is almost beating out of my chest. He remembers. Oh Goddess above, he actually remembers. He is fighting against the hatred in his chest. Even if it's only lust, and not love yet, he is still starting to fight his way back to me.

"Yes," I reply, my voice a fragile whisper.

He slides his hand down the side of my ribs, making pleasure skitter across my skin.

And then he laughs.

It's a harsh and cruel sound that slaps me out of my dazed state like a bucket of ice water to the face.

Drawing back, he locks mocking eyes on me. "Did you really think that I brought you in here because I suddenly realized that

I felt something for you? That I brought you in here because I actually wanted you?"

Pain stabs through my chest, so violently that I forget to breathe.

He wraps a strong hand around my throat, locking it right underneath my jaw so that he can keep me from moving my head as he leans closer. Hatred burns in his beautiful golden eyes as he levels a vicious stare on me.

"I would fuck that insufferable bastard Orion Nightbane before I ever fucked you," he growls in my face.

Grinding my teeth, I glare right back at him. "Liar. If I used my magic on you right now, I would find a massive flame of lust in your chest, and you know it."

"In your dreams."

"Oh really? What a shame. Well, since you're not actually into guys, and Orion isn't into guys either, then maybe I should just go and fuck Orion instead."

His hand tightens around my jaw.

Victory sparkles inside my chest. *That got a reaction out of him.*

But all he says is, "Go ahead. I don't give a shit about who you fuck."

"Right."

He flexes his hand around my jaw again while clenching his teeth. Then he abruptly releases my chin, snapping my head to the side in the process.

"Stay the fuck out of my head," he growls as he spins on his heel and starts stalking away.

I yank against the vines keeping me trapped, but they're surprisingly strong. When they don't budge, a flicker of panic pulses through me.

"Draven," I call while still pulling futilely against the strong vines.

Coming to a halt, he turns around and arches a mocking eyebrow at me. "Yes, little rebel?"

The cruel taunting in his voice when he uses that familiar nickname sends another stab of pain through my heart. It throws me off enough that I only manage a pathetic, "Aren't you going to untie me first?"

"You're the one who wanted me to tie you up. Are you saying that you've changed your mind?"

Frustration rips through me, and I snap, "Goddess damn it, Draven! You—"

"Raise your voice at me again, and I swear to god, I will gag you."

I draw in a long, calming breath through my nose while my treacherous core throbs at the pure command in his words. Utter power seems to roll off his muscular body like smoke as he stares me down, daring me to do it. Fire flickers through my veins.

Holding his commanding stare with eyes full of challenge, I keep my voice level as I retort, "Once I've figured out how to remove that flame of hatred from your chest, I'm going to make you spend an entire night repaying me with your tongue for this conversation alone."

That searing fire of desire flares in his eyes again.

The sight of it snatches the breath from my lungs.

But then he rips off part of a vine and advances on me with vengeance on his face.

My heart jerks, and I try to back away before I remember that there is a thick tree blocking my way. I yank against the vines keeping my hands trapped above my head, but they still refuse to budge. Draven closes the final distance between us.

"No, wait," I blurt out, pressing myself against the tree. But there is no escape from the Shadow of Death. "Draven, wait, I—"

He shoves the vine between my teeth and ties it firmly behind my head. I growl curses at him, but it only comes out as muffled noise, so I try to stomp my heel down on his foot instead. He answers by wrapping his hand around my throat again.

"Here's what's going to happen," he declares, authority

dripping from his dark voice. "You're going to stay here while I go back in there and eat my dinner in peace. Then, I'm going to come back here and do one of two things. Either I'm going to untie you, or I'm going to blindfold you as well and leave you here for the rest of the night. Which option I choose depends on how you behave when I return. Understood?"

I glare back at him and silently promise to make him pay for this when he's back to normal again.

"I suggest nodding." He gives me a look pulsing with command. "Or we're already going to be off to a bad start."

While narrowing my eyes at the domineering bastard, I force myself to nod.

Releasing my throat, he gives my cheek a couple of mocking pats. "Good girl."

Annoyance and desire flash through me. But before I can do anything else, Draven turns around and strides out of the tangle of trees and back down to the dining room.

It takes him twenty minutes to return.

Part of me had begun to worry that he wasn't going to come back. But the smug smirk on his face when he strides back into the woods informs me that he was rather looking forward to this part.

I, however, spent the first few minutes of his absence planning how to play this. I want to bait him. Desperately. Both because I hate losing to his power plays and because I'm hoping that it might trigger another flare of emotions that will tug on our mate bond.

But unfortunately, I know that he is being dead serious with his threats. If I don't do what he wants, he will blindfold me and leave me tied up here. That massive flame of unnatural hatred in his chest makes sure of it.

If he doesn't untie me, it means that I will have to wait for one of our other companions to find me. And I would rather eat a live snake than suffer the mortification of being found like this by any of them. Which unfortunately leaves me with only one choice.

Wicked anticipation glitters in Draven's eyes as he comes to a halt before me. I glare back at him while I still can. Amusement tugs at his lips as he reaches up and starts undoing the knot on the vine that gags me. But when it's free, he doesn't immediately remove it. Instead, he locks commanding eyes on me.

"When I remove this, your first words had better be, *I apologize for my temper.*"

I hold his stare in angry silence since there is nothing else I can do.

At last, he lowers his hands and removes the vine from between my teeth. I draw in a deep breath.

Then I force out, "I apologize for my temper."

"Good." His eyes glint in the now almost entirely dark forest. "Now, beg me to untie you."

I can't stop myself from glaring at him, but I manage to press out, "Please untie me."

He arches a dark eyebrow. "You hold your chin quite highly for someone who is begging."

Curling my fingers into fists, I try desperately to hold on to my temper. After taking a deep breath that does very little to calm me down, I slowly lower my chin and drop my gaze to his boots. "Please untie me."

"Are you going to obey my orders and never bring up that damn rock wall again?"

If he weren't so much taller than me, I would've headbutted him.

"Answer me," he commands. "Are you going to obey?"

"Yes," I grind out, still glaring down at his boots.

"Yes, what?"

My heart skips a beat and heat floods my core. "Yes, sir."

"That's right."

His fingers appear underneath my chin, pushing it upwards. I raise my head right in time for him to shove the vine back between my teeth and tie it behind my head again. Thrashing against the tree trunk, I stare up at him in disbelief.

He lets out a dark chuckle. "I just wanted to hear you beg."

A tearing sound fills the space around us as he rips off another piece of vine. I snap my gaze towards it while a sudden burst of panic pushes out the irritation for a moment. Don't tell me he's going to…? He can't—

"So fucking gullible. Did you really think I would show you mercy?" Shaking his head, he lets out another smug laugh. "I deliberately terrorized the human population in Frostfell for years just to make them do what I wanted. And I didn't even have anything against those people. But you… *You* I hate. So why would I ever show you any mercy?" His eyes glint as he moves the vine towards my face. "Have fun in the dark."

Then he blindfolds me.

And walks away.

I am going to fucking kill him for this.

CHAPTER FIVE

Lingering embarrassment still burns inside me, making it feel like my cheeks are on fire. I don't know what's worse. The fact that Draven humiliated me and left me tied to a tree last night. Or that he is acting now as if it didn't even happen. Both options make me want to simultaneously kill someone and also bury myself so far into the ground that no one will ever find me again.

The one who ended up finding me last night was Isera. Thankfully, she didn't even comment on it. She simply summoned a sharp ice shard and cut me free, and then we just walked back in silence. Thank Mabona for small mercies, at least.

But the experience affected me more than I want to admit. Draven *humiliated* me last night. And that is something that he would never do. Something that the real Draven, *my* Draven, would never do. I just want him back. I want everything to go back to the way it used to be. The way it should be. But I have no idea how to fix it. And worst of all is the poisonous knowledge that sears through my soul like acid. The knowledge that it is all my fault. That I ruined everything.

"Well, that went splendidly," Galen says, sarcasm dripping

from his voice, as he and Draven stalk through the door and drop down on the two empty seats at our table.

We all pause our breakfast and turn to look at them. Draven is scowling. Again. It seems to be the only thing he does ever since I forced that red-violet flame of hatred into his chest. On the other side of the table, Galen pulls his chair in and then leans back to rake his fingers through his blond hair. A disappointed sigh escapes his lips.

"No luck, then?" Lyra asks between bites of fruit.

"No," Galen replies, blowing out another frustrated breath. "Same answer as yesterday. They won't help us fight."

Orion clicks his tongue and shoots Draven an arrogant look. "Told you so."

The scowl on Draven's face deepens as he turns it on the Unseelie King. "Well, we can't all be useless freeloaders. Some of us actually have to contribute." He scoffs. "Maybe you're used to giving up the moment things don't go your way, but just accepting defeat isn't how I do things. We had to at least try to convince them again."

"Doing the same thing over and over again and expecting a different result is the very definition of insanity."

A muscle flickers in Draven's jaw. But before he can retort, or punch the condescending king, Isera cuts in.

"You have two choices," she states in her effortless no-nonsense tone as she locks hard eyes on Orion. "Either you only open your mouth when you have something productive to contribute. Or I gag you."

Dangerous light glints in his eyes as he meets her gaze. "You really shouldn't make threats that you can't back up, little viper."

With her eyes still locked on his, she twists her hand in the air and summons a piece of ice. On one end are two balls of ice while the rest of the ice continues down like a thick, long, and slightly curved rod. Presumably, the two balls would fill Orion's mouth and cheeks, preventing him from speaking, while the curving rod part would be shoved down his throat to truly shut him up. The shape looks distinctly like something else, though.

A smile so sharp that it could've drawn blood spreads slowly across Orion's mouth as he looks up from the suspiciously shaped piece of ice to meet Isera's cool eyes again.

"Oh I didn't realize that you fantasized so much about mine that you have already created a sculpture of it." He tilts his head, making his hair slide over his shoulder, as he studies the piece of ice. "The length looks about right. It should have a little more girth, though." Wicked light shines in his eyes as he meets her gaze again. "Is this the substitute you're using on yourself while you're alone at night, daydreaming about me fu—"

"Alright," Lyra suddenly interrupts, drawing out the first syllable into one long sound. "How about some fruit? Fruit is always good for, uhm… everything. Well, unless you're like dying of a stab wound or something. In that situation, I don't think an orange will do you much good."

Her sudden interruption, and drastic change of subject, stuns everyone so much that we all just turn to stare at her. Apples and oranges and several other fruits that I have never seen before roll across the elegant wooden tabletop as Lyra starts dividing the large pile that the dryads gave us to eat this morning. The rest of the room is thankfully empty this time, since the dryads were apparently satisfied after watching us eat last night.

Draven and Galen exchange a private smile at Lyra's diversion tactic. As if this isn't the first time that she has defused a conflict by doing something entirely unexpected. Orion is now scowling at her instead of glaring at Isera. And our resident ice lady has taken the opportunity to make her little sculpture vanish.

"Uhm, sure," Alistair replies, still looking confused by the sudden change of topic.

Lyra slides him an apple and then flashes him a beaming smile. "Yep. You know what they say. An apple a day keeps the doctor away."

Picking up the apple, he glances down at it in confusion and then shrugs. "Yeah, I suppose it keeps anyone away if you throw it hard enough."

Lyra bursts out laughing. Not a measured laugh either. It's so loud and so abrupt that she accidentally spits a little saliva on Alistair, who is sitting opposite her.

That just makes her laugh even harder.

While still laughing and gasping for breath at the same time, she leans over the table and draws her thumb over Alistair's cheek to remove the specks of saliva before she manages to press out, "Sorry."

Alistair blinks at her, looking stunned that she touched him so casually.

On her other side, Galen is chuckling as well while Draven lets out a huff of laughter. Even Orion appears to be fighting an amused smile. Isera just watches us all with that customary passive mask on her face while Lyra sits back down again.

Alistair and I exchange a confused glance. I have no idea why they're laughing. It was a pretty reasonable comment, in my opinion. Why would an apple, of all things, keep a doctor away? And why would you even *want* to keep a doctor away? If there is one type of person that I would've wanted to have more access to in all my years in the Seelie Court, it's a doctor.

"Alright," Galen says, swallowing down his laughter before clearing his throat. "Should we get back to the problem at hand?"

"Right, sorry," Lyra replies.

But a quick and secret smile, which the two of them share while Orion, Isera, and Alistair are busy stopping the fruit she suddenly shoved at them from rolling off the table, tells me that they both knew exactly what they were doing and that they've probably worked together to steer conversations like this many times before. I glance towards Draven.

A pang hits me in the chest when I see a brief flicker of regret on his features. He lost two hundred years of friendship with these people because of what the Icehearts did to him. They've had a whole life, with private jokes and routines like this, without him.

Quickly wiping that expression off his face, he smoothens his features before Lyra and Galen can see it and instead sits up straighter. "The dryads won't help us, so we need to adjust our plan and move forward without them."

"What about Lavendera?" I say, voicing the plan I've been mulling over since yesterday. "I was thinking that we could try to turn her. If we could get her to switch sides, it would remove the Icehearts' ability to use dragon steel. And she probably also has a lot of really valuable insider information."

Flexing his hand, Draven cuts me a sharp look and growls, "If I want your opinion, I'll ask for it."

The utter disdain in his voice is like a gut punch. My lungs cease working for a second as that crushing wave of black rage and despair and hatred inside me threatens to suffocate me. That small spark of hope flickers dangerously. I cling to it, desperately willing it to survive. Because without it, I don't think *I* will.

"It's a pretty good idea, though," Alistair says, keeping his expression casual as he glances at Draven. "Worth trying."

If I wasn't fighting so hard not to drown in the dark ocean inside me right now, I would've given him a grateful smile.

"It won't work," Draven replies. But the sharp bite is gone from his voice now. Leaning back in his chair, he rakes a tired hand through his black hair. "If there is one thing I'm certain of, it's that Lavendera won't turn against the Icehearts. She's been with them for centuries. She was there before I even became the Commander of the Dread Legion. She's utterly loyal to them."

I want to ask why, but I don't want to hear Draven's perfect voice fill with disdain and watch his eyes flare with hatred again, so I keep my mouth shut. Someone else thankfully asks, though.

"Why?" Isera asks, watching us all through slightly narrowed eyes. "Why is she so loyal to them?"

Draven shrugs. "I don't know."

Silence falls over our table. Morning sunlight streams in through the open door to my left, illuminating the otherwise empty room inside this massive hollowed out trunk. I shift my weight on my chair. Blowing out a small breath, I manage to force the darkness inside my soul back enough that my chest stops aching.

I still think that Lavendera is important to our plans. But unfortunately, Draven is also right. Because I have absolutely no idea how I would go about convincing Lavendera to change sides. I don't know what she wants or why she is loyal to them. I barely even know who she is. After all, every interaction I've had with her has been fake. Just a part that she was playing in order to fool me into thinking that she was one of us. So for now, I push the idea of turning Lavendera against the Icehearts to the back of my mind.

"So," Lyra begins, drawing out the word and glancing from face to face. "What do we do, then?"

"We need to convince the other clans to fight with us," Draven says. "Our clan is powerful, but we won't win a war against the combined might of the Silver Clan and all of the other clans as well. We need to get the others on our side."

"Why do I feel like I've said that before?" Orion cuts in. Then he snaps his fingers, as if suddenly remembering something, and gives Draven a look dripping with challenge. "Oh wait, it's because *I did*."

Draven opens his mouth to no doubt snap back at him, but before another argument can begin, Alistair thankfully interrupts.

"We still also need to figure out what the hell that partnership between fae and dragon shifters is," he says. "If the Icehearts have gone to these lengths to suppress any knowledge of it, it must be important."

"Agreed," Draven replies.

Orion locks intelligent eyes on Isera. "Don't *you* know? You're a descendant of the Seelie Queen. This is the sort of royal knowledge that should have been passed down through the generations. Even in secret." His eyes narrow. "Unless you're not actually a descendant of the Seelie Queen?"

My heart skips a beat. If Orion figures out that Isera lied, he will be gone in a heartbeat. The only reason that he is here is because he must honor the bargain they made. But if he finds out that the entire premise of their bargain was based on a lie, he won't be bound to keep his end of the deal. And if we lose Orion and the Unseelie Court, we will lose this entire war.

To my relief, Isera doesn't panic. Instead, she just flashes him a mocking smile and retorts, "Trying to worm your way out of our bargain, pretty boy?"

"I don't *worm*," he grinds out indignantly.

"You're sounding pretty spineless to me."

"Are you actually a descendant of the Seelie Queen's second daughter?" A dangerous edge laces his voice. "Or just a scheming peasant who has bitten off more than she can chew?"

"I thought we had already established that I have no problem biting things off."

Wicked light flickers in his eyes, and he adjusts his hips almost imperceptibly. But Isera notices, of course, and a villainous smile spreads across her lethally beautiful face. Orion clenches his jaw when he realizes what he did, but he doesn't admit defeat. Instead, he simply changes the subject.

"Why don't *you* know how that infamous partnership works?" he asks, shifting his attention to the three dragon shifters at the table. "They didn't kill you off or imprison you. Your ancestors won the war. So why don't you know?"

"Our ancestors had no riders," Draven replies, somehow managing to sound both smug and annoyed at the same time.

"It's a pretty good question, though," Lyra says, a considering look on her face. "Why doesn't *any* of the dragon clans know? Surely someone must have remembered."

Silence once more descends on the elegant wooden room. I chew my apple carefully while considering the question. They have a point. Our people don't know about the partnership because the Icehearts slaughtered all of the adult fae and then imprisoned the children in the Seelie Court. There was no one left of our people who possessed that knowledge. But why doesn't any of the dragon shifters remember?

And not just that. How come all dragon shifters believe that the Seelie fae enslaved all of them when it was only a few small groups of entitled rejects. How can such a fundamental piece of history be changed so thoroughly?

"Do you think the Green Clan could be involved?" Orion asks, his voice now serious rather than mocking.

"No," Draven replies immediately. "The Green Clan is honest and principled. Always has been."

"Their clan magic is memory magic. They can literally change people's memories."

"They would never use it against their own people."

"Are you sure about that?"

"Yes." Draven cocks his head, a considering look blowing across his handsome features. "But it might be worth asking them about the partnership. Maybe they know. They're suppose to be the keepers of history, after all. Maybe they simply haven't felt the need to keep the knowledge alive among the other clans throughout the centuries since this mythical partnership became useless the moment that the Seelie fae were imprisoned."

Lyra sits up straighter, a smile once again back on her face. "So, we have a plan then?"

"Yes." He nods. "We convince the other clans to fight with us, and we also ask the Green Clan about our shared history."

She slaps her palms on the table excitedly, making a couple of grapes jump in surprise. "Great! Then let's get going."

Finishing my apple, I set down the remains on the smooth tabletop and suck my teeth.

Ideally, I want the other dragon clans, the dryads, *and* Lavendera before we bring the fight to the Icehearts.

Right now, we have none of them.

But I suppose we need to start somewhere.

CHAPTER SIX

"If you come back a third time, we will kill you on sight."

Turning around, I glance back in surprise at the Dryad Queen. Her tone brooked no argument, though. That threat was entirely genuine.

Irritation flickers through me.

"Not a problem," I reply. "Once we've killed the Icehearts and freed this entire continent, I'll just send a messenger bird to let you know instead."

Her gaze sharpens as she locks it on me. I just glare back at her.

Logically, I understand the reason why they won't get involved. But I still can't help the anger burning inside me. Every day, my patience and my goodwill dwindle further. Every day that I have to spend in this cruel new reality where Draven is looking at me with undiluted hatred, I die a little more inside. And part of me wonders if I will ever recover those broken pieces. The other part of me is rapidly losing the ability to give a fuck.

Tension crackles through the air as the Dryad Queen and I stare each other down in silence for another few seconds.

Then a predator's smile curves her lips. "I look forward to it."

And with that, she turns around and disappears back down the hole in the ground that we entered through yesterday.

After blindfolding us, they brought us all the way back to the thorn forest instead of leaving us where they found us inside the underground forest. As if they wanted to make sure that we truly left.

I watch as her flowing dress, made of vines and leaves, ripples across the ground before she disappears from sight. Blowing out a sigh, I shake my head. I don't think I will ever truly understand what goes on inside that dangerous being's head.

"When is your portal guy coming back?" Galen asks from a few strides away.

Tearing my gaze from the hole in the ground and the river that flows up through it, I turn around and look between him and Orion. The Unseelie King brushes his hands down the silver embroidery on his fancy dark blue tunic as if dusting himself off.

"Grey," he states, reminding Galen of the man's name. "I instructed him to open a portal here every hour after sunrise. So it shouldn't be too long."

I turn towards the tree line and the city visible there across the fields, as if I can see the clock tower from all the way out here. The others do the same.

Only the softly rustling leaves and the creaking branches disrupt the silence as we all just stand there, waiting for Grey to open a portal so that we can leave the Seelie Court unseen.

My gaze drifts over the tall stone walls that box in the city while my mind drifts.

Speaking of messenger birds made me think of Fenriel and his magical hawk Talon. I wonder how they are doing. Did our resistance leaders take my advice and recruit him to the rebellion?

I drum my fingers against my thigh as I narrow my eyes at the city in consideration. Should I get the resistance involved? It would be good to have more allies. But is there really anything that they can do from in here, cut off from the rest of the world by a forest of thorns? I shake my head. No. First, we need to deal with the Red Dragon Clan. While they patrol the city like prison guards, there is nothing substantial that the fae resistance can do to help us in this fight.

My gaze once more drifts towards the north side of town where my parents live. I want to go there. I want to know. But at the same time, a terrified part of me doesn't want to know. Because what if my magic isn't there. What if they really do just hate me because of who I am. Right now, I don't think I could handle it if I found out that that's the case. So I'll do it later. I'll do it after I've figured out how to get Draven back. Then maybe, just maybe, I can do the same thing to my parents too.

That tiny light of hope inside me sparkles at the thought. Maybe I can fix it all.

"He's here," Orion announces.

Giving myself a determined nod, I tear my gaze from the city and instead focus on the glittering blue rectangle that has appeared on the forest floor.

Grey bows to his king and then steps aside to let us pass through the portal.

As always, a slight tingling sensation ripples through me when I step through the portal. But it disappears once I'm fully out on the other side.

Bright sunlight streams down from a wide blue sky as I appear in a massive field of yellowing grass. After the gloomy darkness of the thorn forest, I have to blink hard and squint before my eyes can adjust. Warm summer winds wash across the endless plains, tugging at the dry grass and making it rustle. I stare at the open horizon, wondering where we are.

"Your Majesty," Grey says from behind me. "Should I continue to our border?"

"No," Orion replies. "We're not going back home yet."

Now that my eyes have adjusted, I turn around to look at my companions. We have gathered in a loose circle on the now flattened grass. Grey has let the portal disappear, and he is looking at Orion, waiting for instructions.

"Are we really doing the right thing splitting up?" Galen asks, his pale brows creased in worry.

"Yes," Draven replies. "If we're going to meet with all the clans before the Icehearts figure out what we're doing, we need to split up to cover more ground, and you and Lyra need to go together. You have enough authority as my second-in-command to make formal deals, and Lyra is really good at making people do what she wants."

At that, Lyra chuckles and gives him a playful salute. "True that."

Galen, however, still looks worried. "But what if I... mess up?"

"You hated me, truly despised me, for two hundred years," Draven says, though not unkindly. His eyes are serious as he holds Galen's gaze. "But I still chose you as my second-in-command. Even when you hated me, I trusted you with my life. So you need to start trusting your own instincts again."

Embarrassment and a hint of alarm flit across Galen's face, and he clears his throat a tad awkwardly while glancing down at his boots. "I thought we all agreed not to talk about what we accidentally blurted out while we were high on poisonous mist in that pocket reality."

Draven just smiles and claps him on the shoulder. "Chin up. You won't mess up, so stop second-guessing yourself."

Despite the earlier flicker of embarrassment, Galen stands up straighter, and even I can see the tension going out of his shoulders. A sort of steady calm settles over him as he meets Draven's eyes again and gives him a nod. It makes me want to smile. I almost do. But then Orion ruins the moment.

"Well, this is all very touching," he drawls. "But can we perhaps get a move on?"

"We need one more person in our group," Lyra announces before Draven and Orion can get into another fight. Her orange eyes are full of sparkling light as she immediately turns to Alistair. "And since Draven has already admitted that I'm very good at getting people to do what I want, I'm just going to tell you what I want this time. So Alistair, you're coming with us."

Alistair starts in surprise. "I am?"

"Any particular reason?" I ask, arching a sly eyebrow at her.

"Uhm, yeah, have you met the guy? He's funny as hell," she says, giving me a little shake of her head as if that should have been obvious. Then she gives the rest of us a long-suffering look. "And with all due respect, the four of you carry enough aggression to level a medium-sized mountain whenever you're together. And trying to keep the good vibes going in those kinds of circumstances is quite frankly exhausting. So this time, I'll leave you all to sort it out amongst yourselves." She tips her head from side to side and then raises her eyebrows. "Just try not to kill each other, okay?"

A soft chuckle escapes my lips. "We'll try."

"I am making no such promises," Orion declares from my left.

"See?" Lyra stabs a finger in his direction. "My point exactly."

"Fair enough," Draven says. Then he shifts his gaze between her and Galen. "You remember when and where to meet up?"

They nod, and Galen replies, "Yes."

"Good. I'll see you in a few days then."

The grass trembles in fear as both Lyra and Galen shift into dragons. Alistair gives me and Isera a quick nod before he climbs up onto Lyra's back. Gusts of wind slam down against the ground as Lyra and Galen beat their wings hard. My hair whips around my face as I tilt my head back and watch them fly off.

"Well, get to it then, beast," Orion says, mockery dripping from his voice like honey.

Dark clouds seem to gather around Draven as he grinds out, "I'm not carrying any of you. We're using the portal." The same sharp taunting laces his tone as he echoes, "So get to it then, princeling."

For a moment, I think they might actually try to kill each other barely three minutes after Lyra explicitly told us to refrain from that particular activity. But then Orion just turns to Grey.

"Open a portal to the Green Dragon Clan's homeland," he commands.

Grey dips his chin. "Yes, my king."

The glittering blue rectangle appears from the grass again. On the other side of it, I can see what looks like a small copse of trees with a large mountain behind. Draven stalks through it first, followed by Orion, and then Isera. I hold my breath as I step through, though I'm not sure why. Then Grey follows me through it and closes it behind us.

We do indeed end up in a small groove. Thin trees with pale green leaves that droop from the spindly branches form a small barrier between us and the open stretch of grass ahead. On the other side of the grass rises a gigantic mountain that has two massive doors carved into the side. They are framed by gleaming stone pillars, which make the doors seem even grander.

I stare at them.

"The Green Clan lives... here?" I ask, completely stunned.

To my surprise, it's Draven who answers. "Yes."

"*Inside* a mountain? No open sky?"

The usual annoyance fades from his voice and an unreadable expression instead descends on his features as he gazes at the massive doors up ahead. "They're a... strange bunch."

"How do we get inside?" Isera asks, her eyes fixed on the doors as well.

Draven shrugs. "We walk up to the doors and hope that they open them."

"Hope?" Orion sneers.

Draven cuts him a glare but still explains. "This mountain is impenetrable. No one gets in, or out, without the permission of their clan leader."

I frown at him before turning to stare at the mountain again. "But then how did the Icehearts conquer them? How did they get them to swear allegiance and become part of their empire?"

With his gaze still on the closed doors, Draven shakes his head. "No idea. It was long before my time."

"Seriously?" Orion says.

We all turn towards him. The Unseelie King is watching Draven with a smug look on his face.

"This is starting to become embarrassing." Orion gives Draven a vicious smile. "I knew that intelligence wasn't your strongest suit, but it is a sad day indeed when I know more about your culture than you do."

Draven flashes him an equally dangerous smile back. "Spying is easy when you've just been spectating behind your wards like a coward."

"Just tell us how they were conquered," Isera snaps, leveling an annoyed look at Orion.

He shifts his sharp eyes to her. "Say please."

"Mabona's fucking tits," I huff. "I'm starting to think that Lyra was right."

All three of them start in surprise, as if they had forgotten that I was there for a moment. It disrupts the aggression that crackles in the air enough that they don't immediately resume arguing. Instead, Orion clears his throat and volunteers the information without further pressure.

"The Icehearts got the Green Dragon Clan to swear allegiance by threatening to destroy their archives," he says.

I raise my eyebrows. "Archives?"

"This entire world's written history. It's stored in the Green Clan's archives. According to our own historians, the Icehearts somehow managed to get into the archives. Though how they actually managed to do that is still up for debate among different scholars. Some argue that they only managed to steal a section of the archives while others claim that they managed to take possession of whole sections of the mountain." He flicks his wrist. "Anyway, the point is that they threatened to destroy them. That's how they got the Green Clan to bow down." He shrugs. "As far as we know, they did manage to reclaim the archives, though. And they warded them afterwards to prevent it from happening again."

I frown at him. "They reclaimed the archives? But then why is the Green Clan still serving the Icehearts then?"

"My guess? It's simply because they don't go back on their word." He flicks a glance at Draven. "If they're as honest and principled as you say, they probably couldn't simply ignore their vow of allegiance once they had given it."

"You might have a point," Draven says slowly.

Orion blinks, looking completely stunned that Draven agreed with him on something.

"The Green Clan is part of the empire, just like we all are, but they don't really serve the Icehearts," Draven explains. "Not overtly, anyway. They don't rebel. But they also don't use their powers for Bane and Jessina's sake."

"So how do we convince them to fight with us?" Isera asks.

"That's a problem for another day." Draven heaves a deep sigh and turns back towards the imposing mountain. "The more pressing problem is how to get them to even open the door."

CHAPTER SEVEN

"This is a waste of time," Isera announces.

Orion waves a lazy hand. "For once, I actually agree with the little viper. If they were going to open the door, they would have done it four hours ago."

I glance between them and Draven but keep my mouth shut, because I know that if I suggest leaving, then he will argue that we should stay simply because he can't let himself agree with something I say.

It has been over four hours since we stepped through the portal. We have spent most of that time simply standing out there on the grass in front of the massive mountain doors. But a few minutes ago, we retreated back into the small copse of trees that we arrived in because Orion wouldn't stop complaining about how the sun was turning his skin red.

Leaves rustle in the thin trees around us as a warm breeze sweeps across the grasslands. The rippling foliage casts flickering shadows across our faces, but it does indeed give us a nice break from the scorching sun we've been standing in all day. Not that I would ever admit that to Orion, though.

Draven heaves a deep sigh. "Fine." While dragging a hand

through his hair, he shifts his gaze to Orion. "When is Grey's next check-in?"

"He should be opening another portal in about half an hour or so," the Unseelie King replies.

"Alright, then we'll—" He suddenly cuts himself off, his head snapping to the side. "Get down!"

Alarm crackles up my spine as I whip my head in the direction that Draven was looking, but I don't even have time to see the danger before something heavy tackles me from the side.

I slam down on the ground with it on top of me. Air escapes my lungs in a huff as I hit the grass, and I gasp to refill them again. A hand slams down over my mouth. Yanking my arms up, I try to shove at the weight above me while panic pulses through my veins.

Then my gaze meets a pair of gold eyes.

Confused, I stare into them for another few seconds.

It takes me two more to realize that it's Draven.

Draven is the one who tackled me to the ground and who is currently lying on top of me with his hand pressed over my mouth. My heart beats erratically in my chest. Was he... trying to protect me?

As if he can read that question in my eyes, he immediately snatches his hand back and scrambles off me.

"Don't get any ideas," he snarls at me under his breath. "You would've given us away if you'd remained standing any longer." Rolling over on his stomach, he braces his elbows on the ground and then nods towards something to our right. "And I simply didn't want to be fighting *that*."

Tearing my gaze from him, I shift my attention towards the spot he nodded at.

Cold dread washes over me like ice water when I find an entire host of silver dragons flying towards us.

"Malachi's balls," Orion curses from where he is lying on his stomach on my other side.

Isera, who is in a similar position next to him, just stares at the large group of silver dragons through narrowed eyes.

Based on the size of the dragons, Bane and Jessina are not among them, so it must be a squad of soldiers or something.

Their scales glitter like starlight in the bright sun, and their massive wings boom through the air like thunder. My heart pounds as I watch them draw closer. They're flying in formation towards the mountain doors, and they don't look to be in any particular hurry, so they can't be here for us. But I still curl my fingers into the soft grass, gripping it hard, as if that can somehow steady my racing pulse.

The four of us are powerful. But there looks to be at least twenty-five of them, so I doubt we would win a battle against them in these circumstances.

Gusts of wind rip across the landscape as the host of dragons reaches the flat stretch of ground before the mountain doors. The grass trembles in fear as their wings slam down above it when the dragons swoop down to land. Thuds echo across the grasslands as their massive bodies hit the ground.

From under the cover of trees and bushes, I watch as one of the silver dragons hovers over the grass instead of landing straight away.

I suck in a sharp breath as the dragon opens his claws and sets a person down on the grass. Long brown hair whips in the wind from the dragons' wings, revealing a pair of pointed ears.

Lavendera.

The other dragons finish landing. Five of them shift into their human forms while the other twenty remain in dragon form. The dragons face the mountain, standing there in their massive forms as if they can glare the doors open. The five who shifted, however, turn to watch Lavendera. They don't approach her or restrict her in any way. In fact, it almost looks as if they're guarding her. But from a wary distance.

Narrowing my eyes, I study her.

There is no fake iron collar around her neck now. Instead, she is wearing a simple pair of gray pants and a white shirt with silver details that glint faintly in the sunlight. And the way she is standing, the way she is carrying herself, it's as if... As if she is a person of authority.

I furrow my brows.

Why would the Icehearts give Lavendera any authority? I thought they hated all fae. So who—

I almost gasp when a sudden thought strikes me like a lightning bolt.

Snapping my mouth shut, I just barely manage to cut the sound off before it can escape my mouth. But my heart starts pounding in my chest.

Is Lavendera related to the Icehearts? A bastard birthed by one of Emperor Bane's previous life slaves? Based on the way he treated Isera and how he made her dress, and how he talked about her mother as well, it wouldn't surprise me if he actually crossed the line with some of his previous life slaves.

My heart beats hard against my ribs as I stare at Lavendera in a new light.

I don't know for certain, of course, but it would explain a lot. It would explain why the Icehearts give her so much freedom and authority. And it would also explain why she is loyal to them. If she's half dragon shifter, and Bane's bastard to boot, getting her to switch sides might turn out to be impossible.

"It's Bane and Jessina's elite guards," Draven whispers from my right, but his eyes remain fixed on the group of silver dragons. "Which means that whatever they want from the Green Clan is important."

The Green Clan, however, doesn't open the door for them either.

A smug sense of satisfaction pulses through me as we spend the next twenty minutes watching Lavendera and the silver dragons pace impatiently across the grass while the huge mountain doors remain firmly closed.

At last, one of the dragons lets out a roar, and the five people in human form shift back into dragons as well. After once more picking up Lavendera, they fly back the way they came.

Draven lets out a huff of amusement. "Kander didn't open the doors for them? Damn, I'm actually impressed."

Before anyone can reply, Grey opens a portal behind us. I send a silent prayer of thanks to Mabona that he didn't open it while the soldiers were still here.

Clothes rustle as the four of us climb back to our feet and turn towards the glittering blue portal.

"Alright, we'll try the Green Clan again later when we have more of the other clans on our side," Draven announces. "So let's get started with the most important one. The Orange Clan."

Orion gives Grey a nod. He lets the portal sink back down into the ground before opening a new one. Through it, the edge of a forest becomes visible. I suppress a smile as I think about how fortunate it is that Alistair didn't come with us, since we're apparently heading into yet another forest.

That tingling sensation ripples through me again as we once more step through the portal. I study the forest before us while Orion gives Grey instructions. The forest looks wild and messy and muddy. As if it has been raining for weeks on this side of the continent. Tilting my head back, I find that the sky here is indeed covered in dark clouds. I can practically taste the brewing storm on the wind.

Grey bows to his king and then disappears back to what I assume is the Unseelie Court while the rest of my companions turn to look at the forest as well.

A few thick vines swing violently between the trees as a strong wind rips through the landscape. I suppress a shudder even though the temperature is still relatively warm. The wind disturbs the foliage, and drops of water slide down the dark green leaves and fall through the air to land on the muddy ground with muted *plops*.

"The Orange Clan's homeland is on the other side of this forest," Draven says as he starts forward towards the trees. "Let's go."

I follow him. And so does Isera.

"I am *not* going in there," Orion declares in a haughty voice.

Without breaking stride, Draven gives him a mocking glance over his shoulder. "Is the preening little princeling afraid to get his slippers dirty?"

I have to bite the inside of my cheek to stop myself from laughing. Draven is right, though. All three of us are wearing sturdy black boots, and Draven is wearing his dragon scale armor while both Isera and I are wearing the black fighting leathers that Jocasta gave us during the Great Games in the Unseelie Court. But Orion is wearing his fancy formal garments, a pair of stylish shoes, and even his spiky black crown. He's not exactly dressed for a march through a muddy forest.

"Just because you lack any fashion sense doesn't mean that everyone needs to dress down to match your ugly looks, you uncultured beast," Orion retorts, a smile full of sweet poison on his lips.

Coming to a halt, Draven turns around and shakes his head at the Unseelie King. "Or you could've just put on a pair of functional boots like the rest of us so that you wouldn't get stuck in the mud."

"Do I look like someone who owns a pair of *boots*?"

"Fair enough. I do like your shirt, though. It's very stylish."

Surprise flits across Orion's face, and he raises his eyebrows. "Really?"

"No." Draven shoots him a scowl. "What the hell where you thinking putting that on?" Giving Orion a look of utter disbelief, he waves his hand to indicate the king's fancy garments. "Someone can just stab right through it."

Orion lets out a dismissive scoff. "No one would ever be able to get close enough to stab me."

I suck in a sharp breath.

In a heartbeat, Isera has whipped around from where she was standing in front of Orion and pressed a shard of ice against his throat. The Unseelie King just stares at her in shock for a few seconds, his mouth slightly open and one hand still raised.

Isera gives him a slow and incredibly sharp smile. "You were saying?"

That snaps Orion out of his stupor. Revenge glints in his eyes as he locks a glare dripping with challenge on her. She just stares right back.

A huff of laughter escapes my lips.

Oh, Lyra was most definitely right.

CHAPTER EIGHT

When we finally reach the other end of the forest, I'm exhausted, dirty, and sweaty. Partly because it was incredibly humid inside the woods and there was no proper path to follow. But mainly because Draven spent a good portion of the hike secretly summoning his storm magic and using it to blow wind right into me so that I had to struggle to push forward. It took me longer than I want to admit to realize that. Once I did, I used my own magic to increase the spark of exhaustion in his own chest until he was panting with exertion. Only then did we agree to a silent truce.

I glance over at Draven as we trudge the final distance to the end of the forest. His black hair is damp and messy, and mud splatters part of his imposing armor. The sight of it brings a smug smirk to my lips and makes me feel a bit better about the fact that I probably look equally ruffled.

Drawing in a deep breath, I drag a hand through my hair to remove a few stray strands that are stuck to my forehead and cheeks. Part of me can't help but think that Orion had a point. This forest was unnecessarily unpleasant.

I turn towards him and Isera as they catch up to me and

Draven where we have stopped a short distance from the tree line. My eyebrows shoot up when I take in their appearances. I've been so focused on getting through the forest without Draven pushing me into a pile of mud that I have barely been paying attention to our other two companions. But now that I do, I can barely believe what I'm seeing.

Both Isera and Orion somehow look completely unaffected. Apart from the unavoidable mud on their shoes, there isn't a single speck of dirt on their clothes. No drops of sweat line their temples, and I swear to Mabona, neither of them has so much as one strand of hair out of place.

I gape at them. "How the hell are you two so clean and pristine?"

"I don't sweat," Isera and Orion reply in unison.

Surprise flits across both of their faces as they exchange a glance. They quickly break eye contact and turn back to me, but the moment Orion can't see Isera's face, I swear amusement tugs at her lips for a second. I stare at them in stunned disbelief.

"I have ice magic," Isera explains.

Orion shrugs. "I'm royalty."

I frown at him. "What does that have to do with anything?"

"Royalty doesn't sweat." He flicks a nonchalant hand. "Sweating is for peasants."

"Just get a move on," Draven mutters. "We're here."

After shaking my head at our far too unruffled companions, I hurry after Draven as he strides the final distance to the tree line.

Air leaves my lungs in a whoosh when I reach the edge of the forest. My jaw drops, and for a second, my eyes can't comprehend what it is that I'm looking at.

We're standing at the edge of a cliff. The steep side cuts straight down in a sheer drop, and we're so high up that I can't even see the ground. Instead, the side of the cliff disappears down into clouds below us. But that is not the most astonishing part.

Massive islands, which look like upside-down mountains, are

floating in the air before us. The piercing tip is pointing straight down, and each island appears stationary, but they're not attached to anything. They just float there among the clouds, completely free in the air.

The mostly flat surface of each floating island is covered in grass and trees. Sticking up amid the vibrant vegetation are elegant buildings in bright colors. Orange dragons soar through the sky between two of the islands farthest from us.

Dragging in an unsteady breath, I stare at the gorgeous view before me. I thought the Unseelie Court, with its massive waterfalls and glittering canals, was the most beautiful place I have ever seen. But this... This might be the most astonishing thing I've seen yet.

A sharp twinge of longing and regret hits me like a blade to the chest. The world is so big. It's absolutely bursting with incredible things and breathtaking places. And I have seen none of it.

I pull at my collar as the sudden tightness in my chest makes it difficult to breathe.

I've missed so much. I've been *denied* so much.

I want to see it all. I want to experience this world in all its glory and get drunk on new sights and sensations. I want it all. I want fucking everything!

That tightness in my chest intensifies, strangling my throat and squeezing my heart hard, as my gaze is once more drawn back to Draven. I want to experience this beautiful place with him. The real him. Not this unnatural version that looks at me with such hatred.

My eyes burn and my chest aches. I want him back.

"Ryat," Isera begins. "Earlier, you said Tanaka hates you. Why?"

Her timely interruption snaps me out of my spiraling thoughts, and I manage to force the black waves of rage and despair back enough to suck in a deep breath. Dropping my hand from my collar, I shake out my arm and take another steadying breath. With effort, I return my focus to the task at hand. Convincing Rin Tanaka and her Orange Dragon Clan to help us take down the Iceheart Dynasty.

Draven holds Isera's gaze for another few seconds before he turns to look out at the floating islands again. "Because I burned this place to the ground a hundred and forty years ago."

"You did *what?*"

Next to her, Orion chuckles. "Of course you did."

There is no trace of emotion on Draven's face as he watches the beautiful scenery before him. Only that customary expression of confidence and power remains on his features. As if he feels nothing. But I know that that's not true. He feels a lot of things. He's just better than most at hiding it.

"When Rin became clan leader, she launched a rebellion against Bane and Jessina," Draven explains, his eyes still on Rin's homeland. "I broke that rebellion and forced her clan back underneath their heel."

I suppress a groan. This is not going to be easy.

"Great," Isera says, sarcasm dripping from her voice. "So then how do we get her to side with us now?"

"If I just walk up to her, she's more likely to punch me in the face than to speak with me."

I shrug. "Well, you do have a very punchable face."

He cuts me a look from the corner of his eye. "You seemed to like my face just fine last night."

Heat sears my cheeks at the reminder of that humiliating experience.

"So what's the plan then?" Isera asks, mercifully pushing the conversation back on track.

Draven blows out a sigh and lifts one shoulder in a shrug. "Still working on it."

"What?" Orion demands. Raising his arm, he stabs his hand in the direction of the muddy forest we just traversed. "You made us trudge through all of that, and you don't even have a plan?"

"Why do I always have to be the one with the plan?" Draven snaps, anger flashing across his face so suddenly that I jerk back in shock. "God forbid someone else actually used their head for once." He cuts Orion a sharp glare. "You're supposed to be the master of schemes. Pull your fucking weight."

Orion, entirely unfazed by Draven's sudden anger, just arches an arrogant eyebrow. "Need I remind you that I was practically blackmailed into this?"

"Yeah," Draven replies, his voice taking on a mocking edge as he no doubt thinks about how the Unseelie King blackmailed *us* back in his court earlier. He flashes Orion a vicious smile. "Sucks, doesn't it?"

Orion snaps something back at him, but I can barely focus on what, because I can't get that exasperated look on Draven's face out of my head. Because he's right. He has been forced to take on way too much for far too long.

"We can think about how to convince Rin later," I say, interrupting their argument. "First, we need to figure out how to get from here to the floating islands without being seen."

All three of them turn to me. Draven looks caught between being grateful that someone else is forcing our attention back to the problem at hand and angry that I spoke simply because his default mode now is to hate everything I say. Thankfully, his more practical side wins this time.

"I can do a half-shift and fly across that way," he says. "They'll only be watching for dragons, so a small target like that will go unnoticed."

"Good." I nod. "Then you can fly us over as well."

The hatred returns to his eyes in a flash.

Drawing his eyebrows down, he growls, "I'm not carrying you."

I keep my chin raised as I hold his gaze. "You either fly us over or do this all on your own. Your choice."

That unnatural hatred burns in his eyes, trying to override his common sense. He flexes his hand and clenches his jaw for a few seconds. Then he at last grinds out, "Fine."

A yelp slips from my lips as he grabs me without warning. A small cloud of black smoke explodes around us as he shifts into his half-shift form at the same time as he lifts me into his arms. His massive black wings flare out, making the cloud of smoke drift away into the forest behind us before evaporating.

"Wait here," he tells Isera and Orion.

Without waiting for a reply, he simply launches into the air.

My stomach flips at the sudden start, and I wrap my arms around his neck.

His angry gaze immediately snaps to me. "Don't touch me."

"I have to hold on, otherwise I'm going to fall," I retort.

"Remove your arms from my neck, Selena. Or I swear to God, I will drop you on purpose."

"You wouldn't."

"Fucking try me."

I hold his stare. He stares right back. Winds tug at my hair and clothes as he flies us closer to the nearest floating island up ahead. Then he begins lowering his arms, as if he actually is going to let me go. My heart jerks.

With a low snarl, I quickly remove my arms from around his neck.

"You just don't want to be reminded of that night when you flew me through the star-dusted night sky above Frostfell," I bait. "Right after you saved my life and right before you told me that I was your mate."

A sharp tug yanks at my chest.

Draven gasps in what sounds like shock.

And drops me.

My stomach lurches as I suddenly plummet downwards.

Winds rush in my ears and my hair streams up over my head. I want to scream but the sound gets stuck in my throat.

Then a strong hand wraps around my wrist.

I suck in a gasp as my fall comes to an abrupt halt that tears at my shoulder. Tilting my head back, I stare up along my outstretched arm and find Draven hovering in the air above me. His hand is still wrapped around my wrist, and that is the only thing keeping me in the land of the living right now. If he lets go of my wrist, I will fall down through the clouds and die painfully on the ground somewhere far below.

"Draven," I gasp out, my pulse hammering in my ears. "Pull me up."

But he just hovers there, his wings beating the air, and makes no move to pull me farther up so that he can carry me to safety. That unnatural hatred burns like wildfire in his eyes.

"What the fuck did you just do to me?" he demands.

"What?" I shake my head. "I didn't do anything."

"That… tug."

My eyes widen. Right before he dropped me, I felt a sharp tug on our mate bond. I stare up at Draven, my head suddenly pounding. Did he… feel it too? Back at the rock wall in the underground forest, I just thought that he felt some kind of emotion. Not the actual tug that *I* felt on the mate bond. But maybe he has actually started to feel our mate bond again as well.

"You felt it too?" I ask, my voice trembling with hope.

"I…" he begins, looking uncertain for a moment. Then his features harden again. "I fucking hate you. I hate you because nothing makes sense around you. Nothing *about you* makes sense. I hate your voice. I hate how you move. I hate looking at your face. I hate everything that comes out of your mouth. And yet…"

My heart starts beating faster. "And yet?"

He licks his lips. His massive black wings beat the air on either side of his muscular body. Out here, halfway between the cliff and the closest floating island, we're too far away to be seen by anyone else. Right now, it's just me and him.

His grip on my wrist tightens as he clenches his jaw again. I wait, my stupid hopeful heart beating erratically, for him to answer my question.

"It would be so much easier if I just let you fall," he says at last. "Everything would be so much better if you weren't here. Because you ruin everything. You always ruin everything."

Pain slashes through my chest like sharp claws as those words once again hit me with surgical precision. And the fact that they're coming from Draven's mouth make them utterly unbearable.

With his merciless eyes still locked on mine, he begins loosening his grip on my wrist.

My heart leaps into my throat as he begins lifting his fingers from my skin.

"Draven," I blurt out, trying and failing not to sound like I'm pleading. "Draven, please."

"Don't," he snarls. "Fuck, I hate it when you say my name."

But he stops loosening his grip. I don't dare to say anything else, so I just hold his gaze while blood rushes in my ears.

A frustrated noise rips from his throat.

Then he tightens his grip on my wrist again and abruptly flies us the final distance to the floating island. My stomach lurches as he practically tosses me onto the ground and then spins in the air and flies back to Isera and Orion without another word.

I hit the ground hard on my hip, the impact sending a jolt through my entire body. My shoulder aches from hanging by my wrist like that for so long. Waves of black rage and dark despair crowd down on me from all sides. I try to suck air into my lungs, but I can't breathe.

Curling up on my side, I bury my fingers in the soft earth beneath me and grip it so hard that my hand begins to shake.

Draven's words echo endlessly through my skull.

Because you ruin everything. You always ruin everything.

His hate-filled eyes as he glares down at me are burned into my mind. I can still feel his phantom fingers on my wrist. How his grip loosened. Can hear the sincerity in his voice when he told me that everything would be so much better if I weren't here.

I try once more to drag air into my lungs, but the pressure on my chest from that black wave inside me is so intense that I feel like my ribs are going to shatter. I feel like I'm drowning.

I can't keep feeling like this. I need to pull myself together. I need to snap the fuck out of this. Goddess damn it.

Summoning my magic, I create a warm sparkling yellow flame of joy in my mind and then I throw it out across the island. The first person I make contact with gets it shoved straight into his or her chest.

Pleasure immediately floods my body.

I gasp as my lungs finally expand and air fills them. Suddenly, it feels as if I'm floating on a perfect cloud. As if I'm wrapped in the perfect warm hug. I drink in that feeling like I'm starving. It helps force away the endless ocean of suffocating feelings that threatened to drown me.

While drawing in another deep breath, I finally unclench my hand and push myself up from the ground. Dark clouds churn in the sky above me, and the air tastes like a brewing storm. But inside my body, only that addictive pleasure thrums.

I don't even know who it is that I am permanently changing with my magic, just so that I could get this burst of relief and pleasure.

And I don't even care. I feel no remorse. No guilt. No shame. Nothing.

I feel nothing.

Goddess above, it's so fucking nice not to care.

CHAPTER NINE

The rain starts when we reach the main city. Heavy drops fall from the sky. Slow at first. Then picking up in intensity. Harsh winds rip between the elegant buildings, creating a howling sound. Above us, the dark clouds rumble with thunder.

Pushing my wet hair out of my face, I tie all of my hair back in a bun so that I can see properly without the wind whipping hair into my face every few seconds.

The only good thing about this awful weather is that most people who live here have now taken shelter indoors, which means that we've been able to sneak through the city unseen. I glance over my shoulder, but only rain thrums against the wet stone street behind us.

"Rin should be in that building," Draven says, and nods towards a tall red building on the other side of a massive open square.

"Alright." I nod and then look from face to face. "Here's the plan. Isera and I will go in alone and talk to her. She healed us after the Atonement Trials, and if she has tried to start her own rebellion earlier, she probably sympathizes with the two of us more than…" I wave a hand at Draven, who has burned down her home, and Orion, who is just an all-around absolute menace in general. "Well, you."

Draven stares at me, his eyebrows raised. I think his surprise has more to do with the fact that I formulated a plan for us rather than the actual contents of the plan.

But I just couldn't get his exasperated words out of my head. His frustration about how he is always forced to come up with all the plans and make sure that all missions are running smoothly. He deserves better. He deserves someone who takes care of him too. Someone who helps take some of that massive weight off his shoulders. He deserves everything. And I intend to give it to him. Even though he still hates me.

"I agree," Isera says.

Draven looks like he wants to shoot down my idea out of pure habit, but he apparently can't find any actual flaws in it, because he just clenches his jaw and nods instead.

"Okay, good," I begin. "Then we—"

A loud clanging sound, like giant metal bells being rung, splits the air.

We whirl towards the large square to find a mass of soldiers in orange dragon scale armor pouring out of the door to the tall building.

"Fuck," Draven curses. "She knows we're here."

Without hesitation, he stalks out of the shadows and starts out into the open square. The rest of us scramble to catch up with him.

Rain whips down from the sky, stinging my face, as we stride out into the open space. A figure in elegantly decorated armor shoves open both doors to the tall building and walks out onto the short steps outside. Her long black hair whips in the wind as she stares us down from across the wet stones.

"Rin!" Draven calls over the howling winds. "We—"

I shove him forward.

Pain crackles through me as the arrow slams into my side instead. I gasp. Staggering a step forward, I have to blink hard to keep my vision in focus.

Draven whirls around, staring at me in shock. His stunned gaze flits from my face and then down to the arrow that had been meant for him. But before he can say anything, Rin Tanaka's voice cuts through the storm.

"Capture him!" she yells over the howling winds and rumbling thunder.

Another hail of arrows shoots through the air.

Some are ripped away by the winds, and the others clatter against the walls of ice that Isera yanks up around us. Pain pulses through me from the arrow that is still stuck in my side. I glance down at it, dreading this next part.

However, before I can reach towards it with my already trembling hands, Orion abruptly snaps off the arrowhead and yanks the shaft out of my side so fast that I barely have time to gasp. Pain rips through me, but not nearly as bad as it would've been if I'd had to do it myself.

I stare at the Unseelie King in surprise, but he has already spun back to face our attackers.

"Rin!" Draven calls again. "I'm not here to fight! We're here to—"

"Attack!" she screams.

The soldiers around her lurch forward. Their boots slap against the wet cobblestones as they all rush forward. Atop the sloping rooftops all around us, archers loose another volley of arrows.

"Fuck!" Draven snaps.

Summoning his storm magic, he throws it around us in a circle, changing the direction of the already screaming winds and shoving the hail of arrows off course.

"Orion, handle the archers," he commands. Then his sharp

eyes shift to me and Isera. "You two, get me to Rin. And try not to kill anyone."

No one hesitates or questions the orders. Not even Orion. He just summons his nightmare magic and throws it across the square. Bows clatter to the rooftops and archers scream in panic as the Unseelie King blocks out their vision by forcing them to relive their worst memories.

Draven sprints forward. Isera and I flank him as we hurtle across the wind-swept square. Soldiers in orange armor rush towards us from all sides.

Steel rings through the air as Draven draws his massive sword. I yank out my own dagger right before the first wave of soldiers reaches us.

Using the already raging storm to his advantage, Draven directs it with his magic and sends a furious blast of wind crashing into the ranks of soldiers. They call out in shock as a large portion of them are swept to the side as if by a giant hand. I throw out my own magic and latch on to those brass-colored sparks of shock.

While ducking under a blade swung from my left, I blow that shock into massive fires, which in turn triggers a flare of fear. I quickly release my grip on their shock and instead sink my magic into those bone white sparks of fear.

Screams of pure terror echo through the square as I transform those sparks into wildfires. Half of the soldiers in that section flee in blind fear while the rest drop to the ground and vomit as their knees buckle.

But the other ranks who weren't swept away by Draven's wind crash right into us.

Ice shoots through the air as Isera throws massive sheets at them to block their advance. But there are too many of them. And without being able to kill them, we're at a severe disadvantage.

Steel clangs as Draven blocks a sword aimed at his head. With a flick of his wrist, he forces the soldier's sword away from his own and then shoves him back with sheer brute force.

"Tell them to stand down," he snaps at Rin, who is still standing on the steps ahead. "I don't want to kill them. I want to form an alliance."

"Capture him!" Rin yells. Rain pelts her armor and face, and her long black hair is completely soaked as it whips in the wind. "My orders are to capture you!"

"Orders? What ord—"

His words are cut off as two people swing at him from the side. Isera blocks one blade with a sheet of ice while Draven manages to duck the other. Twisting down and around, he spins and drives his fist into the soldier's stomach. Air explodes from the soldier's lungs in a gasp. But three more are already rushing towards us.

Releasing my grip on the section to our left, I focus on the immediate enemies around us instead. I don't want to permanently change any of these people since that would probably destroy any chance we have of getting Rin on our side, so I have to search for emotions that are already there.

Shoving my magic at them in rapid bursts, I test different emotions until I find some that stick. Two people sway and stagger sideways in exhaustion when I find tiny sparks of tiredness that I increase into massive flames. Another hesitates for a second, giving Draven a chance to knock him out with the butt of his sword, when I latch on to that emotion.

Steel clashes and ice shoots through the air as we fight for every step closer to Rin. But the horde of soldiers just keeps coming.

Alarm crackles up my spine as a sword glints right next to me. Yanking my head to the side, I barely manage to evade it before it can slash across my cheek.

A fist slams into my side.

Pain shoots through me, blinding me for a second, as it strikes right where the still bleeding arrow wound is located. I gasp and stagger to the side. Metal clangs against ice right next to my head. Blinking my eyes into focus, I find a sheet of ice blocking the sword that almost took my head off. Stumbling upright, I suck in a shuddering breath and throw my magic at the soldier behind Isera.

With a desperate shove, I force exhaustion into his body. He staggers to a halt and sways heavily, his sword hitting the stones before he could stab it into Isera's back. We exchange a nod.

"Rin!" Draven tries again while parrying two swords and then kicking another soldier in the hip. "I know you hate me, but you need to at least hear me out!"

"No, I need to capture you," she snaps back, her voice laced with tension.

"We're on the same fucking side."

"My orders are to capture you."

"Your orders..." Draven suddenly trails off. Then his mouth drops open as a bolt of realization pulses across his face. "Azaroth's fucking flame, you're wearing dragon steel, aren't you?"

Shock flashes across Rin Tanaka's beautiful features, and she opens her mouth as if to respond. But no words make it out. After working her jaw, she forces out a frustrated breath and then grinds out, "My orders are to capture you."

"The Icehearts are controlling Rin with dragon steel!" Draven bellows across the entire square.

The soldiers from the Orange Dragon Clan hesitate, staring between him and their clan leader in stunned disbelief.

"Capture him!" Rin shouts as she, at long last, runs down from the steps and out into the open square. "Our orders are to capture him."

And then she shifts into a dragon.

"God fucking damn it!" Draven growls while parrying a sword strike and shoving storm winds at another group at the same time as he keeps one eye on the massive orange dragon that appears from the cloud of black smoke.

"If she's wearing dragon steel, there is nothing we can do." He shoves his massive sword back into the sheath that is strapped down his back. "We need to get out. Run like hell to Orion and then get on. Now!"

My mind is still spinning with pain from the wound, so I'm still trying to process what just happened. But Isera doesn't hesitate. Grabbing my wrist, she yanks me with her as she starts sprinting across the square.

The soldiers around us call out in surprise and then scream orders to each other, but they're drowned out when Rin opens her jaws and roars. I gasp as the sound echoes between the buildings loudly enough to make my head ring.

Black smoke explodes behind us.

Stumbling a step, I cast a glance over my shoulder, but the rolling smoke obscures both the soldiers and Draven.

"We're getting out," Isera calls to Orion as soon as we get within earshot.

Rain and winds whip through the square, ripping at the Unseelie King's long dark blue hair and tearing at his fancy clothes. But he stands there with his back straight and his spiky crown on his head, immovable like a mountain, while his eyes glow with powerful magic.

He gives us a single nod.

Then the storm winds blow the black smoke clear, and Draven becomes visible.

Awe fills me as I gaze up at the massive black dragon that now stands between us and Rin. Draven's dragon form is huge, and Isera and I barely managed to get out of the way before he shifted. If we'd been any slower, we would've ended up underneath his body.

His spiky black tail swishes across the ground right next to us.

For a few moments, no one moves.

The soldiers, still in their human forms, stand motionless as they glance between Draven and their clan leader. Rin, in her dragon form, has her black eyes locked on Draven. Rain pelts her orange scales, but she barely seems to feel it. She is much smaller than Draven, and in a one-on-one battle between them, there is no question about who would win.

Unfortunately, though, this is not a one-on-one battle.

Rin lets out a roar.

Black smoke begins exploding across the large square as all the soldiers start shifting as well.

Swinging his massive head in our direction, Draven lets out a deafening roar of his own.

We lurch into motion.

With a flick of her wrist, Isera forms a crude staircase of ice that leads right up to Draven's back. Before it's even fully formed, we sprint up the steps and towards the spikes where Draven's neck meets his shoulders.

Rin attacks.

I gasp and throw myself desperately the final few steps up. Winds rip at my body, trying to throw me off, and my boots slip on Draven's wet scales. Diving forward, I barely manage to reach that spot where his neck meets his shoulders where there is space for someone to sit.

Draven lunges and swipes his claws out to force Rin back. I grab the spike in front of me with both hands right before Isera crashes into my back, almost knocking me off again. Another jolt shoots through me as Orion slams into Isera's back a moment later.

All around us, orange dragons appear in clouds of smoke.

A deafening roar splits the air.

Then my stomach lurches as Draven abruptly shoots up from the ground.

Isera wraps her arms tightly around my waist to keep from sliding off. Thankfully, Orion's back seems to be braced by another spike at least, so I don't have to carry the weight of them both.

The ground rapidly disappears below us as we shoot up through the rain-soaked sky. Rin and an entire host of orange dragons follow us. Thunder rumbles in the dark clouds and winds rip at my body. I cling to the wet spike in front of me while rain hits my face like tiny arrows.

Draven rolls in the air.

My stomach turns and my breath gets stuck in my throat as the world spins around me. Isera's arms tighten around my waist, and Orion curses from behind her.

I scream as a pair of orange jaws snap shut in the air right next to us. Draven roars and levels out again as Rin and the other orange dragons swarm us.

"Help him!" I scream over the rushing winds as Draven breathes a torrent of fire like a long barrier to stop our attackers.

Isera starts shooting blocks of ice at the dragons behind us while Orion focuses on the ones to our right. Twisting to my left, I shove my magic towards the dragons there while Draven fends off an attack from Rin.

Only one of the dragons on the left feels fear, but I latch on to it and increase it to such an awful degree that it lets out a screech and speeds away through the lashing rain.

"Watch out!" Orion snaps.

I don't even have time to turn my head before I feel Isera's body disappear from behind me.

Then a shout of agony rips through the air.

Whipping my head around, I find Orion holding Isera on the left side of Draven's spine. The claw that would've torn through her body now slashes across Orion's thigh instead as he shields her with his body. Pain blooms in his eyes and he gasps in a breath. I quickly help set Isera back down on Draven's scales right before he swerves violently in the air. Isera's shocked face disappears behind my back once more.

I grip the spike before me hard as Draven rolls in the air again to evade three orange dragons. Rin lets out a screeching call.

All twenty dragons around us attack at the same time.

Another deafening roar rips from Draven's chest, making his entire body vibrate from the force of it.

The dark storm clouds around us grow darker, thicker, more violent. The wind thrashes so hard that I'm almost tossed off Draven's back. Lightning splits the air in furious flashes, aimed at the orange dragons.

Isera shoots massive sheets of ice at the dragons that are closing in on us. Two of them appear to have lost their vision as Orion blinds them with his magic, and I manage to force another four of them to flee in fear with my own magic. But the other fourteen keep coming.

Claws slash and teeth snap as they all descend on us.

Draven, who is still trying not to kill anyone, dodges and then tries to force them back with storm winds and bolts of lightning.

A blood-curdling scream splits the air.

Cold terror fills me when I realize that it came from Draven.

Whipping my head from side to side, I find a sight that fills me with both rage and horror. One of the orange dragons has clamped its jaws shut right through Draven's side while another has slashed its claws through his left wing. Draven throws his head back and roars in pain.

Everything inside me goes dead silent and still. Like the moment before an executioner's axe falls.

I don't care that Draven ordered us not to kill anyone. I don't care that it might screw up our chances of forming an alliance with the Orange Dragon Clan. They hurt Draven. They will die.

Summoning a massive flame of fear, I slam it right into the orange dragon who is tearing at Draven's side with its teeth. Pleasure floods my entire body as it connects. I increase the flame into a wildfire.

The dragon releases Draven's side and screeches in fear.

But there is not a single ounce of mercy left in my body.

With cold eyes locked on the orange dragon, I keep increasing the fear in its chest until I can taste blood in my mouth. It thrashes in the air, its mind fracturing from the world-ending fear that I'm forcing into its body. I keep increasing my magic.

The dragon jerks once. Then its movements halt and its eyes grow vacant as its heart stops. I watch, completely detached, as it falls down through the thrashing rain, its orange wings fluttering like useless sheets in the wind as it tumbles down to the ground somewhere far below.

Fire roars through the air as Draven breathes torrents of it in front of himself to keep the others back. But another dragon manages to slip through his flames and Isera's ice to slash its claws across Draven's chest. A moment later, another one claws at Draven's other wing.

Another bellow of pain rips from Draven's chest.

And then the storm completely *erupts*.

Winds and rain and lightning thrash around us like a vicious beast. It's so violent, so intense, that all I can do is to squeeze my eyes shut in order to not get blinded while clinging desperately to the spike before me.

My stomach lurches as Draven suddenly shoots forward.

That furious thunderstorm still rages around us. White light flashes on the other side of my eyelids, and thunder cracks through the air so loudly that I think my eardrums are going to burst. Merciless winds howl around us like wolves. The sheer force of it all is so overpowering that I can barely breathe.

But Draven's desperate push of magic appears to work, because he at last manages to get away from the horde of dragons that surrounded us, the thrashing storm forcing them out of the sky.

Blood drips from Draven's torn wings and runs down his side in thick rivulets as he speeds across the stormy sky. We've barely made it past the forest we trekked through earlier when Draven starts losing altitude.

His wings grow slower and more unsteady with each beat, and he wobbles several times in the air as he tries to put as much distance between us and the floating islands as possible.

A small mountain range becomes visible before us. Draven's entire body is shaking now. A growl rips from his chest as he tries to fly us higher so that we can pass it. We climb what can only be a few short strides upwards.

Then Draven's body gives out.

Winds howl around us as we crash down on the ground.

CHAPTER TEN

I gasp as the impact sends a jolt through my body that rattles my very bones. Black smoke explodes around us, obscuring my vision. Shoving myself into a sitting position, I try to blink my eyes back into focus. But all I can see is the black smoke that now covers the wet grass around us. We were close to the mountain when we crashed, not over it, so at least we didn't hit any of the rocks.

Cold dread washes through me. We *didn't* hit any of the rocks, did we?

"Draven!" I scream over the rushing winds and the crashing rain. "Draven!"

No reply.

Fear spreads through my body like poison.

"He's here," Isera suddenly calls back.

Exhaustion laces her voice, so I can just barely hear her over the winds.

I suck in a shuddering breath of relief. Staggering to my feet, I start in her direction. The storm winds whirl across the grass, blowing the black smoke away, until I can at last see my three companions.

But my blood freezes to ice when my gaze finally finds them.

Isera is standing between two tall figures on the ground. Orion is lying on his back on the grass. His eyes are sliding in and out of focus as if he has hit his head, and there is a long gash across his thigh from where the dragon slashed him earlier.

A short distance from him is Draven.

My heart stops as I stare at my mate.

Draven isn't even conscious. He is lying on his side, completely naked except for those magical bracers that store his armor when he's in his dragon form. As if he was only just barely able to shift back into his human form but didn't have enough energy left to use the magic of the bracers to return his clothes to his body.

Blood wells up from the claw marks across his chest and the massive bite wound in his side. There are deep holes running straight through his body from the orange dragon's teeth.

For a few seconds, I just stand there, staring at him. My mind refuses to process what I'm looking at and my body feels completely numb.

"We need to get them out of the storm," Isera suddenly calls.

Her voice snaps me out of my stupor.

"There's a cave up there," she says. "But I used up almost all of my magical energy in that final push to escape, so I can't summon anything big enough to lift them. We'll have to drag them."

When I had my eyes closed against the blinding lightning, Isera must have summoned a gigantic wall of ice or something to stop the others from following Draven when we escaped.

Bending down, I hoist Draven's chest up and loop my arms under his arms and over his shoulders. He doesn't even stir. My heart aches as I begin dragging him towards the cave Isera indicated.

Orion, who appears to at least be semi-conscious, must have hit his head pretty hard when we crashed because he doesn't even complain when Isera drags his royal ass and fancy clothes across the ground and towards the mouth of the cave.

My muscles shake and the arrow wound in my side pulses with pain as I pull Draven's heavy body as carefully as I can across the grass. Storm wind rips at my hair, pulling strands free from my hair tie and sending them whipping around my face. A few of them stick to my wet cheeks, so I try to wipe my cheek against my shoulder to get them off. Rain washes down over us like an unending flood, and lightning splits the dark heavens above.

Clenching my jaw, I grit my teeth as I make slow progress towards the cave.

A small noise of pure desperation rips from my throat as I haul Draven the final distance into the shelter of the cave. Air escapes my lungs in a whoosh when the harsh winds and stinging rain abruptly disappear. It's cold and gloomy inside the cave, but at least the storm can't reach us in here.

Isera and I place Draven and Orion on their backs in the middle of the cramped space. The Unseelie King blinks repeatedly and shakes his head while his eyes roam across the jagged roof of the cave, as if he is trying to figure out what happened and where he is. Draven is still unconscious.

Worry snakes through my chest, strangling my lungs, as I stare down at his shivering and wounded body. I yank off my jacket. Dropping down on my knees, I pull off the white shirt I wear underneath the leathers. After ripping it into several pieces, I carefully wrap it around his wounds before tying the final piece of it around his hips. Then I pull on my cold and wet leather jacket again to protect my otherwise bare torso.

With my heart aching in my chest, I gently place my hand on Draven's cheek.

"Draven," I say, as if that would somehow wake him up.

It doesn't.

My heart squeezes hard.

"Where am I?" Orion asks, sounding just as groggy as he looks.

"We're in a cave," Isera replies in that no-nonsense tone of hers. "We crashed. Draven is hurt." Her expression softens for a fraction of a second as she adds, "And so are you."

The Unseelie King tilts his chin and looks down at the wound across his thigh. "Malachi's balls. Those were my favorite pants."

Isera laughs.

It's a short and abrupt burst of laughter that seems to just rip out of her.

Both Orion and I gape at her in shock. I don't think I have ever heard her laugh before. It was a surprisingly pleasant sound.

She quickly snaps her mouth shut again, looking equally stunned herself for a moment, before she arches a mocking eyebrow at Orion instead. "How hard did you hit your head? Those pants are awful."

A sly smile curves his lips. "I could take them off, if you want?"

"You probably should."

He blinks at her, looking genuinely stunned, before she turns to me.

"You as well," she says. "These wet clothes in this cold cave all night will give us all hypothermia."

I nod in understanding and then look down at Draven again. Apart from the white shirt I've tied around his hips and wounds, he's already naked. But his body still shakes with either pain or coldness. My throat closes up. I try to swallow down the dread while I start stripping out of my own clothes, but it works poorly. Every glance at Draven's wounded and bloody body sends waves of panic through me.

Like all of us, he has faster healing speed than humans. But his wounds are far too deep. It will take too long to heal on their own. But I still have magic left to use, so if he were to suck it out of my body, it would heal him. However, I have no idea how it works, so I don't know how to give him the magical energy on my own.

Once I'm down to my underwear, I place my hands on Draven's cheeks again and try once more to wake him.

"Draven, please, you need to open your eyes," I beg. "Okay? Just open your eyes and tell me how to transfer my magical energy to you."

He doesn't. And his body continues trembling.

Lying down on the cold stone ground next to him, I carefully wrap my arms around his chest and drape my leg over his as I press myself as close to him as possible. The arrow wound in my side throbs, but I ignore it. If I share my body heat with him, he might at least stop shaking.

"Aren't you going to lie down and hug me like that too?" Orion asks from Draven's other side. He has now stripped out of his wet clothes, and there is a devilish smirk on his lips as he looks up at Isera.

She narrows her eyes at him. "You're lucky I haven't strangled you."

"Choking turns you on, huh? I might be willing to agree to that. Though I'm usually not on the receiving end."

Isera growls something under her breath while yanking off her final garments, leaving her in only underwear.

"Draven, please," I whisper against his cold skin. "Please wake up."

His eyes remain closed, but his body shakes a little less now. I hold him tighter against me, willing my own meager warmth into his body.

"We really should share body heat at least," Orion continues. "Hypothermia and all."

For a few seconds, Isera just glares down at him as if she is fighting the urge to stab him. Then a soft snarl escapes her lips, and she sits down next to him with jerky movements. With a flick of her wrist, she summons that ice gag that looks distinctly like a massive cock and holds it right above Orion's face while she locks threatening eyes on him.

"If you ever tell anyone about this, *this* goes down your throat," she warns. "Permanently."

A sharp smile spreads across his lips, but he says nothing.

Isera dismisses the ice she summoned and lies down next to Orion. He immediately rolls over on his uninjured side and wraps his arms around her body. A low growl comes from her throat, but she doesn't push him off.

Lifting my hand, I gently brush a few wet strands of hair from Draven's forehead. My fingers linger on his cheek.

"Please," I beg again, whispering the words against his skin. "Please, wake up."

He stirs slightly but doesn't open his eyes. And it's a restless stir. Closer to a wince of pain.

I call up my magic. Reaching out, I search for that violet spark of pain in his chest.

When my magic connects, I have to bite my lip hard to stop a gasp. The flame of pain in his chest is so massive that my vision blacks out for a second. Dragging in a long calming breath, I scramble to raise my mental shields so that I can separate his pain from my own.

Once they're in place, I steadily begin lowering his pain.

A shuddering breath escapes his lips.

I almost weep with relief.

The tension bleeds out of his body as I decrease that wildfire of pain inside him until it's nothing more than a tiny spark.

His breathing evens out, and the tense crease between his eyebrows smoothens.

Keeping my arms around him, I continue pouring magic into him to take his pain away.

If he could just wake up and tell me what to do, I could heal him directly. I could give him all of my magic and fix him right now. But because I don't know how it works, all I can do is to lie there uselessly next to him and take away his pain. A temporary fix to deal with the symptoms when I should have been able to fix the entire root cause. Simply because I don't know how.

Goddess above, there is so much I don't know. So much knowledge I don't have, so many lies I've been told, so many skills I lack. All because I've been trapped inside that one city and fed lies all my life. How am I supposed to keep Draven safe when I'm this weak? This pathetic?

I need to get stronger. Smarter. Better. More ruthless.

And I need to do it fast.

Because no one will ever hurt him like this again. I will make fucking sure of it.

CHAPTER ELEVEN

Arguing voices drift through the air. I scowl in annoyance and nestle closer to the warm, muscular body next to me while exhaustion tries to pull me back to sleep. A familiar scent, like night mist and embers, fills my lungs with every breath. It feels so natural. So—

I jerk upright.

Morning sunlight streams in through the cave opening and illuminates the dark gray stone around me.

That sense of familiar comfort is immediately replaced by panic.

Mabona's tits, I must have passed out. I was up all night, using my magic to take away Draven's pain. But my own body must have given in to exhaustion eventually.

Blinking against the sudden light, I snap my gaze to the warm, muscular body that I was nestled against just moments ago.

Draven is still lying on his back, his chest rising and falling with a steady rhythm. The slashes across his chest and the holes in his side have stopped bleeding. But they're still awfully deep. Even with his rapid healing pace, one night wouldn't be enough to fix something like this.

My gaze flits up to the source of the arguing voices that woke me up. Orion is sitting on the ground, inspecting the slash across his thigh, which looks to have mostly healed. I glance down at the arrow wound in my side to find it almost fully healed as well before I return my gaze to Orion. Only a step away from him, Isera is shoving her legs into her pants. The black leather rustles and creaks with her angry movements.

"I don't know why you're so upset," Orion is saying, a sly smile curving his wicked mouth. "You're the one who was cuddling me."

Isera shoots him a glare so cold that it almost gives the entire cave frostbite. "I was not cuddling you."

"You had your arms around me."

She yanks her pants up. "I was trying to push you off."

"You were also lying with your cheek against my chest."

"Because when I had my back against you, that tiny little dagger you keep in your underwear was poking me in the back."

Orion's mouth drops open, and incredulity pulses across his face. "*Tiny little* dagger?"

While buttoning her pants, she gives him a taunting look of challenge. "Yes."

He shoots to his feet. And then winces when it makes his not fully healed wound stretch. He shakes his leg slightly as if to make the pain disperse.

Still only in his underwear, he draws himself up to his full height. It's the first time I've seen the Unseelie King in this state of undress, and I have to admit, it surprises me how toned his body is. In contrast to the almost slightly feminine beauty of his face, his body is made up entirely of lean muscles. It makes him look lethal. And he towers over Isera as he advances on her.

"You take that back," he demands, prowling closer.

Isera, who had bent down to pick up her shirt, is forced to abandon that mission and instead scramble back to avoid being mowed down by him. She has barely managed to stand up straight again when her back hits the cave wall.

Orion places one hand on the wall next to her head and leans closer, his eyes glinting dangerously. "You know full well that there is nothing tiny about it."

With an arrogant expression on her features, Isera tilts her chin up to lock eyes with him. A wicked smile spreads across her lips. "Did I hurt your feelings, pretty boy?"

He clenches his hand. "Take it back."

"Fine. It was slightly above average size."

"You—"

She snickers and shakes her head. "So insecure."

With his hand still on the wall, he lifts his other and traces his fingers over her throat while he rakes gleaming eyes down her shirtless chest. Then he locks eyes with her again and flashes her a lethal smile. "I excel at toying with people until they're on their knees begging for mercy. Are you sure you want to start playing this game with me, little viper?"

"Start playing?" She arches an eyebrow at him and matches his dangerous smile with a villainous one of her own. "We've been playing for months already." Lifting her hand, she gives his chin a condescending push upwards. "Keep up, pretty boy."

Then she ducks under his arm and saunters back to where her shirt is waiting. Orion just remains standing there for another few seconds, his hand still on the wall, as if he can't believe that she just outplayed him like that.

Then he sucks in a sharp breath between his teeth. "*Her?*" With a groan, he throws his hands up in exasperation. "Oh you have got to be fucking kidding me!"

"Would you keep it down?" Draven suddenly growls. "Some of us are still busy trying not to die."

I gasp. Whipping my head back down, I find Draven blinking his eyes open and then squinting against the bright morning sunlight. Relief washes over me like a warm summer wave.

He coughs, scowls, and then sweeps his gaze over his surroundings. "We crashed?"

It's half statement, half question, so I answer, "Yes. Last night."

His attention shifts to me. For one perfect second, he is looking at me like he used to. Then his mind, or rather the unnatural flame of hatred in his chest, catches up and a jolt goes through him. He tries to sit up, as if to scramble away from me. But pain flashes across his features the moment he tries to move, and he collapses back down on the rough stone floor.

"Careful," I snap at him. "Or your wounds are going to start bleeding again."

He huffs and tries to glare at me, but it's ruined by another jolt of surprise when his gaze slips down my body. Drawing his eyebrows down, he grinds out, "Put your fucking shirt back on. I don't want to have to look at your naked body right next to me."

"I would." I shoot him a stare full of challenge. "But my shirt is currently protecting your cock."

He snaps his gaze down to his crotch. Stunned silence echoes between us as he stares at the ripped-up shirt that is currently tied both around his wounds to help stop the bleeding, and around his hips to save him from having to lie here completely naked for all to see.

For a moment, I can't read his expression at all.

Then he rubs a hand over his face and sighs, "Fuck."

Dropping his hand, he tries to sit up again, but it just ends with him sucking in a sharp breath between his teeth and then collapsing back onto the ground. Still on my knees next to him, I try to keep my expression neutral since I know that if I push for an idea too hard, he is going to reject it just out of pure spite.

"I can give you my magic," I say in a casual tone. "So that you will heal."

His gaze snaps back to me. "I don't want anything from you."

Grinding my teeth, I suppress the sudden urge to strangle him. It's starting to get increasingly annoying to try to have a conversation with him when that wildfire of hatred in his chest constantly defaults to arguing with every single thing I say.

"When is Grey coming back?" Draven asks, turning towards Orion instead.

The Unseelie King, who is halfway through getting dressed, pauses with his shirt in his hand and meets Draven's gaze. "I instructed him to open three portals during the night, and if we weren't there, his orders were to return to our court."

"So he's not coming back then?"

"That's what I said."

"It wouldn't even matter," I interrupt. "Because we wouldn't have been able to get all the way back to the edge of that forest with you in this condition." I lock hard eyes on him. "You need to heal."

He clenches his jaw as he glares back at me. But he apparently can't think of any logical arguments to refuse, because in the end, he just forces out an annoyed breath. "Fine."

"Tell me what to do."

"You're not wearing iron, so I can't just take it from you. You need to give it to me willingly."

"And how do I do that?"

"From what I've read, you're supposed to open the gates to your flow of magic and release your grip on it or something."

"What does that even mean?"

"How should I know?" he snaps, scowling up at me. "I'm not fae."

"Fine." I sigh and flick my wrist. "Open the gates and release my grip on it. And then what?"

"Then you breathe it into me while you..." He trails off and looks away.

"While I kiss you," I finish for him.

His angry gaze snaps back to mine. "Having your lips close to mine will suffice."

"We'll be outside," Isera suddenly announces.

"No, we won't," Orion says, and gives her an incredulous look, as if he wouldn't miss prime entertainment like this for the world.

She slides ruthless eyes to him. "When we crashed, your crown flew off your head. I left it out there in the dirt."

His hands shoot up to his head, and his eyes grow wide when he realizes that the crown is indeed not there. Revenge flickers in his eyes as he holds her stare. "The things I will do to you…"

But he stalks out of the cave to retrieve his precious crown anyway. Isera lets out a smug chuckle and then follows him, leaving me and Draven alone.

Nervousness suddenly flutters through my stomach like butterflies. I clear my throat a bit awkwardly before turning back to Draven.

"So…" I begin.

"Just get it over with," he grumbles.

Swallowing, I give him a nod and then push up from my place next to him. Alarm pulses across his face when I instead swing my leg over his body so that I'm straddling him.

"What are you doing?" he presses out.

"Getting into a position where I can place my lips over yours." I arch an expectant brow. "Since you can't even sit up, this is the only way."

Well, it's not actually the only way. But I have ulterior motives.

He scowls, as if he can see right through me, but all he says is, "Just do it already."

Bracing my palms on the cold stone ground on either side of his head, I lean down over him and slant my lips over his.

A sharp breath escapes his lips.

And there is another tug on our mate bond.

This time, I'm the one who almost gasps. Biting my bottom lip, I manage to suppress it. Draven's gaze flits down to my lips, and that dark fire of lust fights with the hatred in his eyes. Lying on his back underneath me, he drags in a deep breath and flexes his hand.

I deliberately let the moment stretch before I finally close my eyes and start trying to figure out how to *open the gates to the flow of my magic* and *release my grip on it.*

Since I'm not sure what to do, I just begin by reaching for my magic. I can feel it there inside me, flowing through my body. On a whim, I try to visualize a pair of doors opening in my chest.

It doesn't work.

I try to visualize the door somewhere between my mouth and my chest instead.

A soft breath escapes me when a feeling of openness washes over me.

"Can you stop breathing on me?" Draven huffs. "It's distracting."

With my eyes still closed, I keep the mental image of the open door while answering, "No, unfortunately I do need to breathe in order to remain conscious."

He mutters something under his breath, and every word caresses my lips. It makes my heart flutter. Suddenly, I realize what he meant by *distracting*. But I don't pull back. Instead, I imagine myself holding my magic in my hand inside of me and then unclenching my fingers so that my palm is open.

A sudden feeling of detachment ripples through me.

I grin.

"Would you hurry it up," Draven complains. "You—"

I crush my lips against his and breathe out.

Magic pours out of me like a flood.

Draven gasps.

Keeping the gates open, I let my magic flow into Draven's body. I don't know how much it will take to heal wounds like that, so I continue to give him more while I move one of my hands from the ground to instead rest on his cheek.

A dark moan comes from deep within his chest.

Then his hands are suddenly in my hair as he abruptly sits up. The sudden move surprises me so much that I break the connection to my magic, but Draven doesn't appear to notice. With me now straddling his lap instead, he curls his fingers in my hair and tilts my head back while his lips at last respond to mine.

Fire flickers through my veins as Draven kisses me back with such furious desperation that I forget how to breathe. His lips ravage mine. Hungrily. Desperately. As if he's starving for my touch. For the feeling of my mouth on his.

I roll my hips and slide my hand down to the back of his neck. Another dark moan rumbles from his throat.

My heart pounds as he dominates my mouth. The desperate, furious passion in every kiss makes me lightheaded, and I hold on to his muscular body as I kiss him back with every ounce of my soul.

And my chest *thrums*.

No. Not my chest.

The mate bond inside me is thrumming. Vibrating in tune with my pounding heart. And through it, I can feel... him.

I can feel the burning lust. The desperate hunger. The confused craving. And the searing hatred. All of it mixed into a raging inferno.

Draven shoves me back.

Disoriented, I topple to the side as he practically throws me off his lap. The sudden end to the kiss and the loss of his lips against mine and the way our mate bond abruptly cuts off again, which happen all at the same time, are so jarring that I actually gasp. Blinking repeatedly, I try to get my mind to focus again as I push myself up from the ground.

"What the hell are you doing to me?" Draven demands. Panic and desperation lace his voice, and his eyes are wild as he stares me down.

I look up as I get my body into a sitting position. Draven is already on his feet. His powerful body is now completely healed, and his muscles shift as he raises his arms and rakes both hands through his hair while he towers over me.

"I could feel you," he continues, his voice still edged with panic, as he holds my gaze with wide eyes. "I could feel... what you feel."

A surge of hope washes through me.

The mate bond.

It was trying to rebuild.

Backing away, Draven shakes his head at me in what looks like both disbelief and warning. "Stay the fuck out of my head."

Before I can reply, he turns around and rips off the scraps of my shirt right before he shifts into a half-shift, which also engages the magic in his bracers. His black dragon scale armor returns to his body with a small puff of black smoke, and his now fully healed wings rustle restlessly on either side of him.

Without another look back, he stalks out of the cave while raking his hands through his hair again.

Still sitting there on the cold stone ground, I stare after him for a few moments. Exhaustion tugs at my body after being drained of so much magic, but I can barely feel it. Because I can still feel Draven's mouth on mine. Lifting a hand, I brush my fingers over my now thoroughly kissed lips.

Draven still hates me. I could feel that massive flame burning mercilessly in his chest when our mate bond briefly reconnected. But by Mabona, it reconnected! Even if it was only for a few short seconds, it was there. I felt him. And he felt me.

That tiny speck of hope that flickers in the dark ocean inside me grows a little stronger, and I dare a small smile. I will find a way to fix this. I will find a way to get him back.

I climb to my feet with a renewed sense of determination.

After getting dressed, I stride out of the cave and join the rest of my companions again.

To no one's surprise, Draven and Orion are arguing.

Again.

"I've already told you," Draven says, hard eyes locked on the Unseelie King. "I don't want to carry any of you."

"Tough luck, you brooding beast," Orion replies with a vicious smile. "Grey doesn't know where we are. So we either fly all the way back to my court and then portal back from there. Or we just fly straight to the Purple Dragon Clan's homeland. Which, as I've already pointed out, is much closer than my court."

"Stop calling me *brooding beast*."

"Stop calling me *preening princeling*."

"Stop arguing," Isera snaps, cutting them both off. "Or I swear to Mabona, I will kill you both myself."

Draven cuts her a look. "You're one to talk. All you and he ever do is argue."

"Like you and Selena," Orion interjects with a pointed look at Draven.

"Like you and him," Isera snipes back at the Unseelie King.

I heave a deep sigh.

This is going to be a long day.

CHAPTER TWELVE

"Seriously?" Orion blows out an annoyed sigh. "Another forest?"

"Yes," Draven replies. "Except this time, it's not something we just need to cross. This forest *is* the Purple Clan's homeland."

Tilting my head back, I stare up at the majestic trees that form the border between the forest and the grasslands behind us.

It's much warmer here than it is in the Seelie Court at this time of year. The air also feels different. It's heavier, in a way. More humid. The vegetation is different as well. The leaves are wider, thicker, and more deep emerald green in color. Dotted among them are flowers in elegant shapes and bright colors. The sounds of thousands of birds chirping and insects trilling drift out from the vibrant forest.

"So how do we sneak in?" Isera asks. She looks a lot less impressed than I am as she regards the forest before us.

"We don't," Draven replies. "The moment we set foot on the other side of that tree line, they will know we're there."

"Then how do we get past them?"

"We don't. We walk inside and wait for them to come to us."

"Sounds like an awful plan," Orion says.

"Based on your extensive knowledge of dragon shifter culture?" Draven challenges. "Or perhaps your astounding contributions to our other missions so far?"

The Unseelie King cuts him a dark look.

Draven flashes him a lethal smirk but then simply forges on. "When they ambush us, because they *will* ambush us, you three keep your mouths shut and let me do the talking." He turns to me and Orion. "And you two, no matter what happens, do not summon magic."

I blink at him in surprise. "Why?"

"Diana is incredibly distrustful of outsiders. And your magic isn't visible. So if she sees your eyes glowing, she will immediately assume that you're messing with her mind, and then she will try to kill us."

"She will probably try to kill us anyway," I point out. "Well, you, at least."

"And she's right." Orion lifts his toned shoulders in a nonchalant shrug. "Our magic would be messing with her head."

"My order still stands," Draven grinds out, annoyance flitting across his face. "You two do not use your magic."

Orion narrows his eyes. "A king does not take orders."

"This one does. Or he will find himself with my sword through his spine."

"One of these days, I'm going to take you up on that challenge, beast."

Draven just lets out a condescending huff of laughter and then turns to Isera. "You can use magic since yours is clearly visible in the air but try to use it for defense only. Unless you want to get torn apart."

Isera raises one eyebrow in question. "Torn apart?"

"You'll see."

The chirping birds and trilling insects seem to grow louder the longer we stand outside the border. I cast another glance at the thick forest while fighting a very untimely smile. I really am glad that Alistair went with Lyra's group instead.

"Everyone clear on the plan? Good," Draven says without actually waiting for a reply. "Then let's go."

The moment we step across the tree line and into the forest, all the birds and insects go abruptly silent all at the same time.

I cast an alarm glance at Draven, but he just continues forward.

Once we've taken a few steps in, the birds and insects start singing again. I draw in a deep breath. The air in here tastes like thick fog and smells strongly of flowers. Flicking my gaze from side to side, I watch for any members of the Purple Dragon Clan. But all I can see is dark green leaves, trees covered in vines, and colorful flowers that almost seem to glow from within.

We continue forward in silence.

The farther we walk, the louder the birds and insects seem to get. Or it might just be because of our own prolonged silence. I'm not sure. But it's starting to give me a headache. It feels like my entire head is buzzing.

"Is the sound getting louder?" I ask at last, while rubbing my temples to relieve the headache building behind my eyes.

"Yes," Draven replies from where he walks next to me. "It's so that we won't hear them move closer when they ambush us."

"Oh."

I don't know what it says about me that I somehow now consider statements like that entirely normal. It hasn't even been an entire year since I left the Seelie Court, but I think I've changed more as a person during that time than all other one hundred and sixty-seven years combined.

"Let's try to keep this ambush brief then," Orion says. "So that we can head back to my court before the day after tomorrow."

I arch an eyebrow at him. "That's an oddly specific deadline."

"If we wait any longer than that, Haldia won't be able to heal the scar on my thigh. And I won't have a scar tarnishing my perfect—"

A *bang* splits the air.

I whip my head in Orion's direction, and my mouth drops open. A massive black panther has slammed right into a thick sheet of ice that Isera raised beside Orion. The Unseelie King is also gaping. But not at the panther that almost killed him. Instead, he stares from Isera to the ice that saved him from the animal attack and then back again.

Isera, however, isn't looking at him. Dropping the sheet of ice, she instead summons a sharp spear and shoves it towards the panther.

Before it can connect, Draven slams his palm down on Isera's arm, shoving it downwards. The ice spear buries itself in the rich soil instead.

"What the fuck did I just say?" Draven growls at her. "Defense only." Exasperation blows across his face as he gives her an incredulous look. "It's like being surrounded by children."

Low, animalistic growling echoes from all around us. I flick my gaze from side to side, and my stomach drops.

"Uhm... Draven?" I begin.

That massive black panther wasn't alone. An entire pack of them has crept out of the vegetation and now surrounds us in an impenetrable circle. The animals bare their teeth and let out low snarls.

"You killed my people," a hard voice suddenly cuts through the rumbling growls.

Spinning around, I find a tall woman with brown hair and green eyes striding out from the shadows. Her purple dragon scale armor sports faint carvings that depict a variety of lethal-looking animals. She tosses her thick, wavy hair back behind her shoulder as she comes to a halt outside the ring of snarling panthers.

"That's pretty rich, Diana," Draven replies, giving her a

knowing look. "Even for you. Considering that you sent them to that mountainside to kill *me*."

She clicks her tongue but doesn't argue. Instead, her suspicious eyes slide over me, Isera, and Orion. "You certainly keep strange company."

Draven flicks a pointed glance at the panthers around us. "I could say the same about you."

The animals growl in response but don't attack. Diana cocks her head.

"You've grown pretty big balls lately, Shadow of Death," she says. "First, you betray the Icehearts. And now you've wandered into my woods of your own free will. Why?"

"Because we need to talk."

"No, I meant, why did you betray the Icehearts?"

"Because someone finally figured out that they have been controlling me with dragon steel for two hundred years and cut it out of my arm."

Her eyes widen.

Draven flashes her a knowing smile. "Yeah? That make you curious enough to have a conversation like adults?"

For another few seconds, she just watches us with an unreadable expression on her face. Then she clicks her tongue again.

"Come with me."

CHAPTER THIRTEEN

The Purple Dragon Clan doesn't live in one city. Or even a handful of cities. Instead, their homeland seems to span this entire forest. Beautiful wooden houses are nestled between the trees in what feels like an entirely random pattern, and some have even been built on the branches above. The only places where there are never any buildings are the open glens that are scattered across the woods. That surprises me, since they would seem like ideal locations, until I realize that those are probably left open intentionally so that they can use them when they shift into dragons.

A low snarl rumbles from my left. I glance down at the panther that is prowling there. Other jaguars have joined as well, though they're sticking more to the edges. Their yellow eyes watch us intently, but after that first lunge at Orion, they haven't done anything to attack us. I assume it's on Diana's orders, since her clan magic is the ability to control animals.

I study her where she walks ahead of us. She carries herself with effortless pride, her spine straight and her chin raised, and she moves through the woods like a predator. Since she rarely visited the Seelie Court, I've had very few opportunities to study her before now. But based on this limited interaction, and the fact that she sent twelve people to assassinate Draven on the mountainside outside the Ice Palace last year, I get a feeling that Diana Artemisia is an incredibly dangerous person.

Taking a right, she strides towards a building that has become visible between the trees. It's a long one-story building with warm firelight dancing in the windows. Smoke rises up from a chimney on one end. It drifts up towards the canopy in swirling rivulets.

The jaguars and panthers trail to a halt.

I glance at them over my shoulder, but Diana just walks up to the door of the long building and pulls it open. The sounds of chatter and laughter spill out from the room inside.

Holding the door open, she at last turns back to us. "I have things I need to finish first. You can wait in here."

Draven gives her a nod. "Alright."

Without hesitation, he strides across the threshold and into the building. I hurry after him, in case there is some kind of trap waiting inside. Isera and Orion saunter in after me.

The moment we enter the room, all conversations stop and all laughter dies out. Clothes rustle as forty-odd people turn around to stare at us. Anger darkens their features the moment they lay eyes on Draven.

We appear to have entered some kind of tavern. Even though it's only midday, the canopy of the forest outside makes the light dim enough that candles have been lit on the tables. The flickering candlelight dances over the dark wooden walls, making the polished surfaces shine. Tables are spread out across the large rectangular space. The ones on the sides are made for two, or four, or six people. But along the very middle of the room, two massive tables run the length of almost the entire room. There is a bar to our right, and a door that appears to lead into a kitchen. The scent of cooking food drifts out of it.

Draven sweeps his gaze over the room before he finds an

empty table for four. We start towards it in silence while the tavern's patrons stare daggers at us. Conversations start back up again, but they're whispered and full of anger now.

Wood scrapes against wood as the four of us pull out chairs and sit down. To my surprise, Draven chooses one of the seats where his back is against the rest of the room. I sit down opposite him so that I can see what is happening behind his back.

Isera eyes the other unsafe seat that has its back against the glaring dragon shifters, but Orion casually plops down on it before she can make a decision. She gives him a questioning look that he either doesn't notice or pretends not to notice, so she just rounds the table and sits down in the final chair without commenting.

Tension crackles through the room like lightning bolts. It's so intense that I can almost hear it vibrating in the air.

"So," I begin, drawing out the word, as I meet Draven's gaze. "How long before someone tries to stab you in the back?"

For a fraction of a second, I swear I can see amusement tug at his lips. But all he says is, "I'd give it five minutes."

Orion casts a sideways glance at the tables to his right. "I bet a night in my castle on two."

"I say less than one," Isera adds, her sharp gaze gliding across the room.

"When it happens, don't hurt anyone," Draven says.

Orion arches an eyebrow in silent question.

"She's testing us," Draven explains. "And remember what I said. The two of you can't use your magic or she'll—"

A knife shoots towards the back of Draven's neck.

Whirling around, Draven yanks his arm through the air and manages to slam his forearm into the wrist of the man holding the knife. The guy lets out a grunt of pain at the impact, and the blade goes flying from his fingers. It clatters to the floor a short distance away.

Isera lets out a smug huff of laughter. "Called it."

Half of the tavern lurches towards us.

Shooting to our feet, we spread out side by side as the shifters from the Purple Clan attack us with a mix of proper knives and simple dinner utensils. I duck as a blond guy swipes a blade at my face and then twist out of reach when he tries to hit me on the way back.

My pulse thrums in my ears. How am I supposed to fight when I can't use my magic? And since we're not supposed to hurt anyone, I can't use my dagger either. So what the hell am I supposed to do? I'm not a brawler.

I flick a glance at Draven.

My heart leaps into my throat when I see that he is surrounded by five people who are all attacking him at the same time. I gasp as one of them rams a knife right into Draven's shoulder.

Thankfully, it only gets stuck in his dragon scale armor. But just the thought of it makes that furious rage that is always burning inside me now rip free. Summoning my magic, I shove it at the purple sparks of worry that I hope are present in their chests. After all, they're fighting the Shadow of Death. They have to be at least a little worried.

To my relief, almost all of our attackers feel at least a flicker of worry.

I pour my magic into them.

The sudden massive flames of worry in their chests make them hesitant and clumsy. Around Draven, three of the attackers stumble and the remaining two pull back instead of striking.

Draven cuts a look in my direction.

I just shoot him an unapologetic look back, knowing that he can see my glowing eyes.

Clenching his jaw in annoyance, he whirls back to our attackers and summons his own magic. A storm wind speeds through the room and slams into the now incredibly worried and uncoordinated group of dragon shifters. The force of the wind, and their slower reflexes, completely bowls them over and they hit the floor like a heap of sticks.

Ice shoots through the air.

And suddenly everything is silent.

Quickly releasing my grip on my magic, I turn to look at our attackers. All of them are on the floor. Some managed to get to their knees while others are still on their backs. But all of them have a lethal shard of ice positioned against their throat.

Draven yanks out the knife that was still stuck in the shoulder plate of his armor.

Fear suddenly washes through the room.

After giving Isera a look, Draven tosses the knife on the floor. The shards of ice vanish as well a moment later.

"We are not your enemies!" Draven growls at the now thoroughly stunned crowd.

They all just stare back at him, apparently shocked that he just let them go instead of taking revenge.

"The Icehearts controlled me with dragon steel for two hundred years," he continues. "And they're doing the same to Rin Tanaka and god knows how many others." His golden eyes blaze with fire as he sweeps his gaze over them. "I hate them more than you do. We need each other to break free."

Only stunned silence answers him. It's so loud that it almost echoes between the smooth wooden walls. Dancing candlelight flickers over the surprised faces all around us.

Then the door opens.

And Diana strides in.

"Smart choice," she says, her shrewd eyes on Draven.

Turning to face her, he narrows his eyes at her with an incredibly impressive look of suspicion on his face. "This was a test?"

It takes great effort not to smirk. *As if he didn't already know that.*

He really is a great actor.

A sharp smile plays over Diana's lips as she shrugs.

"And?" Draven arches an eyebrow at her. "Did I pass?"

Everyone glances between the two of them while they continue watching each other. Then Diana lets out a breath of amusement and flashes him a smile. Sweeping her arm out, she motions towards a table closer to the back of the tavern.

"Have a seat."

CHAPTER FOURTEEN

When Draven told us that Diana was suspicious of outsiders, I didn't expect it to be to this ridiculous degree. Every time we try to convince her to help us, she brings up a new reason for why we can't trust each other. It's almost evening by the time Draven has dismantled all of her arguments.

"Fine," she presses out at last. Blowing out a weary sigh, she waves her hand in defeat. "When the time comes, my clan and I will help you in whatever way we can. But not before you have more people on your side."

"Good." Draven gives her a nod in acknowledgement. "And we will have more people. It's just a matter of time."

She opens her mouth as if to argue again, but then just closes it and heaves another deep sigh. Leaning back in her seat, she rakes her fingers through her wavy brown hair.

The patrons who are eating and drinking in this tavern have come and gone several times since we first stepped across the threshold. I'm not sure how they structure their society here, but I'm assuming that most people can't just sit around and drink all day.

This last group of people to visit the tavern is the most cheerful of the bunch so far. Laughter rings out from most corners, and they have even pushed aside the two long tables in the middle to make space to dance. From chairs by the bar, two people play a pair of instruments that I've never seen before in my life. Several couples dance a very passionate-looking dance to the dramatic notes.

"You left a damn mess behind after you betrayed the Icehearts," Diana says. Dropping her hands from her hair, she sits forward again and instead wraps her hands around her mug. "A damn fucking mess."

"I know," Draven replies, his eyes serious. "I can imagine."

"No, I don't think you can. Your betrayal sent shockwaves across the whole continent. And then you just... disappeared." Her green eyes slide to Orion. "I never could've imagined that you had gone to the Unseelie Court, of all places."

The way she says it sounds almost like an insult, so before Orion can retort with something cutting, Draven smoothly changes the topic. "Who did they name as the new Commander of the Dread Legion?"

"Gremar."

I suppress an annoyed scoff. Gremar Fireclaw is the leader of the Red Dragon Clan, which is responsible for managing the Seelie Court, and he has always gone about his duties in a brutal and merciless way. I'm not exactly his biggest fan.

Draven lets out a mocking chuckle. "Oh I'm sure he's feeling very pleased with himself now."

"He sure is." She clenches and unclenches her hands around her mug for a few seconds. Then she adds, "There is something else I have to tell you."

"What?"

She looks up to meet his gaze head on. "The Icehearts are searching for the Gold Clan."

My eyebrows shoot up. Gold Clan? There is a Gold Clan?

Opposite me, Draven gives Diana a dubious frown. "The Gold Clan is a myth."

"No, they're not," Orion cuts in, speaking for the first time in hours.

We all turn to blink at him in surprise. He just leans back in his seat and sweeps his gaze over all of us before lifting his shoulders in a casual shrug.

"They're the ones who put up the wards around my court," he explains.

My mouth drops open. "What?"

He nods.

"Wait, so the Gold Clan… has shield magic?" I ask, my mind spinning.

The ability to raise wards and magical shields is incredibly rare. I've always wondered who raised the wards around the Unseelie Court all those millennia ago. Since they're so massive, it would've required far more power than one single fae should be able to produce. But since there was no other explanation for it, I've just assumed that there must have been a ridiculously powerful fae born in the Unseelie Court thousands of years ago.

"Yes," Orion confirms. He lets out something between an amused huff and a scoff. "To this day, it remains the single most expensive bargain we have ever made." His intelligent eyes shift to Draven, and a knowing smile curves his lips. "But it has been so worth it."

Draven just rolls his eyes at him.

"Where are they now?" Isera asks, her eyes on the Unseelie King. "Do you know?"

He shakes his head. "Couldn't tell you even if I wanted to, love."

She starts slightly at the term of endearment, but Orion has already picked up his glass of wine and is taking a casual sip.

"Anyway, I just had to warn you about that," Diana continues. "From what I've been told, they have Lavendera working on it."

My gaze snaps back to her at the mention of Lavendera's name. Then I have to grip the table hard to keep from gasping as a sudden thought strikes me. Was that why she was trying to get into the Green Clan's mountain? Draven said that they are the history keepers. If anyone knows what happened to the Gold Clan, it's them.

I flex my hand. We really need to talk to them.

But at least they refused to open the doors for Lavendera too, so the Icehearts don't possess that knowledge either.

"Look, I really must be getting back to work now," Diana announces, and gives Draven a pointed look. "I was in the middle of something when you suddenly strolled into my woods and demanded that we talk."

He arches an eyebrow back at her. "I didn't *demand*."

"You *only* demand and give orders. It's what makes you... you." She lets out a short chuckle. "Anyway, you're welcome to stay the night. But don't cause trouble."

"Your people are the ones who attacked us," he points out.

"Fair." She shrugs. "I've let everyone know that we're on the same side now, so that shouldn't happen again."

"Shouldn't."

"Yes."

Draven shakes his head and flashes her a knowing smile. "Good talking to you, Diana."

"I look forward to escorting you out in the morning."

But there is a slight smile on her lips as she pushes her chair back and stands up. With a nod to the rest of us, she strides across the floor and out the door.

The moment she's gone, Draven picks up his mug of ale and immediately moves to another table. A table that lets him sit with his back to the wall. Isera moves as well, but I suspect that it's more because she wants to put some distance between her and Orion than anything else.

Left alone at our current table, the Unseelie King and I exchange a glance.

"*Love?*" I question, arching an eyebrow at him.

"I knew she would hate it," he replies with a devilish grin.

"Uh-huh."

I cast a glance at Draven. My heart jerks and then squeezes painfully when I find him glaring at me with that hate-filled fire in his eyes. Snapping my gaze away, I instead stare out at the dancing dragon shifters.

It's an incredibly impressive dance. Both dramatic and sensual at the same time.

My gaze drifts back to Draven, and then to Orion, as a plan starts forming in my mind.

Meeting the Unseelie King's eyes, I declare, "Dance with me."

He draws back in stunned surprise and then frowns at me. "Why?"

"To remind Draven of his true feelings."

Understanding dawns on Orion's lethally beautiful face, but the look he gives me is full of sly calculation. "Why should I help you?"

"Apart from the fact that you are responsible for this mess by cursing that damn portal so that it would kill the person who loves me?"

His eyes glint sharply. "You *chose* to do that on your own. I didn't force you."

"He would've died otherwise."

"Still. Not reason enough for me to owe you anything."

"Fine." Leaning back in my chair, I stretch out my legs and cross my ankles nonchalantly. "If you dance with me to make Draven jealous, I won't mention to Isera that you mumbled her name in your sleep when you were injured last night."

His eyes widen in what looks like shock or alarm. Quickly wiping that expression off his features, he raises his chin in a haughty expression. "I didn't murmur her name."

"I was awake almost the entire night since I was taking away Draven's pain with my magic, so I heard *everything* that happened in that cave."

That hint of alarm flits across his features for a moment again, but all he says is, "You're bluffing."

I just look back at him, keeping my gaze steady.

Clenching his jaw, he grinds his teeth while no doubt calculating if he can take the risk that I'm not bluffing. In the end, he lets out something between an irritated snarl and a huff of approval.

"Cruel," he says. His black and silver eyes glint as he flicks his gaze over me. "I still don't particularly like you, but I have to admit, I respect this new ruthless you a little more."

A vicious smile curls my lips.

"Fine." He flicks his wrist. "We have a deal."

"Excellent."

I *was* bluffing, of course.

But Orion doesn't need to know that.

CHAPTER FIFTEEN

Both Draven and Isera start in surprise when Orion stands up from the table and holds out his hand to me. Without looking in their direction, I take his hand and let him lead me to the makeshift dance floor. The dragon shifters who are already dancing there flick a glance at us but thankfully don't make an issue of it.

"Just a heads-up," I begin as we position ourselves on the floor. "I don't actually know how to dance."

Orion gives me a look that is somewhere between incredulity and exasperation. Heaving a sigh, he rolls his eyes. "Of course you don't. Malachi's balls, you really are uncultured, aren't you?"

Without waiting for a reply, he simply places one hand on my waist, moves mine up to his shoulder, and then takes my other one in his. I suck in a sharp breath between my teeth as he suddenly pulls my body incredibly close to his. Then he starts moving us in the same dramatic and passionate way in which the other people are dancing as well.

He is an incredibly skilled dancer. Which, I suppose, shouldn't surprise me since he is the king. I don't know if this style of dance is common outside the Purple Clan or if Orion is simply excellent at adapting the way he moves so that it is in tune with the current music, but we spin and twist across the floor as if he has performed this dance thousands of times before.

And all the while, his body remains close to mine. His hand even slides a little lower down my back. It makes my skin crawl, but I block out the emotion because I know that it serves a purpose.

"Just so we're clear," Orion begins, leveling a haughty stare on me. "I'm quite repulsed by this."

"Oh trust me, the feeling is entirely mutual," I reply, shooting him a pointed look back. "But let's make it look good anyway so that we can make the people we actually care about jealous."

He clicks his tongue. "Fine." Then alarm suddenly flashes across his face, and he practically blurts out, "I mean, I don't care about Isera."

"Sure." The word practically drips with sarcasm.

"I don't."

"You know, I never specified Isera. That was all you."

Clenching his jaw, he tightens his grip on my hand while frustration flickers in his eyes. "She is the most infuriating, stubborn, arrogant, unbending woman I have ever had the misfortune of meeting. I most certainly don't care about her."

"Really? Then I suppose you don't care that she is currently glaring at me through narrowed eyes?"

Orion misses a step.

I grin. "Thought so."

Quickly recovering his step, he clears his throat and tries to appear unaffected. We have deliberately refrained from looking in their direction since this dance began, but his gaze now darts towards Isera for a second. When he turns his head back to me, he is smirking like a satisfied cat after seeing that Isera is indeed watching us through slightly narrowed eyes.

Keeping my gaze on Orion, I ask, "And my target?"

He flicks a glance at Draven. A knowing smile plays over

Orion's lips when he shifts his attention back to me and replies, "Currently deforming this establishment's cutlery."

I risk a quick look in Draven's direction while Orion spins us around again. Just like the Unseelie King said, my mate is currently gripping the fork in his hand so hard that it has started to bend in half. Pressing my lips together, I suppress a wicked smile.

"Excellent," I say.

Orion's gaze slides back to mine. "Let's finish this off with a bang then, shall we?"

Before I even have time to reply, he spins us around and then bends me over his arm while leaning down so that his face is right above mine. His long dark blue hair falls down around us like a curtain. Since no one can see our facial expressions at the moment, we just look back at each other in mutual disgust.

Then Orion is abruptly ripped away from me.

It happens so fast and so violently that I don't even have time to straighten. His arm just disappears from behind my back, making me topple backwards towards the floor.

However, before I can fall too far, a strong hand grips my arm and yanks me back up. Blinking, I toss my hair out of my face and whirl towards the person responsible for the sudden interruption.

Draven releases my arm and instead buries his fist in Orion's collar.

The Unseelie King, who looks like he was just about to straighten after being thrown aside, doesn't have time to react before Draven has yanked him back up by his collar and locked furious eyes on him.

"If you ever touch her like that again, I will cut off your fucking hands," Draven growls in his face.

A truly villainous smile spreads across Orion's mouth. But before he can say anything, Draven shoves him back and instead whirls towards me. My breath gets stuck in my lungs as his blazing eyes lock on me.

"You," he grinds out. "With me. Now."

Not waiting for me to reply, he simply takes my arm in an iron grip and hauls me with him out the door. Still standing in the middle of the dance floor, Orion flashes me a satisfied smirk and winks.

Warm air smelling of rich soil and sweet flowers fills my lungs as we exit the building and step out into the forest outside. Since the sun has almost set now, and the thick canopy above blocks out most of the light, the shifters from the Purple Clan have lit torches all across the forest. Secured to poles that have been sunk into the ground, they fill the woods with warm orange light at regular intervals.

Draven pulls me with him as he stalks around the back of the building to a place with no windows and no other people around. Then he practically throws me up against the wall and gets right in my face. Both of his hands are braced against the dark wooden wall on either side of me, caging me in.

"What the fuck was that?" he growls, his golden eyes burning with anger and hatred and... something else.

I let a mask of innocence descend on my features. "What was what?"

"You know exactly what I'm talking about."

"Me dancing with Orion."

"Yes."

"And?"

"And what?"

A note of challenge creeps into my voice, and I tilt my chin up in an arrogant expression as I hold his stare. "And why is that a problem?"

"Because..." he grinds out, but then trails off. Opening his mouth, he tries again. But only a frustrated growl escapes his lips.

"Because it made you jealous," I finish for him.

"No," he snaps. "I did not feel jealous."

"Possessive, then?" Arching an eyebrow, I lift a hand and draw teasing fingers along his jaw. "I'm yours, aren't I?"

With his hands still planted on the wall on either side of me, he clenches his jaw and curls his fingers into fists as if he has to physically stop himself from touching me. "No. You're a menace. That's what you are."

"Oh, I know. It's part of why you love me."

His eyes flash. "I don't love you."

"Yes, you do."

"You need to stop spewing delusional nonsense and start obeying my fucking orders."

An unapologetic smirk spreads across my lips. "Is that right?"

"Yes." He draws in a frustrated breath through his nose. "I very specifically told you not to use your magic during the fight. But you did it anyway."

"Because they tried to hurt you. Anyone who hurts you *dies*." That final word rips from my lungs like a snarl.

Draven draws back a little in surprise.

And the mate bond vibrates in my chest again. It's only for a fraction of a second. But it's there.

Panic pulses across Draven's handsome face.

Yanking one hand away from the wall, he instead places it across my collarbones and shoves me all the way back up against the wall again, as if he needs to physically keep me away from him. But he doesn't remove his hand. It remains there over my collarbones, pinning me to the wall.

"Stop messing with my fucking head," Draven growls at me, his eyes wild.

"Admit it," I retort, holding his stare with eyes full of steel. "You want me. Badly."

He drags in a highly controlled breath.

I show him no mercy. Grabbing his collar, I yank his face closer to mine. That desperate hunger fights with the burning hatred in his eyes as I pull him so close that I can feel his erratic breaths dance over my lips.

"You want me," I repeat, my voice pulsing with command. "You want to crush your lips against mine and rip my clothes off and fuck me hard against this wall, because deep down, you know that what I'm saying is true. I am yours. And you are mine."

The muscles in his arm shift as he flexes the hand he still has braced on the wall next to me.

"You know that the hatred you feel isn't natural," I press. "You know—"

"Did you kiss him?" he interrupts, his voice cutting the air like a blade. "Orion. Did you kiss him there at the end of the dance?"

"Why does it matter?"

"It matters."

"I thought you didn't care."

"Just answer the fucking question, Selena." His hand on my collarbones grows firmer. "Did you kiss him?"

I hold his fiery gaze with serious eyes for a few seconds before at last replying, "No, I didn't kiss him."

He forces out a jagged breath and unclenches the hand he still has planted on the wall. I tighten my grip on his collar and pull his face even closer to mine. Our lips are so close now that I swear I can feel tiny bolts of lightning crackle between them.

Another unsteady breath is forced out of his lungs. Dropping his hand from the wall, he takes my waist in a firm grip instead while his other hand slides up from my collarbones and towards my jaw. A ripple of pleasure rolls through my spine when his commanding hand caresses my throat before he places it along my jaw. With a firm push, he tilts my head back. His chest heaves.

My heart beats erratically as he curls his fingers around the side of my waist, tightening his grip on me possessively. His breath dances over my lips with every jagged exhale as he slants his lips over mine. I draw in an unsteady breath.

Something like a moan escapes from deep within his chest

when his lips almost brush against mine. He flexes his hand on my waist. I tilt my head back a little more to close that final distance between us.

But right before our lips can touch, he tears himself away and stumbles back across the ground. A frantic mix of panic and hatred and desperation and a terrible, world-ending hunger burns on his entire face as he stares at me with wide eyes. His chest rises and falls with rapid breaths.

I open my mouth to speak, but before any words can make it out, he suddenly whirls around and strides away.

Slumping back against the wall, I stare after him as he disappears around the corner.

My chest heaves and I feel completely breathless after the almost kiss. Lifting my hands, I rake them through my hair and then tilt my head back. It hits the wall behind me with a soft thud. I heave a deep sigh.

Well, fuck.

CHAPTER SIXTEEN

Warm morning winds sweep across the grasslands and fill my lungs with the taste of fog and damp grass when we walk out of the forest and back out into the open fields beyond. Diana stops at the tree line, so we all turn back to face her.

"I will send one of my animals with a message if anything changes," she says, sweeping her gaze over all of us. "But if you need my assistance with anything, all you have to do is to let me know."

Draven gives her a nod in acknowledgment. "Good. I'm glad to have you on our side, Diana."

"I never said that I was on your side." She gives him a pointed look. "I said that I will offer assistance if you need help with anything."

"Yeah, yeah, I know, we need to convince more of the other clans first."

She just looks back at him in silence.

He lets out something between an amused huff and an exasperated sigh. "Always great talking to you."

There is an expression I can't read on her face, and for a moment, I'm worried that she was insulted by the friendly jab.

But then she just lets out a small sigh and says, "I will be seeing you, Shadow of Death."

And with that, she turns around and walks back into her forest.

"Alright, we need to get going," Draven says as he turns back to us. "It's almost time to meet up with the others."

"Yes," Orion agrees. "And I need to get back to Haldia before the ugly scar on my thigh becomes permanent."

Draven rolls his eyes but just starts striding out onto the grass without commenting.

Black smoke explodes into the air as he shifts into his dragon form. With an impatient growl at us, he moves his tail into position. We all hurry up it and take a seat in the same place as last time.

My stomach lurches as Draven launches into the air. His massive wings boom around us, and winds rip at my hair and clothes, as he flies away from the Purple Clan's homeland and back towards the Unseelie Court.

I spend the entire flight alternating between a renewed sense of hope and an even more crushing sense of despair.

The fact that I've managed to make Draven feel something other than hatred towards me, even if just briefly, makes that tiny spark of hope in my chest flutter. He was jealous when I danced with Orion. And he wanted to kiss me, desperately, outside in the woods afterwards. It's proof that his real feelings are there. Buried deep inside him.

But at the same time, the hatred isn't going away. No matter how furiously he kissed me in that cave or how jealous he was in the tavern or how badly he wanted to kiss me again outside, it doesn't change the fact that he also still hates me with every fiber of his being. That flame of hatred that I put in his chest is still there. It's still as strong as ever. I even checked this morning just to make sure.

Regardless of what I do, I can't remove that hatred, which is the source of the problem. And that awful knowledge, and the crushing sense of hopelessness that comes with it, is eating me alive from the inside.

When we at last land outside the wards around the Unseelie Court, I feel so restless that I'm tempted to reach out with my magic and create an emotion in someone's chest just so that I can feel that comforting sense of pleasure that comes with it. But I thankfully manage to suppress the urge. And besides, we are the only four people out here on the plains anyway.

"Home at last," Orion says. A satisfied smirk, tinged with the hint of a threat, blows across his lips. "Or at least, I am. Would you like me to invite you inside the wards as well, or would you prefer to sleep out here on the ground?"

Isera cuts him a knowing look. "You bet a night in your castle on two minutes. You lost."

To my surprise, he lets out a short laugh of approval. "Fine." He flicks his wrist nonchalantly. Then a mocking expression settles on his features as he looks Draven up and down. "You all need proper baths anyway."

Draven flashes him a taunting smile back. "Aww, you got a little blood and dirt on you? Should I find you some pearls to clutch, princeling?"

"Should I find you some mud to roll in, beast?" he retorts.

Next to me, Isera almost smiles but then suppresses it at the last moment. I just shake my head at all of them.

We thankfully manage to get through the next half hour without killing each other while we wait for our other companions.

At last, two black dragons become visible across the plains.

Galen, Lyra, and Alistair.

I smile.

Let's see how many dragon clans we've managed to get.

CHAPTER SEVENTEEN

The door to the elegant dining room bangs open. I jump and whirl around, thinking that we're about to get attacked. We're not. Well, *I'm* not about to get attacked at least. Someone else is, though.

Amusement gleams in Orion's eyes as he watches Isera storm into the room with a murderous expression on her face. A garment in dark blue and silver is clutched in her fist, and she shakes it in the air before throwing it at Orion's chest.

"What the hell is this?" she demands.

The ball of rich blue silk and gleaming silver threads hits Orion in the chest and then flutters down to land on the floor before his feet. He doesn't glance down at it, though. Instead, his glittering eyes are fixed on Isera.

Amusement plays over his dangerously beautiful face. "It's a dress."

"I can see that," Isera retorts. "What was it, and a note with a command on it, doing on my bed?"

"It wasn't a command."

"The note said, *wear me*."

He waves his hand nonchalantly and flicks a glance up and

down her body while he gracefully steps over the discarded dress and closes the distance between them. "I just thought you might want to wear something other than fighting leathers."

I suck in a sharp breath.

In a heartbeat, Isera has grabbed him by the collar and summoned a shard of ice. Her blue and silver eyes flash dangerously as she yanks Orion's face down to hers and presses the shard of ice against his throat.

"If you ever presume to think for me, or give me orders, again, I will slit your throat," she warns.

A slow smile spreads across his lips, full of unapologetic challenge. "It's just a dress." He slides his tongue lightly along his bottom lip while raking his gaze up and down her body. "And you would look lethally beautiful in it."

Tension crackles through the air like lightning as they just stare each other down in silence for another second. Then Isera abruptly dismisses the shard of ice and uses her grip on Orion's shirt to shove him back a step. However, because the Unseelie King is both taller and more muscular than her, he only lets her shove him back less than half a step. His eyes glitter with wicked amusement as he watches her.

"If you like the dress so much, *you* wear it," Isera snaps.

"Sure." That devilish smile on his lips widens as he begins unbuttoning his fancy shirt. "But if you wanted me to take my clothes off... *again*," he adds with a knowing look, "you really could've just said so."

My jaw almost drops when Isera actually *blushes*.

Heat flushes her cheeks, and her mouth opens a little, but no words make it out.

Orion stops trying to unbutton his shirt and instead cups her cheek. A truly villainous smile decorates his gorgeous face as he slides his thumb over her bottom lip and then across her flushed cheek.

"Perfection," he murmurs.

She slaps his hand away.

Across the room, Lyra, Alistair, and Galen look between the two of them in confusion.

"Uhm, did we… miss something?" Alistair asks.

Isera flicks her gaze to him. Her eyes widen in surprise when she realizes that he is wearing a fancy tunic in Orion's signature dark blue and silver. As is Galen. And both Lyra and I are wearing elegant shirts in the same colors as well.

When I got to the room that Orion assigned to me here in the castle, I found a set of fresh clothes waiting on the bed. A pair of nice black pants and an elegant dark blue shirt, with a few silver details on it, in a style that leaves my shoulders bare. I destroyed the white shirt that I wear under my fighting leathers when I wrapped it around Draven in that cave, so I gratefully put on the fresh clothes that Orion provided, since I didn't want to wear the thick leathers while eating dinner.

The only person who apparently insisted on wearing his own clothes is Draven, who has been standing by the wall in his black dragon scale armor and watching the unfolding events with an amused smirk on his lips.

When Isera realizes that everyone else received clothes to wear as well, she starts in surprise and then snaps her gaze down to the dress on the floor. For a fraction of a second, I swear I can see a wave of embarrassment crash over her face before she manages to hide it behind that impassive mask that she usually schools her features into.

Clearing her throat, she simply strides over to the table and takes a seat. Behind her back, Orion lets out a silent chuckle while absolute victory shines on his face. Whatever weird game they're playing, he apparently won this round.

Chairs scrape against the rich dark blue carpet as we all sit down around the beautifully decorated dining room table. It's the same private dining room that we gathered in when we first came to the Unseelie Court several months ago now.

The chandelier filled with faelight gems casts sparkling light across the room, making it look like stars are dancing over the beautiful landscapes and night skies that are shown in the paintings on the walls. Just like last time we were here, there are nine chairs around the table. Four plain ones on either side of the table, and then one grand high-backed one at the head of the table.

This time, however, Isera doesn't insist on sitting as far from Orion as possible. Instead, all six of us claim the chairs closest to Orion's fancy one.

A moment later, a group of smartly dressed fae men and women walk through the door with plates of food and pitchers of wine. Once we have all been served, they bow to their king and then retreat again.

"Well then," Orion begins, and swirls his wine while glancing towards Galen and the others. "How did our other group fare?"

Galen looks to Draven, who nods.

"It took some convincing, but the Blue Clan will stand with us," Galen announces with a small smile on his lips.

Across the table, Draven mirrors the smile and gives his friend another nod in acknowledgement. "Good work."

I have to suppress a smile when that small gesture makes Galen hold his head a little higher. To his left, Orion just arches a dark brow.

"And?" he prompts.

Galen clears his throat and glances back at the Unseelie King before sweeping his gaze over all of us. "And that's it. We also managed to visit the Brown Clan, and we tried to convince them, but well... They were very stubborn."

Draven lets out a huff of laughter. "Shocker."

"Right?" Galen smiles before his expression turns serious again. "They admitted that they might be open to the possibility, but they won't seriously consider joining us unless we have the Green Clan on our side."

A groan escapes me.

He shifts his attention to me. "I take it that means you had no luck with the Green Clan?"

I shake my head. "They didn't even open the door."

Tilting his head to the side in a half nod, he lets out a small sigh. "Can't say I'm surprised." His gaze shifts to Draven, and a hint of hope fills his voice as he asks, "And the Orange Clan?"

"Rin is wearing dragon steel," Draven replies, his expression grim.

Both Galen and Lyra curse.

"I should've known." Draven heaves a deep sigh and rakes both hands through his hair. "Or at least suspected. Of course Bane and Jessina would have more than just the single piece of dragon steel they were using on me. And if they were going to use it on anyone, it was definitely going to be Rin. Controlling the only person with healing magic is vital."

Silence descends over the dining room. For a few moments, only the faint dings from our utensils as we continue eating fill the room.

"But we did manage to convince Diana," Draven continues eventually. Then he grimaces. "Mostly, anyway. She's willing to join us once we have more clans on our side." He looks from Galen to Lyra. "Did you visit anyone else?"

"No." Lyra takes a large gulp of wine and then lifts her shoulders in a helpless shrug. "We didn't have time."

"Alright, so that leaves the Green Clan, the White Clan, and the Red Clan." He drums his fingers on the dark wooden tabletop. "The Green Clan probably still won't open the door if we go back now."

"They respect Rin, though," Galen adds with a considering look on his face. "So if we can somehow get the Orange Clan on our side, the Green Clan will probably be willing to listen. And then if we get the Green Clan, we'll also get the Brown Clan."

"I never realized how much politics there is among all your

clans," Alistair suddenly says. His pale brows are furrowed in what looks like genuine surprise and confusion. "I thought you were all... I don't know? United. Like, one cohesive nation who collectively agree on everything."

Draven, Galen, and Lyra all burst out laughing. Even Orion snickers into his wine before taking a long sip.

"Azaroth's flame, no," Lyra presses out between bursts of laughter. "There are tons of culture differences between all the clans, which have created a lot of both conflict and collaborations over the years. Some clans have more history with each other than others, but we've all tried to outmaneuver each other in different ways more than once. It's quite fun, actually." A mischievous grin spreads across her mouth. "Especially when you know exactly which social norms to break in order to create maximum chaos."

Alistair lets out an approving chuckle and raises his glass at her in salute.

"What did I tell you last time we were here?" Galen begins. "And again at the Blue Clan's capital? And outside the walls of the Brown Clan's lands?" He gives Lyra a pointed look full of exasperation. "Don't rope him into your craziness. You alone are enough of a menace. Together, the two of you would level cities to the ground."

Lyra and Alistair just exchange a devilish grin across the table.

"Shall we get back to the point?" Orion interrupts, and arches an expectant eyebrow at the rest of us.

"Right." I swallow a bite of food and set my fork down. "So have I got this right? We need the Green Clan, for multiple reasons, but to get them, we first need to get the Orange Clan? And we can't get them unless we somehow neutralize the dragon steel that Rin Tanaka is wearing? Which we also can't do because she will try to capture or kill us if we come near her?"

"That about sums it up," Galen agrees.

"Which then brings us back to Lavendera," I continue.

Draven shoots me a scowl. "I've already told you, we won't be able to turn Lavendera against the Icehearts."

Pressing my lips together, I drum my fingers on the table but don't argue since I'm pretty sure that he's right. Especially if my suspicions are correct that Lavendera is Bane Iceheart's bastard child. It would also explain what Diana said. That Lavendera has been given the important task of locating the mysterious Gold Clan. If they—

I gasp out loud.

The others, who had apparently continued the discussion while I was lost in thought, turn to stare at me in confusion.

Slamming my palms down on the table, I look from face to face. "By Mabona! *That's* why they're looking for the Gold Clan." I turn to Orion. "You said that the Icehearts were able to subjugate the Green Clan by threatening their archives, but that the Green Clan managed to get the wards back up and therefore don't really do the Icehearts' bidding anymore."

Understanding dawns on his face as well. "The Gold Clan could destroy the wards around the archives." His already pale face suddenly grows even whiter. "And around my court as well."

Draven curses under his breath. "If they get the Gold Clan, and then the Green Clan as well, we're screwed."

"He's right," Galen agrees, and draws a hand through his blond hair. "Kander von Graf could change all of our memories. He could make it so that we don't even remember that we know each other. He wouldn't normally do something so dishonorable, but if they threaten to destroy his archives..." He shakes his head, leaving the rest of his sentence unspoken.

Isera takes a sip from her wine and then studies us all from over the rim of her glass, but she says nothing, and the impassive mask on her face makes it difficult to know what she's thinking. Light from the faelight chandelier casts glittering light across her face.

"Can *we* get the Gold Clan?" I ask into the now tense silence.

Everyone looks from face to face. In the end, it's Draven who replies.

"I wouldn't even know where to start looking," he says.

The silence around the table tells me that the others were thinking the same thing.

"So Rin Tanaka is the key, then?" Lyra says, shifting the conversation back to a more realistic plan.

"No, Lavendera is the key," I argue.

Draven shoots me an incredulous look. "How many times do I have to tell you? We won't be able to turn her."

"What we really need is the Red Clan," Alistair interrupts before I can retort. "They control the Seelie Court. So if we can get them on our side, we will also get the entire Seelie Court." He turns to me. "You were in some kind of resistance group, right? They should be able to contribute a lot more once they don't have to worry about Gremar Fireclaw breathing down their necks."

Draven draws a hand over his jaw. "That's... actually a good idea."

Alistair shoots him an indignant scowl. "I'll pretend I didn't hear that tone of surprise in your voice."

On the other side of the table, Orion smirks into his wine glass.

"Alright," Draven says, letting his hand drop and sitting up straighter. "We'll focus on the Red Clan next. But Gremar is... tricky to deal with. Especially now that he is the new Commander of the Dread Legion. We can't just show up. We need to draw him out, without him knowing that it's us, and get him to meet with us alone."

The others nod in agreement.

I draw in a deep breath and nod as well.

And then, we start scheming.

CHAPTER EIGHTEEN

By the time I return to my room in Orion's castle, my entire body is vibrating with restless energy. I don't know why, but I feel like things are moving too slowly. Months have already passed since we first escaped the Ice Palace. Who knows what wicked plans the Icehearts have been able to cook up during that time?

Pacing back and forth across the floor of my room, I can't help but feel that time is running out. All of it. The time to mount a proper attack on the Icehearts. The time to prepare our own defenses. The time to fix what I did to Draven.

My heart squeezes painfully.

Every day that passes is another day where Draven only focuses on how much he hates me. Soon enough, he will have spent more time hating me than he did loving me. Even if I can somehow figure out how to remove that hatred from his chest, will it be enough? Will everything actually go back to normal? Or will our relationship already have changed too much by then?

A sudden wave of dread and panic threatens to overwhelm me, so I pull anger around me like a shield. I will make Draven remember how he feels about me if it's the last fucking thing I do.

Stalking over to the bed, I throw myself down on my back and unbutton my pants. He told me after our kiss in the cave that he could feel my emotions through the mate bond. Well, let's see how he handles this, then.

With that furious anger still burning through me, I slip my hand into my panties and start pleasuring myself. A moan escapes my lips as I rub my fingers over my clit in exactly the way I like it. While imagining that it's Draven doing it, I continue moving my fingers until pleasure builds like a storm inside me.

There is a tugging sensation in my chest, and suddenly, I can feel a mix of hatred, yearning, and panic through what used to be our mate bond.

Throwing my head back, I grin up at the pale stone ceiling while I continue bringing myself towards an orgasm.

The door is yanked open.

Storm clouds and lightning crackle around Draven's powerful body as he stalks into my room and throws the door shut behind him.

"What the fuck do you think you're doing?" he snarls at me.

Slowly tilting my head back down, I meet his gaze head on while I nonchalantly continue pleasuring myself. "What does it look like?"

Just as I calculated, that exact phrasing of the question makes his gaze dart down to the hand between my spread legs. Burning hunger flares up in his eyes. Clenching his jaw, he flexes his hand and drags his gaze back up to my face.

"Stop doing that," he growls at me.

Holding his gaze with a smug stare, I just continue pleasuring myself. "Why?"

"Because I can feel your... lust. And pleasure."

"Huh. Interesting." I run my tongue along my teeth. "It must be because I'm imagining that it's your hand doing it."

Desperate longing flashes across his face like a bolt of lightning. The actual lightning around him crackles in the now even more violently churning storm clouds that ripple out from his broad shoulders. Threats glint in his eyes as he suddenly starts moving forward, stalking towards me where I'm still lying on the pale sheets of the bed.

With one elbow braced on the mattress underneath me and my other hand still rubbing my clit, I just watch him advance on me while I raise my eyebrows in arrogant challenge.

The bed creaks as Draven places a hand on it, right next to me, and then leans down over me. There is a dangerous expression on his face, which just makes my clit throb harder.

"I said," Draven grinds out, his voice dark. "Stop doing that."

"Or what, Shadow of Death?" I taunt, my fingers still moving.

"Trust me, little rebel, you don't want to play this game with me."

My heart stutters at that nickname. He has barely called me that since I put the hatred in his chest. And hearing it now makes that boldness inside me swell.

Cocking my head, I flash him a smirk full of challenge. "You're the one who came into my bedroom. The way I see it, you have two choices. You can either leave." I flick a pointed glance down between my legs. "Or you can help."

He drags in a highly controlled breath and flexes his hand again. Hatred and anger and desperate passion fight for supremacy in his eyes.

I rub my clit harder.

Pleasure spikes up my spine, and I throw my head back and gasp.

My heart jerks as a pair of strong hands suddenly grab my ankles and yank me farther down the bed. Snapping my head back up, I now find myself closer to the edge where Draven is towering over me. His hand shoots up and wraps around my wrist, yanking my hand away from my clit before releasing me, and then he grabs the top of my already unbuttoned pants with both hands and shoves them down my thighs along with my underwear.

"Oh." I flash him a satisfied smirk. "You've decided to help, I see."

"You infuriating little…" he growls under his breath while continuing to strip me naked.

Fabric flutters through the air as he yanks off my pants and underwear and tosses them down on the floor. Grabbing me by the hips, he pulls me all the way to the edge with one firm yank. My spread legs are now draped down over the edge of the bed on either side of Draven's legs where he's standing before me.

Leaning down over me again, he grabs the collar of my shirt.

And then rips it open.

I gasp, and fire crackles through my veins while my clit throbs.

After throwing the scraps of my shirt aside, he pauses for a second and just stares down at my now utterly naked body. He is still dressed in full dragon scale armor. And the complete difference in vulnerability between us somehow makes that fire in my veins even hotter. I squirm against the sheets as my clit throbs with the need for him.

Deep desire burns in his eyes as he rakes his gaze over my naked body. The sight of it makes my heart skip a beat.

"Are you going to fuck me in full armor, or…?" I raise my eyebrows expectantly. Then a wicked smile blows across my lips as I spread my legs wider. "I'm already wet, so you—"

"Shut up." It sounds more like a desperate plea than a command.

Dragging in deep breaths, it looks like he is frantically trying to convince himself to leave instead.

"I hate you so fucking much," he says.

But a small cloud of black smoke appears as he shifts out of his fully human form and into his half-shift form. Though I think the sudden shift had more to do with getting his clothes off efficiently than anything else. While shifting, he can store the clothes he is wearing inside the black bracers on his forearms. He does that now, leaving his muscular body entirely naked except for those black bracers.

His imposing black wings flare out on either side of him as he grabs me by the hips and slams into me with all the fury and desperation that the hatred inside him is still making him feel.

Gasping, I arch up from the bed as pleasure pulses through me.

Draven's hand locks around my throat while he pulls out and then thrusts back in again.

"Did you think I was going to *make love* to you?" he taunts, that anger and hatred still burning along with the desire in his eyes. His hand flexes around my throat as he starts up a commanding pace. "No, I'm going to *fuck* you. That's what you wanted, isn't it?"

A moan escapes my lips as he thrusts in again, creating the most incredible friction.

"That's what I thought," he says. "So don't mistake this for anything other than what it is. I'm only here to prove that you are the one who is desperate for my cock. For *me*. So I'm going to fuck you until you're nothing but a trembling mess begging me for another orgasm."

Dark desire washes through me, and my clit throbs. I grin up at him. "Do your worst."

His eyes gleam as he picks up the pace, fucking me dominantly and without mercy. He keeps one hand around my throat and the other on my hip to stop me from sliding up the sheets with every firm thrust of his hips.

Pleasure builds like a wave inside me.

I rake my gaze over his perfect body. His muscles flex with every commanding move, and light from the faelight gems glitter in his beautiful golden eyes. A deep sense of possessiveness burns through me. *Mine.* He is *mine*.

The mate bond thrums in my chest.

Draven gasps. Desire drowns out the hatred in his eyes for a fraction of a second before the two emotions are back to their unending battle again. He drags in a shuddering breath and flexes his hand around my throat.

A smirk tugs at my lips. He can feel it. He can feel what I feel right now.

That knowledge brings forth an idea. A wicked idea. But one that I'm going to use anyway.

While sliding a hand around my breast, I cast a lazy glance towards the ripped shirt on the ground. "You didn't need to destroy the shirt, by the way. It was a gift from Orion."

Draven's eyes flash. "Don't say his name. Don't you fucking dare say *his* name while *my* cock is inside you."

"Whose name?" I ask in my best innocent voice. "Ori—"

His hand shoots up from my throat to my mouth. I suck in a startled breath as he shoves his middle finger and ring finger into my open mouth. With them pressing down on my tongue, and his thumb pressing up underneath my chin, I can no longer form words.

While still fucking me hard, Draven leans closer and locks commanding eyes on me.

"You moan *my* name," he growls. "Only my name. Or you lose speaking privileges. Understood?"

Heat pools at my core, and I squirm against the sheets as another wave of dark desire crashes over me.

Since he's still keeping me gagged with his fingers, all I can do is nod in acknowledgement.

"Good," he says.

But he doesn't remove his hand.

Instead, he slides his other hand up from my hip and towards my breasts.

With him no longer keeping me in place, I begin sliding along the sheets with every firm thrust of his hips, so I throw my own hands out and grip the sheets hard to stay in place. That incredible tension builds inside me as Draven keeps fucking me like he wants to carve his name across my soul.

I gasp as something zaps my nipple.

Since Draven is still keeping my head immobile, I can't tilt my chin down to look. But I know exactly what it is. Draven's eyes glitter as he holds my gaze while using his storm magic to zap my nipple with a tiny bolt of lightning again.

A garbled moan rips from my throat.

Pleasure curls around my spine as he zaps my other nipple as well at the same time as he hits a spot deep inside me with his cock. I moan around his fingers again. Gripping the sheets hard, I squirm underneath him as the thrumming tension inside me reaches unbearable levels.

He smirks down at me. "Look at you. So utterly at my mercy."

With that devilish look in his eyes, he shifts his free hand down from my nipple and towards my clit instead. While still fucking me senseless, he brushes his fingers over my clit. And then zaps it with a tiny bolt of lightning.

Lights flash before my eyes as pleasure shoots up my spine. I moan his name, but it only comes out as unintelligible mumbling because his fingers are still keeping my tongue trapped underneath them. His cock keeps hitting that perfect place inside me while he zaps my clit with lightning again.

Desperation floods me. Goddess above, I want to moan his name when I come. I want *him* to hear me moan his name.

My hand shoots up and wraps around his wrist instead. But because of the sheer power difference between us, I know that I will never be able to remove his hand unless he allows it. With that incredible tension vibrating inside me like a storm, I grip his wrist hard and plead with my eyes while I tumble uncontrollably towards an orgasm.

"That's it." He strokes his thumb over my jaw. "Beg me for it."

But he still doesn't ungag me.

Pitiful noises escape my throat as I try to hold back the orgasm. Draven shows me no mercy. While fucking me from that perfect angle, he zaps my clit with lightning again.

Release explodes through my body.

I gasp around his fingers and arch my back as pleasure crackles through my every nerve. Garbled moans spill from my lips, and my limbs shake as the waves of pleasure wash through me. Gripping his wrist hard, I once more plead with my eyes while my legs tremble around his hips.

He flashes me a smug smirk full of victory.

And then finally removes his hand.

I gasp in a deep breath as he continues fucking me through the orgasm, intensifying it with every thrust of his hips.

"Draven," I moan.

He comes.

Hard.

The moment I moan his name, release explodes across his features so intensely that his eyes shutter. His cock pulses inside me, and his wings flare out while he grips my hips hard to keep himself upright.

The mate bond suddenly thrums inside me like a violent storm, and for a few seconds, I can feel his intense pleasure through it as well. The sheer force of it momentarily blinds me.

Then the connection is broken again, and only my own fading orgasm remains.

When his release has faded as well, he just remains standing there, staring down at me with wide eyes. His hands are still gripping my hips and his cock is still buried deep inside me.

I stare up at him, but I can't read the expression on his face.

That tiny spark of hope inside me flutters. Did it work? Did this somehow break through the flame of hatred?

His chest heaves as he stares down at me, his imposing black wings still spread wide behind him.

Then reality seems to snap back into him, and he abruptly pulls out and staggers two steps back.

A small cloud of black smoke explodes into the room as he shifts back into his fully human form in order to quickly put his armor back on.

I remain lying there naked on the bed, drawing in unsteady breaths to calm my thundering heart.

For a moment, we just watch each other while tension crackles through the room like lightning. Then Draven spins on his heel and simply starts towards the door without another word.

My heart jerks.

"Wait!" I call, scrambling up from the bed.

But my legs are still wobbly from the intense orgasm that has barely left my body, so I stumble the first two steps and end up crashing down on my knees on the floor.

Draven turns around, but when he meets my gaze again, there is only a mocking glint in his eyes and a cruel smile on his lips. "And there it is. You on your knees, a trembling mess, begging me for another orgasm."

Heat flushes my cheeks. But it's more anger than embarrassment.

Raising my chin, I level a knowing stare full of challenge back at him. "Who are you trying to fool, oh Shadow of Death? I could feel *your* pleasure too. Remember?"

His eyes flash.

I try to get to my feet as he suddenly stalks back towards me again, but my legs are still too unsteady. Still on my knees, I have to settle for arching a cocky brow at him.

He stops with his boots right in front of my knees so that I have to truly crane my neck if I want to keep eye contact. A ripple of pleasure rolls down my spine as he draws soft fingers along my jaw.

Then he suddenly takes my chin in a punishing grip and locks hard eyes on me. "If you ever pull a stunt like this again, I will make sure that you spend every night for the rest of your life with your hands shackled above your head. Understood?"

I flash him a lethal smile and make my voice deliberately seductive as I reply, "Yes, sir."

Desire flares in his eyes again.

With a growl, he snaps my head to the side as he releases my chin and whirls around. His boots thud against the floor as he stalks back out the door and slams it shut behind him. I watch the poor slab of wood vibrate in the door frame while I draw in a deep breath.

Well, that went… mostly according to plan.

I think?

CHAPTER NINETEEN

There is a tightness in my chest that I wasn't expecting. As I look out over the darkened streets of the Seelie Court, I suddenly feel trapped. Even though I'm currently lying atop a roof with the open night sky above me, I still feel as if walls are closing in on me from all sides.

I suppose it makes sense, given that I have literally been trapped in this city for most of my life. But it's more than just the feeling of being physically trapped in a specific place. The tightness in my chest and the uncomfortable emotions that twist inside me like cold snakes have more to do with who I used to be when I lived here.

When I'm in this city, it makes me feel like everyone is trying to force me back into a mold that I no longer fit inside. Because this city only remembers the person I used to be when I lived here. It has no idea who I have become after leaving it.

It's ridiculous. I know that. Cities don't have emotions or an agenda. They're just a collection of buildings. But still, as I look out across the darkened streets below, I can't help but hate this city. Once this is all over, I never want to return here again. I want to leave this place and the person I used to be behind.

"Any sign of him?" Orion whispers from below.

I scan the streets around me again, but from this angle, I can't actually see properly down into all of the streets, so my surveillance abilities are somewhat limited. With a sigh, I roll over, grab the edge of the roof, and then drop down to the stone street below.

After dusting myself off, I take up position next to Orion and at last answer his question. "No. But Alistair said that he saw him heading in this direction earlier. So he should pass by here within ten minutes or so."

Orion nods.

Since we can't just walk up to Gremar Fireclaw in his own homeland, we had to devise a strategy to get him to come to us. But if he knows that we are the ones who want to talk to him, he is more likely to contact the Icehearts so that they can ambush us rather than actually coming to talk to us. So in order to get him here without risking a trap, we need to use someone else to lure him in. And I know exactly who.

"Ah yes, by the way," Orion begins. His eyes gleam as he gives me a knowing look. "Next time you and Draven have wild hate sex, would you mind being a little quieter?"

I whip around to stare at him, my cheeks blazing. "I… we… what do you… we didn't…"

He lets out a smug chuckle, clearly very pleased with himself. "Yes, you did. My staff could barely sleep because of all the noise."

"That's not true! He gagged me, so there's no way we were loud enough to disturb anyone."

"Good for you, living out your wicked little fantasies." His smirk is positively villainous. "But I was referring to how the bed kept banging against the wall."

Mortification crashes over me. I feel like my entire face is on fire.

"Uhm, well, that's…" I stammer before drawing my eyebrows

down and instead huffing, "Well, it's your fault anyway, so you don't get to complain."

He arches an eyebrow at me. "How could it possibly be my fault that your hate sex is noisy?"

"It's your fault that we're having hate sex."

"Oh dear. I'm flattered that both of you find me so irresistibly hot that you had to release your frustrations by fucking each other instead."

I shoot him a scowl. "I meant that it's your fault that he hates me."

"That isn't my fault."

"Yes, it is. If you hadn't rigged the game by cursing that final portal, I would never have been forced to make Draven hate me."

"You made a choice."

"Because the choice was either to let him die or to make him hate me!"

"It was still your own choice."

"It doesn't matter! If we could've just stepped through that portal when we reached it, none of this would've happened. But you made sure that if I stepped through the portal, the person who loves me would die. And that's—"

"I was bluffing!" The words rip out of him, suddenly full of desperation.

Jerking back, I blink at him in stunned surprise. He lifts a hand as if to rake it through his hair. But then halfway up, he seems to remember that he is still wearing that spiky black crown on his head, because he freezes with his hand in the air like that. Dropping his hand back down, he just turns back to meet my gaze instead and heaves a deep sigh.

"I was bluffing," he repeats, his voice softer this time.

"What?" I breathe.

Some of that desperation flickers in his eyes again for a second. "How could I have set that kind of restriction on a portal? Grey only has portal magic. I only have nightmare magic.

Neither of us has the magical capacity to set a curse that could determine which specific person loves another person who steps through a portal. Let alone kill that person instantly from what could've been halfway across the continent for all we know. It's not possible to set that kind of restriction on a portal!"

I just stare at him, my heart beating painfully in my chest. Those massive waves of dark despair threaten to crash over me. And I know, without a doubt, that if I let them hit me right now, I will drown. Fully and irrevocably. So I block everything out. I block out all the horrible implications of this new information. I can think about it later. Later when I'm alone. Later when I don't need to function properly.

"So I was bluffing when I carved that message into the branch above the portal," Orion continues. "I was *bluffing*, God damn it. I thought you had figured that out. When you stepped through the portal and back onto the sands of the arena, I thought you had seen through my deception." Regret washes across his beautiful features for a moment as he motions towards where Draven is standing in the shadows farther down the street. "I never thought that you would…"

"Make my fated mate and one true love permanently hate me?" I finish for him, the words tasting like blood and iron in my mouth.

"Yeah." He heaves another sigh and slides his gaze back to me. "That was ruthless."

I give him an annoyed look.

"That wasn't an admonishment. It was a compliment." That hint of regret is gone from his face. Instead, there is something almost like respect in his eyes. "Not everyone is able to make those kinds of brutal decisions. Especially under pressure." He lets out a small huff of both amusement and approval. "Maybe you really will win this war."

"Maybe *we* really will win this war," I correct, holding his gaze.

He scoffs.

Silence falls over the street for a few seconds. Since it's the middle of the night, all the windows are dark. Only the silver light from the moon illuminates the deserted street around us.

"This is..." Orion begins, but then trails off. Clearing his throat, he tries again. "Did you know that this is the first time that I've been part of a... group?"

I raise my eyebrows in genuine surprise. "What about your friends back in the Unseelie Court?"

For a moment, I swear I see a flicker of deep longing in his eyes. But then he breaks eye contact and instead stares at the dark wooden wall across the street. "Being the king comes with a lot of power. But it's also a very... solitary position."

"You don't have friends? Or people who can give you advice at least? People you trust?"

"Trust?" he scoffs. "What is trust?" Letting out another huff of disbelief, he shakes his head. "No. Power is everything in our court. And if I'm not powerful and intelligent and strong and ruthless enough to keep it, someone else will take it from me. So all my life, I have only ever been able to rely on myself."

"That sounds... lonely."

A small sigh escapes his lips. "Yeah."

Another second passes. Then alarm flashes across his face and he snaps his gaze back to me. Threats practically pulse in his eyes as he locks them on me.

"If you ever tell anyone I said that, I will trap you in your worst nightmares for two days straight," he warns, his voice low and vicious.

I just flash him a wicked smile back. "If you try to trap me in my bad memories, I will shove a wildfire of fear into your chest and increase it until your mind breaks."

He blinks, looking surprised that I threatened him back instead of caving. Then he lets out a short laugh and shakes his head. "You know, I'm actually starting to like you a little bit."

"Ah, now it makes sense."

"What does?"

"You're attracted to women who hate you." I bait him with a knowing smile. "That's why you're so obsessed with Isera."

"I'm not obsessed…" he splutters, barely getting the words out without tripping over his own tongue. "With her. Obsessed? She's… That's not—"

I chuckle and turn around to reach for the edge above me. "I'm going to check from the roof again."

While Orion continues huffing threats below, I pull myself up to the roof again and then roll over so that I can see the streets around us. Shifting my gaze from side to side, I scan the area for our target.

Surprise flickers through me when I find someone else instead.

Barely a few steps away, right around the corner from where Orion and I were talking, is Isera. I had no idea that she was there, because we couldn't see her from where we were standing. But from up here, I can.

Silver moonlight falls across half of her face as she stands there in the shadows of the building, looking in our direction rather than at the rest of the street. She's leaning her back against the dark wood, and her arms are crossed over her chest. But there is a thoughtful expression on her face as she studies Orion without him knowing that he is being observed.

I wonder how much of our conversation she overheard.

Movement suddenly catches my eye on the street next to ours.

My heart leaps.

He's here.

CHAPTER TWENTY

Wood clatters against wood as Imar is thrown in through an open door by Draven's wind magic and hits the table and chairs that were arranged on the floor inside, knocking them over. Imar gasps, shaking his head and blinking furiously as if trying to figure out what just happened.

Draven simply stalks in after him and yanks him up from the floor before slamming him down into one of the few chairs that still remain upright. Air explodes from Imar's lungs, and before he can recover his breath, Isera covers his arms and legs and torso in ice, trapping him to the chair.

From my place by the wall inside, I just keep leaning back against the dark wooden panels with my arms crossed over my chest and watch them unseen from the shadows.

"Here's what's going to happen," Draven declares. "You're going to send a message to Gremar and tell him that there has been some kind of emergency and that he needs to come to the Golden Palace straight away."

Imar, who is a member of the Red Dragon Clan and who was the chief administrator responsible for organizing the

Atonement Trials, snaps his head up and stares at Draven in shock. "You... What the fuck do—"

"The only words that should be coming out of your mouth right now are *yes, sir*."

Anger flickers in Imar's blue eyes, and he yanks against his ice bonds. "Fuck you. You think you can torture me into betraying my clan leader? You underestimate my strength, Shadow of Death."

"Torture you? Why would I waste time and energy torturing you," a vicious smile curls Draven's lips as he jerks his chin in my direction, "when I can just have *her* change your entire personality instead?"

Summoning my magic, I straighten from the wall and walk out of the shadows with my eyes glowing. "Remember me?"

All color drains from Imar's face.

I let a cruel smile settle on my lips as I advance on him.

Just like most people, Imar believes that I can change someone's emotions so much that they become an entirely different person. And... well, to be fair, I *can* actually do that now, since I can create permanent emotions out of nothing and just force them into people's chests. But anyway, the point is that Imar has always believed that and has therefore always treated me with a level of wariness. When I registered for the Atonement Trials, he barely took his eyes off me once he learned that I had emotion magic. So I knew that simply seeing me with glowing eyes was going to create a spark of fear in his chest.

And it sure did.

I quickly latch on to that bone white spark of fear that appeared in his chest when he saw me, and then I begin increasing it rapidly.

"No, wait," Imar blurts out, and yanks hard against Isera's ice shackles again. "Don't. Don't—"

I shove more magic at him, increasing his fear even more.

"Please," he stammers. "Please, don't change me. I like who I am. Please, don't make me—"

Bracing my palms on his forearms, I lean down over him with that cruel smile still on my lips. "After all the shit you put us through in the Atonement Trials, do you really think I would show you mercy now?"

He thrashes in his seat. My magic keeps pouring into him, intensifying his fear, until he is yanking so hard against his restraints that the chair wobbles even though I have my palms pressing down on his forearms.

The power I have over his life right now makes a dark sense of craving burn through me. I drink in that absolutely intoxicating mix of fear and pleading in his eyes while I keep increasing the strength of my magic. I've never held this kind of ruthless authority before. It's making me feel drunk on power.

"Please." Imar's frantic gaze snaps to Draven. "Please, I'll do whatever you want. Just don't let her change me. Please, don't let her change me."

A smirk spreads across my face as I turn my head and glance back at Draven over my shoulder. My heart skips a beat when I find him watching me with both desire and hatred in his golden eyes. When my gaze meets his, he starts slightly and then quickly shifts his attention to Imar instead.

"Do as you're told," Draven replies. "And I might ask her to back off."

"Yes, yes, I'll do whatever you want!" He yanks against his restraints again. "I'll send a message to Gremar and ask him to come to the Golden Palace."

And he sure did.

Half an hour later, Imar has sent an emergency message to Gremar, and we are hauling his unconscious body across the grasslands and towards the Golden Palace outside the city.

Orion casts a glance at Imar's unconscious body, that Galen is carrying slung over his shoulder, before he shifts his gaze to me and gives me an unimpressed look. "I could've broken him faster."

I snort. "Sure you could."

"And speaking of ineffective uses of our limited time on this world," Orion continues, his eyes narrowing as he slides a suddenly suspicious look at Isera. "Why are we using the main entrance instead of the secret path that leads straight to the heart of the castle?"

"What secret path?" I ask, frowning at him even though his gaze is still fixed on Isera.

"It's a design feature present in both of our castles. With the exact location kept secret from the masses, of course." Challenge creeps into his suspicious stare as he holds Isera's gaze. "As a descendant of the Seelie Queen's second daughter, you should know that much, at least."

"Of course I do," Isera replies smoothly as she levels a look of challenge back at him. "But I'm not about to disclose the location of it to three dragon shifters and the ruler of an enemy court, am I?"

He holds her stare for another few seconds, suspicion still swirling in his eyes. Then he clicks his tongue and presses his hand to his chest in an overly dramatic gesture. "Enemy? You wound me, little viper. And here I was, thinking that you trusted me."

Tension crackles through the air as they hold each other's gaze in silence. Then, to my surprise, both of them let out a short huff of laughter that is barely more than an amused snort.

Behind their backs, Alistair and I exchange a quick glance.

That was close.

If Orion ever finds out that Isera isn't actually royalty and that their entire bargain is based on a lie, we're going to be in deep shit.

Thankfully, though, Isera is apparently an incredibly smooth liar.

Once we reach the Golden Palace, we split up into smaller groups to prepare the ambush for Gremar Fireclaw. And to prepare the four contingency plans that Draven devised as well, in case everything goes to hell.

I lead Galen into a small storage room that I discovered back when I was scouting out the Golden Palace during the Atonement Trials all those months ago. Once he has deposited Imar inside the room, I look down at Imar's unconscious body. With the potion we forced him to drink, courtesy of Haldia, he's probably going to sleep all the way until the day after tomorrow.

Closing the door to the storage room behind us, we exchange a nod and then start back towards the room where the others are getting ready. But once we draw close to it, I hesitate.

After telling Galen that I need to handle something else first, my feet start drifting in the direction of the main entrance again.

Since Gremar first needs to receive the message that Imar sent, and then also needs to fly all the way here, it will be hours before he actually shows up. Which means that I have time to sneak back to the city, if I want to.

Trailing to a halt in a corridor, I glance towards the hallway that will take me to the main entrance before I shift my gaze to the one that will take me back to my friends.

We're right here. In the Seelie Court. And I have time. I can go and visit my parents, if I want. I could go and check with my magic and finally get my answer.

Panic lurches inside me at just the thought of it.

What if I'm wrong? What if there is no manufactured flame of hatred in their chests? What if they really do simply resent me?

Glancing down the gold-glimmering corridor, I bite my lip as indecision rips at my chest.

Then I shake my head. No. I can't risk it. Not right now. When Orion admitted that he had been bluffing about the portal, I almost drowned in that black ocean that is just one second away from crashing down over me at any given time. If I go there now and find out that my parents do in fact hate me, I won't be able to handle it. It will be the final drop that makes that tiny light of hope inside my chest go out. I need to focus on the mission at hand. I can find out the truth about my parents later. When I'm in a better place mentally.

Giving myself a nod to confirm my decision, I start back towards the room where the others are.

The hallways inside the Golden Palace are dark. Since all the faelights in the corridors have been ripped out and replaced by torches on the walls, the only illumination right now comes from the moonlight that streams in through the windows. So when I see faelight spilling out from a small gap in a door up ahead, I frown in suspicion.

Moving quietly, I sneak the final distance to the room and glance in through the gap in the door.

My heart skips a beat.

Draven.

He is sitting on a chair that seems to have been dragged away from the desk in the corner. His head is turned slightly away from me, and he has buried his face in his hands. Light from a lone faelight gem falls across his body where he sits, drawing in deep breaths.

Then he looks up.

And my heart almost stops.

Dragging in another deep breath, he tilts his head back and rakes both hands through his hair. There is an expression of utter tiredness on his face. I have never seen him look this exhausted before. It makes him look both like a weary thousand-year-old man who has seen too much and an overwhelmed twenty-year-old boy who just wants to go home at the same time.

Pain stabs right through my chest at the sight of it, and I stifle a sharp intake of breath.

But not fast enough.

Draven whips his head towards me.

In a heartbeat, that exhausted expression disappears from his features as his usual mask of control and authority slams back down over his face.

Because that's what it is, I realize with another painful pang. A mask. This composure and power that he always exudes is a mask so that we won't see what he is really feeling. But now, when he thought he was alone, he let his mask slip for a few seconds so that he could catch his breath.

And I saw it.

And he knows that I saw it.

Anger pulses across his face as he shoots up from the chair and stalks towards me.

"I'm sorry," I begin, raising my hands as I take a few tentative steps into the room. "I didn't mean to—"

"Were you spying on me?" he demands, anger and embarrassment lacing his tone.

"No, I was just..." Trailing off, I just meet his gaze, my eyes soft, while worry and pain and a terrible sense of helplessness strangle my chest. "Are you okay?"

"Am I okay?" He lets out a harsh laugh.

Embarrassment and anger over the fact that I saw him like this mix with the usual hatred in his chest, and the combination of it all makes him look more unhinged than I have ever seen. He paces across the pale stone floor in front of me while an entire host of emotions fight for prevalence in his eyes.

At last, something inside him seems to snap.

"No, I'm not okay. I'm fucking tired!" His eyes wild, he swings out his arm and stabs it in the general direction of where everyone else is gathering. "Do you have any idea how fucking exhausting it is to always be the one in charge? To always be the one who needs to come up with all the plans and make sure that everything runs smoothly? To make sure that everyone else is working together and doing what they need to be doing instead of getting into fights over every fucking thing? To be the one responsible for seeing everything through. For checking everything. Planning. Organizing. Mediating. Delegating. Doing everything. Always being responsible for everything. While half of the world hates me for something that I couldn't even control!"

Pain and a large amount of shame crawl up my throat, and I can't get a single word out. I should've done more. I should've helped more. Taken on more responsibility. Planned more. Executed more. *Done* more.

His chest heaves. He rakes his hands through his hair again before shaking his head at me. Desperation pulses in his eyes when he looks at me.

"And what makes it even worse is that I can't even make sense of my own emotions anymore!" The words rip out of his chest, full of pain and confusion, as he stares at me. "I hate you so much, and I don't even really understand why. I just *hate* everything about you." That terrible desperation creeps back into his eyes. "And at the same time, I want you so fucking badly that I can barely breathe. Which just makes me hate you even more. I'm just so fucking tired of it all!"

Each word hits me like a gut punch.

Because this is all my fault.

I am the reason why he is struggling right now.

If I hadn't forced that hatred into his chest, he wouldn't be feeling this exhausted and confused and torn and overwhelmed right now. *I* did that. I forced this hard existence onto him.

And completely without reason.

Because Orion was bluffing.

There was no curse on the portal. If I had stepped through it, Draven would've been fine. But I didn't figure that out. I wasn't smart enough to see through the lies and deceit. I just believed him. Just like I always believed everything that I was told while living in the Seelie Court. Like an ignorant child.

I thought I had grown. Changed. Become smarter. Better.

Stronger. But I hadn't. I ruined our relationship over nothing. I ruined it. I ruined everything.

That darkness inside me rises up like black tidal waves on all sides.

I hurt Draven. He is struggling and in pain because of what I did to him. And I can't even try to comfort him. Can't even try to help him. Because he hates me. Everything I do and everything I say will only make it worse.

I ruined it.

I ruined everything.

I always ruin everything.

That endless black ocean presses in on me, threatening to suffocate me, and that tiny light of hope flickers desperately in the darkness.

"Draven," I begin, and I have to choke his name out through my strangled throat.

I don't even know what I'm going to say. What can I say, at this point?

His wild eyes meet mine. Anger and embarrassment and exhaustion and panic and desperation still pulse across his face, making him look like he is one second away from snapping completely.

"Oi!" Alistair suddenly calls from somewhere down the hall. "We're ready! Come on."

In a heartbeat, Draven wipes that desperate expression off his features and slams his usual mask back on. Only power and complete control remain on his face as he abruptly spins on his heel and stalks out of the room without a second look back.

I stand there, feeling like my heart was just ripped out of my chest.

Dragging in an unsteady breath, I try to force those black waves back by sheer force of will. It works. Barely.

Once again blocking out all of my emotions, I try to pull

myself together as efficiently as Draven did while I walk back towards our friends as well.

We have a job to do.

Gremar is on his way.

The plan is set.

Now, we just have to hope that we're not about to get screwed over.

CHAPTER TWENTY-ONE

Torchlight burns in the main entrance hall, right inside the closed doors that lead into the Golden Palace. I watch the light dance over the pale walls, which makes them shimmer like gold. I have no idea what this room looked like before the dragon shifters conquered our court, but now, there are no decorations in here. No royal carpets. No furniture. Nothing. It surprises me since most of the castle remains unspoiled, but I think the Icehearts might have deliberately stripped this first room bare as a cruel reminder that this beautiful castle is now a deserted relic.

I flick another glance at the closed doors. My heart beats nervously in my chest. We have four contingency plans, but I still can't entirely suppress the worry that ripples inside me. Out of all the clan leaders, I know Gremar the most since he and his clan have been responsible for maintaining order in our court all my life. He is ruthless, prideful, and he hates fae with every fiber of his being. Which really doesn't bode well for this conversation.

The doors are yanked open.

"It's the bloody middle of the night," Gremar Fireclaw growls as he stalks into the room. "What's so important that you couldn't—"

He jerks to a halt as he finds Draven standing there in the middle of the gold-glimmering entrance hall. The torches cast flickering light over Gremar's brown hair and red dragon scale armor as he just stands there for a moment. Behind him, the doors that he so violently yanked open swing shut again with a thud.

The sound seems to snap him out of his surprise. His expression darkens, and he begins summoning his lava magic.

Draven lets out a huff of amusement. "I really wouldn't, if I were you."

With his gaze still locked on Gremar, he nods in our direction. Gremar casts a quick glance around the room.

By the left wall, Isera and I summon our magic while Alistair and Orion do the same on the opposite side of the room. Orion and I don't do anything with ours, for now, but Isera and Alistair let their ice and fire magic crackle along their arms.

A hint of genuine surprise pulses across Gremar's face before he manages to hide it. Indignant rage roars up in his eyes instead as he glares at us for another few seconds before shifting his furious stare back to Draven. However, he does the smart thing and lets his lava magic fade out.

"Oh, you really have sunk low, haven't you?" Gremar says, shaking his head at Draven in disapproval. "Consorting with the fae." He practically spits out the final word. "Have you no pride left?"

"Says the guy who is forced to make parts of his clan *live* with the fae," Draven replies, a cruel smirk on his lips. "Have *you* no pride left, Gremar?"

Anger flashes in his brown eyes. "My clan doesn't live *with* them. We rule over them."

"Bane and Jessina rule over them. Not you. And they rule over you as well. Which is why you're forced to spend so much time here in the Seelie Court even though you hate it."

He opens his mouth to retort, but since Draven is right, he

apparently can't figure out how to refute that statement, so he just closes his mouth and grinds his teeth instead.

Draven lets out a long breath, and the vicious cruelty bleeds away from his features. Instead, he meets Gremar's frustrated stare with serious eyes. "Your clan shouldn't be ruled by a different clan. And neither should mine. Or any of the other clans. You *know* that."

"You talk of treason."

"Yes."

"The Iceheart Dynasty has dominated this continent for millennia. It's the natural order."

"Natural order? Just because our society is structured like this now doesn't mean that this is the way it *should* be structured. Just because we were born into the time and age that we were, we think that this is the normal way to live. But what's normal isn't always right."

"And what do you want to do instead?" Gremar shoots a look full of disgust at the four fae around him. "Trust the fae? They enslaved us! They used dragon steel to control our minds so that we had no free will. Have you forgotten that?"

"They're not the ones with a boot to your throat now." Draven gives him a pointed look. "In fact, they are the ones who will help us all overthrow Bane and Jessina and take back authority over our own clans."

"Overthrow the Icehearts?" He lets out a scoff of utter disbelief. "Have you lost your mind? It's because we are united that we are strong. Without a united force of dragon clans, without the Dread Legion, the Seelie Court would try to rebel and the dryads would try to take over the woods again and the Unseelie Court would be attacking us instead of cowering behind their wards like whipped dogs."

Searing rage flashes across Orion's face, and I think it's by sheer force of will that the Unseelie King doesn't start torturing Gremar right then and there.

"We're not meant to be a monolith!" Draven snaps, frustration lacing his voice. "We're separate clans with different cultures. We're not meant to be ruled by one set of leaders as if all dragon shifters are the same." He stabs a hand towards Gremar. "Your clan has their own culture and their own traditions, but you barely get to practice them now because two people in an ice castle halfway across the continent is deciding what you're allowed to do in your own homeland."

"We still have our own culture."

"Really? Didn't Fire Night used to be a huge tradition among your clan? A rite of passage even?" Challenge shines like steel in Draven's eyes as he stares Gremar down. "When was the last time you got to practice that?"

Gremar opens his mouth, but no retort makes it out. Standing there on the pale floor, he just looks back at Draven, his mouth still slightly open.

"The Red Clan is fierce and proud," Draven continues, his voice echoing with conviction through the high-ceilinged hall. "And it's supposed to be ruled by *you*."

Across the floor, Gremar hesitates.

"Azaroth didn't choose Bane and Jessina to lead the Red Clan." Draven holds Gremar's gaze with blazing eyes. "He chose *you*. It's time to take your clan back."

For the first time ever, Gremar Fireclaw's iron conviction wavers. He opens and closes his mouth several times, but no words make it out. So instead, he licks his lips and swallows while that uncharacteristic uncertainty flits across his face.

Still standing by the left wall, I watch it all in stunned silence.

Mabona's tits, he's good. This entire conversation, Draven has deliberately been hitting Gremar precisely where it will hurt the most. His pride. It's like watching a master archer shoot the wings off a fly. I've always known that Draven is excellent at making people do what he wants, but watching him manipulate

Gremar this thoroughly is so hot that I can feel the fire flickering through my veins.

"It's, uhm..." Gremar begins, indecision still pulsing in his brown eyes.

The massive doors to the entrance hall are yanked open.

I whip my head towards them.

Ice spreads through my body like cold poison as two dragon shifters in elegant silver garments saunter in through the doors.

A slow smile spreads across Empress Jessina Iceheart's face. "Well, isn't this a lovely little reunion."

CHAPTER TWENTY-TWO

Across the room, Alistair flinches at the mere sound of her voice. It breaks my heart to see it. Since I was living with Draven in the Ice Palace, I don't know the full extent of the physical and mental torture that the Icehearts put Alistair and Isera through. But given the complete breakdown that I witnessed in the kennels last year, and his reaction just now, it must have been even worse than I could have imagined.

"Well done, Gremar," Emperor Bane Iceheart says as he strides into the room next to Jessina. His long black hair ripples down his back when he moves. "I was doubting your intelligence when you sent word. But you were right." Bane's black eyes gleam in the torchlight as he sweeps his gaze over us. "We really do have rats in the castle."

Isera's expression darkens. Standing next to her, I can practically feel the murderous rage and hatred radiating from her entire body. Not only did Bane torture *her*, he also tortured and humiliated and drained the life out of her mother for a hundred and fifty years until she died from it.

Grabbing her wrist discreetly, I begin backing us away from the door and towards the side of the room where Draven and

Gremar are standing. Across the shining floor, Orion and Alistair do the same.

The previous hesitation is completely gone from Gremar's face as he inclines his head and says, "Thank you, sir."

Draven lets out a mocking snort.

Anger flickers in Gremar's eyes as he snaps his gaze back to Draven and gives him a taunting smile back. "Did you really think that Imar and I don't have protocols in place? The moment he sent his message, I knew exactly what was going on."

"Of course we did," Draven replies, a smirk ghosting across his lips.

Gremar blinks in surprise, apparently not having expected that answer. But before he can say anything, Empress Jessina loses the final shreds of her already incredibly limited patience.

"Now, are you going to surrender quietly?" she asks, her pale gray eyes full of both haughty arrogance and vicious threats. Sweeping her long white hair back over her shoulder, she arches a pale brow at Draven. "Or are we going to have to kill all of your friends before we drag you back to make an example out of you?"

"I choose option four," he replies.

My heart leaps. Four. We're going with contingency plan number four. It's the riskiest one. But also the plan that, if we succeed, will bring the most substantial reward.

"Four?" Jessina echoes, her delicate brows scrunching in confusion. "What do—"

Galen and Lyra, who are hiding in the other room just inside the open doorway behind us, flip their levers.

A white stone wall slams down from the ceiling, cutting the room in half and separating the Icehearts from the rest of us.

I smile. Since the levers were well hidden in the walls, and there was nothing visible in the ceiling either, none of us knew that this very convenient contraption existed. No one except Orion, who apparently has a similar mechanism in his own castle. It looks like the Seelie and Unseelie Courts used to share knowledge and ideas before we became rivals.

The moment that the wall hits the floor, Gremar whips around in shock.

But the rest of us have known what to do since the moment Draven said the word *four*, so we are already moving. Next to me, Isera summons a mass of ice and slams it straight into Gremar, pinning him to the wall and trapping him there. Orion yanks open a door behind him and darts into it while Draven runs into the room where Galen and Lyra are waiting. Windows are slammed open inside that room.

Yanking out a piece of steel, I sprint towards where Isera is keeping Gremar trapped. Alistair runs towards me from the other side.

Deafening roars echo across the palace grounds outside as Draven, Lyra, and Galen jump out of the windows and shift into dragons. Massive black bodies are briefly visible on the grass outside before they lurch into the air.

"I will kill you for this, you filthy fae bitch," Gremar snarls while he starts trying to melt Isera's ice with his lava magic. "And then I'll—"

She yanks the ice up over his mouth.

Dark red lava bubbles under the thick ice, and water runs down it as it starts to melt. Gritting her teeth, Isera keeps building the ice up over and over again.

Alistair and I skid to a halt in front of Gremar. While still pouring ice magic over his body, Isera suddenly removes the block of ice that was trapping his wrist.

I shove the piece of dragon steel against the naked skin of his wrist, right below the edge of his armor. Gremar's eyes widen in shock, and his lava magic falters. Not hesitating a second, Alistair summons his fire magic and rapidly heats the metal.

A hiss rips from my lips, and I almost drop the piece of dragon steel.

"Shit, sorry," Alistair blurts out, and grabs the metal from my fingers. "I forgot that you can feel the heat too."

Since he is immune to the effects of his own fire magic, he doesn't get burned when he holds the searing piece of dragon steel. Gremar thrashes against the ice bonds, and if Isera wasn't silencing him with ice, I'm pretty sure that he would be screaming.

Alistair awkwardly bends the metal rod with only one hand while keeping a blue flame in his other and using it to heat up the material. At last, he manages to get the two ends together so that he can weld them together.

The moment it's done, Isera yanks down the ice over Gremar's wrist again to cool down the metal. A hissing sound fills the room as the cool ice meets the hot dragon steel.

Outside the walls, dragons roar as Bane and Jessina fight Draven and the others. The noise is so loud that the windows around us rattle in their frames.

"Go!" I tell Alistair. "Help them. We've got it from here."

"See you on the other side," he replies, and then whirls around and sprints into the other room.

A moment later, he leaps out the window and onto the grass outside.

Fire roars into the sky in a massive torrent.

I channel my magic and shove it straight into that piece of dragon steel. "Don't fight back."

Gremar immediately stops moving.

I suck in a sharp breath. This was the only part of the plan that we couldn't really test beforehand, so I was worried that it wouldn't work. That I would mess this up and ruin it for everyone. But it worked. Goddess above, it worked.

My heart beats hard in my chest as I stare at Gremar. I'm bending him to my will with dragon steel. The mere thought of it should horrify me. But it doesn't. This is the man who has tormented and punished us all my life. The man who has killed and hurt and humiliated any fae who dared to step out of line. And now, I hold *his* life in the palm of my hand.

Vicious revenge burns inside my soul, adding more fuel to the wildfire of rage and hatred that I let loose inside me when we left the Unseelie Court.

A few steps away, Isera lets her ice magic fade out and instead walks into the room with the levers.

Gremar only stands there, glaring at me with murderous eyes.

"You are not allowed to take off the dragon steel, and you are not allowed to tell or show anyone that you are wearing dragon steel," I declare. "You are not allowed to tell anyone what we did to you in this room. And you are not allowed to hurt me, Isera, Alistair, Draven, Galen, Lyra, or Orion."

Since I don't know how specific I need to make my orders, I make them as detailed as possible to avoid loopholes.

"You will lead Emperor Bane Iceheart into that room," I point to the room that Orion disappeared into earlier. "And you cannot let him, or anyone else, find out that it is a trap. Understood?"

He opens and closes his mouth for a few seconds, as if he wants to say something else, but in the end all he grinds out is, "Yes."

"Good. Then go and find him now and start convincing him to come here."

Hatred burns like black flames in Gremar's eyes, but he jerks his chin down in a nod. Isera flips the levers, one at a time, which will make the wall retract into the ceiling again. Gremar turns towards it and waits.

All the orders that I have just given to Gremar are swirling around somewhere in the back of my mind. They don't distract from my present thoughts, but they float there like glowing words.

Stone groans as the wall begins lifting. Slowly at first, but then it picks up. It disappears into the ceiling again with a bang.

And leaves us face to face with Lavendera.

I jerk back in surprise. But Gremar's orders were to leave now, so he just strides past her and towards the main entrance.

For a few tense seconds, nothing happens. Lavendera just stands there, staring unseeing at the wall above my shoulder. As if her body is here but her mind isn't. She looks exactly like she did the last time I saw her. Flowing brown hair rippling down her back, and the scar across her cheek and jaw that mars her otherwise extraordinarily beautiful face. Her pink and purple eyes have that faraway look in them that she seems to get from time to time.

After we left the Ice Palace, I thought for a while that she might have been faking her weirdness so that we would be less likely to suspect that she was actually a traitor. But she actually is this strange.

"Selena," Isera calls from the room behind me. "I'm going to…"

She trails off, and I think she might be glancing through the doorway and into this room, but I can't tell for certain because I don't dare take my eyes off Lavendera.

Ice shoots through the air.

It speeds through it so fast that I barely have time to flinch.

Lavendera, however, sees it coming.

A massive tree shoots up from the ground in front of her. The ice slams into it with such force that the wood cracks and the tree topples halfway forward. It suddenly sinks into the ground again.

Behind it, Lavendera blinks hard a few times, her eyes still unfocused.

Then her gaze at last seems to lock on me. It takes another moment for recognition to spark in her eyes. When it does, she heaves a deep sigh.

"I gave you a head start," she says. "You should have used it."

"I did."

"Not well enough."

"I thought you were my friend. I confided in you. I tried to help you. And you betrayed me."

Her eyes show no emotion as she simply replies, "Yes, friends tend to do that."

"No, they—"

Branches shoot towards me.

I suck in a sharp breath and throw myself to the side. The branches slam into a block of ice while I roll across the floor and reach for my own magic. Shoving it forward, I aim for the peach-colored spark of confusion in Lavendera's chest. With her erratic way of behaving, she must be feeling constantly confused.

A hiss rips from my lungs, and I lose the grip on my magic the moment it connects.

Scrambling backwards, I leap out of reach of another branch while Isera shoves a second block of ice at her.

My head is ringing, and a flicker of fear blows through me as I stare at Lavendera.

When I tried to connect my magic to her emotions, something went wrong. No, something *is* wrong. With her. The moment my magic connected with her, it was like being hit by a wall of tens of thousands of screaming people. It was almost physically painful.

"They're coming soon," Isera hisses at me under her breath while she continues throwing sheets of ice at Lavendera. "If they come back and see this, our whole plan is ruined. We need to get her out of here."

We need to get her on our side, my mind immediately insists instead.

"Why are you working for them?" I call to Lavendera while ice and wooden branches crash against each other. "You could help us. You're one of us, so why are you helping *them*?"

Her gaze slides to me. "Because you can't give me what I want."

"And what is that?"

She doesn't reply. Only doubles the number of branches that she shoots at us. But a terrible craving flared up in her eyes when I asked that question. Whatever it is that she wants, she wants it *badly*.

"Fuck this," Isera growls under her breath. "We're taking this outside." She shoots a pointed look at me. "Make sure we get the bastard."

Before I can so much as nod, she slams a sheet of ice towards Lavendera's side. She yanks up a tree to block it, but Isera has already thrown a second attack. A massive ice wall crashes into Lavendera from the front, barely cushioned by a tangle of branches, and the force sends her flying backwards and out through the main entrance behind her.

Without a second look back, Isera sprints after her.

Outside, wings boom and dragons roar while fire lights up the night sky.

Giving my head a quick shake, I try to get my wits back as I spin around and run over to the room that Orion disappeared into earlier.

The Unseelie King jerks back, and his eyes abruptly stop glowing.

"Malachi's balls, you couldn't have announced yourself or something?" he huffs. "I was about to blast you with my full power."

"Sorry," I give him a smile full of sarcasm. "Next time, I'll make sure to hire a master of ceremonies to announce me."

He rolls his eyes in a very unkinglike way. "Everything is ready on my end, so we should—"

Cutting himself off midsentence, he suddenly yanks me the final half step out of the doorway and in behind the wall.

"They're here?" I guess, keeping my voice soft.

He nods in confirmation.

My heart leaps and then starts pounding in my chest.

This is it. Our entire plan hinges on this moment. If we screw this up, we're doomed.

Two pairs of feet thud against the floor in the entrance hall outside, getting louder with every step as they draw closer. But I can barely hear them over the pounding in my ears.

Please, Mabona. This has to work.

Summoning my magic, I get ready to shove it forward at a moment's notice. Next to me, Orion's eyes begin glowing as well. I resist the urge to fidget. Every nerve inside my body is strung so tightly that I can barely breathe.

The footsteps reach the doorway.

I hold my breath.

A silver pant leg appears across the threshold.

And then Emperor Bane Iceheart strides in through the door.

CHAPTER TWENTY-THREE

Orion hits him with the full power of his magic. Bane gasps. Whipping his head from side to side, he desperately tries to figure out what just happened as the room around him disappears and is instead replaced by whatever horrible memory Orion is showing him.

I'm just about to slam him with my own magic when Gremar lurches towards Bane as if to protect him, which is when I realize that I didn't tell him that he couldn't help Bane after the trap had already been sprung. Panic shoots up my spine, and I shove my magic into the dragon steel around Gremar's wrist instead.

"Don't move!" I blurt out.

He immediately stops halfway through a stride. I suck in a breath of relief. It's followed by a sense of wicked satisfaction. All my life, other people have been ordering me around. Everyone from the dragon shifters who patrol our court to the master of the Fishing Guild to the leaders of the fae resistance to random strangers in town who simply want their own needs met. So to have this kind of absolute power over someone, where they obey my every word, feels shockingly good.

"Selena," Orion snaps.

Giving my head a quick shake, I yank myself out of that weird feeling and once more focus on the problem at hand. Gremar is still standing there, frozen mid-step, but Emperor Bane has staggered several steps to the side. And not the side that we want him to be on.

Summoning my magic again, I shove it at the flame of fear in his chest.

I jerk back in shock when it isn't there. The memories that Orion shows people usually involve fear in some way.

Quickly releasing that emotion, I shove several more at his chest until something sticks. To my surprise, the one that I find blazing in his chest when he watches those memories is despair. Latching on to that black flame, I start pouring even more magic into it.

Bane sucks in an unsteady breath and stumbles. I force more magic into him, turning that black flame of despair into a raging wildfire that is big enough to consume his whole body.

His knees buckle.

Somewhere outside, a dragon roars.

Part of me, an incredibly big part of me, still thinks that we should just kill him now while we have the chance. But Draven said that if we kill Bane, Jessina will feel him die through their mate bond. And then, all bets are off. Apparently, if we kill him before we've been able to trap or at least neutralize Jessina, the final thin thread of her restraint is going to snap completely and she is going to fly straight over the Seelie Court and kill every single person in the city with her ice flames.

So instead of shoving my dagger into Bane's throat, which is what I really want to do, I simply keep pouring my magic into him while Orion grabs his now trembling body and starts hauling him towards the portal on his right.

The Unseelie King said that everything was ready on the other side, so I turn towards Gremar instead. But in order to command him through the dragon steel, I need to first sever my connection to Bane. Glancing over my shoulder, I find Orion shoving him in through the portal. There should be soldiers waiting in there to help their king, so he should be fine with just his own magic for a few seconds.

Cutting off the magic to Bane, I spin back to face Gremar. His body is shaking slightly, and sweat rolls down his temple, as he has to strain his muscles to keep the unnatural pose that my previous order trapped him in.

"Now, you are going to lead Jessina through this portal as well," I begin. "Without her finding out that it is a trap and without helping her in anyway."

He just glares back at me in silence.

That's when I realize that the order not to move is still in effect. I cast another stressed look back at where Orion is waiting for me to come and help him while I quickly flick through those orders floating at the back of my mind. Once I find the one that prevents Gremar from moving, I imagine myself snuffing out those glowing words the way I would a candle.

Gremar immediately staggers forward and then straightens properly.

"I will kill you for this," he growls at me, and the utter fury in his brown eyes informs me that he means every word of that.

But he can't do anything else, because I ordered him to go and get Jessina now, so he simply spins on his heel and stalks back out the door.

Once he's gone, I dart through the portal.

On the other side, I find a dungeon filled with chaos. Grey is standing right next to me, keeping the portal open. But across the rough stone floor, Orion and four guards are trying to shove Bane into a sturdy chair that has been bolted to the floor, but the emperor is fighting back even though he is still trapped in his memories as well.

Summoning my magic, I slam it into his chest.

Something almost like a sob of hopelessness rips from his

throat, and his body goes limp, as I turn that black flame of despair into a raging wildfire again. Orion and his soldiers at last manage to shove him into the chair and shackle him to it.

The Unseelie King flicks his long dark blue hair back behind his shoulder and turns to arch an eyebrow at me. "Selena, how nice of you to finally join us."

"I had to order Gremar to get Jessina," I reply, giving him a pointed look back.

He clicks his tongue but doesn't argue, since he knows that I would need to cut the flow of my magic to do that and therefore couldn't help him with Bane this past minute.

I glance back at the portal that Grey is still keeping open.

When Draven and the others see Gremar returning for Jessina, they will know that the plan is on track and will start making their way back to the portal as well so that they can ambush Jessina when she gets here while Orion and I focus on keeping Bane down.

Faelights have been set into parts of the dark stone ceiling. They, along with the faint blue glow coming from Grey's portal, provide the only illumination in this otherwise darkened cell. I'm not sure exactly where, but I know that this dungeon is located somewhere underneath Orion's palace in the Unseelie Court. The gleaming gems cast harsh shadows across Bane's face where he sits shackled to the metal chair in the middle of the room. I study him.

The emperor thrashes in his chair, throwing his head from side to side while those pitiful sounds escape his throat. Seeing him like that honestly shocks me. He has always been so confident and powerful and in control. But now, when Orion is forcing him to relive his worst memories, he looks disturbingly like a real person with real emotions.

"What are you showing him?" I find myself asking.

Orion glances at me from the corner of his eye before shifting his attention back to our prisoner. "His worst memories from when he was enslaved by some of the fae from your court."

My heart jerks and then starts pounding in my chest. Biting my lip, I try to suppress the sudden flash of morbid curiosity. No one in our court knows anything real about that time period since all the history books were destroyed and all the people who were involved were killed. But here is a firsthand witness whose memories are still intact.

"Can you…" I begin, and then clear my throat a little self-consciously. "Can you show me too?"

"Are you sure you want to know?" Orion asks, still keeping his eyes on Bane.

"Yes."

He nods. "I can make you a spectator in the memory. Grab my wrist. It will keep you from moving here in the real world. Squeeze it when you want out."

"Okay," I breathe.

My heart hammers against my ribs as I move closer to Orion's side and grab his wrist in a firm grip.

Without warning, he thrusts me into Bane Iceheart's memories.

The abrupt shift stuns me so much that I almost lose the grip on my own magic. With immense effort, I manage to keep my connection to the black wildfire of despair in Bane's chest while the dungeon around me is now replaced by a muddy field. I keep a tight grip on Orion's wrist to stop myself from trying to walk forward.

Bane and Jessina are standing on the grass in front of me, but they look nothing like how I'm used to seeing them. Instead of carrying themselves with royal grace while wearing glittering silver garments, they're practically cowering where they're standing on the grass. Dressed in worn rags, they look dirty, exhausted, and terrified.

I appear to be looking through the eyes of a fae man, and there are three more fae standing next to me on the grass.

"Please, sir," Bane is saying, his voice trembling. "We just flew all the way to the Green Wilds and back. We need to rest before we can shift and carry you again."

"I don't care what you need," the fae man to my right snaps. "We've got things to do." His eyes begin glowing. "Now, *shift*."

The memory ends and is immediately replaced by another one. The sudden change makes me almost tilt forward, and I'm glad that Orion told me to hold on to his wrist. When the world around me keeps changing like this, it's difficult to remember where my body actually is.

When the next memory stabilizes, we're inside what appears to be a dark stable. Rotting hay covers the floor, and short wooden walls frame the box where the horse should be. Except there is no horse in it. Instead, Bane and Jessina are kneeling there on the hay.

"Please don't make us sleep in here," Jessina is saying, her voice soft and pleading.

"Why not?" a fae woman replies with a snicker from my left. "This is exactly where you belong. Did you really think that you could refuse a partnership with us? That you were so high and mighty that you could deny us a chance to be dragon riders? That you could tell us that we weren't worthy of you? You are animals. No better than horses. *This* is where you belong."

"Don't talk to my mate like that," Bane growls. "She—"

I gasp as the fae man closest to him punches him in the face. But the person whose eyes I'm watching through merely continues leaning his back against the stable wall, watching it all while keeping his arms casually crossed over his chest.

Bane yanks his arms up as the guy punches him again. Next to him, Jessina lurches forward and grabs the fae man's arm.

"Stop!" she calls. "Don't—"

He backhands her across the face. The sudden hits snaps her head to the side and sends her stumbling into the wall.

Rage pulses across Bane's face as he starts to leap up from the ground to attack the guy. But before he can so much as get off his knees, the fae man summons some kind of magic that makes his eyes glow.

"Stay on your knees," he orders. "And keep your mouth shut."

Bane immediately stops moving as the dragon steel overrides his free will.

The fae man grabs Jessina's collar and yanks her upright again. Her hand is pressed against her cheek where he backhanded her, and tears line her eyes as she stares at him in fear. He looks back at Bane with cruel eyes. And then slaps Jessina across the face again.

I jerk back in shock.

Jessina gasps in pain, and rage burns in Bane's eyes. But with the dragon steel keeping him silent and on his knees, he can do nothing to protect her.

The memory shifts again. This time, we're in a small cabin. It's dark outside the windows, so I can't tell where we are.

"Drink," a fae woman orders from where she is standing in front of Jessina, who is sitting at the table with Bane. The woman's eyes glow in the dim light inside the cabin. "All of it."

Forced by the dragon steel and the woman's magic, Jessina picks up the wooden tankard and starts drinking. Bane looks between her and the three fae who are standing on the other side of the scratched wooden table. Worry pulses across his whole face.

On the chair beside him, Jessina grimaces while she continues drinking. Whatever it is that they're forcing her to drink doesn't taste well.

Once she has swallowed every drop, she sets the tankard back on the table and drags in a deep breath.

"What was that?" she asks. "It tasted… strange."

The fae woman shrugs. "A potion. To make you sterile."

My heart jerks hard in my chest.

In the memory, Bane's mouth drops open while horror spreads across Jessina's face.

"What?" she gasps out.

The fae woman shrugs again, as if it's no big deal. "We can't have you getting pregnant, can we? It would make everything so messy and ruin all our plans."

Tears well up in Jessina's eyes as she presses a hand to her stomach.

I squeeze Orion's wrist in rapid succession.

He immediately pulls me back out of the memory.

Staggering backwards, I suck in unsteady breaths while very uncomfortable feelings twist inside my chest like thorny vines. My back hits the cold stone wall of the dungeon, and I brace myself against it gratefully while my heart continues slamming in my chest.

That was… not what I was expecting.

In theory, I knew that it must have been horrible for the dragon shifters who were enslaved by that small group of entitled fae who trapped them with dragon steel when they refused to form a normal partnership with them. But this was worse than I was expecting.

My head spins and my chest tightens uncomfortably. Because I suddenly *understand*. I understand exactly why Bane and Jessina slaughtered the people who enslaved them. I understand why they trapped the remaining fae inside the Seelie Court. I understand why they made us live in filth and poverty. I even understand why they began sterilizing us. It wasn't just about keeping the population growth under control and strengthening the magical bloodlines. It was for revenge.

I press a hand to my mouth as bile rises up my throat.

Oh Goddess above, I actually understand why the Icehearts

hate us all so much. And they're right to. They are right to hate the people who did all of these awful things to them.

My stomach turns as I stare at Bane with new eyes. I used to look at him and Jessina as monsters who were just evil simply because they wanted to be. But they're not. They were humiliated and violated and tormented too. How am I supposed to—

"Remember what they've done," Orion says.

His strong voice, so full of confidence and authority, cuts through the dread inside me like a blade. I suck in a sharp breath, trying to reorient myself again. Blinking, I tear my gaze from Bane and instead meet Orion's hard eyes.

"I've seen *your* worst memories too," Orion continues, holding my gaze. "Remember what they've done."

Even without his magic, memories suddenly start flashing through my mind. Memories of how my stomach has ached all my life when I've only been allowed one single meal a day. Memories of all the drunk and ragged people who are drowning their sorrows in alcohol all across our court. Memories of how we were forced to kill and hurt each other during the Atonement Trials. Memories of Isera and Alistair, half-naked and shackled in iron, kneeling blindfolded in the middle of a crowded banquet hall. Memories of them being led around half-naked in a collar and chain. Memories of them locked in dog cages. Memories of Draven standing on a mountainside while the Icehearts whip his wings to shreds. Memories of the blood that ran down his ruined wings and the world-ending pain that he had to endure. Memories of them using dragon steel to take away Draven's free will for two hundred years.

I drag in a shuddering breath.

That panic and dread evaporate inside me as the sympathy I briefly felt is replaced by hatred and rage that is even stronger than before.

Yes, that small group of entitled fae assholes who enslaved them and did all of those horrible things to them deserved everything they got. But *we* did not. The way they were treated by those people doesn't justify how they have treated all of us who are completely innocent of those crimes. They have been punishing fae for generations for a crime that we have not committed. And they've even done the same thing that the fae did to them to other dragon shifters. Like Rin Tanaka. And Draven.

The final flicker of sympathy inside me is crushed into oblivion as I once again remember the feeling of that world-ending pain that Draven had to endure after his wings were whipped to shreds. And it wasn't the first and only time they did that. They whipped his wings like that every day for *six years*.

That massive black ocean of rage and hatred roars up inside me like tidal waves.

Every day. For six years.

I'm going to fucking kill them for that alone.

Screaming suddenly echoes through the room.

I whip my head towards the portal to find Isera and Alistair practically throwing Lyra and Galen in through that glittering blue rectangle before diving through themselves.

"Close it!" Isera screams at Grey.

Grey's gaze immediately darts to Orion, who jerks his chin down in a nod. Roars and clanging sounds come from the other side of the portal for a second, drawing closer at an alarming rate. Then it collapses into the ground, and deafening silence falls over the room.

I flick my gaze over all of them, looking for Draven.

Ice spreads through my chest.

"No!" Galen screams, shoving Alistair away from him. "We can't just—"

"Where is Draven?" I demand, my voice cutting through the room like lightning.

Galen turns towards me. His violet eyes are filled with panic and dread and guilt.

"He's… gone."

CHAPTER TWENTY-FOUR

The dark fury inside me is swallowing my whole soul. That small spark of light and hope is now nothing more than a tiny pinprick in a stormy ocean full of thrashing black tidal waves. I can barely hear anything over the roaring in my ears as Orion ushers us all out of Bane's cell and into the dimly lit stone corridor outside. The door closes behind us with a thud. The four soldiers remain inside, keeping Bane under control, while Grey quickly disappears into the stairwell up ahead.

"What do you mean *gone*?" I demand as soon as we're alone.

"We could've gotten him back!" Galen snarls at Isera. "We could've—"

"No," she snaps, cutting him off. "We couldn't. You know it as well as I do. There was nothing we could've done to take him back at that point."

"But the—"

"We barely managed to get the two of you out! She was already halfway across the city when—"

"Just tell me what happened!" I scream at them, panic still thrashing inside my chest.

Deafening silence falls over the rough stone corridor. It's so loud that it almost echoes between the walls.

"It was as if Jessina could feel it the moment that you took Bane," Lyra begins, her orange eyes full of dread and worry.

"She probably could," Alistair adds from where he is standing next to her. "Through their mate bond."

My heart slams against my ribs, and I barely manage to press out, "What happened?"

"She just... went berserk," Alistair continues. Disbelief shines on his face as he shakes his head. "She *cut off* Gremar's hand with a sword to get the dragon steel off."

A jolt shoots through me, and I reach towards those glowing orders that are supposed to be floating in the back of my mind. They're no longer there. My mouth is dry as sand as I try to swallow through the storm of emotions that is building inside me.

"Once that was gone, the entire Red Clan showed up as well," Isera picks up. "Along with the soldiers from the Silver Clan who were already there. Draven was swarmed. He shifted into a half-shift to try to escape in the chaos, but Jessina in her dragon form somehow managed to knock him out."

My heart pounds painfully as I whisper, "Where is he?"

"She took him. Alistair and I can't fly, and she was halfway across the city by the time Galen and Lyra managed to get free from the horde of dragons that was swarming them as well." For the first time since she stepped through the portal, her eyes soften a fraction as she holds my gaze. "There was nothing we could do."

Panic thrashes inside me, and those massive black waves that threaten to crush me wobble precariously inside my soul. I drag in short, jagged breaths.

"We need to go back," I declare. Whipping around, I lock eyes with Orion. "Call Grey back. Tell him to open another portal to the Seelie Court."

Orion's gaze slides to Isera, and he says nothing.

"Open another portal!" I scream at him.

"No," Isera replies from behind me. "The castle is already overrun. And Draven isn't there anymore."

I whirl around to face her, rage burning through me like wildfire. But the expression on her face stops the threat on my tongue before I can spit it out. Pain and sympathy, emotions that I've almost never seen on her face before, shine in her eyes as she just holds my gaze in silence.

"Selena," Lyra suddenly says from where she's standing next to Alistair. Her voice is also laced with pain. "We all want him back. But he's not in the Seelie Court anymore. Going back there isn't going to help him. First, we need to figure out where she took him."

On my other side, Galen paces the stone floor like a snarling wolf. But even he doesn't argue.

"We still have Bane," Alistair says, addressing the entire room. "We can use him to get Jessina."

"How?" I ask. "How are we—"

Pain suddenly spikes through my chest.

It's so violent that I double over and gasp out loud.

Another stab of pain hits me.

Sheer horror washes through me when I realize where it's coming from.

The mate bond.

I can feel Draven's pain through our flickering mate bond.

Jerking upright, I gasp out, "She's hurting him!"

"What?" several of the others reply at the same time.

Another burst of pain hits me through the mate bond. And I know from experience that the intensity of the emotions that I feel through our mate bond is only a tiny fraction of what Draven feels.

Blind rage hits me like a boulder. It's so intense, so all-consuming, that my vision actually blacks out for a second.

Lurching forward, I yank open the door to Bane's cell.

The four guards inside jump in surprise, but Orion must signal to them from behind my back because they do nothing as I storm into the cell. Before we left a few minutes ago, I increased Bane's small spark of tiredness until he passed out from it. Now, I shove my magic into his chest and smother that flame of tiredness again. He jerks awake.

"Show him those memories again," I snap at Orion, my words coming out like an order rather than a request.

Thankfully, Orion doesn't make an issue of it. He just summons his magic and hits Bane with it without question. Bane yanks hard against the thick manacles that keep him trapped, and he throws his head from side to side as he is forced back into his worst memories.

Standing there before him, I summon my own magic and slam it into that black flame of despair in his chest. Then I start increasing it. And increasing it. And increasing it.

Bane thrashes hard in the chair as I amplify his emotions over and over again. Desperate whines rip from his throat, along with broken sobs, and his limbs shake violently.

I keep increasing the strength of my magic, knowing that Jessina can feel all of this through her own mate bond with Bane.

She thinks I'm cruel? Oh, we have only scratched the fucking surface of just how cruel and vicious I can really be.

Another burst of pain stabs through my chest. Stronger this time.

"Selena," Galen calls from somewhere behind me. "What's going on?"

"She's torturing him!" The words rip out of my lungs, full of desperation and tasting like blood.

Rage and hatred and undiluted terror tear through my chest, and I force more magic into the flame of despair in Bane's chest. He screams. His body shakes violently, and he starts banging the back of his head against the chair.

Another massive spike of pain shoots through my and Draven's mate bond.

I increase the strength of my magic until Bane's mind almost breaks. I can feel it, like a fragile eggshell that only requires one more tap to shatter. That ruthless ocean of unforgiving hatred inside me almost makes me do it. But reason manages to break through first.

If I kill Bane, Jessina is going to kill Draven. And I didn't do all of this for no reason. I did it so that she would *stop* torturing Draven.

With immense effort, I pull myself back from the edge and cut off the flow to my magic.

"Stop showing him the memories," I tell Orion.

Yet again, the Unseelie King thankfully does what I tell him without issue.

Bane slumps back in the chair, his chest heaving. I reach out with my magic and connect to the spark of tiredness again. Then I steadily increase it until he passes out.

The moment that Bane's agony stops, so do the bursts of pain from Draven. For another minute, I just stand there, watching Bane sleep slumped in the chair like that. But no more spikes of agony come through my and Draven's mate bond.

"What... happened?" Galen asks hesitantly from behind me.

Dragging in a deep breath, I try to pull my sanity back together again. It's getting harder and harder every time. After raking my fingers through my hair, I draw in another breath and then turn around to face the others.

"Jessina was torturing Draven," I explain. My voice comes out shockingly flat. As if I'm just reciting last week's weather. "I could feel it through our mate bond, which has started to reconnect at times lately. So I showed her what will happen if she hurts Draven. And now, she knows."

Several of them exchange a glance that I can't muster enough fucks to interpret.

"So," Lyra begins. "She's not torturing him anymore?"

"No."

Both she and Galen let out a shuddering breath of relief.

I start towards the door. "I'm getting him back."

To my surprise, it's Orion who grabs me by the arm to stop me. "No."

That horrible flat emptiness in my voice remains as I glance down at his hand on my arm and simply declare, "I suggest you take your hand off my arm."

"Stop and think for a moment," he grinds out, but he does release my arm. "Jessina Iceheart is viciously smart. This is what she wants. She wants you to get emotional and charge in there to save him so that she can capture you too. So we need to be smarter."

Galen forces out a long breath, his pale brows drawn down in a scowl. "I hate to admit it, but he's right. If we just charge in there now, we're only going to get Draven and all of us killed. It's the middle of the night. We're all angry and exhausted and worried. We need to get some sleep to clear our heads. Then, we will make a proper plan."

"If she was torturing him just now, it means that she can't have flown all the way back to the Ice Palace," Isera adds, her sharp gaze moving across all of our faces. "She must have landed somewhere else."

"That's a good point," Lyra agrees. "Based on the average flight speed and time that has passed…" She trails off for a few seconds while staring out at the wall, as if counting in her head. "The only other village within that distance is Hunter's Marsh."

"Okay." Galen nods several times, but it looks more like he's trying to settle his own nerves than reassure us. "So Draven and Jessina are in Hunter's Marsh. That's good. That's a start. Let's get some sleep to clear our heads, then we make a proper plan in the morning."

The others nod in agreement.

I just stalk past them and out of the dungeon without another word.

In the morning? I don't fucking think so.

I am getting him back.

Tonight.

CHAPTER TWENTY-FIVE

The halls of Orion's castle are silent as I make my way towards a room farther down. The faelight gems that are scattered across the ceiling like stars have been turned low, only giving off a soft white glow. It's enough to see by while still making it feel like I'm walking underneath a starry night sky rather than inside an elegant hallway.

I cast a glance over my shoulder. But only grand paintings of beautiful night skies with northern lights watch me as I sneak along the lush blue carpets. When I reach the intended room, I pause with my hand on the handle. I really hope I'm not about to get my throat slit.

Shoving down the handle, I pull open the door and stride into the dark bedroom beyond.

I only make it two steps across the threshold before something sharp is pressed against my throat. I freeze. Behind me, the door swings shut again with a soft thud.

Then white faelight fills the room as its occupant turns the gem in the swirling steel holder on the nightstand.

"Mabona's tits, Selena," Isera says while leveling an

exasperated stare on me. "We're supposed to be getting a few hours of sleep."

Glancing down, I study the sharp shard of ice that is pressed against my throat before Isera flicks her wrist and dismisses it. The coldness disappears from my skin as I look up to meet her gaze. She is standing on the soft blue carpet in the middle of her elegant guest bedroom, wearing a very short silk nightgown. Her long black hair falls down over her mostly bare shoulders, and she looks incredibly put together, despite the fact that the rumpled bedsheets announce that she was most likely sleeping when I broke into her room.

"I thought you were..." Trailing off, she shakes her head and then draws a hand through her smooth hair. "Never mind." Suspicion enters her silver and blue eyes as she looks me up and down, no doubt noting the fact that I'm dressed in my black fighting leathers and have a dagger strapped to my thigh. "What are you doing here?"

"I need your help," I announce.

"With what?"

"I am getting Draven back."

"We're making a plan for that in just a few hours."

"No. I am getting him back tonight." Steel creeps into my voice. "I am not leaving him at the mercy of that sadistic bitch for one second more than absolutely necessary, so I'm going to Hunter's Marsh tonight. I need you to help me threaten Grey into opening a portal and then stay with him to make sure that he keeps the portal open instead of running to Orion to rat me out."

She gives me an incredulous look. "You can't be serious."

"I am."

"You're going to get yourself killed."

"I don't care."

"Ryat will care."

My heart squeezes painfully. "Draven hates me."

"For now. Once you figure out how to fix your little magic

problem and he returns to normal, he's going to be furious with you. And with *me* for letting you endanger yourself like this."

I forget how to breathe as my heart suddenly stutters. The absolute certainty in her voice when she said that sends a surge through me that makes me feel lightheaded. As if there is no doubt in her mind that I will somehow be able to remove the hateful magic in Draven's chest.

Giving my head a quick shake, I push aside those dangerous thoughts and instead focus on the problem at hand. First, I need to get him back. Then, I can worry about everything else.

"You owe me," I remind Isera.

She shifts her weight on the carpet but doesn't say anything.

"During the Atonement Trials, I blocked out your fear so that you could get through that tunnel inside the maze," I press on. "And in return, you said that you would owe me a favor."

"Getting yourself killed is a stupid way to call in that favor."

"I won't get myself killed."

"We're going to make a plan for this in the morning. A proper plan, which we will all execute together. Can't you just—"

"I am not leaving him alone with *her*!" I growl at her. "You know how vicious and cruel she is. I need to get him out." Challenge drips from every word as I finish with, "You owe me, and I am calling in that favor right now."

A soft snarl rips from her throat. "Ryat is going to kill me for this."

"That sounds like a *you* problem."

Shaking her head, she lets out something between an exasperated sigh and a huff of amusement. "If this is what it's like from the other side, I'm starting to get why people are so pissed off at *me* all the time."

In spite of everything, I smile.

She just heaves a resigned sigh and flicks her wrist. "Fine. Let's go threaten Grey."

To my surprise, she doesn't even change clothes before

leaving her room. She just walks out into the corridor barefoot and wearing only that tiny dark blue nightgown. Though I suppose that she is lethal enough even without any equipment.

When we reach the door to Grey's room, I pull out a pair of lockpicks and start working on the lock. Next to me, Isera raises an eyebrow in surprise. I just shrug in reply.

After we assassinated that Wolfstalker guy when we first came to the Unseelie Court, I asked Draven to teach me how to pick locks. So in the weeks while we played the Great Games, he did just that. He was right that it's a very useful skill to have when you need to assassinate someone. Or simply get through a door without having to kick it down.

The lock clicks open.

Straightening again, I motion for Isera to enter first since she will be doing most of the threatening. She sweeps her hair back behind her shoulders and then pulls the door open silently. I follow her as she slips inside, and then I close the door softly behind me.

Grey's bedroom is large and surprisingly luxurious. Though I suppose it makes sense given that people with portal magic are incredibly rare, which makes him invaluable to the Unseelie King.

The portal-wielder in question is lying on the left side of a large double bed. White sheets are tangled around his legs in a way that makes it look like he kicked them off during the night. He is only wearing a pair of underwear, and the clothes he wore earlier tonight are draped messily over a chair by the desk. His mouth is slightly open and his chest rises and falls with steady breaths.

Isera strides up to the bed and positions herself right next to the edge. Then she summons a shard of ice, puts a hand on Grey's bare chest to keep him down, and then unceremoniously places the shard against his throat.

His turquoise and yellow eyes snap open, and he tries to jerk upright. But Isera's hand on his chest keeps him pressed down against the mattress, preventing him from accidentally slitting his own throat on the shard of ice. He struggles for a second. Then his gaze focuses on Isera.

"Oh, Malachi's fucking balls," he blurts out. "Not you." His chest starts rising and falling faster while he stares at Isera with wide eyes. "He's going to kill me for this."

"We need a portal," Isera simply announces.

"Alright, alright," Grey presses out so fast that he almost stumbles over the words. Fear flickers in his eyes. "But please take your hand off my chest, and for God's sake, put on some more clothes. If he finds out that I saw you like this, he's going to carve my eyes out."

For a fraction of a second, I swear I can see a smug smile ghost across Isera's lips. But she does remove her hand from Grey's chest and takes a step back.

He immediately scrambles out of bed. After dragging a panicked hand through his brown hair, he snatches his rumpled clothes off the chair and yanks them on while flicking his worried gaze between me and Isera.

"I need a portal to Hunter's Marsh," I say, locking eyes with him.

"Only His Majesty can grant permission to open portals," Grey replies.

Isera smirks. "You can tell *His Majesty* that I forced you."

"Oh, I plan to. But I still won't open any portals without his permission."

"Not a problem. Selena will just go and bring him here right now then." She gives him a knowing look as she sits down on his bed and crosses her bare legs. "I'll wait here."

Panic pulses across his face.

"Selena?" Isera prompts.

I start towards the door.

"No, wait!" Grey calls, and lurches forward as if to stop me.

Both Isera and I pause and raise expectant eyebrows at him. Indecision flashes across his face. For a moment, it looks as if he even considers opening a portal for himself to escape through. But that would still leave Isera in his bedroom dressed like this, and we all know how Orion would react to that.

A frustrated noise escapes his throat. "Fine. I'll open a portal to Hunter's Marsh." He shoots Isera a hard look. "But when I report this later, you were wearing proper clothes when you came in here and you never touched me. Agreed?"

Her eyes gleam with amusement, but she flicks her hand and says, "Agreed."

Drawing in a steadying breath, he seems to compose himself again. Then he starts moving his hands in the air as he summons a portal. I check that my dagger is secure in its sheath while I watch that glittering blue rectangle rise up from the floor.

Once it's in place, I can see a dark field through it.

"If you die over there, Ryat is going to try to kill me, which means that I will be forced to kill him," Isera begins while giving me a pointed stare. "And you don't want that, do you?"

I shoot her a flat stare back.

"So come back alive." She flashes me a sharp smile. "Or things will start to get messy."

I'm rapidly losing the ability to care about consequences, so I just give her a nod.

And then I step through the portal and into Hunter's Marsh.

CHAPTER TWENTY-SIX

Crickets are buzzing in the grass when I step out onto a darkened field just outside a small village. I sweep my gaze across the cluster of buildings up ahead. There is a barn and a stable to my right, but the rest of the houses look like normal homes. Nothing that appears grander, like a city hall or something, which would be the most likely place for Jessina to be staying.

As promised, the portal remains open behind me while I start sneaking across the damp grass and towards the closest buildings up ahead. I don't have time to search through them all. Not to mention that I'm unlikely to succeed without getting spotted if I go through every single house in this village.

Soft clouds drift over the dark sky above and temporarily obscure the moon while I close the final distance to the nearest house. If Jessina and an entire host of silver dragons landed here and took temporary possession of a house, everyone in this village must know exactly which house it is. There is no way something like that would escape notice. Not in a village this small.

Sliding out my lockpicks again, I walk up to the door in front of me and then drop down on one knee. Somewhere across the village, a sheep bleats. I cast a glance over my shoulder, but the dirt road behind me is empty.

After about a minute, I finally manage to get the finnicky lock open.

Impatience pulses inside my chest like thrumming lightning. Every second I waste here is another second that Draven is at the mercy of Jessina fucking Iceheart. I need to get him out. Now.

A darkened hallway becomes visible before me as I sneak across the threshold and into the house. Several open doorways branch off from that one hallway. I glance through them as I move quietly across the worn wooden floorboards.

The doorway to my left holds a small kitchen while the one on my right leads into a tidy but well-used living room. I scan the frayed yellow couch and scratched wooden table before continuing deeper into the house. Staying close to the wall, I try to prevent any of the floorboards from creaking underneath my feet.

Another open doorway on my right shows what looks like a workshop. Carpentry tools litter the wooden bench by the wall, and unfinished pieces of furniture are scattered across the floor.

I continue on to the final door, which is thankfully also open.

Remaining in the hallway, I glance through the door and into the dark room beyond. Satisfaction courses through me when I find a bedroom. Two people are sleeping on the bed in the middle of the room. One man and one woman. Humans, by the looks of it.

While sliding the dagger from my thigh holster, I approach the man's side of the bed. Since he is physically stronger, he is the biggest threat. Once I reach the bed, I position myself so that I'm standing right next to him and summon my magic. Then I place the dagger across his throat.

A jolt shoots through him, and he starts blinking his eyes open.

"If you move, I will slit your throat," I say.

All traces of sleep disappear from his features in a flash as fear instead pulses across his face. "Eva!"

The woman next to him jerks awake. I grind my teeth in annoyance and press the dagger harder against the man's throat while Eva's panicked eyes land on me.

"Scream and I'll kill him," I warn her.

Fear flickers in her eyes as she scrambles out of bed, sending sheets flying and tumbling down on the floor in her haste. But she wisely keeps her mouth shut.

"Eva, don't—" the man begins.

"Shut up," I growl. "Tell me where Jessina Iceheart is keeping Draven Ryat."

By the wall, Eva gasps, which all but confirms that they are indeed staying somewhere in this village. However, the man quickly presses his lips together, as if that would somehow save him from having to answer.

Reaching out with my magic, I connect it to the bone white flames of fear that are now burning in both of their chests. They're already pretty big, but I start increasing them anyway.

"Tell me where they are," I order again, my voice coming out shockingly hard.

"I don't know what you're talking about," the man replies while shaking his head.

That terrible impatience burns through me again, and I flex my fingers on the hilt of the knife to release some of the tension trapped inside me. It doesn't work. So I just slide my gaze to Eva instead.

"I would really hate to get blood all over these white sheets," I say, holding her stare with merciless eyes. "Such a nuisance for you to wash out, don't you think?"

All color drains from her face, and her terrified eyes dart between me and her husband.

"Don't tell her anything," he snaps before Eva can break.

A low snarl threatens to rip from my chest. I don't have time for this. Those dark waves of unending hatred and rage wobble inside me, threatening to crash down and at last drown me fully, as the image of Draven, shackled and defenseless with Jessina's foot on his neck, flashes through my mind again.

"You know what she will do to us if she finds out we betrayed her," the man continues, his pleading eyes on his wife.

That cold mercilessness is spreading through my veins like poison, but I don't know how to stop it. And truth be told, I don't think I want to stop it anymore.

"Ah, I see," I say. "You're more afraid of her than you are of me." A vicious smile curls my lips. "That can be fixed."

Before they can so much as open their mouths to respond, I throw open the floodgates of my magic and flare those flames of fear into wildfires.

Eva's knees buckle, and she crashes down on the dark bedroom floor while terrified whimpers escape her lips. Below me, a dark stain spreads across the front of the man's underwear.

"Tell me where she is keeping Draven Ryat," I command. "Or I will make you wish that someone as merciful as Jessina Iceheart was here instead of me."

"The green building," the man stammers, his eyes wide with terror as he stares up at me. "In the middle of town."

"Which green building?"

"There's only one green building."

"Excellent."

With a flick of my wrist, I remove the blade from his throat and slide it back into its holster. I keep the magic connected for another few seconds, though. Fear shines in their eyes as they stare up at me, one from the bed and the other from the floor, too afraid to move.

"If you tell anyone that I'm here, I will come back and kill you both," I warn. "Understood?"

They nod frantically.

"Good."

At last, I let my magic fade out. Since they didn't know me beforehand, this encounter will likely shape their entire view of me, so they will continue to fear me even after the magic is gone.

Spinning on my heel, I start towards the door.

"You're a monster," Eva whispers, her voice full of anger and fear, from where she is still kneeling on the floor.

Once upon a time, a comment like that would've paralyzed me. Knowing that someone disliked me enough to call me something like that would've made me fret and worry and feel sick. It would have hurt me beyond belief to be called a monster. Once upon a time.

Now, I find that I have, at long last, officially run out of fucks to give about other people's opinions.

So instead of feeling anxious about how these two humans see me, I embrace the monster label as I turn back to lock eyes with Eva.

"Yes, I am." I flash her a cold smile, full of cruelty and threats. "So make sure that I don't have a reason to return."

Another whimper slips from her lips, and she cowers down on the floor.

I stalk out the door and back out into the night.

Neither of them raises the alarm.

Warm night winds wash over the countryside, making the crops in the fields around the village sway. I quickly leave them behind as I jog towards the center of this village and the green building that is supposed to be there.

I slow down as I reach the middle of the village. It's difficult to see in the darkness, but I think the building up ahead is green. There is only one problem. It's surrounded by dragon shifters in silver armor.

Biting back a curse, I throw myself in between two houses before they can spot me. Sneaking along the wooden wall, I peer around the corner on the other side. The ring of dragon shifters continues around the whole building.

I suppress a frustrated sigh. How am I supposed to get through without any of them seeing me? I could use my magic to connect to some emotion in their chests, but for that to work, they all need to be feeling the same thing. Unless I create an emotion out of nothing, of course. But the problem is that I have no idea if I'm able to do it to this many people at the same time.

Before, I've only ever done it to one person at a time.

Or two people, my mind corrects. If I did make my parents hate me with magic, that would mean my current maximum for creating emotions out of nothing is two people at the same time. Not one. Goddess, I really need to visit them soon to find out the truth.

I cast another glance around the corner. But of course, nothing has changed. An entire circle of dragon shifters still stands between me and the green building.

Drumming my fingers against my thigh, I consider my options. But impatience still tears at my chest, and I'm finding it hard to concentrate. I flick a glance up at the roof. Would it be possible to jump from this roof to the roof of the green building?

It's worth a shot.

However, I'm not skilled enough in the art of scaling walls that I can just climb up the side of a two-story building without any handholds. At least not without the very convenient climbing gear that I got from the human resistance in Frostfell. I really should've brought that with me when we escaped. Though I suppose I had a lot more urgent things to prioritize back then. Like Isera and Alistair. And Draven.

That tiny light of hope inside my soul flickers as those dark waves threaten to crash over me again at just the thought of him.

While trying to block out the pain in my chest, I hurry over to the door that leads into the building I'm currently hiding behind. If I can just sneak through the house instead, I will be able to reach the windows on the second floor, and from there, it will be much easier to get to the roof.

After picking the lock, I sneak inside. A short hallway and a large living room meet me inside. I sweep my gaze over the deserted room but draw my knife just in case. There is no way for me to know where the staircase is, so I just cross the living room and move towards the doorway at the back of it. Soft carpets muffle my footsteps as I sneak forward.

Impatience thrums inside me like a storm.

Too long. Everything is taking too long.

Picking up the pace, I hurry the final distance to the door and round the corner.

And come face to face with a dragon shifter in silver armor.

He jerks back, looking just as startled as me.

Then his gaze snaps up to my face, and recognition dawns in his eyes. He opens his mouth to sound the alarm, but I was already moving. Jerking his head back, he barely manages to avoid the dagger I thrust towards his throat. The blade misses its target but slams right through his jaw and tongue instead.

Pain crackles across his stunned face.

I yank the blade again to free it from his jaw, but he jerks his head in pain, which ends up cutting parts of his tongue in half instead. A gurgled scream makes it past his lips. Panicked, I yank the blade out while praying to Mabona that there is no one else inside this house. His scream wasn't loud enough to be heard from outside. But if someone else is awake in here, they would definitely have heard it.

Trying to press the advantage, I lurch forward and swing at the soldier's throat again.

He kicks me in the chest.

Air explodes from my lungs, and the sheer force of it sends me flying back into the living room. I hit the side of the couch and crash down on the floor. Rolling over, I try to gasp in a breath through my throbbing body.

Steel rings into the dark room.

Alarm screams inside my skull, and I barely manage to roll out of the way before the soldier slams a sword down into the wooden floorboards where I used to be. Blood drips from his mouth as he snarls at me through his shredded tongue.

Blinking hard, I try to focus enough through the pain to summon my magic.

He swings again.

I scramble backwards over the floor. But not fast enough. The sword whooshes down towards me. I yank my legs apart. The blade slams into the floor between my spread legs a moment later.

Still trying to gasp air back into my lungs, I scramble the final distance away while he is busy yanking the sword back out of the wood. Leaping to my feet, I reach desperately for my magic. But I don't even have time to visualize it before a sword speeds for my face. Panic blares inside me, and I throw myself backwards to evade it.

A foot appears behind mine, yanking my leg forward.

The move pulls me off balance and sends me crashing down back first on the floor. I gasp as the hit knocks the air from my lungs again. Blood drips down over my face as the wounded man bends down over me and rams the sword towards my throat.

My mind screams at me.

I slam a massive pale pink wildfire into his chest.

Pleasure floods my body.

And the sword stops moving towards my throat.

While still increasing the wildfire of sympathy that I created and shoved into his chest, I crawl out of range and gasp in deep breaths to refill my lungs. The soldier straightens, and lowers his sword, while I quickly climb back to my feet.

Pleasure continues thrumming inside me, washing away the

terrible rage and hatred that is always strangling my chest, as I continue to increase that pale pink wildfire of sympathy that the soldier now feels towards me even though I almost cut his tongue in half.

He watches me, his eyes sad and indecisive.

I ram my dagger into his throat.

Shock pulses across his face, and he drops his sword as his hands instead fly up to his throat. I yank the dagger back out and keep increasing his sympathy for me. Pleasure continues vibrating inside my soul like a cloud of golden sparkles while I watch the man die without trying to hurt me in return since he now has too much sympathy for me.

When he dies, the connection of magic is broken.

Cold emptiness crashes over me as that warm sparkly feeling disappears. I drag in a strangled breath, suddenly desperate to feel it again so that I don't have to feel everything else.

"You really shouldn't have come here," a voice suddenly says from the same doorway that the soldier appeared from.

I snap my gaze up to it.

Ice sinks into my stomach as I find Lavendera standing there. Out of all the people who could have been staying in this house tonight, she is by far the worst for me. Because for some reason, she is so messed up in the head that she seems to be immune to my magic.

Briefly, I wonder what kind of torture the Icehearts have put her through to make her mind snap like this. But that just makes me think about what Jessina is putting Draven through right now. Which, in turn, makes the searing rage and hatred inside me flare up dangerously again.

"You took Draven," I retort while wiping the bloody knife on my pants.

Lavendera's eyes soften for a moment. "Yes." Then that blank mask returns to her features again. "But you still shouldn't have come here. Because now, I need to capture you."

"No, you don't."

I hold her gaze while starting to discreetly back towards the front door. This earlier fight with the dragon shifter yet again proved that I can't win a sword fight against trained soldiers. I'm simply not skilled enough with a blade for that. What gives me an advantage is my magic. But if that doesn't work against Lavendera, my chances of making it out of here are very slim.

"You don't have to serve them," I continue while I keep discreetly edging backwards. "You can join us instead."

"I don't want to join you."

"Why not?"

"Because only they can give me what I want."

"And what is that?"

The front door gets closer behind me. Lavendera doesn't seem to notice. She just walks after me across the floor at an unhurried pace. She hasn't drawn a weapon or summoned her magic. But there is no hesitation in her eyes. She is going to capture me because that is what Jessina has ordered her to do.

"Please, Lavendera." Desperation bleeds into my voice. "I need to rescue Draven."

"I know you want that. But your want is a drop in the world's oceans compared to how deeply I want what I want. And I need it. I need it."

Shaking my head in confusion, I stare at her as I edge the final step to the front door. "What do they have on you?"

Her eyes go out of focus for a few seconds. I reach for the door handle. Then her vision snaps back into focus with her eyes glowing.

"So fucking crowded!" she growls.

Branches shoot out from her in every direction, shoving furniture aside as if they were toys and shattering every window in the room. Fresh night air washes inside.

I bolt out the door.

"Intruder!" Lavendera yells.

Her voice carries through the broken windows and echoes across the village.

My heart jerks as I skid out between the buildings and onto the next dirt road.

Black smoke explodes from behind.

And then ten silver dragons are climbing into the sky.

I run.

CHAPTER TWENTY-SEVEN

My heart pounds as I watch a portal form a few steps away. They shouldn't be back this soon. Why are they back this soon?

The glittering blue rectangle rises to its full height. Then a room becomes visible on the other side.

I can barely breathe as Orion, Galen, and Grey step through the portal and back into the meeting room in Orion's castle that I have been pacing impatiently for the past ten minutes.

After my disastrous rescue attempt in Hunter's Marsh last night, I barely managed to make it back to the portal without being killed. When I did, I was in such bad shape that poor Grey ended up getting blood over half of his bedroom. Orion was so furious that I had blackmailed Grey in that way that he made me grovel for his permission to let Haldia heal me. Which, to his complete surprise, I did without question. I don't give a fuck about my pride. I just needed to be in perfect health today so that I can help get Draven back.

Lyra and Alistair stand up from where they were sitting at a table by the wall when they see Galen, Orion, and Grey walk through the portal. Across the room, Isera is leaning against the wall, her arms crossed over her chest and her sharp eyes watching our returning friends.

"What happened?" I demand as soon as they're through the portal.

Morning sunlight streams in through the windows of the elegantly furnished meeting room, and one of them has been left open a crack. Air smelling of morning dew and blooming summer flowers swirls in through the small opening, making some of the documents that are scattered across the tables flutter. In the distance, the waterfalls that surround the Unseelie Court's capital rumble steadily as the water flows down into the lakes below.

Grey closes the portal behind him and, after a nod from Orion, bows and then leaves the room.

"She left a note," Galen at last replies to my question.

His expression is grim as he holds up a folded piece of paper. My heart starts beating faster.

"She wasn't there?" I ask.

Galen shakes his head. "No."

This morning, we agreed that we would sneak back into the Golden Palace in the Seelie Court. Since Jessina no doubt despises staying in some backwater village which lacks all the comforts that she is used to, we guessed that she would return to our castle in the Seelie Court instead. She might have been able to knock Draven out when she first captured him, but transporting him all the way back to Frostfell would no doubt be difficult. And besides, I doubt she would ever leave Bane behind. As unhinged and cruel as she is to everyone else, she does seem to genuinely love her mate.

But apparently, she didn't go back to stay in the Golden Palace. Instead, she left a note in there, no doubt assuming that we would return there as well.

"What does the note say?" I ask, staring at the piece of paper in Galen's hand while my pulse continues thrumming in my ears.

"It's a time and a meeting place.

"For what?"

"For a hostage exchange." His violet eyes are serious as he sweeps them over all of us. "She wants to trade Draven for Bane."

My heart skips a beat. "Good. Let's do it."

By the table, Alistair draws his eyebrows down in a skeptical frown. "Can we trust her to actually do it, though?"

"We're not doing it," Isera growls from the wall on the other side. "We're not giving Bane back."

Anger spears through me as I turn to glare at her. "We need to get Draven back."

"So we rescue him instead. That way, we get both Draven and Bane."

"That might be difficult," Galen interjects, glancing between the two of us. "As reckless as Selena's rescue attempt last night was," he gives me a pointed look before softening slightly and continuing with, "it was actually a great way of testing their defenses. Now, we know that Draven is guarded by not only their elite soldiers, but also by Lavendera. Which means that dragon steel is no doubt in play. Since she cut off Gremar's hand to remove the dragon steel we put on him, she now controls that piece. And she has no doubt put it on Draven's wrist instead."

"Which means that if we try to rescue him," Orion picks up, his gaze sliding to me and Isera, "the same thing that happened when we tried to talk to Rin Tanaka will happen again. Except that this time, it will be Draven who is trying to kill us."

"Not to mention that we would need to pull all of this off before the hostage exchange deadline she gave us, which is in three hours," Galen finishes.

By the wall, Isera's expression has darkened into a murderous thunderstorm. Cold fury laces her voice as she once again grinds out, "We are *not* letting Bane go."

"We don't have any other choice," Galen replies while shaking his head at her. "If we want Draven back, we need to agree to trade."

"Which brings us back to *my* question," Alistair interrupts before Isera can retort. He shifts his gaze between all of us while raising his eyebrows pointedly. "Can we actually trust Jessina to go through with the trade? What if it's a trap?"

"Oh, it's most definitely a trap," Lyra says.

We all turn to stare at her.

Outside the windows, two birds make playful loops over the manicured garden. Their cheerful chirping drift in with the warm breeze through the small gap in the window.

Lyra lifts her shoulders in a shrug in response to our questioning stares. "It's Jessina Iceheart. All she ever does is to scheme and plot traps and try to outsmart people. Of course she is going to have something else planned for us at that hostage exchange."

"See?" Isera stabs a hand in her direction. "Yet another reason for why we shouldn't go through with it."

"Oh, I didn't say that. We're definitely going through with it. She won't spring her trap until after she has Bane, so we need to have a plan for how to get Draven, and ourselves, out of there as soon as the exchange is done."

Orion flicks his wrist. "Not an issue. Grey will open a portal, and as long as we have that open right behind our backs, it won't matter what kind of trap she is planning to spring."

"Just make sure that Grey is staying on this side of the portal," I begin. "So that she can't target him."

"Of course I will order him to remain here." He shoots me a pointed look. "As opposed to you, I actually think things through before I go around blackmailing someone else's subjects into opening portals so that I can rush into danger without a proper plan."

I just roll my eyes at him. For someone who is supposed to be all kingly and refined, he can be surprisingly petty.

"We're agreed, then?" Galen picks up, pushing the conversation back on track. He looks from face to face. "We don't risk another rescue attempt. Instead, we trade Bane for Draven."

All of us nod. Well, everyone except Isera. Rage burns like blue flames in her eyes as she leans against the wall, glaring at us all in silence.

"Alright, good." Galen gives us all a nod. "Then we need to start making plans for different scenarios. Depending on how she—"

Isera shoves off from the wall and stalks across the room. We all watch in stunned silence as she storms out the door and throws it shut behind her. I understand why she's angry. She hates Bane more than anyone else. But we need to get Draven back, and she probably understands that as well, which is why she didn't argue when we made the decision. I still wish she would've stayed and helped us plan out the different scenarios, though. She's usually levelheaded in a way that most of the rest of us aren't always.

I keep glancing towards the door while we sit down and start planning how to handle different traps that Jessina might try to spring on us, but Isera doesn't return.

Once we're halfway through the first plan, pain suddenly spikes through my mate bond.

I gasp out loud.

The others whip around to stare at me, but I can barely see them because the room around me sways when another burst of pain slams into my chest through the mate bond. Panic and rage sear through me.

Pushing up from the table, I shove my chair back so hard that it topples over. Wooden clattering fills the meeting room behind me as the chair hits the floor, but I'm already running. My feet pound against the dark blue carpets as I race through the castle and towards the dungeons.

Pain stabs through the mate bond over and over again.

I throw myself down the stairs to the dungeon.

My heart leaps into my throat when I find the Unseelie fae who were supposed to be guarding Bane lying unconscious on the dark stone floor. Sprinting the final distance, I burst into Bane's cell.

Isera doesn't even turn to look at me. She just rams her shard of ice into Bane's thigh again.

Bane, who is still shackled to the metal chair and drugged with a potion from Haldia so that he won't be able to focus enough to access his magic, hisses in pain but then tilts his chin back and laughs up into Isera's face.

"Keep going, little slave," he taunts, his voice slightly slurred due to his drugged state. "When we win this war, I will pay you back for every stab."

Isera just slams her ice shard into his thigh again and twists it.

A gasp of pain rips from his throat, and his eyes slide in and out of focus from the agony and the drugs.

Another spike of pain hits my chest through the mate bond.

"Stop!" I scream at Isera. "She's taking it out on Draven."

She just stabs him again.

He throws his head back and gasps before letting out a maniacal laugh. "Did I tell you that I made your mother crawl naked through our entire throne room while my whole court watched and laughed and kicked her as she crawled past on her hands and knees?"

Dark fury explodes across Isera's face. Yanking the shard of ice from his thigh, she swings it towards his throat. I throw myself forward. With a scream of panic, I barely manage to grab her wrist before her shard of ice can hit his skin.

"Stop!" I yell at her again.

Standing right next to her, I tighten my grip on her wrist. My heart pounds like a battle drum, and my chest is heaving from the long run across the castle and the sheer panic inside me. In the chair, Bane just lets out another vicious laugh.

"After we win, I will do the same to you," he says, his cruel eyes locked on Isera. "But I think I'll break your legs first, so that it will take you even longer to crawl through the whole room."

"Every time you hurt him, Jessina hurts Draven," I snap at Isera before she can retort. "So back the fuck off."

She just keeps her utterly merciless eyes on Bane. I tighten my grip on her wrist to stop her from trying to slit his throat. She simply dismisses the shard of ice from that hand and summons it in her free hand instead.

A cry of desperation rips from my throat when she rams that shard into Bane's other thigh and twists it hard.

Another blast of pain hits me through the mate bond.

I yank out my dagger and place it against Isera's throat. Threats drip from my voice as I growl, "Stop."

She doesn't even look at me. Her cold eyes remain solely focused on Bane, who is gasping and laughing like a maniac again.

"If you want me to stop, you'd better be prepared to use that," Isera at last replies, and flicks a detached glance down at the blade I'm holding to her throat.

Her voice is so cold that I swear I can see frost crackling through the air around her when she speaks.

"This man tortured my mother for a hundred and fifty years before he killed her," she continues, that freezing hatred lacing her voice like ice. "This might be my only chance at revenge. I'm taking it."

Yanking out her ice shard, she rams it through Orion's shoulder instead. He gasps in pain, and his head lolls to the side while his eyes slide in and out of focus.

"I've already told you," Isera continues. "I hate them more than I care about you and much more than I care about my own life. So if you're going to kill me, kill me. I will continue torturing him regardless."

A shockingly large part of me almost does it. Almost slits my friend's throat. The realization of it stuns me so much that I actually stumble a step back, lowering my knife.

She simply stabs Bane again.

Abandoning my attempts to convince Isera, I instead desperately summon my magic. I have never tried anything like this before, but by Mabona, it has to work.

Pain pulses through the mate bond again.

The moment I feel it, I shove my magic down through our mate bond.

Normally, I can only connect to someone's emotions when they are within a certain geographical distance. But through the mate bond, I can already feel his emotions, even when he is out of range of my magic. So this should work. It has to work.

I gasp as my magic connects.

It feels different than usual. Stronger. And more complex. Like two separate threads, the mate bond and my magic, woven together to form one braid.

World-ending pain hits me like a boulder as my magic latches on to the violet wildfire of pain in Draven's chest. The force of it is enough to make me stagger back, my vision blacking out for a second, before I manage to raise my mental walls to protect myself. Once they're in place, I decrease his pain in one massive push.

A shuddering breath escapes me when I can almost feel a sigh of relief through the mate bond.

Isera slashes Bane across the chest with her ice shard.

Pain tries to spike in Draven's chest, but I keep my magic pouring down our mate bond so that he can't feel it.

Isera lifts her shard again.

But then she is suddenly wrenched away from Bane.

Snapping my gaze towards her, I find Orion pulling Isera

away before setting her down on the floor far out of reach from Bane.

"That's enough, little viper," he orders.

She fights against his arms around her chest before managing to tear herself free. Death flares in her eyes as she locks them on him. "Get out of my way."

"No." He stares her down with equally commanding eyes. "Unfortunately, we need the brooding beast in order to win this war. So you need to stop stabbing our hostage."

"I won't—"

"Yes, you will. *For now.*" He takes a firm grip on her chin. "We need Draven. You know that. But once we have him back, I swear to both Malachi and Mabona that I will help you get your revenge."

It looked like she was about to snarl back at him, but that apparently surprises her enough that she hesitates. Confusion flits across her face for a second, and her mouth remains slightly open, as she just stares back at him.

"I know what it's like to never have anyone to lean on," he continues, his gaze searing into hers. "To always have to do everything yourself. To always be alone and unapproachable. But I will help you shoulder this." A truly wicked smile spreads across his lips. "Trust me, if there is one thing I do really well, it's revenge."

She blinks. Then her gaze darts to me, and a flash of guilt flickers in her eyes. Slowly lowering her hand, she lets the shard of ice fade into nothingness.

In the chair, Bane is still bleeding. But since no new stabs of pain hit him, Jessina stops hurting Draven as well. I still keep my magic pouring down our mate bond until our flickering connection is once more broken on its own.

"I want them hurt," Isera says, her voice full of both pain and anger. "Both of them."

"Oh, they will be," Orion promises. "We will make sure of it."

The memory of what Bane just told Isera, of what he did to her mother, echoes through my mind and mingles with the memories of the pain that Draven is currently enduring. I squeeze my hand into a fist.

Yes. Yes, we will make them both hurt. For this. For everything.

But first, we need to get Draven back.

CHAPTER TWENTY-EIGHT

When we step through the portal, my mind is calm and clear. I have been able to wrest the black rage and dark hatred back behind the walls inside me again so that I will be able to make smart decisions during this hostage exchange instead of letting Jessina provoke me into making stupid mistakes.

Or so I thought.

It only takes three seconds for that roaring fury inside me to come crashing back.

The meeting place that Jessina specified is the ballroom in the Golden Palace where we had the commencement ball during the Atonement Trials. However, all the side tables, white tablecloths, gleaming silver decorations, pitchers, and wine glasses have been removed. Now, only the glittering golden chandeliers in the high ceiling remain, making the large room feel cavernous.

But that is not what makes my vision flash red due to undiluted rage. It's what meets me when I come to a halt on the floor a few steps from the portal.

Jessina Iceheart is standing there in the same silver-sparkling dress that she wore when she and Bane ambushed us in this castle yesterday. Her white hair has been pulled back from her face in a simple braid this time, and the hem of her dress is slightly muddy. No doubt from her unglamorous visit to Hunter's Marsh.

Next to her is Lavendera, who is currently staring at the wall across the room with that strange blank look she gets on her face when she is disassociating from the world.

To their left and right, ten of the Icehearts' elite soldiers are spread out.

But my gaze goes straight to the man kneeling in front of Jessina.

Draven.

He is still wearing his black dragon scale armor, but his face is bloody and his eyes are glassy with pain. His hands have been shackled in front of him. And his wings...

Bile crawls up my throat.

Not only has she whipped his wings again. She has also *chained* them together. Thick iron manacles encircle the bones that frame the top of his wings. They have simply been locked right through his wings in those places, tearing the thin membrane that is supposed to be there. A short chain runs from one manacle to the other, trapping his wings together behind him and preventing him from spreading them out to his sides.

The black rage and dark hatred surge up inside me like tidal waves as I stare at him.

That lone speck of light that remains inside my soul flickers precariously.

I can barely hear anything over the roaring in my ears.

I'm going to kill her for this.

I'm going to kill them all for this.

"What have you done?" Galen demands in a horrified voice as he comes to a halt on the floor next to me.

We have already planned exactly how we are going to stand so that we will be able to get Draven out of here as quickly as possible regardless of what the trap might be.

Across the polished floor, Jessina flashes us a vicious smile. "I've done far less to him than a traitor of his caliber deserves. I would've done much worse," her pale gray eyes slide to me, and her expression sharpens like a blade, "if you hadn't started playing your little game of tit for tat."

I just stare back at her, my head still roaring with fury, while suddenly wishing that Isera had been even more brutal while she was already at it.

Lyra clenches her fist and grits her teeth where she is standing a little behind and to the left of Galen. Orion remains closest to the portal, while Alistair is closer to the front. Isera hauls Bane with her through the portal and shoves the drugged-up emperor down on his knees between me and her. Galen, who is standing a little ahead of us, remains as a barrier between Bane and Jessina, in case she is going to try something very direct.

Fury pulses across Jessina's face when she sees the blood on her mate's body.

"When we win this war, I'm going to make you all watch as I torture the person you love most until they're begging for death," she promises, threats dripping from her voice like acid.

Isera holds her stare with cold eyes. "You already have."

That vicious smile on Jessina's lips widens. But all she says is, "Let's trade, then."

"One person leads the hostage to the middle of the room," Galen begins. "They trade and then walk back to their side."

"Fine." Jessina flicks her wrist and then looks to Lavendera. "Remove the dragon steel from his wrist."

My gaze darts down to Draven's shackled wrists. But because the manacles are in the way, I can't see anything.

Lavendera just stands there for another second, staring unseeing at the wall across the room. Then she blinks hard and at last returns to the world around her. Moving gracefully across the floor, she crouches down in front of Draven and pushes the manacles up higher. It reveals the thin bracelet of dragon steel that Alistair bent with his fire magic. However, it looks to have been cut on one side so that it could be wedged onto Draven's wrist.

With efficient moves, Lavendera pries it from his wrist and then stands up again.

"Thank you for returning that to me, by the way," Jessina says, her smug smile directed at me.

On the floor, Draven drags in a deep breath and tries to blink his eyes into focus. But he is clearly too severely wounded to be able to fight back.

"Take him to the middle and complete the exchange," Jessina orders as her gaze returns to Lavendera.

Lavendera says nothing. She just gently slides her arm underneath Draven's and helps him to his feet.

On our side, I simply grab Bane's shoulder and yank him to his feet. We had to let Haldia partly heal his thighs so that we wouldn't have to drag him. But we left most of the wounds untreated.

Only the slow thudding of our feet puncture the silence as the four of us start walking towards the middle of the room. I keep my gaze shifting between Jessina, Draven, Lavendera, Bane, and the elite soldiers ahead. We have several plans in case she tries something, but I need to be able to see what it is before it actually happens in order to be of any use.

However, Jessina doesn't do anything. She simply stands there in her slightly muddy dress, watching me with sharp eyes.

Lavendera and I reach the middle of the room.

We pause for a moment, then we push our hostage forward at the same time.

Draven stumbles into me.

My heart skips a beat at just feeling him close to me again. All I want to do is to hug him and tell him that everything will be okay. But I can't. First, we need to get him to safety.

I shift my gaze to Lavendera as I start backing across the floor while supporting Draven with a firm arm around his waist.

"I will never forgive you for this," I tell her as she starts doing the same with Bane.

"I don't want forgiveness," she replies. But she doesn't say it in a challenging way. Instead, her voice sounds… sad.

Not knowing how to respond to that, I just continue backing across the floor. My gaze flits from face to face as I try to anticipate where the trap will come from. We have almost reached our own sides of the room now. Whatever Jessina has planned, it's going to happen soon.

My heart thunders in my chest as I back the final distance to Galen.

The moment I'm within reach, he grabs Draven, spins them both around and shoves his best friend straight into Lyra's arms. Lyra does the same, whirling around and maneuvering Draven into Orion's range. Within a heartbeat, the Unseelie King has disappeared through the portal with Draven.

The whole thing took barely more than a few seconds.

Across the floor, Jessina jerks back slightly in surprise. Then annoyance flits across her face as she glances at the portal while her elite soldiers take Bane from Lavendera.

I let out a shuddering breath of relief as the rest of us start quickly retreating towards the portal as well. Whatever happens now, at least Draven made it out safely.

"And where do you think you're going?" Jessina calls, and raises her hand. "We're not done yet."

Lyra slips out through the portal, shortly followed by Galen. Isera, Alistair, and I have almost reached it as well.

There is movement from the side of the room as another group of people suddenly start moving across the floor.

"Go!" I hiss.

Isera darts through the portal.

"There is someone who wants to see you, Selena," Jessina calls right before I can step through the portal as well.

My gaze flits towards the new group of people.

And my heart stops.

"If I see either of your eyes glowing, they die," Jessina warns from across the room.

Alistair has stopped next to me instead of going through the portal, but I can't spare him even a glance, because my eyes are locked on the two people who are being led over to where Jessina is standing.

My parents.

Fear pulses across their faces as they are forced to their knees in front of Jessina, but resentment quickly joins that emotion in their eyes when their gazes land on me.

"Mom." The panicked word escapes my lips without permission. "Dad."

Terror crashes through me as Jessina summons two blades of ice with her magic and positions them in front of my parents' throats. They flinch, fear pulsing across their faces again. I drag in an unsteady breath.

Rooted on the floor, all I can do is to just stare at them.

"Selena," Alistair whispers from next to me.

But I don't reply. And I don't move. The portal is right behind us. Two more steps, and we're through it. But I can't leave them. They're... they're my parents. I can't leave them.

"Let them go," I snarl, rage ripping through my soul, as I snap my gaze back up to Empress Jessina.

A cruel smile curls her lips, and her pale gray eyes harden. "Do you really think you're in a position to make demands?"

The ice blades press tighter against my parents' throats. I cast a panicked look down at them. Fear and hatred shine in their eyes as they stare at me accusingly from across the floor.

It makes my chest twist in pain.

I drag my gaze up to Jessina. "What do you want?"

"What do I want?" She lets out a vicious, mocking laugh. "I want you to learn a lesson, slave."

"What lesson?"

She glances towards Bane, pain and anger in her pale eyes, before her merciless gaze locks on me again. "A lesson in how a war against me works."

"Which is what?"

"You take one of mine." She motions towards the portal where Draven disappeared and then towards my parents. "I take *three* of yours." Her eyes sharpen like unyielding steel. "So don't you ever dare touch my mate again."

Dark rage flares inside me. "I could say the same to you."

"No, you can't. Because I'm the one with the hostages. And you're not ruthless enough to back up your threats." Her eyes glint as she raises her hand slightly. "But guess what, slave?"

I just hold her stare with eyes full of rage and hatred.

She flashes me a smile dripping with malice. "I am."

My parents suck in a sharp breath.

She slits their throats.

CHAPTER TWENTY-NINE

Time slows until every second feels like an hour. Fear drowns out the resentment in my mom's yellow and lavender eyes for a second. For one second. The last second. Her entire face is lined with utter terror and her mouth is still slightly open from that final gasp. And her terrified eyes remain locked on me. Next to her, my dad is staring at me in shock, his silver and turquoise eyes wide.

And for that one moment, time seems frozen. As if this one second lasts for an age.

Then a deep red cut appears across their throats.

Blood bursts out and runs down their necks like a flood, staining their worn shirts red.

They topple to the side.

Light from the white faelight gems in the chandelier above paints silver highlights in my dad's blond hair when he falls. His eyes are still wide with shock, but the light in them is fading. Fast. Too fast.

Thuds echo into the cavernous ballroom as my parents hit the floor. Lying on their sides, they stare at me from across the polished stone floor while their bodies convulse. Once. Twice.

The wounds across their throats are so deep that the ice blades almost decapitated them. Blood pours out of the brutal cuts, forming pools around them and turning my mom's long silver hair red at the ends.

Then the last flicker of light in their eyes dies.

I can see the moment it happens. The moment that the final spark of life leaves their eyes. The moment that they change from being people to being bodies on the floor. Even in death, that terrified expression remains on my mom's features as her unseeing eyes stare at me from across the bloodstained floor.

My throat hurts.

And someone is screaming.

It takes me another second to realize that my throat hurts because *I* am screaming.

Time snaps back into place.

Another scream tears from the very depths of my soul, splitting the air like an explosion.

Ice shoots through the air.

I stumble as I'm shoved backwards while a massive wall of fire roars across the room. Shards of ice slam into the flames, and hissing steam explodes across the room as the two forces hit.

"Selena!" Alistair yells at me while sending another wave of fire across the room. "We need to go!"

"NO!" I scream.

Or continue screaming. I don't think I've stopped screaming since she slit their throats, but it's difficult to tell because I can barely hear anything over the ringing in my ears.

"No, I need to get them!" I scream, staggering a step forward again. "I need to—"

Alistair wraps a strong arm around my waist and yanks me back while sending another torrent of fire across the room. Ice slams into it, creating another cloud of hissing steam.

"No!" I scream again, struggling against Alistair's grip.

With one arm wrapped around my waist and the other shooting fire at Jessina, he backs towards the portal. Panic clangs inside me. I can't just leave them. I can't leave them. My parents. I can't just—

Twisting to the side, Alistair throws me through the portal while sending a massive wave of fire in the other direction. I fly through it like a limp doll and crash down on the floor of a small study inside Orion's castle. Alistair leaps through the portal a moment later.

"Close it!" he screams.

Ice shoots towards us from the other side of the portal.

Grey immediately slams the portal back into the ground, shutting it right before a hail of ice shards could get through.

"NO!" I cry. Scrambling to my feet, I run over to where the portal used to be. "Open it!"

"What happened?" Galen yells over the chaos that erupts inside the room.

Or it might just be inside my own head. I can barely see what's happening around me. All I can see is the fear and shock in my parents' eyes as Jessina slit their throats.

"She killed them!" I scream. My throat is raw and every word tastes like blood and iron. "She killed them! Take me back! I have to go back!"

"Her parents," Alistair is saying from somewhere right next to me. "Jessina killed her parents."

Just hearing those words from someone else shatters everything inside me. As if I could pretend that it wasn't real, that it wasn't too late, until someone else acknowledged what happened.

A broken cry rips from my lungs, and I whip around towards Grey. "Open the portal! I need to go back! Take me back! I need to get them! I need to—"

"Selena!" Alistair grabs me by the shoulders and spins me back around to face him. "They're already dead." His orange and green eyes are filled with pain and sorrow as he holds my gaze and repeats softly, "They're already dead."

Tears well up in my eyes. Shaking my head, I try desperately to unhear his words while a broken whimper escapes my lips.

"I'm sorry." His eyes are filled with agony as he holds my gaze. "I'm so sorry."

My knees buckle.

I crash down on the floor so hard that it sends a jolt through my body. But I can barely feel it. Pressing my palms against the floor, I bow forward and try to gasp air back into my lungs. My chest feels like it's being crushed by a boulder. Broken sobs escape my lips, and my entire body trembles.

"Selena," Isera says, her voice gentler than I have ever heard.

Still on my knees, I look up to meet her gaze. But she is standing right next to Draven, and my eyes immediately go to him. Galen and Lyra must have removed the iron chains that bound his wings, because he has now shifted into his fully human form. His face is still pale with pain, and Galen is bracing him with an arm around his back where they stand close to the door. As if they were just on their way to Haldia when Alistair and I returned.

There is a war going on behind Draven's eyes as he looks at me. As if he wants to rush over and comfort me but at the same time doesn't even want to touch me because of how much that flame of hatred in his chest is still telling him that he wants nothing to do with me.

Desperate longing and unyielding hatred fight in his eyes.

For one single moment, it looks like he's about to rush over and wrap me in his arms.

But then the hatred wins out, and he looks away.

The final shard that remained of my already broken heart shatters into a million irreparable pieces.

"Get out," I whisper, my voice hoarse.

Galen glances between me and Draven, pain evident on his face. "Selena, he doesn't—"

"Get out."

They all just look back at me with eyes full of sympathy and pain. I can't bear it. I can't bear it. I can't breathe. I can't—

"Get out," I press out, my chest suddenly heaving. "Get out. Get out! GET OUT!"

My screams echo against the pale stone walls of the small study, but I can barely hear it over the blood roaring in my ears. I need to be alone. I hate having people around me when I'm in pain. I want to be left alone. I just want to be left alone. Oh Goddess, it hurts.

Alistair strokes a gentle hand over my back as he starts towards the door. The others thankfully follow him.

I gasp out broken sobs as they all leave the room and close the door softly behind them.

The moment the door clicks shut, everything inside me shatters.

Another desperate scream rips from my soul. Still on my knees, I bow forward and slam my fist against the ground while screaming my lungs out. Tears stream down my face like unstoppable floods.

They're gone. My parents are gone. In less than five seconds, my entire world changed forever. And I can never get them back.

Agony slashes through my chest like claws.

I gasp in a panicked breath. Then another scream tears out of me, and I pound my fist against the floor over and over again while tears continue flowing down my cheeks. Broken sobs escape my lips before more screams rip out of me.

She killed them. Jessina *killed* my parents.

Pain slashes through my throat as I scream my fucking lungs out.

She killed them. She slit their throats like they were nothing. She wiped out their futures with one flick of her wrist.

Shooting to my feet, I whip my head from side to side in search of something to break. Anger courses through my veins like crackling fire.

I need to break something. I need to hear something break. I need to feel something break. Something other than my own heart.

Grabbing the chair next to me, I hurl it into the wall on the other side.

Wood snaps as it crashes into the stone wall.

The satisfying sound fuels my rage, and I snatch up the already cracked chair and slam it into the wall again while another scream rips from the depths of my soul.

Rage and agony tear through my chest like feral wolves.

She killed them.

I slam the chair into the wall again.

She killed them. She killed them.

Chips of wood fly through the air as I shatter it against the thick stone wall. There isn't a lot of furniture in this room. Only the now useless chair, a bare desk, and an empty bookcase by the wall. I break everything I can get my hands on.

But no matter what I do, I still can't stop my own heart from being ground into dust beneath the mountain of grief and regret that is crushing me.

My knees buckle, and I crash down on the floor again. This time, I don't even bother catching myself. I just lie there among the broken pieces of wood and stare at the light that falls in from the window to create bright rectangles on the floor. My chest aches.

Curling into a ball, I wrap my arms around myself

And then I cry my eyes out.

CHAPTER THIRTY

Lying on the cold stone floor, I stare at the fading light on the ground. It's almost gone now, which means that night has almost fallen. The small study around me is dim, the deep shadows hiding all the furniture I ruined. Too bad it can't hide everything else that I've ruined.

I know that I should get up. I know that I should rejoin my friends. I know that I should apologize to Orion for destroying his chair and some of the shelves in his bookcase. But I can't bring myself to care.

So I just lie there on the cold stone floor and stare at the sliver of golden light on the ground that fades into darkness with every passing second.

Pain pulses inside my chest like a second heart. I try to draw in deep breaths, but it feels as if someone is sitting on my chest, crushing it, while a pair of brutal hands are locked around my raw throat.

But worst of all is the regret.

It sits inside my stomach like a block of ice, poisoning everything with freezing tendrils that twist between my ribs like snakes and turns my entire body cold.

Curling up on my side, I squeeze my eyes shut and try to shield myself from the horrible regret that is eating me from the inside.

It doesn't work.

Because regret, I've come to realize, is the most brutal emotion of them all.

Fear fades as soon as you remove the thing you're afraid of.

But regret…

Regret is permanent.

Either you said or did something that you can't take back. Or you didn't say or didn't do something that you should have. Either way, the result is the same. It's too late now. Too late to go back and redo it.

That irrevocability of it is what makes it so horrible. No matter what you do from now on, it's too late to change what you should have done before.

And I know exactly what I should have done.

I should have gone to see my parents straight away. As soon as we left the Unseelie Court, I should have visited them and checked if they had my magic burning inside their chests.

But I didn't.

And now, they're gone.

They're dead. They died within seconds. Without warning. And now, I will never know.

I will never know if my parents actually hated me or not. I will never know if they truly resented me because of who I am and what I did, or if they actually loved me and only hated me because I had accidentally forced a flame of hatred into their chests when I was a child and couldn't control my powers.

I wanted to know. Knowing the truth was vital to me. It could have changed everything. It would have *meant* everything to me.

But now, I will never know.

I will never know if my parents loved me.

Agony and paralyzing regret crack through my chest like a whip.

Curling my fingers into a fist, I gasp out broken sobs while waves of darkness crash over me.

I should have gone there straight away. I should have checked on my parents straight away. But I was just so busy. I kept saying that I would do it later. Later when things weren't so chaotic. Later when I had more time. Later when I wasn't dealing with a crisis.

But that's the thing. There will never be enough time. There will always be another crisis. There will never be a perfect time to do something.

I should have prioritized them.

And now, it's too late.

Now, there is nothing left.

No one left.

My parents are gone. My mate is gone.

All that is left is guilt and hate and rage and regret.

Suffocating, all-consuming regret.

Those massive black waves inside me crash through my soul like a storm-plagued ocean. Crushing everything. Tearing everything down. Beating that small spark of hope inside me with merciless force.

Broken sobs slip from my lips.

That tiny light inside my soul flickers.

And then it goes out.

Dark rage and searing hatred rush in to fill the void, burying me whole.

I feel like I'm drowning. I can't breathe. I can't feel anything but agony and regret.

It's going to kill me. These emotions are going to kill me.

In a burst of sheer panic, I draw upon that dark rage and searing hatred. Drawing it to me like a raft. Clinging to it.

Infusing the black waves themselves with it. Until everything inside me is just a burning black ocean of rage and hatred.

If I thought I was angry and ruthless when I left the Unseelie Court, it is nothing compared to the utter mercilessness that now consumes me.

Shoving myself up from the floor, I dust myself off and roll my shoulders back.

My head is now terrifyingly silent and clear.

I stalk towards the door and throw it open.

A guard in Orion's dark blue and silver colors jumps in surprise.

"Where are they?" I demand.

"Dining room," he blurts out. Uncertainty shines on his entire face as he flicks his gaze up and down my body. "I can show you—"

"No. I know where it is."

He stares after me as I stride past him and start towards the dining room. Outside the windows, the final red and orange rays of sunlight have disappeared beyond the horizon. Darkness now blankets the heavens, and the glittering faelights have been turned on inside the castle to light the way.

That unending rage burns inside me as I stalk through the castle.

I'm going to kill the Icehearts. I'm going to kill every single one of them. Their entire clan. I will wipe them all from the face of this world and then burn every page in every history book that contains their names until it will be like they have never existed.

Reaching the door to Orion's private dining room, I simply yank it open and storm inside.

Clothes rustle as every head snaps in my direction.

All six of them are there, but the table looks nothing like it usually does. There are no decorations. No fancy platters of extravagant food and no mass of different utensils. Only one plate and one knife and one fork in front of each person. Half of the plates are practically untouched, as if my friends have been poking at the food rather than eating it.

As usual, Orion is sitting in his grand chair at the head of the table. Alistair and Isera are seated next to each other on his right, while our three dragon shifters are sitting on the other side. Draven is now wearing a simple black shirt with his sleeves rolled up instead of his armor. There is no blood on his skin, and no pain on his face, so Haldia must have healed all of his wounds. He watches me with those conflicted eyes of his as I stalk up to the table. As if he both hates me and wants to comfort me at the same time.

But then his expression changes slightly when he takes in my appearance. Or rather, the look on my face.

In fact, all six of them are staring at me as if a demon has just stormed into the dining room, trailing fire and brimstone. To be fair, I feel like a demon. And fuck, it feels good.

"We need a new plan," I declare.

"Uhm," Galen begins, casting uncertain glances between me and the rest of them. "Are you... okay?"

"I'm fine. Like I said, we need a new plan." Bracing my palms on the smooth tabletop, I lean forward and meet their eyes. "The dragon steel is a problem. As long as the Icehearts have access to that, we will never be able to hit them with everything we have. So we need to fix that by solving the root cause of the problem."

"Lavendera," Isera supplies.

I nod. "Yes."

"So, we need to capture Lavendera and turn her against the Icehearts?" Lyra guesses.

"No. We need to *kill* Lavendera."

Everyone jerks back a little and stares at me as if they have never seen me before. Everyone except Draven, who is watching me with eyes I can no longer read. I meet his gaze with a hard stare.

"You've said it yourself," I begin. "Multiple times. Lavendera won't betray the Icehearts. So let's not waste time trying."

"But didn't you say that she might have important information too?" Galen asks in a careful voice. As if I'm a vicious animal that he is trying to calm down.

"I don't care," I reply, shifting my hard stare to him. "She is the only one among them who can use dragon steel. She needs to die."

"Are you sure you've thought this through?"

"Yes."

"But what if we—"

"I'm going to kill them." I growl. Fire blazes in my eyes as I stare them all down. "Do you understand? I'm going to kill them all."

"Look, Selena. I promise, we will get justice for your parents, but—"

"I don't want *justice*!" I snarl. "I want *revenge*!"

Galen draws back and stares at me as if he has no idea who I am anymore. Next to him, Lyra just looks like she's worried about me. Draven continues watching me with those unreadable eyes while Orion actually raises his glass at me in approval. On the other side of the table, Isera holds my gaze and gives me a slow nod. Alistair tilts his head in a nod towards her, as if to say, *what she said*.

"I still think we should—" Galen begins.

"I'm going to kill Lavendera." I push off from the table and stalk towards the door. "Either help me. Or stay the fuck out of my way."

CHAPTER THIRTY-ONE

Our prediction was right. Because of Isera's torture session in Orion's dungeon, Emperor Bane was too injured to fly back to the Ice Palace straight away. They're most likely waiting for Rin to get here so that she can heal him, and probably Gremar too, if they're feeling merciful. Regardless, it means that Lavendera is still in the Seelie Court as well. And that means that we can finally kill her.

"Why don't we just kill her from a distance?" Orion asks, for the third time in as many minutes. "It feels like we're making things more complicated than they need to be."

The trees around us rustle restlessly as a warm wind sweeps through the thorn forest. Shielding my eyes from the sunlight that filters down through the canopy, I watch as Lavendera walks along the path from the Golden Palace and towards the city to do whatever it is that traitors do. Five dragon shifters in silver armor follow her. I recognize them from the fields outside the Green Clan's mountain. They're part of the Icehearts' elite guards.

"I've answered this twice already," Draven replies to Orion's repetitive question. "She has tree magic. I have never, not once in the two hundred years that I've known her, seen a ranged attack on her actually hit her. She always manages to block it with her tree magic. It's like she has a sixth sense or something."

"I still think luring her to us is unnecessarily risky," Orion counters.

Draven scoffs and flashes him a mocking smile. "Yeah, well, we can't all be cowards."

Orion's eyes flash. Taking a step closer, he locks a stare full of challenge and suspicion on Draven. "You've been pushing pretty hard for this plan. How do we know that you're not leading us into a trap?"

"Why would I lead you into a trap? We're on the same side, asshole."

"Are we?" Suspicion glints like blades in Orion's eyes as he comes to a halt right in front of Draven and looks him up and down. "How do we know that you're not wearing dragon steel again? They could've put it back on you while you were in captivity and ordered you to lead us into a trap."

"They did put dragon steel on me while I was in captivity. But she took it back before she traded me for Bane, remember?"

"There could be a second piece. Hidden somewhere."

"That doesn't—" Draven's retort is cut short as he sucks in a sharp breath.

I snap my gaze to Orion to find his eyes glowing. Anger surges through me like fire. Grabbing his arm, I yank him towards me instead. "What the fuck are you doing?"

He yanks his arm out of my grip while his eyes continue glowing. "I need to be sure."

"Back the fuck off," I order while summoning my own magic in warning. "He has been through enough."

His eyes continue glowing for another couple of seconds before he finally releases the grip on his magic. After a hard look in my direction, he lifts his toned shoulders in an unapologetic shrug. "He's clean. No dragon steel apart from the piece Jessina took back."

Draven grabs him by the collar and yanks him closer before growling in his face, "If you ever rifle through my head like that again, I will fucking kill you."

To my surprise, it's not anger or threats or even indignation that flashes across Orion's face. It's frustration.

"I had to be sure!" he snaps, his voice laced with exasperation.

Raising his forearm, he shoves Draven's hand away from his collar. Draven lets him. That strange expression of helpless frustration remains on Orion's dangerously beautiful features as he smooths his fancy shirt down again and looks from face to face.

"I've staked my entire court on this!" he snaps, and there is a hint of desperation in his eyes as he looks at us. "On *you*. On six insane idiots who have nothing left to lose. Well, guess what?" He stabs his hand against his own chest. "*I* have something left to lose. I have an entire court whose safety I'm responsible for." His hard eyes shift to Draven. "So I had to be sure."

Next to me, Isera cocks her head slightly and watches him with a considering look on her face. Draven says nothing, just stares back at Orion. The Unseelie King blows out a frustrated breath.

"I wouldn't even be here if it wasn't for that damn bargain you forced me into," he continues, sliding his gaze to Isera. His eyes narrow slightly as he watches her. "And I'm still waiting for you to actually prove that you're a descendant of the Seelie Queen's second daughter. The fact that you also didn't know about the kill box wall in your own castle is very suspicious, little viper. It's not the first time. And it's making me think that there are a number of things that are not adding up about this."

My heart skips a beat. If we lose Orion and the Unseelie Court, we'll be back to square one. We can't let that happen. We can't ever let him find out that Isera lied about being royalty.

Luckily, though, there is no way to fully prove it either way. Isera might not be able to prove that she is a descendant of the Seelie Queen, but Orion can't prove that she *isn't* either.

"Guys," Alistair says before Isera is forced to answer. "Lavendera has reached the city."

Clothes rustle as everyone turns back to watch Lavendera walk through Golden Gate and into the city. While Orion's attention is elsewhere, Isera slides a grateful glance in Alistair's direction and dips her chin. Alistair, who is a lot more perceptive than people give him credit for, just suppresses a small smile. Behind him, Lyra is grinning openly, her orange eyes glittering in a ray of golden sunlight as she watches Alistair while he can't see. Galen just shakes his head with a knowing look on his face.

"Alright, get everything ready out here," I begin. "Alistair and I will go into the city."

"I'm coming too," Draven announces.

Turning towards him, I raise my eyebrows in surprise. "That's not part of the plan."

"It is now."

"We've already agreed. You will stand out too much, so you will stay here."

His eyes gleam, and he steps closer. "How interesting. That almost sounded like an order."

I raise my chin. "That's because it was."

"I see." He slides two fingers along my jaw. "Would you like me to remind you what usually happens when you try that?"

A pleasant shiver rolls down my spine. For a few precious seconds, I can see *him*. I can see Draven in his eyes. The way he used to look at me. The way he used to touch me. The way he used to tease me and flirt with me and banter with me.

Then the hatred snaps back into his eyes, and he yanks his hand back down from my face as if he had been burned. Taking a step back, he gives me a vicious look.

"I'm going into the city as well," he declares. "Wanna know why?"

My head is still spinning from the sudden switch in personality, so I don't manage to respond. Draven answers anyway.

"Because you always ruin everything," he says. "And I don't trust you not to screw this up."

Pain spears straight through my chest. It couldn't have been a better precision strike if he tried. I truly do always ruin everything. My parents. Him. Us. Everything I touch.

And I will never get it back. I will never get any of it back. So now, all I want is revenge.

That all-consuming rage inside me burns like black wildfire as I turn away from Draven and start towards the city. Alistair quickly jogs to catch up. Unfortunately, Draven does follow as well.

I get a suddenly overwhelming urge to use my magic to create an emotion. Just so that I can feel that wonderful pleasure that comes with it. But I manage to suppress the urge as we sneak in through North Gate and make our way across the city.

We intercept Lavendera and her guards a little sooner than we had planned for, so we stick to the shadows and trail them while we wait for them to reach the location we have preselected for our ambush. I can feel Draven glaring at me from where he looms behind me, but I don't even care anymore. I just want someone else to feel the pain that I constantly have to live with. And soon, I will.

Lavendera has stopped at the edge of a small square. People are hurrying across the open space, desperate to finish whatever task they're in the middle of. Others are seated at the worn tables that have been placed out in the sunlight. Empty cups litter the tabletops as they try to drink their hunger and sorrows away. All of them cast fearful glances at the dragon shifters in silver armor, but no one seems to realize that they're there for Lavendera since she is standing a short distance away.

"Stop," she suddenly snarls.

The people around her jump in surprise. Then they notice who said it, and the fear is quickly replaced by ridicule. They all still believe that she is just a weird person who lives out in the thorn forest. They have no idea who she really is. What she really is. A traitor.

"Enough!" She blinks hard and shakes her head. "It's so fucking crowded!"

Next to me, Alistair stares at her with his eyebrows raised.

"Huh," he whispers. "So it wasn't just a cover to fool us. She really is crazy."

Since I came to the same conclusion earlier as well, I just nod and reply, "Yes."

Waves of burning rage crash inside me as I watch her and the soldiers from the Silver Clan stand there out in the sunlight. The people who chained Draven's wings together. The people who murdered my parents.

Regret hits me like a gut punch.

I should have prioritized them. I should have gone to see them while I could. And now, it's too late.

Those black waves crash over me again, threatening to suffocate me.

Panicked, I pour more fuel on the burning hatred and rage inside me until it's so intense that it overshadows the sickening regret again.

Alistair cocks his head as he studies Lavendera from across the street. "I wonder what the Icehearts put her through to make her like this."

I drag my gaze to the strange woman who I thought was my friend. Merciless death roars inside me.

"I don't care. She needs to die." I jerk my chin. "Get the plan in motion."

CHAPTER THIRTY-TWO

Standing in the messy living room of a house one street down from the square, I watch through the window as Alistair sneaks through the crowd on the other side and makes his way towards a wagon filled with hay. Lavendera has snapped out of her crazy state and is now making her way towards the street where Draven and I are hiding. The soldiers from the Silver Clan trail her from a distance.

Draven is standing behind me, watching our targets through the window as well. His chest is so close to my back that I swear I can feel the tension crackling like lightning in the air between us. He leans forward a little and tilts his head in order to keep Alistair in view when the fire wielder slips in behind a group before returning to the street in a place between Lavendera and her five guards.

When Draven twists his body like that, it makes his breath caress the side of my neck. Every time it happens, my spine tingles and my skin prickles. I squeeze my hand into a fist, trying to block out the sensation. Having his body this physically close when his heart is so far away is making me want to scream.

Out on the street, Alistair reaches the wagon filled with hay right after Lavendera has passed it. He pauses. With his face hidden underneath a hood, he watches Lavendera and counts down the distance. Once she has reached the spot we planned for, Alistair throws a fireball at the pile of hay.

"Death to the Icehearts!" he screams, and then bolts down the street.

The hay catches fire with a whoosh, sending a huge column of flames surging up into the air. Behind the wagon, the soldiers lurch into motion. Rushing forward, they dart around the burning wagon to locate the person responsible and protect Lavendera. But Alistair has already slipped inside a house across the street. He will jump out the window on the other side and then run back out through North Gate and out to the thorn forest where the others are waiting.

On the street, people scream as the massive pillar of flames stretches towards the blue summer sky.

I let out a huff of amusement. "Alistair still hasn't learned the definition of *a small fire*, I see."

A laugh rips from Draven's chest.

And there is a violent tug on the mate bond.

I whip around to stare at him in stunned surprise. He snaps his mouth shut and casts a panicked look down at his own chest. Conflicting emotions battle in his eyes like a churning storm.

"You felt that," I say. It's not a question. "That's—"

The door is kicked open.

I suck in a sharp breath between my teeth as I'm yanked back and whirled around. My heart skips a beat as I find myself pressed against Draven's chest with his arm wrapped protectively around my back right before a sharp thud rings out above me. I snap my gaze up.

A sword has slammed into Draven's shoulder, his armor stopping the blow. Time seems to slow to a crawl as I stare at the sharp blade that now rests on Draven's shoulder, wielded by the soldier behind his back who had aimed the sword at my neck.

Draven's arm is still wrapped around my waist as he holds me tightly while shielding me with his own body.

My heart beats hard against my ribs as I stare up into Draven's face.

Fear and desperation flit across his features for a second as he stares back at me with wide eyes.

Then the soldier yanks his blade up to strike again.

A blast of wind slams into the soldier. He flies backwards and crashes into the wall behind him so hard that the table beside him rattles on the uneven floorboards while another gust of wind slams the door shut.

Draven shoves me out of his arms and shoots me a disgusted look. "Told you that you would screw it up."

Fury roars through me, so intense that my vision flashes red for a second. Fury at the world. Fury at the whole universe. At the cruel gods and goddesses who let me have a small taste of happiness and love before ripping it all away and turning it into a constant mental torture that is worse than anything I've ever experienced.

Shoving past Draven, I stalk up to the Silver Clan soldier and slam my boot into his jaw before he has a chance to regain his wits and struggle to his feet. His head snaps to the side from the hard kick. I call up my magic and slam a bone white wildfire of fear straight into his chest.

Pleasure immediately floods my body.

Closing my eyes for a moment, I drag in a small shuddering breath of relief as that sparkling warmth drowns out the agony in my heart.

I increase the fear in the soldier's chest and relish in the feeling of pleasure that continues surging through my body. Beneath me on the floor, the soldier trembles and whimpers in fear.

A vicious smile curves my lips as I stare down at him

cowering at my feet. This is where he belongs. This is where they all belong.

"Please, stop," he gasps out, staring up at me with terrified eyes. "I'll do whatever you want."

I shove a massive burst of power down the magic connection, blowing his fear into an inferno.

Another broken whimper rips from his lips, and he cowers down further.

"Please, I'm begging you," he blurts out, his voice shaking and his entire body trembling before my boots.

It gives me a sick sense of satisfaction to know that this man would never have begged and whimpered like this of his own free will. Nothing would make an elite soldier of his caliber break down like this. Nothing natural. But what is natural, and what is free will, when I can literally change the way he feels?

A desperate whine slips from his lips.

I pour more magic into him, increasing his fear until I can feel that his mind is about to break.

And then I push some more.

I can see the moment his mind breaks from fear. It's in his eyes. Like a light suddenly going out, leaving only an empty shell. An empty, *obedient* shell.

After lowering his fear back down to make sure that he can still function enough to carry out my orders, I reluctantly cut off the flow of my magic.

That warm sparkling sense of pleasure immediately vanishes, and the cold black waves of pain and the searing flames of fury rush back into my soul. The contrast is so sharp that I forget what we're doing for a second.

Then the plan flows back into my mind.

Alistair sets the fire and runs off. The soldiers chase him and search the houses. We ambush one of the soldiers when he steps inside. I break him with my magic.

My mind churns to catch up while also screaming at me to

create another emotion so that I can feel that warm pleasure again.

What was the next part of the plan again?

Get Lavendera where we want her.

Right.

"You're going to go out there and tell Lavendera that she needs to hide inside the thorn forest until you find the person responsible for the fire," I order the soldier who is now sitting limply on the floor before me. "Tell her to follow the old road and wait for you just inside the tree line. And act normal. Then you come back here. Understood?"

He just stares up at me as if I'm the Queen of Hell herself who has come to claim his soul.

I kick him in the thigh to snap him out of it. "Understood?"

"Y-yes," he stammers.

"Good." I jerk my chin. "Get to it."

Boots scuff against the floor as he scrambles up from the ground. He casts another terrified look at me, followed by one at Draven, and then hurries out the door. Draven and I walk up to the edges of the window so that we can peer out without being seen from the outside.

Out on the street, one of the other soldiers from the Silver Clan darts out of the building that Alistair escaped through earlier. But he has apparently not figured out that our little pyromaniac jumped out of a window at the back, because he just runs to the next building and kicks that door down before darting inside to search for a fae man who is long gone by now.

Lavendera is standing a little farther up the street, frozen in the place she was in when Alistair set the fire. Her pink and purple eyes are surprisingly clear and focused as she stares at the door that Alistair ran in through. If she saw that that was where he went, she hasn't shared it with her guards.

The soldier that I broke runs up to Lavendera. Since people are still screaming and running around a short distance away while trying to put out the fire in the wagon, I can't hear what the guard says. But he points in the direction of North Gate and then makes a motion for her to hurry. She frowns at him but then starts in that direction.

My heart leaps into my throat when she takes off at a run instead of walking.

The others can technically handle the next part on their own. But I want to be there. I want to be the one who kills her. But to do that, we need to somehow get there before her.

Silver armor appears in front of me as the soldier runs back in through the door. His eyes, still a strange mix of terror and emptiness, are wide when he skids into the room.

I slam another wildfire of fear into his chest.

Pleasure washes over me again.

Closing my eyes, I draw in a deep breath as it drowns out all the hurt and pain and rage and that awful, awful regret that is poisoning me from the inside.

It's cut off abruptly as the soldier's heart gives out.

Grinding my teeth in annoyance, I open my eyes and glare at him as his body topples to the floor in a heap of limbs. His face is white with fear and his glassy eyes stare unseeing up at me, terrified even in death.

I feel nothing but satisfaction.

"You killed him?" Draven says.

"I couldn't risk him telling the others," I snap back, feeling suddenly both guilty and defensive.

And I also needed to feel that burst of pleasure again, my treacherous mind adds silently in my head.

But Draven just shoots me an annoyed look. "I know. I wasn't lecturing you. I was confirming that he's dead."

"Oh."

Blinking, I just stand there for a second. Then I glance down at the very dead man at my feet. I clear my throat, feeling both embarrassed that I snapped like that and grateful that Draven's moral compass is as broken as mine.

"Yes, he's dead," I confirm.

"Good." He jerks his chin. "Then let's go."

We spin around and dart through the messy living room until we reach the windows on the other side. After shoving one open, we leap out onto the deserted street beyond.

"We won't be able to overtake Lavendera," I say as Draven and I start running down the street so that we can circle the building and make our way towards North Gate.

"The others can handle it," he replies.

"*I* want to handle it," I growl back, fury streaking through me.

I want to be the one who kills Lavendera. I *need* to be the one who kills her.

He slides his gaze to me, glancing at me from the corner of his eye, while we continue running.

A small cloud of black smoke erupts beside me. I suck in a sharp breath as Draven suddenly hauls me up into his arms and shoots down the street, his wings beating hard on either side of him. My stomach lurches as he swerves around a corner and flies down the next street at full speed.

My mind has barely managed to catch up with what happened, so I draw in a deep breath and wrap my arms around his neck while houses flash past on either side of us. Lying in his arms, I look up at his handsome face and try to read the expression there. But only his usual mask of ruthless power and authority is visible on his features.

"Thank you," I whisper.

"Don't thank me." He shoots me a look dripping with threats. "You will owe me severely for this. And when I come to collect, I expect complete obedience. Understood?"

"You can always have whatever you want from me. I thought you already knew that."

His gaze darts down to mine, and there is another violent tug at the mate bond.

Draven sucks in a sharp breath between his teeth. Shaking his head, he snaps his gaze back to the street ahead and forces out, "Shut your mouth. Right now. Or I swear to God, I will drop you right here and leave you behind."

A violent storm thrashes inside me, but I slowly close my mouth again.

Apparently satisfied, Draven picks up speed and flies around another corner.

My heart jerks hard in my chest when I realize which street we're on.

But before I can scream at Draven to go back, to take any other road, any road except this one, we're already halfway down it. And right next to *it*.

The house.

My parents' house.

Regret crashes over me like merciless tidal waves. I stare at the door. The windows. The peeling paint on the outside walls.

A whimper of agony rips from my lips, thankfully drowned out by the booming of Draven's wings, when I catch sight of the potted plants in the window.

They're still there. My mom's plants. Which means that all of their other things are still inside too. No one probably even knows that they're dead. The house doesn't know that they're gone. That they're never coming back.

My throat closes up as I twist my head and stare back at the doorstep when we fly past.

The doorstep where I have stood so many times when I've knocked on the door.

The doorstep I should have been standing on weeks ago.

It would've taken me less than five minutes. Less than five minutes to go and see them. Less than five minutes to talk to them. Less than five minutes to reach out with my magic and find out if they truly hated me or if they, deep down under a flame of magic I accidentally created, actually loved me.

I should have done it. I should have—

The house disappears behind me as Draven swerves around another corner and shoots straight for North Gate.

I gasp in a breath. It feels as if my heart was ripped out of my chest again. As if it's now lying there on that doorstep outside my parents' house, torn and bloody. Regret claws at my insides like vicious talons.

They might have loved me. All my life, they might have actually loved me. And now, I will never know.

The feeling of regret is so all-consuming that I barely realize that we've made it out of the city and across the grasslands outside.

When we reach the tree line, Draven simply dumps me on the ground. Since I still haven't recovered from seeing my parents' house like that, I just collapse down on the ground.

"How did it go?" Galen asks from somewhere above me.

Dragging in a deep breath, I try desperately to push the regret back. It doesn't work, so I just let more of the hatred and anger into my soul so that I don't feel the regret as sharply.

While Draven explains what happened, I stagger to my feet and dust myself off.

Alistair is already there too. Though, it looks like he has only just returned, because he is leaning against a tree trunk while his chest heaves. Lyra is looking at Draven while he speaks, but Isera's far too intelligent eyes are locked on me. I quickly break eye contact. Out of all the people here, she alone understands my current feelings the most.

"She's coming," Alistair suddenly presses out between deep breaths.

We all whirl around to look at the road that leads from North Gate and straight into the thorn forest. Lavendera is jogging along it, heading towards us.

"Get into position," Draven orders.

While Lavendera makes her way towards us, we quickly spread out so that we're covering all angles in case something goes wrong. I move to a position behind a thick tree trunk so that I can step out right behind Lavendera once she crosses the tree line.

My heart slams against my ribs as I watch her get closer.

Once she is almost at the tree line, she slows down.

There is a soft smile on her lips as she sweeps her gaze over the trees before her. For the first time in all the time that I've known her, she looks genuinely happy.

If she only knew what is waiting for her in here.

I slide the dagger from my thigh holster.

Lavendera strolls closer.

Blood pounds in my ears and a storm of rage and hatred thrashes through my soul.

Lavendera Dawnwalker, traitor to the entire Seelie Court and my former friend, will die in ten seconds.

I will kill her in ten seconds.

And I feel no guilt whatsoever.

I flex my fingers on the hilt of my knife while bitter rage claws at my chest.

If I can't have my happily ever after, no one can.

CHAPTER THIRTY-THREE

Lavendera strolls into the thorn forest. Her beautiful pink and purple eyes are bright and clear, completely in the present, and she has an almost excited spring in her step. I have never seen her look this happy before. I'm not sure if it comes from being in the woods or from simply being away from her dragon shifter guards.

In the end, it doesn't matter. All that matters is that she dies.

Sunlight filters down through the green canopy above, painting bright highlights in Lavendera's flowing brown hair as she walks past the tree that I'm hiding behind. The leaves around us rustle restlessly again. I turn with her when she moves, getting into position.

Isera steps out from the trees a few steps in front of Lavendera. Her sudden appearance makes Lavendera stop short. But to my surprise, she smiles as she locks eyes with Isera.

"It's her, isn't it?" she says, that strange smile still on her face. "I knew it would be."

I slip out from my hiding place and quickly close the short distance between us.

"Who is what?" Isera asks, keeping Lavendera's attention fixed on her.

Only cold calculation remains inside me as I sneak up behind Lavendera's back and raise my blade.

I ram it towards the side of her neck.

"NO!"

Vines shoot out from every tree around me. They curl around my wrists and ankles like whips and yank me away from Lavendera.

"No!" that same furious voice repeats in a vicious snarl.

Chaos erupts as thick vines strike at my friends as well, leaving them battling opponents they can't see that seem to be coming from every direction.

Lavendera whirls around to face me.

But to my utter shock, her eyes aren't glowing. Which means that the vines are not her doing. And what's even more baffling is that she looks as shocked as I am.

"Do not touch her," that same voice hisses. "If you hurt her, you will face the wrath of every forest on this world."

It all suddenly clicks in my head. The voice. The words. The vines.

Twisting my head to the side, I find the Dryad Queen gliding out of the trees. Fury flashes in her brown eyes as she glares at me. The intensity of it is enough to make my heart skip a beat. It feels as if I'm facing down the merciless power of nature itself.

Two steps away, Lavendera whirls towards her as well.

Anger, as old and terrible as the woods themselves, darkens her beautiful features when she lays eyes on the Dryad Queen.

"No!" she growls. "Not you!"

The Dryad Queen hesitates, the anger in her eyes disappearing when she shifts her gaze from me to Lavendera. "You can't—"

"How could you do that to me?" Lavendera demands, insanity starting to bleed into her voice. "How could you?"

"You know that—"

"I don't care!" Desperation and insanity lace her voice, making it sharp and high and unhinged. "You don't know what it's like!"

The vines trapping my limbs abruptly disappear as the Dryad Queen yanks them back and slams them up to protect herself instead. I hit the ground hard and jerk back in shock as Lavendera starts attacking the Dryad Queen. Branches shoot through the air, slamming into the Dryad Queen's wall of vines. I throw myself backwards as one of them bounces off and almost spears through my eye.

Across the forest floor, my friends stagger upright again when the trees stop fighting them to instead focus on Lavendera. Trees and branches and vines shoot up from the ground and flash through the air and crash into each other as Lavendera throws her magic at the Dryad Queen in mad fury.

I adjust the grip on my knife. "We should—"

A dragon roars from the city.

Whirling around, I snap my gaze towards the city across the grass.

Four silver dragons have appeared above the rooftops. Their wings boom through the air as they climb higher, letting out another series of bellowing roars.

Lavendera shoots a tree into the air, right through the tree line and out into the open air outside. It sails gracefully through the warm summer air before crashing down on the ground.

All four dragons whip their heads towards it. Towards *us*.

With a roar, they speed forward.

Oh shit.

"Come with us," the Dryad Queen calls to Lavendera while still blocking her furious attacks. "They won't—"

"No," she snarls back. "I'm staying with them! It will happen soon now. I know it will. They said so."

"They're lying."

"No, they're not! They promised. They promised."

Wings boom through the air as the silver dragons shoot towards the tree line.

"Orion," Draven yells over the cracking branches and snapping vines.

"He's not opening the next portal for another half hour," the Unseelie King calls back.

"Fuck."

I snap my gaze between the rapidly approaching dragons and the woman I was supposed to have already killed. She said it herself. She's going back to the Icehearts. I can't let her do that. I can't let her keep helping them with something as dangerous and important as dragon steel. This might be my only chance to kill her. I need to take it.

Adjusting the grip on my knife, I flick my gaze over Lavendera's body and calculate the best moment to stab her while she's focused on attacking the Dryad Queen.

There.

I lurch forward.

"NO!" the Dryad Queen screams again.

Vines shoot towards me. I dive to the side, barely escaping them. But the Dryad Queen can't try again because Lavendera has increased the intensity of her attacks and begun backing towards the tree line. Towards the four silver dragons who are almost here.

Leaping to my feet, I get ready to make one last attempt.

"Don't!" the Dryad Queen yells, desperation pulsing in her voice. "We'll help you! We'll help you if you don't hurt her!"

I hesitate. We need the dryads on our side. But we also need to neutralize Lavendera.

"Draven!" Lyra calls. "Orders?"

Before he can reply, the four silver dragons reach the tree line.

Deafening roars echo across the landscape as they open their jaws and bellow. A shimmering starts at the back of their throats.

"Isera! Alistair!" I yell.

Lavendera slams a massive wall of trees towards the Dryad Queen and sprints out into the open grasslands.

Ice flames shoot towards us.

I gasp.

Fire roars through the air. It's followed by storm winds and a massive wall of ice.

My heart thunders in my chest as the ice flames from the silver dragons crash into the storm of defensive magic. Alistair's fire burns through the ice flames, making mist explode into the air, while Draven's winds blow the attack back towards the dragons. In the middle, those crackling ice flames slam right into Isera's thick wall. Ice shatters against ice, sending chunks flying through the air.

Underneath it all, Lavendera sprints across the grass, heading straight towards the Golden Palace. Indecision flashes through me. I could still try to shove my magic into her to kill her that way. But my magic doesn't seem to work on her. And we also need the dryads.

"Selena!" Isera calls.

I snap my gaze back up to the dragons. Ice flames stream through the air as they attack again. Alistair shoots another torrent of fire to cancel it out while Isera blocks her side with another ice wall. Draven shoots a bolt of lightning at the dragon on the left.

The dragon screeches but manages to mostly get out of the way.

Summoning my magic, I shove it straight at that dragon. Just as I anticipated, a flame of violet pain has flared up from the partial hit from the lightning strike. I pour magic into it, forcing it into a wildfire.

An earsplitting scream tears from the dragon's chest.

Outside the city, more silver dragons, along with red dragons, appear in clouds of black smoke. Wings boom as they climb into the air and shoot towards us.

"We need to get out of here!" Galen calls over the roaring magic and beating wings.

Trees shake around us as the four silver dragons hover right at the tree line, breathing ice flames with furious intensity. I increase the strength of my magic, and the dragon on the left screams in pain.

"Grey isn't—" Orion begins.

"Then we retreat deeper into the woods," Galen interrupts. "We can't stay here!"

Above the Golden Palace, a massive silver dragon explodes into view.

Icy dread and burning fury rip through my soul at the sight of it. At the sight of *her*.

Jessina Iceheart.

The rage makes me pour even more magic into the dragon on the left. He screams in agony and wobbles in the air. The other three roar in fury.

"RUN!" Orion screams.

Disconnecting my magic, I whirl around and sprint towards the thicker trees.

Ice flames crackle behind us.

My heart jerks as I hurtle across the uneven ground.

"Follow the lights," the Dryad Queen's voice suddenly echoes through the twisted woods.

Ice flames clink and roar through the air right behind my back.

I gasp.

A muscular body slams into me.

The force of it sends us both flying sideways.

Ice flames shoot through the air where I used to be a second later.

Holding my breath, I brace myself for a hard landing. But the ground never comes.

My stomach lurches as we continue plummeting down through the forest floor and into the unknown depths beyond.

CHAPTER THIRTY-FOUR

Instead of slamming into the hard ground, our fall is broken by a sloping net of tangled vines. That powerful body is still pressed against mine, muscular arms wrapped tightly around me, as we hit the vines and then roll down along them before finally reaching the thick grass below.

Dragging in a deep breath, I try to calm my pounding heart as I blink and look up at the person who slammed into me up there in the thorn forest. The person who saved me from the ice flames one second before they could hit me.

Draven.

Of course it's Draven.

It will always be Draven.

His beautiful golden eyes are wide as he stares back at me, and there is a storm of conflicting emotions pulsing in there. One moment, he's looking at me with hatred. The next with fear. Then with desperation. Then anger. Confusion. Longing. Back to hatred.

Above us, the ground rumbles as the hole that the Dryad Queen must have opened in the forest floor closes itself again. The sunlight that filtered down through it disappears, but the underground forest we've ended up in isn't pitch black. All around us, spheres of light are floating between the trees, giving off a warm golden glow.

It's breathtaking.

For a few seconds, I feel utterly at peace as Draven and I lie there on the soft grass, gazing into each other's eyes while his arms are wrapped around me.

Then panic flashes across his face.

Shoving me out of his arms, he scrambles to his feet.

The loss of his body around me makes me feel even more cold and empty than before.

"This is your fault," he says, anger lacing his voice. "If you had been faster, Lavendera would be dead by now. If you hadn't just left that dead soldier on the floor, the others wouldn't have found him so quickly. If you hadn't—"

"That's not really why you're angry," I interrupt.

Brushing blades of grass from my black fighting leathers, I climb to my feet as well and raise my chin to lock hard eyes on Draven. The black waves inside me are thrashing like a violent ocean in a storm.

I can't do this anymore.

I can't fucking take it anymore.

It's enough.

It's all just fucking *enough*!

This ends right now.

One way or another.

"You're angry with me because you protected me from the ice flames just now," I continue while I start advancing on him.

He takes a step back.

"You're angry because you protected me from that sword back in the city too," I press, striding closer. "You're angry because you wanted to comfort me after my parents were killed."

Panic flashes across his face again, and he continues backing away.

"You're angry because you are constantly fighting against your instincts." I hold his gaze with a commanding stare. "Against who you really are. But your soul hasn't forgotten. Your heart hasn't forgotten. It's only your mind that is trying to rewrite all of your feelings for me."

"Stop," he grinds out, shaking his head at me. But that panic remains on his face. "Stop talking."

"Why? Are you afraid that the things I'm saying actually make sense?"

"I hate you."

"Yeah, I know. Because I used my magic to force a wildfire of hatred into your chest so that I could save your life."

"No. I hate you because I finally realized who you truly are."

"What I am is your mate."

"I don't care. The mate bond is broken." He takes another step back. "I don't want anything to do with you."

"Then why do you keep protecting me?"

"Because you're messing with my head!" The words rip out of his chest, full of panic and desperation. His eyes are wild as he shakes his head at me and backs away again. "I can't think straight! Whenever you're around me, my head is a gigantic fucking mess of conflicting thoughts."

"So stop thinking and start *feeling*!"

"Stop moving closer!" Yanking out his dagger, he slams it up against my throat. Fire rages in his eyes as he stares me down. "Stop. Moving. Closer. I can't fucking breathe when you're this close."

Holding his gaze, I raise my chin as I stand there with his blade across my throat.

Then I take a step forward.

Panic flashes across his face again. Pulling the blade towards him, he rapidly moves it with me so that I don't slit my own throat on it.

"See?" I challenge, holding his stare. "You're still protecting me."

"Next time, I won't."

That thin thread of patience inside me snaps.

Slamming my palms against his chest, I shove him backwards and rip out my own blade. Insanity burns through me like wildfire as everything inside me shatters. Like the walls of a dam before the fury of an unstoppable flood.

"Then prove it!" I scream at Draven as I swing my blade at him.

Shock crackles across his features, but his battle instincts immediately take over and he blocks my strike. Steel clangs as my blade smacks into his. I shove it off and then lunge at him again.

He parries it easily. I just stab at him again. And again. Rage roars in my ears as I attack Draven with everything I have until he finally snaps as well.

Ducking under my next swipe, he slams his shoulder into my chest. I gasp as air explodes from my lungs when Draven tackles me.

We hit the ground hard with him on top of me.

I swipe my blade towards him again while trying to suck air back into my lungs. His hand shoots out, and he smacks the side of it straight into my wrist. The precision hit makes my fingers spasm, and the dagger flies out of my hand. It hits the ground a short distance away.

Throwing my arm out, I try to grab it, but Draven's free hand shoots out again. Strong fingers wrap around my wrist. A thud echoes into the gold sparkling forest as he slams the back of my hand down against the ground beside my head.

With his knife in his other hand, he shoves it up underneath my chin again. He pushes the flat of the blade so hard against my chin that the sheer power behind it forces me to tilt my head all the way back.

Anger crackles in Draven's eyes as he leans down over me. "What the fuck did you think that was going to accomplish?"

"It proved what I was saying! That you can't hurt me. Because you *love* me."

"Not anymore."

"Yes, you do, you thickheaded overgrown bat!"

There's a sharp tug on the mate bond, and he jerks back slightly as he no doubt remembers what we shared the day I last called him that. Panic flashes across his face once more. I press my advantage.

Summoning my magic, I draw forth that massive inferno of love that I feel for Draven.

And then I shove it straight at him, attaching that emotion to his chest.

It makes the intensity of it decrease in my own chest as Draven instead feels half of that love that I feel.

He gasps.

"Remove it!" he blurts out, panic and dread flashing like lightning in his eyes.

"No. This is half of the love I feel for you. Half. And you love me just as much."

"Remove it *now*!"

"Fight, Draven! Goddess damn it, fight back!" Desperation bleeds into my own voice as I scream the words up at him. "Fight for me! Fight for us."

My magic continues pouring into him, forcing him to feel all the endless love that I have for him.

There is another violent yank on the mate bond.

Terror washes over Draven's features. Still straddling my chest, he tightens his grip on my wrist as he pins it harder against the ground. "Stop it!"

"No." I stare up into his panicked eyes. "I will keep my magic connected to you like this every second of every day for the rest of my life. I will force you to feel what you really feel!"

The mate bond pulses hard inside me.

It feels as if there is a rope attached to my chest on one side while the other side is hanging down inside a dark abyss, and someone is trying to haul himself back up that rope.

No, not someone.

Him.

Draven's chest heaves as he shakes his head at me while anger and panic and hatred and fear fight like wolves behind his eyes. "Cut off your magic right now."

"No." It's a simple word. Full of defiance. Full of challenge. Full of threats.

"Cut it off!"

"No." I keep my love pouring into him through my magic. "Since your heart is still lost, I will make you feel *my* heart for the rest of our lives. My love is strong enough for the both of us."

"Then I will cut it out!" he screams at me, his voice almost breaking from the panic that fills it.

His desperate eyes are wild and full of insanity as he yanks the blade down from my throat to instead press it against my chest, right over my heart.

"I will cut your fucking heart out," he snarls at me. "So that I never have to feel it again. So that I never have to feel like *this* again."

"Then do it!" I scream back at him.

Yanking up my free hand, I grab his wrist. He jerks in surprise, but I keep my grip firmly around his wrist and use that to press his knife harder against my chest. My heart beats out of control as I hold his knife hand steady there, one simple push away from killing me.

"Do it!" All the weeks of loss and pain and agony come crashing down on me at the same time as I scream up at Draven in defiance and challenge. "Cut it out! Rip my heart right out of my chest. It's yours anyway, so do whatever the hell you want with it!"

Anger roars through his eyes.

Yanking his wrist out of my grip, he raises his hand above my chest.

A scream of fury rips from his throat and splits the world around us as he rams the blade straight towards my heart.

I keep my eyes on his beautiful golden ones as a sense of peace settles over me.

At least it will be over now. At least I won't have to hurt any more after this.

The blade slams down with a thud.

I gasp.

Draven stares down at the knife in his hand, the blade buried deep in the grass right next to me. My heart stutters.

There is a massive pull on the mate bond.

One last desperate heave over the edge of the abyss.

My magic slams back into my own chest with such force that my vision blacks out. But it's not just the love that I attached to Draven's chest that shoots through the air towards me. An explosion of hatred bursts from his chest. I can feel that flame of hatred shatter like a glass sculpture that explodes from the inside, the sharp edges pelting against my magic like shrapnel.

Our mate bond slams back into me.

Light and color and burning unending love floods my chest as Draven's side of the mate bond restores itself like a lightning strike straight to my chest.

A cry of pure relief tears from my throat.

Still straddling my chest, Draven stares down at me while one hand is still wrapped around the knife that he drove into the grass instead of my heart. Pain and longing and a love so fierce it could've burned the world down shine in his perfect golden eyes.

I reach out with my magic and gently prod at his chest.

The red-violet flame of hatred is gone.

Utterly and completely gone.

CHAPTER THIRTY-FIVE

"Draven," I gasp out his name like a prayer.

The moment his name leaves my lips, he drags in a long shuddering breath, as if it's the first breath he has taken in years. His golden eyes are burning with emotions. But not hatred. Not anymore. Instead, he is staring into my eyes while relief, longing, and deep unending love pulse in his beautiful eyes.

"Selena," he breathes.

Yanking the blade out of the grass, he tosses it aside and releases his grip on my other wrist. Still straddling me on the ground, he cups my cheeks with both hands and presses his lips against mine in a desperate kiss.

It sets my whole soul on fire.

I gasp into his mouth and slide my hands into his hair. Curling my fingers in his soft black hair, I press his lips harder against mine as I kiss him back desperately.

The mate bond thrums inside me, inside *us*, flooding my senses with his burning need and inflaming my own until I can barely see the deep forest and the glowing golden spheres floating among the trees around us. All I can see is him. All I can *feel* is him.

And I want more. I want everything. I want everything that the cruel universe has denied me these past weeks. I want my mate. I want all of him.

Sliding my hands down his neck, I start pulling at the collar of his armor while still kissing him furiously. My heart stutters when he breaks the kiss but quickly starts fluttering again when he begins stripping out of his armor. I start doing the same with my fighting leathers, but I only manage to get the jacket off before he stops me.

"No." He grabs both of my wrists, stopping my movements when I reach for my shirt. Desperate longing burns in his eyes as he drags his gaze over my body. "I'll do it."

He places my hands back down on the soft grass above my head. I keep them there as he finishes removing the rest of his clothes and then settles himself on his knees between my legs. Pleasure skitters down my spine as he draws his fingers along the sliver of bare skin visible between the top of my pants and the edge of the shirt that has slid up my stomach.

I arch my back, pushing my hips forward slightly as he begins unbuttoning my pants. His gaze rakes across my body again, as if he wants to brand every curve of my body into his mind forever. My skin prickles at the exposure as Draven curls his fingers over the top of my pants and underwear and starts sliding them down my legs.

The leather scrapes against my bare thighs as Draven takes his time pushing the fabric down. I squirm on the ground as need burns through me.

He stops when my pants reach my knees and leans down while his eyes glint in the golden light.

I suck in a shuddering breath as he kisses the inside of my bare thigh. He smiles against my skin. While kissing his way down my thigh, he starts sliding my pants down my legs again. The contrast between the scraping leather and the soft brush of his lips against my sensitive skin makes my clit throb with need. A desperate whimper escapes me as I squirm on the grass.

Draven smiles against my skin and then slides my pants and underwear all the way off my legs. A shiver ripples through me even though the air inside this underground forest is warm. I suck in a sharp breath as Draven suddenly grabs my ankles and spreads my legs wider. Fire flickers through my veins.

Arching my back, I bite my lip to muffle a moan as Draven kisses his way back up my legs again. My heart pounds as his lips reach the inside of my thigh once more, moving higher at an excruciatingly slow pace. Burning lust thrums inside me, amplified by Draven's own which is flooding my senses through the mate bond, until it feels as if my entire soul is vibrating.

He flicks my clit with his tongue.

I gasp, pleasure zapping through my spine.

A dark laugh rumbles from his chest, making his breath dance over my throbbing clit.

My hands shoot down and slide into his messy hair, gripping it hard to keep his sinful mouth down there. Tilting his head back, he gazes up along my body and locks eyes with me.

"I said *I'll* do it," he reminds me, his eyes gleaming. "So put your hands back over your head and keep them there."

Heat pools inside me at the effortless command in his voice. Drawing in another shuddering breath, I unclench my fingers from his hair and force myself to move my hands back so that they're resting on the soft grass above my head again.

"Good girl," he murmurs.

Pleasure crashes through me, and I squirm desperately on the grass.

Draven shifts his position between my legs and draws his strong hands up the side of my thighs until he reaches my hips. The fabric of my shirt bunches above his hands as he starts pushing it upwards. My skin prickles as he bares my stomach.

Leaning down over me, he kisses the spot right above my pussy.

I whimper.

But he only smirks against my bare skin and starts kissing his way up my stomach instead. His strong hands slide up the sides of my ribcage before stopping right underneath my breasts. With a possessive grip on the side of my ribs, he holds me firmly in place as he teases me with his tongue and lips. Another desperate moan escapes my mouth, and I roll my hips, seeking friction.

He just lets out another low laugh that dances over my bare skin, clearly enjoying the sweet torture he is inflicting on me.

A jolt shoots through my body as he suddenly slides his hands up over my breasts, pushing the fabric of the shirt upwards as well. My nipples harden at the exposure. Draven flicks one of them with his tongue.

Throwing my head back, I gasp up into the lush green canopy.

My clit is throbbing and my entire body aches with need.

Draven slides his tongue around my nipple while he continues pushing my shirt up over my collarbones. I tilt my chin back down as the fabric slides up over my face. But once it reaches my eyes, Draven stops.

Leaving the shirt blocking my vision like that, he draws one hand along the curve of my breast and moves the other down between my legs. Something between a whimper and a moan rips from my lips as he teases his fingers over my clit.

He pinches my nipple.

I gasp. Throwing my head back, I squirm hard underneath him, but the shirt remains like a blindfold over my eyes. It heightens my senses and makes every brush of his lips and every teasing move of his fingers send lightning crackling through my nerves.

While rolling one nipple between his fingers, he takes the other into his mouth at the same time as he rubs his thumb over my clit.

Pleasure pulses inside me.

Dragging in unsteady breaths, I clench my hands into fists above my head to stop myself from touching him. He toys with my clit and torments my nipple with slow luxurious strokes of his tongue until I can barely think straight. Tension thrums inside me, and I'm so wet that it takes all of my willpower not to grind myself harder against his hand.

Lust, from both sides of the mate bond, crashes through my soul like a storm.

"Draven," I gasp out. "Draven."

A moan rips from his chest, vibrating against my nipple. Raising his head, he demands, "Say it again."

"Draven," I breathe, my voice hoarse.

He drags in a shuddering breath. "Fuck, I love it when you say my name."

Sliding his hands up my body, he finally pushes my shirt all the way up over my head and then tosses it aside. I blink against the warm light from the glowing spheres and then meet his beautiful eyes. They glitter even brighter in the golden light.

At last lifting my hands from the grass, I lock them behind his neck and pull his mouth down to mine. He moans into my mouth as I claim his lips.

Bracing one hand on the ground, he moves the other down to my thigh. With a firm grip, he raises my leg while his cock presses against my entrance. I lift my hips. He thrusts inside me.

Pleasure crackles up my spine as his cock slides into me in one commanding thrust that fills me completely. I gasp into his mouth. After drawing out slightly, he slams back in again. Another desperate moan drips from my lips.

Draven rests his forehead against mine. "I love you, little rebel. I love everything about you."

My heart stutters in my chest. With my hands still locked behind his neck, I hold him close to me as I kiss him again. "I love you too, Draven. I love you more than life itself."

He kisses me back with a desperation that takes my breath away. Love and lust and pleasure and desperate need thrum inside our souls, shared by our mate bond, as he fucks me with a possessiveness that burns like wildfire. Every thrust of his hips is a primal claiming. A defiant scream to the world that I am his. A threat and a challenge to anyone who would dare try to take me from him again.

My entire body vibrates with pleasure as he worships my body. Tension pulses inside me, thrashing like a storm, as every commanding thrust of his hips and every stroke of his tongue brings me closer to an orgasm. His cock slams into me, hitting deep inside. I gasp in desperate breaths as lights flicker before my eyes.

Draven's fingers dig into my thigh as he fucks me possessively. Pleasure shoots up my spine with every dominating thrust, making the building tension inside me thrash like a thunderstorm.

I slide my fingers down from his neck and rake them across his back.

A moan rips from his lungs.

The sound of it shoves me straight over the edge.

I gasp as the intense orgasm crashes through my body with enough force to make my legs shake. Draven tightens his grip on my thigh, holding me firmly in place as he continues fucking me through the waves of pleasure. His beautiful eyes sear into mine, as if burning the expression on my face into his mind forever.

A groan tears from his chest as he comes as well.

I yank his mouth down to mine, stealing that deep groan from his lips while his cock pulses inside me. He kisses me back furiously, biting my lip and dominating my mouth with his tongue. Pleasure crackles through my every vein.

The mate bond pulses inside us like a glowing tether, connecting his soul to mine. Forever.

When the intensity of the orgasm has faded out, Draven rests his forehead against mine again. Still buried deep inside me, he remains like that for a few seconds. His chest heaves. So does mine.

Then he gently pulls out and lies down on the soft grass next to me. Wrapping his arms around me, he pulls me tightly against him. The desperate longing in the way he holds me makes my fragile heart crack all over again.

I press my body harder against his. "I missed you so much."

"I missed you too." With his arms still tightly around me, he kisses my forehead and draws in a deep breath as if breathing me in. "I missed *us*."

A sob rips from my lips, and before I know it, the floodgates crash open and tears flow down my cheeks. "I'm sorry. I'm so, so sorry. I was trying to save you, but instead, I ruined everything."

"No. You *did* save me. I would have died back in that pocket reality if you hadn't done what you did." He kisses my forehead again. Insistently. Urgently. And he tightens his arms around me, as if he wants to physically press his words into my body. "You never ruin anything. And you could never ruin us."

Another broken sob escapes my lips.

He edges back slightly and moves one hand up to my jaw, tilting my chin up so that I meet his eyes. They're overflowing with love, which just makes more tears stream down my cheeks.

"I told you that I would destroy the barriers of the afterlife and battle both of our gods to find you." A soft smile tugs at his lips. "Did you really think that I would let something as trivial as a little magic keep me from you?"

Something halfway between a laugh and a sob rips from my lungs.

"You're mine." He strokes his thumb over my cheek, wiping the tears away. "You have always been mine. You will always be mine. Now and forever. And God help anyone who tries to take you from me."

I smile. The sight of it makes his eyes brighten, and he brushes a soft kiss against my lips. A contented sigh escapes from deep within my chest.

Relief and love and pain and longing thrash inside my ribcage, making my chest ache with the intensity of it all. Wrapping my arms around Draven again, I press my cheek against his chest and nestle closer to him. He holds me tightly.

For a while, we just remain like that.

With my cheek pressed to his firm chest, I listen to the steady beat of his heart.

The wild passion through the mate bond has simmered down to a steady flow of love. It fills me like a warm sparkling sea.

But to my surprise, that dark rage and hatred inside me doesn't disappear. They remain there inside my soul, thrashing about like the merciless waves of an endless, storm-plagued ocean.

Even though Draven is back, I still can't return to who I was before I stood there on the plains outside the Unseelie Court and threw open the massive gates to all the rage and hatred inside me.

I suppose it makes sense, though. Because it wasn't just about losing Draven. It was decades, centuries, of being treated like crap. A hundred and sixty-seven years of hunger and pain and humiliation at the hands of dragon shifters and fae alike. An entire life of being distrusted, punished for crimes I haven't committed, and blamed for all the wrongs of this world even though I am not responsible for them.

Losing Draven wasn't the cause. It was the final drop in a massive dam that has been ready to burst for decades. The final drop that at long last shattered the walls. And now, the walls are broken. The flood is already out, crashing over the world and sweeping away everything in its path. It's too late to put it back behind the walls again.

The sound of my dad's final gasp echoes through my head and the sight of my mom lying in a pool of her own blood that has turned half of her silver hair red flashes before my eyes.

That black rage and hatred inside me roars like a crashing thunderstorm.

No, there is no stopping the flood now. I am no longer the person I used to be. The Selena Hale who left the Seelie Court last year, ignorant like a child and so full of hope, is dead and gone.

Panic and dread suddenly stab through my chest.

The Selena Hale that Draven fell in love with is gone.

Pulling him tighter against me, I drag in an unsteady breath while my heart starts thundering in my chest.

"What's wrong?" Draven asks.

My heart almost breaks all over again. He could feel the moment I tensed up. Of course he could. He sees me, all of me, in a way that no one ever has before.

"I, uhm..." I begin hesitantly. "I'm not... the same. As I was before." Clearing my throat, I try to compose myself enough to speak in complete sentences. "What I said in Orion's dining room before we left... I meant it. I don't want justice anymore. I want revenge. I don't care who I hurt. I just want revenge." Anger creeps into my voice, making it hard and sharp like a blade. "I want my fucking revenge!" My chest heaves, and I drag in an unsteady breath as that flicker of dread hits me again. I swallow. "So I'm not the person you fell in love with anymore."

He slides his hand up to my jaw again and cups my cheek. Edging back slightly so that he can see me, he tilts my head back until I meet his gaze again. His eyes are dead serious as he locks them on me.

"You want to destroy the world? I'll help you burn it down. You want to kill everyone? I'll help you slit their throats. There is *nothing* you can do that would make me stop loving you. I love you, little rebel. All of you."

My heart stutters, and I drag in another unsteady breath as I gaze up into his serious eyes. "Even the really fucked up parts?"

"Especially the really fucked up parts." He gives me a knowing look. "Because I have them too."

A short laugh full of relief and gratitude escapes my lips. With his hand still on my jaw, keeping my head tilted back, he leans down and steals that laugh from my mouth with a possessive kiss.

When he draws back and meets my gaze again, his eyes burn like golden flames. He flashes me a devilish smile.

"You wanna be villains? Let's go be fucking villains."

CHAPTER THIRTY-SIX

When the Dryad Queen told us to follow the lights, she apparently meant those glowing golden orbs that float between the trees. After putting our clothes back on, Draven and I found a trail of those shimmering spheres running straight into the forest in one direction. I glance at them as we follow them towards where I'm assuming the Dryad Queen is waiting for us.

The small balls seem to almost pulse, making me wonder if they're actually some kind of living creature rather than a product of magic. It's hard to tell, though, since my knowledge of the dryads and the strange woods they live in is incredibly limited.

We walk for a surprisingly long time before we finally see a group of people standing inside a large ring of those floating orbs. Lyra is inspecting a glowing sphere next to her. There is a smile on her face as she watches it. From across their loose circle, Alistair watches *her*.

Galen is pacing back and forth, trampling the soft grass underneath his boots, while Orion simply stands there with his back straight, looking effortlessly regal and unbothered. A few steps away, Isera is leaning her back against a tree, her arms crossed over her chest.

All of them turn their heads to look at us when we come into view.

Relief washes across Galen's face. "You're okay."

Draven nods, a smile on his face. "Yeah."

All our friends glance between the two of us, noting how close together we're walking as we make our way over to them. A mix of confusion and hope flits across both Galen's and Lyra's features, but neither of them clearly dares to ask the question.

"You sure took your sweet time getting here," Orion drawls, cocking an impatient brow.

"We, uhm…" I glance over at Draven before finish with, "Got lost."

Isera slides a knowing look at me. "Your pants are buttoned incorrectly."

Heat stains my cheeks when I snap my gaze down to find that I did in fact button them wrong in my haste to put them back on.

Orion lets out a dramatic sigh and gives us a reproachful look. "Not only did you waste all of our time by stopping to have hate sex, you also make us look like a ragtag group of losers with no fashion sense. Delightful."

"Not hate sex," Draven replies, his eyes glinting. "Just… sex."

Galen and Lyra suck in a sharp breath. Even Alistair stands up straighter and stares at me with his eyebrows raised in silent question.

"You found a way to remove the magic?" Galen asks, flicking his gaze between me and Draven.

"No," I reply. A wide smile spreads across my lips as I nod towards Draven. "He shattered it on his own."

Even Isera raises her eyebrows now.

"But I thought that wasn't possible," Alistair says, staring between the two of us. "I thought it was permanent."

"It is," I reply. "It shouldn't be possible. But…"

Trailing off, I look to Draven as we at last come to a halt in front of our friends. Glowing spheres float around us all in a wide circle, bathing the lush green woods in golden light. Draven slides an arm around my waist, resting his hand on my hip possessively.

"It wouldn't have been possible without the mate bond," he explains. "Everything Selena was doing, every time I was near her, I could feel our mate bond fighting to reconnect. I was trapped underneath that mass of hatred burning in my chest, but eventually, the connection between us grew so strong again that I could use the mate bond like a rope to haul myself out of that burning hatred."

"Yes!" Lyra exclaims, a wide grin on her mouth.

There is a glint in Alistair's green and orange eyes as he levels a knowing look on Draven. "Not surprised."

Draven raises his eyebrows at him in silent question.

"Someone as annoyingly bossy as you would never let some random magic tell you what to do." He shrugs. "You earned the nickname I gave you, you know."

A surprised laugh escapes Draven's chest, and he pulls me a little closer to his side.

From her place by the tree, Isera meets my gaze and gives me a nod while the hint of a smile shines on her lips. I smile back.

"You're all finally here, I see," the Dryad Queen suddenly says from my left.

Twisting my head in that direction, I find her gliding out of the woods. Her hair and her dress, all made of leaves and vines and branches, ripple behind her as she moves. When she reaches the circle of floating lights, the glowing spheres part before her without a word or even a glance from her. They pulse slightly, casting that glittering golden light over her pale green skin.

Draven slides his arm from my waist as we turn to face her fully. Galen, Lyra, and Alistair do the same while Orion, who was already looking in her direction, just remains standing there with that customary royal and slightly cocky tilt to his chin. Isera remains leaning against the tree, her arms crossed over her chest, but she narrows her eyes slightly as she watches the Dryad Queen who comes to a halt in front of our now loosely formed semi-circle.

"And *you* have some explaining to do," I reply, some of that anger returning to my soul. Standing up straighter, I level a hard stare on the Dryad Queen. "Why did you stop me from killing Lavendera?"

Indignation flashes across her ancient face, and she raises her chin but doesn't respond.

"You promised to help," I remind her, that sharpness still lacing my voice. "In exchange for us not hurting Lavendera, you promised us help, so the least you can do is answer my question. Why did you stop me from killing her?"

"She's..." The Dryad Queen clenches her jaw before finishing the sentence with a vague, "One of us."

I frown at her. "What does that mean?"

She just looks back at me in stubborn silence.

"Lavendera is obviously not a dryad," I press. "She's fae. Or half fae, at least."

My friends raise their eyebrows at me in surprise.

"I think she might be the child of Emperor Bane and one of his previous fae life slaves," I explain.

Lyra sucks in a sharp breath.

Next to her, Alistair stares at me with eyebrows raised while thoughts churn behind his eyes. "It would certainly explain her weird loyalty to them."

"Yes. Though it's still just a theory." I shift my gaze back to the Dryad Queen. "Regardless, she's clearly not a dryad. So what did you mean by *she's one of us?*"

The leaves and vines in her hair continue rippling around her as if on a phantom wind as she just keeps looking back at me in silence, her jaw stubbornly clenched.

"Is it because she has tree magic?" I push.

"The reason is irrelevant," she finally replies. Power and command both lace her voice and gleam in her brown eyes as she stares me down. "What matters is that we want her. And we want her unharmed."

My head spins. What could the dryads possibly want with Lavendera? They already have tree magic. And tree magic which is no doubt much stronger than Lavendera's. They also hate the Icehearts, and she is stubbornly loyal to them. So why do they want her? She does whatever the Icehearts want, which has no doubt harmed the dryads in some way. So do they just want her in order to punish her for that? But then why stop me from killing her up there?

"I can read the questions in your eyes, young fae," the Dryad Queen says. "But I will not answer them. All you need to know right now is that we want Lavendera brought to us. It is our most desired wish, and one we are willing to strike a bargain for. So tell me, what is it that you would want?"

"We want what we came here for last time," I reply, holding her gaze. "An alliance. We want you to help us take down the Icehearts."

She throws her head back.

The abrupt move startles me enough that I jerk back a little, but she only spreads her arms wide while keeping her head thrown back like that. Her hair streams out both to the sides and behind her, and her dress seems to almost grow down into the ground. The sight of it all is shockingly terrifying.

A hissing, rippling sound fills the woods for a second.

My heart slams against my ribs, and fear trails an icy finger down my spine.

Then it stops just as abruptly as it began.

The Dryad Queen tilts her head back down, and her hair returns to flow more normally down her back. She locks those ancient eyes of hers on me, and I am once more reminded that this being isn't mortal. This being isn't a normal person who lives and dies while the world continues moving. This being is part of the *fabric* of the world.

"We accept," she declares. "If you bring us Lavendera, the dryads will go to war. For you. For us." Her eyes sharpen like lethal blades. "And for revenge."

My heart pounds at the unforgiving fury in her voice.

I truly wonder what the Icehearts did to the dryads all those millennia ago.

It seems like a reckoning is coming. An unholy alliance between the Seelie Court, the Unseelie Court, the dragon clans, and the dryads. All of it coming for the Icehearts. Like a boulder rolling down a mountain, picking up speed.

First though, we need to get Lavendera. Not just for the dryads. For the dragon shifters too. Somehow, this strange and certifiably insane fae who stares at walls with blank eyes half of the time is the key to the entire war. She is also utterly loyal to the Icehearts.

So the question is, how in Mabona's name are we supposed to save someone who doesn't want to be saved?

CHAPTER THIRTY-SEVEN

Water splashes as Draven slams his arms down into the river to catch the fish that swam past. It shoots out of reach right before he can grab it. On the riverbank, Galen chuckles and casts a glance at Draven over his shoulder while he continues towards the rest of us with the fish that he himself caught.

"Amateur," Galen calls to Draven, a smile on his face.

Straightening in the water, Draven turns towards the riverbank and gives his best friend a dark look that is completely ruined by the smile that threatens to spill across his lips. "I could always just fry the entire river with lightning."

"You could. But it would just prove that your reflexes really are worse than mine."

Draven's eyes glitter in the golden light from the spheres floating between the trees. "Wanna come down here and say that to my face?"

"Not to mention that a lightning strike would probably kill all other marine life in the river too," Lyra adds.

She is also standing in the river, her eyes scanning the clear water as she searches for another fish. All three dragon shifters have stripped down to their underwear so that their armor doesn't get wet while they try to catch fish in the slow-moving river. There is no direct sunlight down here in the dryads' underground forest, but the air is warm. And so is the water, from what Lyra has said. Apart from us and the glowing orbs in the air, the lush green forest around us is peaceful and still.

Galen laughs and wiggles his eyebrows at Draven. "When *she* comes in and urges you to act responsibly, you know you've lost."

Still standing knee-deep in the river, Draven mutters under his breath, but amusement tugs at his lips as well. "I still dispute your claim that your reflexes are better than mine."

"And yet..." Galen drops his newest prize on the pile of ice next to Isera before turning back to smirk at Draven. "I'm the one who keeps catching all the fish."

"That's just because you always aim for all the grandfather fish who swim so slowly that even Orion could've caught them."

"Keep telling yourself that if it helps you sleep at night. I've simply developed excellent reflexes because I've spent two hundred years in close proximity to that," he points at Lyra, "absolute maniac who keeps jumping off cliffs and shifting mid-air right in front of me."

Draven tips his head to the side. "Good point."

"For the record," Orion interrupts. "I could catch fish if I wanted to. I simply choose not to."

Everyone turns towards the Unseelie King, who is standing on the grass halfway between me and Isera. I continue my work while I turn to glance at him as well. My knife thuds steadily against the flat piece of wood before me as I continue gutting and chopping the fish without looking at it. On my other side, Alistair is frying the freshly cut fish with his fire magic.

Orion keeps his chin raised as he looks back at us all.

"Remind me again what it is that you are actually contributing with here?" Draven says, and arches an eyebrow at him.

"My presence is contribution enough." His black and silver eyes gleam as he flashes us a devilish smile. "You're welcome."

In the water, Lyra rolls her eyes while Draven looks like he is contemplating whether to shoot a lightning bolt at the Unseelie King or maybe to create a rain cloud right above his head. Galen straightens after dropping off his fish on the pile of ice and then starts back towards the water.

"And besides," Orion continues. "I'm not the only one who isn't doing anything." Twisting slightly, he looks over at Isera, who is standing two steps to his right. "What are you contributing with, little viper?"

Isera just points down at the pile of ice that the fish is resting on.

"I've gotta agree with *squeamy* on this one, ice lady," Alistair calls while moving the flame in his palm around the fish before him. "You could probably catch more fish than Draven."

"Squeamy?" Orion demands, looking completely outraged. "Is that supposed to be a nickname?"

"I am perfectly capable of catching fish," Draven huffs from the water.

"I've already done my job," Isera replies to Alistair's comment. Arching a dark eyebrow, she gives him a knowing look while I swear a smile lurks at the corner of her lips. "Just focus on yours, *Flambé*."

Alistair's mouth drops open. "Flambé?"

She shrugs, her silver and blue eyes gleaming. "You keep giving everyone else ridiculous nicknames. You could use one of your own. And you do excel at pouring alcohol over things and setting them on fire."

A laugh bursts out of me. While still continuing to cut the fish before me, I laugh so hard that my shoulders shake. Alistair just shakes his head at the both of us and then shoots a glance down at the dagger that keeps flying across my makeshift cutting board.

"Careful with the knife, Soulstealer," he says.

"Nah, she's good," Lyra calls from the water while stalking a fish. "Just look at how her hands move. She's a pro."

Galen meets my eyes from over his shoulder while he walks back into the river. "You are actually surprisingly good at that."

"I used to be a fish cutter," I explain with a casual shrug. "I've literally been doing this exact thing almost every day of my life."

To my right, Orion scrunches his nose. "This is why I decimate anyone who even thinks of taking my crown. I would die before I ever touched a dead fish, let alone—"

"Here," Isera suddenly calls.

Since I'm assuming that she's talking to me, I turn towards her.

A dead fish smacks into the side of Orion's face.

The riverbank goes utterly silent.

I gape at the Unseelie King as the dead fish falls down from his cheek to hit his shoulder before landing on the grass right next to his fancy shoes.

For a moment, no one moves. No one even breathes. I swear the river itself stops flowing.

Then Orion slowly turns towards Isera.

"Sorry." She flashes him a completely unapologetic smile dripping with challenge. "My hand slipped."

In a flash, Orion has closed the distance between them. With a firm grip on her collar, he slowly draws her face closer to his. "Your hand slipped?"

She summons a shard of ice and presses it against his throat before he can pull her all the way to him. Their lips are so close that they're almost touching.

Another villainous smile slides across Isera's mouth as she replies, "Yes."

"If there is so much as one single stain on my clothes from that fish, I will make you spend the rest of the night washing it out."

"You seem to spend a lot of time fantasizing about taking your clothes off around me. Desperate much?"

"Let's not forget who cuddled whom in that cave."

Heat flushes Isera's cheeks for a second as she presses out, "I did not cuddle you!"

"No? So you're saying that you didn't wake up with your arms around me and your cheek snuggled into my chest?"

"That was only to prevent hypothermia!"

"Sure." His eyes gleam with devilish light. "Just admit that you want to fuck me."

"You're the one who couldn't keep control of his cock when I climbed onto your lap while stealing the dragon steel back there in your court."

"You're the one who got down on your knees and offered to suck my cock for all eternity."

"In order to trick you into a bargain and then trap you in it so that you have to obey my will. Which I managed to do anyway." With the shard of ice still against his throat, she rises up on her toes and slants her lips over his. "You belong to me now, pretty boy. Don't forget it."

"A bargain that I'm becoming increasingly certain is based on a lie. And once I prove that, the deal will revert and I will win our bargain by default." He slides his tongue along his bottom lip, only a breath away from hers. "And then *you* will belong to *me*, little viper."

From the river, Lyra suddenly calls in a cheerful voice, "Why don't you just fuck each other and release all of this tension between you?"

Orion and Isera practically leap apart. Brushing his hands down his embroidered shirt, he turns away from Isera and tries to appear unaffected while she draws her eyebrows down in a scowl and moves to pick up the fish she threw.

"What?" Lyra laughs, and her orange eyes glitter as she flicks a glance towards Alistair. "A nice fuck is good for the soul."

His cheeks flush bright red, and he almost drops the fish. Snapping his gaze down to it, he clears his throat while the flame in his hand gets inexplicably larger.

"Azaroth's flame," Draven mutters from the river. "It really is like being surrounded by children. At this point, summer will be over before we get this done."

"I don't mind," I call back to him. A teasing smile spreads across my lips as I deliberately rake my gaze up and down his body. "I'm enjoying the view."

Draven, who is still standing knee-deep in the water in only his underwear, slides his gaze to me. Drops of water run down his skin, and his muscles shift with every move he makes. My grin widens. At long last, that smile that he has been holding back spreads across his handsome face. Shaking his head at me, he gives me a look that lets me know exactly what we will be doing the moment we're alone again.

He was right, though.

Catching enough fish for all seven of us took longer than we had expected. It was only once Isera's patience ran out and she froze part of the river that we could finish our task more efficiently.

Once dinner is finally ready, we can start focusing on what we actually need to discuss.

How to get Lavendera.

But just as I suspected, figuring out how to save someone who doesn't want to be saved is not easy.

"If she won't come willingly, we'll just knock her out," Isera says, and shoots an impatient look at Orion, who yet again pointed out our target's unwillingness to be saved. "The important part is *how* we get to her. If she's not trailing the Icehearts themselves, she's followed by elite guards."

"We can handle the guards," Draven says. "As long as Bane and Jessina aren't there. So what we need is a way to draw them out while leaving Lavendera behind."

Sitting on the grass next to him, I swallow another piece of fried fish, which tastes surprisingly good, and then tap my fingers against my thigh in thought. "Do they always bring Lavendera with them when they leave?"

"No. She doesn't leave the Ice Palace that often, so my guess is that they only bring her when they need her to control someone with dragon steel."

"Alright," Isera picks up, shifting her gaze between Draven and the rest of us. "So what about the Purple Clan?"

"What about them?" Galen asks from where he is sitting next to Lyra.

"We need to create some kind of problem that the Icehearts need to fly out and handle. Artemesia said that she was willing to help us earlier. What if we ask her to create some kind of problem close to her clan's homeland? It would force the Icehearts to fly out there, but since they're not controlling her with dragon steel the way they're controlling Tanaka, there would be no reason for them to bring Lavendera."

Silence falls over the deep forest as we all consider her suggestion. For a while, only the gentle rippling of the river disturbs the quiet.

"I don't think it will be enough," I admit, and flick an apologetic look in Isera's direction. "Jessina and Bane have outsmarted us time and again. Even if they fly out, we won't just be able to stroll into the Ice Palace and take Lavendera. She's too important. Without her, they can't use dragon steel. So they'll make sure she's thoroughly guarded."

Isera sucks her teeth and then nods in acknowledgment.

"What if we just overwhelm their senses?" Lyra says. Raising her eyebrows, she looks from face to face. "It's what I do when I need to get away with something I shouldn't be doing. Create enough chaos in the same place at the same time, and no one will notice what I'm doing in the middle of all of that."

"Smart," Alistair agrees with an impressed nod.

Draven just arches an eyebrow at her. "Done that a lot in the barracks, have you?"

She just gives him a sheepish grin that is most definitely a *yes*.

"Okay, so what if after the Icehearts have left," I begin, nudging the conversation back on track, "we make it seem like all of the other clans are attacking Frostfell?"

"How?" Galen asks. "They have patrols all across the grasslands outside the city. If there's a legion of dragons flying towards them, the scouts would know."

I shift my gaze to Draven. "The commander in charge of all those scouts, do you know who it is?"

"Yeah." He nods. "His name is Ferver Osteria."

"Do you know where he lives?"

"Yes." Confusion pulls at his brows. "Why?"

A smirk slides home on my lips as I explain what I had in mind.

The others nod in approval.

"We still need to actually locate Lavendera, though," Alistair reminds us. "She might be strolling through the city or hiding in a bedroom while going through one of her crazy-pants moments, for all we know."

"The elite guards who are responsible for watching her will know where she is," Draven replies. "Even the ones who aren't actively watching her. So as long as we get to one of them, we'll know her current location."

Isera nods, her intelligent eyes full of schemes. "That just leaves one problem. How do we get her out of the city without being seen?"

Silence falls over our group again. I eat some more fried fish while I ponder the problem. If Lavendera turns out to be inside the Ice Palace, we can't just walk inside and get her. Everyone in there knows exactly what we look like and that we're traitors who should be captured or killed on sight.

To my surprise, the one who offers a solution is Orion.

Up until now, he has just been sitting there on the grass, eating his fish while scowling down at the unrefined manner in which he is forced to dine. But now, he stretches his legs out before him and crosses his ankles. A sly smile curves his lips.

"Leave that to me."

CHAPTER THIRTY-EIGHT

Being back in Frostfell is strange. I feel like I was an entirely different person when I lived here. No, actually, it feels like the person I was back then is *two* entire personalities ago. I changed a lot when we were stuck in the Unseelie Court. And then I changed again, even more, after we left it.

Standing in the shadows of a building, I lean my back against the cool stone wall and gaze up at the gleaming Ice Palace above. Stars glitter in the black night sky above, making the palace shine even brighter.

When I first arrived here after the Atonement Trials, I was like an ignorant child who stubbornly thought she had everything figured out but who in reality knew nothing of the world. I still blindly believed that everything I'd been told all my life was the truth because it hadn't even occurred to me that I was living in a bubble where all the available information was censored by someone else. And on top of that, I was angry, hurt, and terrified of my feelings for Draven.

Looking back on it now, there are things I wish I hadn't said. Like when I called him a coward for not standing against the Icehearts. Or how I reacted when he told me that I was his fated mate. And some things that I wish I had said sooner, like—

Regret hits me like a gut punch.

My parents' lifeless eyes flash before my eyes.

The pools of blood.

The silver hair turning red.

The fear and shock on their faces.

The hatred in their eyes when they looked at me right before they died.

The empty doorstep.

The potted plants still in the windows.

Throwing my hand out, I brace it against the cool stone wall behind me in order to keep myself upright as the darkened street around me suddenly sways. I try to gasp in a breath, but my lungs no longer seem to work. Agony stabs through my chest as waves of grief and regret crash down over me. I feel like I'm suffocating.

"You okay?"

It takes enormous effort to get my eyes to focus on the face in front of me. Alistair has rounded the corner and stopped short right in front of me. Worry flickers in his eyes as he looks at me, waiting for an answer.

Oh Goddess, pull yourself together.

Straightening from the wall, I pretend to dust off my clothes while looking down so that he can't see my eyes. After summoning a small flame of warm yellow joy, I shove it into the building across the street and straight into the chest of whoever is in the upstairs room there.

Warm sparkling pleasure wraps around me like a hug, and I drag in a deep breath of relief as my lungs finally start working again.

With effort, I cut off the connection to my magic, and look up to meet Alistair's gaze. I know that I just altered whoever is inside the house forever, but I still can't bring myself to care. I desperately needed that boost. In fact, my entire soul is pulsing insistently, begging me to do it again. It takes all of my willpower to ignore that urge.

"Yeah, I'm fine," I reply, trying to sound as casual as possible.

Alistair holds my gaze for another second, looking unconvinced. But in the end, he just shrugs. "Alright."

I send a silent prayer of thanks to Mabona that he didn't press the issue.

Goddess above, I really need to get it together. The devastating grief and the suffocating regret about not prioritizing my parents have been hitting me more frequently than I expected. I thought that I would just feel that overwhelming sense of regret that afternoon when I broke down in Orion's castle and then I would move past it.

But it's not that easy.

I can go hours without thinking of it, without even remembering that they're dead, and then the smallest thing can just set it off. Seeing some random stranger with her parents. The smell of a certain type of wood smoke that my dad came home smelling after work. Hearing a metallic rattling sound because it sounds like when my mom grabbed her box of needles to mend something. Or, like just now, when I was thinking about the things I wish I had told Draven sooner.

Another stab of agony hits my chest, and I clench my jaw to suppress the urge to use my magic again.

Goddess fucking damn it. I need to keep it together. I need to be stronger.

Forcing the regret back, I instead breathe in the roaring fury and hatred inside me until I feel that merciless fire crackling through my whole soul.

I am not the weak link. I refuse to be the weak link.

So I will pull myself together.

And I will get my fucking revenge.

"She sure is pretty," a sly voice suddenly says from my left.

I almost jump in surprise. Trying to compose myself, I give

my head a quick shake and then flick a glance in the direction of the voice. However, I am not the one who looks most startled.

Opposite me, Alistair snaps his head in the direction of the voice.

Orion Nightbane has glided out of the shadows unseen, as if he is a living breathing slice of the night itself. Sly amusement glitters in his eyes as he nods towards Lyra while meeting Alistair's gaze.

"What?" Alistair replies. Blinking, he shifts his gaze between the Unseelie King and the three dragon shifters who are making their way towards us along the darkened road. "Lyra?"

Since Isera is leaning against the wall a little farther down behind us, and therefore isn't even in the direction Orion nodded, the only person he could possibly have been referring to when he said *she* is Lyra.

Orion smirks at Alistair. "You blush a lot when you look at her."

I flick a glance at him, and sure enough, our threatening fire wielder has a hint of red staining his cheeks.

"No, I don't," he splutters.

Orion arches an eyebrow. "So you don't think she's pretty?"

"No. I mean, yes. I mean—"

"That's not what a woman wants to hear."

"Of course I think she's pretty! Look at her." Alistair throws his arm out, pointing in her direction, while that adorably flustered look on his face intensifies. "She's like the sun. All bright and warm and gorgeous and—"

The sly smirk on Orion's face deepens, and Alistair starts blushing again.

"You…" Alistair growls, and a ball of fire flares up in his palm. "I will fucking incinerate you."

"Stop tormenting him," Isera says from her place by the wall. Her eyes gleam as she slides her gaze to Orion. "Or I'll show you what real torture looks like."

"Oh, I've tortured far more people than you ever have, little viper." Orion flashes her a sharp smile. "So don't make threats you can't back up."

"Do you think she heard me?" Alistair hisses to me under his breath while casting a panicked look towards Lyra.

I briefly shift my gaze to her, Draven, and Galen, trying to estimate the distance, before meeting his eyes again and shaking my head. "No. They're too far away."

Relief washes over Alistair's face, and he extinguishes the fire in his palm.

When they reach us, Draven shoots him an exasperated look. "Getting along fine, I see."

"Like fire and highly flammable alcohol," Alistair replies.

A short chuckle escapes Draven before he snaps his mouth shut and cuts off the sound. He wasn't a big fan of Alistair and Isera in the beginning, but it looks like they've really grown on him.

"What did Artemesia say?" Isera asks from where she's still leaning against the wall a short distance away.

"Diana is with us," Draven confirms. "She has agreed to create a distraction that will draw out Bane and Jessina."

Relief flows through me. Followed by wicked anticipation that makes my blood sing. The first preparation is in place. Soon, I will take the Icehearts' most precious person from them. And that is just the beginning. I will take everything from them. Their power. Their clan. Everyone they have ever cared about. I will wipe every trace of them from this earth until it will be as if they never existed at all. And then, I will have my revenge.

"Good," Isera replies. "Then let's get this over with."

"Selena and I will head to Ferver's house so I can show her where it is," Draven says. "Galen, you take Lyra and Alistair to scout out the taverns. I trust your judgement in finding the one that best suits our needs."

Confidence seems to flow through Galen, making him

straighten his shoulders a little more, as he nods in acknowledgement.

Draven shifts his gaze to Orion and Isera. "And I trust you two not to kill each other while you handle *your* mission."

She just meets his eyes with stone cold seriousness. "I can't promise that."

A groan rips from Draven's chest, and he rubs his forehead. "Azaroth's fucking flame."

"Don't worry, you brooding beast," Orion says, a devilish smile on his dangerously beautiful face as he flicks a look full of challenge back at Isera. "I can handle her."

She just snickers. Still leaning against the wall with her arms crossed nonchalantly over her chest, she watches him with sharp eyes but thankfully doesn't escalate the conflict.

"Alright," Draven says. Drawing himself up to his full height, he looks from face to face while that effortless power that he wielded as the Commander of the Dread Legion rolls off his shoulders like pulsing black storm clouds. "This is it. We've played defense until now. Recruiting allies. Trying to make plans to stay one step ahead of them. Now, it's time to strike. So I expect all of you to keep your head in the game."

A thrumming sense of anticipation mixed with solemn seriousness sweeps over us all as we stand there gathered in the shadows on a darkened street far below the glittering Ice Palace. Warm night winds smelling of stone and ice roll down from the mountain. I draw in a deep breath.

Draven meets each of our eyes in turn.

"It's time to take the fight to them."

CHAPTER THIRTY-NINE

Anticipation courses through me as I reach up to unhook the latch on the window. I have spent too many years allowing other people to have power over me. Now, I will finally start taking it back. Instead of worrying about what everyone will think of me, I will finally shove the real truth right in their faces. I shouldn't be worried about them. They should be worried about me.

Pulling the window open on silent hinges, I rise up onto my toes and cast a quick look inside. A smile blows across my lips.

This tavern is perfect. Galen really did know what he was doing when he picked it.

It's close enough to the Silver Clan's barracks to be convenient, but not so close that it's full of off duty soldiers. Instead, only three people are sitting at the scratched wooden tables inside. Three male dragon shifters who apparently have nothing better to do during the day than to chug flagons of ale, one of whom appears to own this less than reputable establishment.

After checking to make sure that they are all still focused on the mugs before them, I grab the frame and climb onto the windowsill. Moving silently, I climb in through the window and drop down on the floor at the back of the tavern. We need to make sure that the rats have nowhere to run when we spring our trap.

I quietly close the window behind me again and then sneak across the stained floorboards and towards the open doorway that I'm assuming leads into a kitchen. Given the overpowering smell of spilled alcohol and sweat, and the distinct lack of food scents, I'm assuming that it's empty, but I glance inside anyway. Just as I predicted, only dirty pots and pans meet me when I look inside the kitchen. Twisting back around, I shift my attention back to the owner and his two patrons.

The tavern keeper is sitting by the table closest to the bar. His thick brows are furrowed as he writes something in a ledger that barely fits between the three mugs of ale that take up most of the space. A short distance away, the two patrons are seated at separate tables. Both of them have their backs to me, but based on the way they're sitting, they're in a bad mood. The one on the left is gripping his mug as if he is trying to strangle it, and the other guy sets his down with a hard thump after taking a swig.

Anger crackles through me with shocking force. What could they possibly have to be angry about? They didn't watch their parents get murdered right in front of them. They don't have to live with the devastation of never knowing if their parents loved them. They haven't been forced to stand helplessly in another city while someone whips their mate's wings and then shackles them together. They're members of the Silver Clan who rules more than half of this world. They have no idea what it means to be angry.

The door is yanked open.

From my place at the back of the tavern, I watch all three of them jerk upright at the sudden disturbance.

"Careful with the door," the owner growls from his table. "I just had it replaced after…"

He trails off, and his gray eyes widen, as Draven Ryat prowls into his dingy tavern. All color drains from the tavern keeper's face as Draven comes to a halt right inside the threshold. The door swings shut behind his muscular back with a thud.

For one single second, the entire tavern is frozen in time. I swear even the candles on the tables stop flickering for that one moment.

Then all three Silver Clan members scramble to their feet. Wood scrapes against wood as they leap out of their chairs so fast they almost knock them over. Mugs wobble on the rickety table as the guy to my right hits the table leg with his foot on the way up.

"Gorden, alert the Icehearts," the tavern keeper snaps while whipping his head towards the blond patron on my left. Then he jerks his chin at the dark-haired guy who almost knocked his table over. "Kil, get the guards."

"Oh, I wouldn't do that, if I were you," I say.

Whirling around, they stare at me in shock where I'm standing behind them, leaning one shoulder nonchalantly against the wall. Then panic flashes across their faces, and they immediately spin around again so that they don't have their backs to Draven. But since they can only face one direction, that of course leaves their backs unprotected from me. Pushing off from the wall, I start towards the three dragon shifters who are now keeping their eyes firmly on Draven.

My mate just leans back casually against the door, crossing his arms over his chest and one ankle over the other. His entire body language is practically dripping with nonchalant power and lazy arrogance. A smirk spreads across his lips, and he lets out a chuckle.

"What's so funny, traitor?" the tavern keeper snarls at him.

"The fact that you have it all wrong. I am not the most dangerous person in here." His golden eyes glint as he nods towards me. "*She* is."

The three of them quickly twist towards me again. Confusion, and a hint of wariness, flits across the tavern keeper's face as he looks me up and down. The blond patron, Gordon, does the same. The third guy, Kil, is neither convinced nor intimidated. He lets out a mocking scoff as he flicks a dismissive glance over my body before meeting my eyes. His boots thud against the stained wooden floor as he starts towards me.

"I'd recommend simply obeying our orders," I tell him while he advances on me. Sliding out my dagger, I flash him a vicious smile. "Or this is about to get messy."

Anger pulses across his face. "I will not take orders from some skinny little fae bitch who thinks she's—"

I slash my knife at him.

He jumps back, surprisingly fast for someone who has four empty mugs of ale on his table, and twists to the side to avoid the blade. It misses his chest but nicks his upper arm instead. And that is all I need.

Summoning my magic, I shove it straight at that violet spark of pain that flares up in his chest. He cries out in pain as I pour a flood of magic into it, increasing that flame until it roars like a wildfire. Screams of pure agony rip from his chest, and he collapses down on the ground.

I stand there over him, increasing the strength of my magic, and watch him writhe in pain at my feet.

"Please," he gasps out. "Please, stop."

Staring down at him with merciless eyes that are glowing with magic, I keep increasing his pain until he screams and breaks into panicked sobs. He reaches a shaking hand towards my boots.

"Please, I'm begging you," he sobs.

I kick his hand aside and continue increasing my magic.

"I'll obey," he cries. "Please, I'll do whatever you want."

A vicious smile curls my lips, but I finally cut off my magic. "See, that wasn't so hard, was it?"

He just curls in on himself and sobs on the floor.

I slide my gaze to Gordon and the tavern keeper. "Anyone else?"

Fear crashes over their features, and they quickly raise their hands and drop to their knees.

My whole soul pulses with satisfaction. All my life, I have been at someone else's mercy. So watching three grown men get down on their knees and surrender is so deeply satisfying that it makes me feel drunk on power.

Across the room, Draven watches me from where he is still leaning nonchalantly against the door. His eyes burn with such hunger that it snatches my breath right out of my lungs. It looks like he wants to shove me up against the wall and fuck my brains out right here.

The sight of it makes my soul vibrate with pleasure.

I was so worried about what Draven would think when he found out about the endless rage and hatred that have been building inside me for decades. I was worried that it would change the way he looks at me. That it would make him stop loving me.

But it hasn't. It's the exact opposite.

He loves this ruthless side of me. He loves seeing me powerful and in control. He loves the darkness in me as much as the light.

"What do you want?" the tavern keeper stammers while casting panicked glances between me and Draven.

"We want you to run up to the elite soldiers' barracks and tell Sharptail that his cousin is brawling here in your tavern," Draven says, locking eyes with the terrified man. "Bring him, and only him, here straight away."

The tavern keeper jerks his chin down in a couple of frantic nods.

"If you even think about betraying us…" A cruel smile spreads across Draven's lips.

"I won't," he stammers. "I swear, I won't."

"Excellent." Draven at last uncrosses his arms and pushes off from the door. Taking one single step to the side, he jerks his chin towards the door. "Then get to it."

The terrified tavern keeper flicks a glance at me. I nod, giving my permission as well. Scrambling up from the floor, he swallows and then starts edging towards the door.

"Today, if you don't mind," I say in response to his slow pace.

He jumps and then hurries forward with quicker steps. On the floor before me, Kil continues sobbing where he is still lying curled up on his side. Gordon, still on his knees with his hands raised, is white as a sheet. The tavern keeper cringes and bows his shoulders when he is forced to pass by right in front of Draven to reach the door.

Smug satisfaction pulses inside me as I watch him run out the door to do our bidding. Across the dirty floor, Draven and I exchange a villainous grin.

Goddess help the rest of the world when Draven and I are on the same side.

CHAPTER FORTY

"Azaroth's flame, Tim, if you get into one more brawl, I will—"

Lightning crackles through the room.

Before the door has even finished closing behind the tavern keeper, the elite Silver Clan soldier known as Sharptail is struck by Draven's lightning. His muscles spasm, and he hits the floor hard.

Summoning a bone white flame of fear, I slam it into his chest.

The tavern keeper and his two patrons are one thing, but an elite guard trained to protect the Icehearts' most precious asset is quite another. He will be too well-trained to break from just a little torture the way the others did earlier. And I'm not taking any chances.

A strangled gasp rips from Sharptail's throat as my magic slams into him while he is still trying to regain his wits after Draven's lightning strike. Pleasure immediately floods me.

Leaning against the edge of a table, I watch him try to make his muscles work properly again while I continue to increase my magic. Draven stalks up to him and grabs him by the collar.

With a firm yank, he pulls him up to his knees and locks commanding eyes on him.

Fear pulses in his eyes as he meets Draven's gaze. Most of it is mine, but I think a part of him is terrified of Draven all on his own. After all, Draven didn't earn the name *Shadow of Death* for nothing.

"Where is Lavendera?" Draven demands, his fist still buried in Sharptail's collar.

"W-what?" Sharptail stammers. "I don't—"

"Keep wasting my time, and I'll go find your precious cousin Tim instead."

I flare the wildfire of fear in his chest.

A panicked cry of terror escapes his mouth. Next to me, Gordon and Kil watch him with wide eyes from where they're kneeling on the floor. The tavern keeper remains pressed against the wall on the other side.

"She's in the library!" Sharptail presses out. "Please, don't hurt my cousin. Lavendera is in the library."

"What library?" I ask.

"That building halfway between our barracks and the palace. The one with the green door."

I glance at Draven, who is scowling down at Sharptail, before I ask, "Do you know it?"

"I've never been inside," Draven replies. "But yeah, there is only one building with a green door between the Silver Clan barracks and the Ice Palace, so I know where it is." He shifts his gaze back to the guard before him. "How often is she there?"

"All the time." Sharptail stares back at him, his eyes wide with fear as I continue to increase my magic. "It started like two days ago. She's being kept in there all the time. I think there is some kind of massive, important project she's working on. I don't know. I'm not responsible for guarding her this week. Please. That's all I know."

Cold dread washes through my veins as understanding dawns inside me.

"The Gold Clan," I blurt out.

Draven flicks his gaze to me, and realization hits him as well. "Fuck."

My heart pounds, but I say it out loud anyway as I try to combat the feeling of suddenly being incredibly pressed for time. "She's looking for information about what happened to the Gold Clan. What else would she be doing in a library?"

"Yeah," Draven agrees. "We need to get going."

I nod. Spinning the knife in my hand, I slit Kil's throat.

Across the room, Draven does the same to Sharptail.

The moment Draven cuts his throat, my magic detaches from his chest and that warm sparkling feeling of pleasure disappears. I suck in a shuddering breath at the cold harshness that replaces it, but the sound is thankfully drowned out by the crack of lightning.

Gordon and the tavern keeper drag in synchronized gasps, but they're cut off when white bolts of lightning hit them in the chest. They tense up and then hit the floor. Dead.

I blink hard a couple of times, still trying to push aside that jarring feeling when the pleasant effects of my magic disappeared. My mind urges me to connect my magic again. Just for a little while. To make the transition smoother. I manage to suppress the urge with great effort. We have a job to do.

"Let's go," I say, more to get my own head back in the game rather than to Draven, while wiping off my knife and sliding it back in my thigh holster.

Draven does the same with his blade before shouldering the door open. Once we're outside, he pulls out a pair of lockpicks and locks the door behind us to prevent anyone from going inside and seeing the dead people on the floor. No prying eyes watch him as he finishes his task.

Since it was nighttime when Galen and the others scouted out this place last night, it was impossible to know if this street would be busy now during daytime. Thankfully, it's as deserted now as it was yesterday. Only silent stone houses watch us as Draven and I pull up the hoods of our cloaks again and start jogging down the street.

Though, the reason for the strange emptiness on a lot of streets in this city is quite sinister. I realized it when we first arrived. There are no humans in Frostfell anymore.

I have no idea what happened after I lit the spark of the human rebellion here last year, but since the Icehearts still control the city, the humans obviously didn't win. And now, there are no humans at all in this city. I don't know if that means that the Icehearts executed them all or if they just banished them.

And I simply cannot bring myself to care. I know that I am partly responsible for whatever happened to them. But I don't feel bad about it. I'm so done feeling bad about doing what needs to be done. So I push the thought of it out of my mind and instead focus on our more pressing problem. Our incredibly time-sensitive problem.

"If Lavendera finds the Gold Clan..." I begin while we hurry towards our rendezvous point. "If the Icehearts get the Gold Clan, and then the Green Clan too, it's over."

"I know. We need to finish this before she succeeds."

My heart pounds as I feel that sudden time limit hit me. We've made a plan, and we always wanted to execute it as fast as possible, but now that unexpected stress of fighting against the clock is making me jittery.

I have no idea what is going on inside Lavendera's head most of the time, but what I do know is that she is smart. Dangerously smart. She managed to fool not just me, but every single contestant in the Atonement Trials, into thinking that she was one of us. And even afterwards in the Ice Palace, she managed to trick me into trusting her and caring about her and sharing my plans of escape with her. And all the while, she was working undercover for the Icehearts. Despite being halfway insane, she is also viciously intelligent.

If she has been locked in that library for the past two days with the sole task of finding out what happened to the Gold Clan, there is no telling how much she might have already pieced together. So we need to get her out of there. Right now. Before she gives the Icehearts the key to winning this war.

Disbelief ripples through me, and I even shake my head at the absurdity of it all, as Draven and I jog the final streets down to our meeting spot. I knew that Lavendera was an important player in this game, but I never expected that that crazy girl would end up being the key to the whole thing.

If we get Lavendera, we will take away the Icehearts' ability to use dragon steel, which means that we will be able to get Rin Tanaka on our side. And once we have her on our side, we will have half of the other clans on our side as well. Including the all-important Green Clan, who might even be able to tell us how the partnership between dragon shifters and Seelie fae works. It will also get us the dryads, who are both terrifyingly powerful and also connected to the entire continent.

And all of it comes down to one certifiably insane fae woman who is blindly loyal to our enemies.

How the hell are we going to get this done in time?

"Do you have a location?" Galen calls as Draven and I draw closer to our prearranged meeting point.

Alistair is casting worried glances up and down the street while Lyra is practically bouncing on her feet in anticipation. Orion and Isera are nowhere to be seen.

"Yes," Draven replies as we run the final few steps and skid to a halt before them. "She's been locked in a library for the past few days."

"Searching for the Gold Clan, we think," I finish with a grimace.

"Shit," Galen curses. "Where?"

"That building with the green door halfway between the Silver Clan barracks and the palace," Draven says. "I was never stationed there myself, for obvious reasons, so I don't know what the security is like around the building. Do you?"

He shakes his head. "No."

"Lyra?" Draven asks.

"No, that was always Silver Clan territory," she says with an apologetic shrug.

"Fuck. Alright, we need to head there right now and scout it out. We've made plans for how to handle the abduction if she was in the Ice Palace or out in the city. This changes everything. We need to know what we're looking at before all hell breaks loose, otherwise this will never work."

Alistair continues flicking his gaze up and down the street. "What about Isera and Orion? They're not back yet."

"We'll have to meet back up with them afterwards instead. We can't afford to waste any more time. We have no way of knowing how close Lavendera is to figuring out what happened to the Gold Clan, and if she succeeds before we can get her—"

"We'll lose this war," Alistair finishes with a grim nod.

"Yeah." Draven jerks his chin. "Let's go."

We take off up the street and towards the area between the Silver Clan barracks and the Ice Palace. Our cloaks flutter behind us as we run. My heart pounds as a few people glance our way in surprise when we hurry past, but with our faces partially hidden underneath hoods, no one should be able to recognize us. I still throw my magic out across every street we pass, aiming for those yellow-green sparks of suspicion in people's chests, and decrease their suspicion until they don't even think twice about a cloaked group hurrying up the street.

Draven, who immediately figures out what I'm doing, gives me a grateful nod.

"So, you think I'm like the sun, huh?" Lyra suddenly says in a light voice as we round another corner.

Alistair chokes on his breath. Coughing desperately, he casts a panicked look at her.

So, she apparently did hear him earlier.

"Focus," Draven says, flicking a pointed glance at Lyra.

From her other side, Alistair casts a relieved look at Draven. I have never seen him look that grateful for Draven's orders before.

"We'll split up to cover more ground," Draven continues as we draw closer to our target area. "I'll scout out the north side. Selena, you'll handle the west."

I shoot him a sly smile. "Yes, sir."

His eyes glint as he meets my gaze for a second before shifting it to Galen. "You and Lyra, take the south side. And Alistair, you'll handle the east."

"Why can't I team up with Alistair?" Lyra complains. "He's so much more fun than grumpy over here."

"Because I need Galen to keep your recklessness in check," Draven replies before shooting a pointed look at the fire wielder on her right. "And Alistair is just as crazy as you. This is a stealth mission. An important, time sensitive stealth mission. And together, the two of you are as subtle as a fucking volcano eruption."

Alistair looks caught between a scowl and an unapologetic grin.

Lyra just laughs. "Well, can't argue with that, I suppose."

"Alright, split up," Draven says, and jerks his chin. "We'll meet back at the rendezvous point."

We take off in different directions as we reach the next crossroads.

My heart patters in my chest as I follow a small winding path between two houses, heading towards the west side of the large building up ahead. Most houses in this section of the city have painted their doors in shades of blue. Everything from pale sky blue to royal midnight blue. So it's thankfully easy to deduce which building is our target.

I slow down as I draw closer to the grand structure made of white stone.

That terrible sense of stress tears at my insides.

Lavendera is in there somewhere. She could be one single minute away from finding something that will tell her where the Gold Clan is, and there is no way for me to know.

With my pulse thrumming in my ears, I sneak around the final building and peer out at the library ahead. Dread sluices through my veins.

There are at least ten guards from the Silver Clan standing in the open area between my hiding spot and the library. And on this side, there is no cover between it and where I am. Nothing at all to hide behind while sneaking closer.

Summoning my magic again, I throw it across the entire area. Not just the west side but all the other sides as well. More dread crawls up my throat when my magic connects with yellow-green sparks of suspicion in over thirty chests. There must be around ten guards watching every side of the building.

"Mabona's tits," I curse under my breath.

While decreasing their sparks of suspicion, so that none of us will be spotted, I remain there pressed against the wall while studying the area in front of me.

The grand library sits on a flat stretch of stone. There are no other houses or buildings or any types of structures close to it as far as I can see. I had kind of expected it to at least have a wall or something around it. That way, we would've had some kind of cover to hide behind at least. But there is nothing. The guards who surround the library have a clear and completely uninterrupted view of their surroundings. Getting past them unseen is going to be difficult.

I shift my gaze to the library itself. There are no windows on the building. Which is no doubt great for the books since it protects them from being damaged by sunlight, but it makes breaking into the damn thing very difficult. To get in, we will need to go through the door. I can't see it from the west side, but I suspect that it's closely guarded and probably locked as well.

It's frustrating as hell, but at least it proves one thing. Lavendera really is in there. There is no other reason for why they would guard a library this heavily.

My heart thumps as I flick my gaze from side to side, trying to figure out how in Mabona's name we're supposed to get inside before that insane woman can find the answer to a problem that would win the Icehearts the war.

From my vantage point, I can't see any possible way for us to get inside the library and abduct Lavendera without having to fight forty Silver Clan guards, which would just alert the whole city to our presence and screw up our entire plan.

So in the end, it will all come down to Isera and Orion.

If they can succeed with their part of the plan, we might have a shot at this. If not, we're screwed. Which brings us back to the worrying fact that they weren't at the meeting point.

Hopefully, they haven't killed each other.

CHAPTER FORTY-ONE

By the time afternoon arrives, I'm so stressed out that I have to actively suppress the urge to crawl up the walls. I just want to get this over with, but we can't begin until Diana starts her distraction. Pacing back and forth in the shadows of a deserted alley, I try to calm my pounding heart.

"It's time."

I jump as Draven comes running into the alley. Since we can't cluster together without drawing attention, we've had to spread out across several streets so that we just look like individual people loitering about instead of a group of traitors who are planning for a heist.

"It's time," Draven repeats as he comes to a halt in front of me. "Diana sent word that the distraction has begun. Bane and Jessina should receive word of it within the hour. And they should fly off straight away once they do."

Should.

Worry twists inside my stomach like cold snakes.

They *should* hear about it within the hour. They *should* fly off. Our entire plan is based on a whole lot of *shoulds*. Specific people need to react in specific ways to specific events, and all of it needs to happen in a very specific order. If even one of those things goes wrong, half of my friends could end up dead.

Draven slides his strong hands along my cheeks, tilting my head back so that I meet his gaze. "Be careful. If anything goes wrong, send up the signal immediately. Don't wait. Don't hesitate. Because no matter where you are, I will find you and I will get you out."

My heart squeezes tight, and I reach up to grip his wrist as worry crashes through me again. "*You* be careful. The three of you have the most dangerous job."

"Just promise me." He holds my gaze. Insistent. Urgent.

I swallow at the intensity in his eyes. "I promise."

"Good." Leaning down, he presses his lips against mine in a desperate kiss. With his eyes still closed, he rests his forehead against mine for a second. Then he lets out a shuddering breath. "Let's go get everything."

A short laugh full of desperation and hope and worry rips from my lungs. "Yes, let's go get fucking everything."

He steals one last kiss from my lips before tearing himself away and running back down the street the way he came. I watch his perfect body until it disappears around the corner. Nausea rolls through me the moment he's gone. I don't want to let him out of my sight. I don't want to lose him again. We've lost so much time already, and there are so many things that could go wrong with this plan.

I try to swallow down that sense of dread. I suddenly have a really bad feeling about this.

Trying to block it out, I give my head a hard shake and spin on my heel. I don't have time to worry right now. I need to get Alistair and then we need to get going. Sprinting around the corner, I hurry onto the next street.

"It's time," I call.

Alistair, who was lounging casually against the wall, jerks up straight and snaps his gaze to me. "Now?"

"Now." Running up to him, I continue past and down the street. "Let's go."

He scrambles to catch up and then falls in beside me as we make our way towards our target. People on the streets blink in surprise and frown at us. Keeping my head slightly bowed, I make sure that my eyes aren't visible as I latch on to those yellow-green sparks of suspicion with my magic and decrease them until everyone just shrugs and continues going about their day.

Anger courses through me like crackling lightning. Anger at myself. At the pathetic person I used to be. I was born to do this. Alistair and I can run through a dragon shifter city in very conspicuous cloaks without people even thinking twice about it because I can manipulate them into not feeling suspicious. I possess incredibly powerful magic, and I'm incredibly skilled at using it. I should never have let the fae resistance keep me stuck as a lookout.

Instead of being so concerned with other people's opinions, with wanting them to like me, I should have just marched into our leaders' meeting and demanded my place among them. Demanded respect and responsibility.

So much wasted time. So many wasted opportunities. Just because I wanted to be liked. Just because I wanted people to approve of me and accept me.

But growing up the way I did, it was impossible not to seek that approval. In school, our teachers taught me that everything bad that has ever happened in the history of this continent was my fault. That I was wicked and cruel and that I needed to atone.

And on top of that, my parents also—

Pain and regret slam into me with such force that I feel like my chest caved in. Stumbling a step to the side, I have to throw out my arm and push off against the wall to straighten myself as I continue to run. I can feel Alistair glance at me in silent question where he is running next to me, but I can't concentrate enough to even look at him.

The street around me blurs as I try to focus through the agony-filled regret that tears at my chest like vicious claws.

That unfinished sentence echoes inside my skull.

And on top of that, my parents also hated me for ruining their marriage.

Or they didn't.

I will never know.

Regret squeezes my lungs, strangling every drop of air from them. I try to suck in a desperate breath, but I can't make my chest expand. It feels like my chest is trapped in a massive vise which just keeps tightening.

Releasing my grip on my magic, I stop lowering people's suspicion and instead summon an emotion from nothing. This time, I don't choose a positive emotion such as joy. No. This time, I summon a black flame of despair and slam it right into the closest dragon shifter's chest while Alistair and I run past.

That warm sparkling pleasure immediately floods my entire body. I suck in a deep breath as that horrible strangling sensation finally disappears from my chest.

On the street behind me, the dragon shifter lets out a sob of despair. I cast a glance at him over my shoulder as we continue down the road. He crumples to the ground with another sob, pulling attention away from me and Alistair and instead drawing it to himself. That wasn't the reason I chose despair, though. I did it because he deserved it. It's high time that the Silver Clan feels what the rest of us have been forced to endure under their rule.

I continue increasing his despair for another few seconds before I manage to sever the connection. The more I create emotions from nothing, the harder it becomes to let them go.

"You okay?" Alistair asks in a casual voice that somehow holds absolutely no judgement at all.

Mabona's tits, I really did misjudge Alistair when I first met him back in the Seelie Court.

"Yeah," I reply as we round a corner. Then I nod towards a house halfway down the street. "This is it."

"Alright. Same plan as we talked about?"

"Same plan."

"I'll wait two minutes."

I nod and then take a sharp right into a narrow alley while he continues straight ahead. Darting between two tall stone houses, I slip around the row of buildings so that I'm instead approaching our target from the back.

My chest heaves from the long run and the temporary issues I had with breathing, so I slow to a walk once I get closer to the house up ahead so that I can properly scan the area for threats. While drawing in deep breaths to calm my thrumming pulse, I study the buildings around me. They look empty. I shift my gaze to my target building as it appears before me.

Ferver Osteria, the leader of the scouts, lives in a two-story house with a sizeable garden and a stone fence around it to give him privacy from his neighbors. Though according to Draven, it's not actually Ferver's house. It's Papa Osteria's house. Apparently, the powerful leader of the scouts has no interest in starting a family of his own, so he still lives with his parents and his younger sister, despite the fact that both he and his sister are over two hundred years old.

I flick a glance over the well-kept lawn and the immaculately trimmed bushes and artfully planted flowers as I edge open the back gate and sneak through the garden. Someone either loves gardening or has way too much time on their hands.

The back door is locked, but thanks to Draven's earlier tutoring, I manage to get it open with a pair of lockpicks.

Cheerful voices drift out as I edge the back door open and slip inside.

"Can you hand me the bowl?" a woman's voice calls.

I close the door softly behind me while clanging and clinking sounds echo from what I assume must be the kitchen.

"No, not that one," the woman replies with a laugh. "Azaroth's flame, honey, we've been married for four hundred years, and you still don't know which bowl is the salad bowl?"

"It's a bowl," a man's voice responds. "They all look the same."

"Honestly, Dad," another female voice says in a teasing tone. "You really are hopeless."

He chuckles. "Says the daughter who refuses to move out."

Anger streaks through me, and I have to squeeze my hand into a fist to stop myself from moving closer. Why do they get to have a happy family life when their clan has destroyed mine forever? By Mabona, I want to kill them all.

The front door is pulled open.

"Ferver?" Mama Osteria calls from the kitchen. "You're early, darling. We weren't expecting you for another half hour."

Alistair strides in through the front door and closes it behind him. I shift my gaze to him from where I'm standing at the other end of the hallway. He gives me a nod. Moving on silent feet, I sneak closer to the doorway that all the voices are coming from while Alistair walks towards it with more determined steps.

"Dinner isn't quite ready yet," Ferver's mother calls as we draw closer. "Do you need to get back early?"

Just as Draven said, Ferver comes back to eat dinner with his family every night before he returns to his post at the scouts' headquarters. Though, as his mother just commented, he usually arrives half an hour from now.

Alistair and I reach the open doorway at the same time. I give him a nod to indicate that the garden outside is empty and that there were no signs of their neighbors either. He returns it, confirming that it was the same at the front of the house. Since this might get a little loud and messy, we had to make sure that no one would hear us and sound the alarm.

Once we've confirmed that we'll have as much privacy as we

can get inside a crowded city, we round the corner and step inside the spacious kitchen.

It's much bigger than I would have expected. There is a stove and an oven connected to a chimney on the back wall, and lots of counters on both sides that provide ample space to work. Logs crackle and pop in the fire underneath the metal stove, and two pots are resting on top of it. The scent of herbs flows through the air as the food in the pots bubbles merrily.

Between the kitchen section and the doorway is a large table for six. Four places have been set with shining plates and cutlery. I sweep a quick glance over everything before fixing my gaze on the three dragon shifters in the room.

Mama Osteria is chopping salad that she is scooping into the bowl next to her while her husband stirs one of the pots. Ferver's sister is searching for something in one of the drawers, which makes a rattling sound.

My heart jerks and then squeezes painfully as that rattling sound triggers a memory of my mother. I panic as my lungs threaten to cease working again, so I quickly throw open the doors to the rage burning inside me and breathe it in.

"Ferver?" his mother says and starts lifting her head to look up towards the doorway. "Did you—"

She gasps.

The bowl is knocked clean off the counter as she jerks back. It hits the floor with a wooden clattering and rolls to the side, sending salad and beans tumbling out onto the pale stone floor.

Papa Osteria whips around, the ladle in his hand flinging drops of stew through the air, and Ferver's sister jerks upright from the drawer with a knife in her hand.

"Put the fucking knife down," Alistair warns, his voice as vicious as it was back when we were living in the Seelie Court. It has been a long time since I heard him sound like that.

"You—" Papa Osteria begins.

Fire roars through the kitchen. The entire family gasps and

stumbles back as Alistair sends flames rushing up all around them.

Summoning my own magic, I latch on to the bone white sparks of fear in their three chests and blow them into wildfires. Panicked cries rip from their lungs as they throw their arms above their heads to protect themselves.

"You heard him," I snarl at them, rage still coursing through my chest like a living breathing thing. "Put the fucking knife down."

Metal clatters against stone as Ferver's sister drops the knife in her hand. Even Papa Osteria drops his ladle.

"Kick it towards me," I order.

With terrified green eyes staring at me as if I'm a demon, Ferver's sister kicks the knife towards me. It slides across the stone floor, the scraping sound almost drowned out by the flames that still crackle in the air around them.

I just stare her down with merciless eyes. "Kneel."

With my magic still increasing their fear, they're too terrified to resist so they just drop to their knees. Alistair finally lets his fire magic fade out, but the Osteria family still doesn't dare to move. I keep my magic connected to them, increasing it until all three of them are shaking with terror, while Alistair stalks up to them and pulls three lengths of rope from his belt pouch.

Whimpers escape Mama Osteria's lips as Alistair efficiently ties their hands behind their backs. Once they're all tied up, he walks back around them so that he is standing in front of them. I join him and then increase their fear a little more as Alistair summons a crackling ball of flame in his palm.

"Stay on your knees and keep your mouths shut," he orders. The fire in his palm grows larger. "I would hate to have to burn this house down with you in it."

Terrified whimpers spill from their lips, and they cower down before us.

A rush of power soars through me. I drink it in greedily. This is how it's supposed to be. Them, on their knees, before us. Before *me*. It's their turn to be afraid. It's their turn to kneel and bow and grovel. It's their turn to feel what it's like to be truly powerless.

Alistair strolls over to the table and pulls out a chair. It scrapes loudly against the floor in the otherwise dead silent room. I join him. Dropping down on a chair, I swing my feet up and cross my ankles as I rest my boots on the edge of the table.

"And now, we wait," Alistair says to me in a low voice.

I nod. *And now, we wait.*

Ferver should be coming here in less than thirty minutes.

And there it is again.

Should.

He *should* be coming.

My heart starts pounding in my chest as that stress thrums inside me again like a violent storm.

Ferver should come home for dinner tonight.

But if he doesn't, Draven, Galen, and Lyra are going to die.

CHAPTER FORTY-TWO

When forty minutes have passed and Ferver still hasn't shown up, I'm ready to burn the entire house down. The Osteria family watches me with worried eyes as I pace back and forth across their kitchen. Whatever they were cooking is now likely inedible since the fire in the stove when out twenty minutes ago, so the scent of food and herbs has now been replaced by the sharp tang of fear.

The front door is yanked open. Whirling around, I snap my gaze to the open doorway that connects the kitchen and the hallway while hope and anticipation pulse through me.

"The Icehearts just left," Alistair calls as the front door thuds closed behind him.

Disappointment and worry tear at my chest. Both at the fact that it was only Alistair, rather than Ferver, who walked through the door and at the news he brought. He rounds the corner and walks into the kitchen.

"I just saw the two of them fly away from the Ice Palace," he says.

I curse under my breath.

"There is still time," he adds, his voice low enough that only I can hear. "As long as he arrives within the next ten minutes, we're fine."

If he arrives, my mind corrects silently. He has to arrive. Goddess fucking damn it, he has to. Because I will not lose Draven again. If the Icehearts and the Silver Clan try to take Draven from me again, I swear by every god and goddess and every demon in hell that I will burn this entire world down until there is nothing left but ash.

With great effort, I manage to nod in response to Alistair's statement. But I immediately begin pacing again. Stress and worry rip through my soul like vicious beasts. Flexing my hands, I stalk back and forth across the floor while I increase and decrease the Osteria family's fear just to pass the time.

They whimper and cower down, and then suck in deep breaths, over and over again as I toy with their fear levels. They deserve it. Goddess damn it, this entire fucking clan deserves to suffer after everything they have put me through. They—

The front door is pulled open.

"I'm back!" a man's voice calls while hurried footsteps move towards the kitchen. "Sorry I'm late. The meeting ran long."

Snapping out of my anxiousness, I yank out the dagger from my thigh holster and quickly move so that I'm standing behind Ferver's mother. She whimpers in fear as I place the knife across her throat. Alistair moves so that he is standing by the wall right inside the doorway. That way, he can move up behind Ferver once he steps inside.

"I hope you didn't..." Ferver continues as he rounds the corner and enters the now messy kitchen. Trailing off, he staggers to a halt a couple of steps inside and stares at the scene before him with wide eyes.

I get a sudden overwhelming urge to slit his mother's throat, just so that he can feel what I felt when Jessina killed *my* mother. But we still need Ferver to do what we want, which means that we need all the hostages alive, so I manage to ignore the sudden murderous urge.

"Here's what's going to happen," I begin, my voice coming out shockingly hard and cold. "You're going to run up to the Silver Clan barracks and tell every soldier you come across that your scouts have seen four different clans flying in to attack Frostfell at the same time. You're going to tell them that the Icehearts have been alerted and are on their way back, and that every available soldier needs to shift and fly out across the plains in all directions to defend the city."

For a few seconds, he just stares at me in shock and utter incredulity. Then anger crackles across his face, and he reaches for the sword at his hip.

A wall of fire roars up behind him. He gasps and whirls around while staggering away from it. On the other side of the flames, Alistair flashes him a cruel smile.

"If you disobey even one single part of those orders," I continue. "We will burn down this house with your entire family in it."

His parents and sister let out terrified whimpers where they remain on their knees before me.

Ferver whirls back around to face me. Fear battles the anger on his face. I run out of patience.

Releasing the grip on the magic I have flowing into his family, I summon a bone white flame of fear out of nothing and slam it into Ferver's chest.

He sucks in an unsteady breath, and his knees almost buckle. Throwing out a hand, he has to brace himself on the back of a chair to keep himself upright.

"Alright, I'll do it!" he blurts out, his green eyes wide and desperate.

Pleasure thrums inside me, both from creating an emotion out of nothing and also from the sheer satisfaction of finally being the one in control. The one with all the power.

"Good." I stare him down from where I'm still standing with my knife to his mother's throat. "If you deviate even slightly from your orders, or if you tell anyone about this, you will come home to a burnt-out house with three charred skeletons inside. Understood?"

With every word out of my mouth, I increase his fear even more. His face is ashen as he nods desperately.

Satisfied, I lower his fear back down again as much as possible so that he will be able to carry out his orders. Leaving the rest of the flame that I still can't remove, I force myself to cut off the flow of my magic. Coldness rushes in to replace the sparkling warmth. The sharp contrast just makes the anger and fury inside me even stronger.

Across the room, Alistair lets his fire magic fade out as well. I jerk my chin at Ferver.

After casting a fearful glance at his family, he pries his fingers off the back of the chair and staggers towards the door. Alistair slides his gaze to him. Ferver flinches, but when no more flames appear, he quickly hurries out into the hallway and then back out the front door to do our bidding.

"Alright, let's get them into that closet in the hallway," Alistair says.

It takes enormous effort to force my knife away from Mama Osteria's throat. I fucking hate this family. This happy, loving family that has a future together even after all of this is over. That roaring rage and hatred inside me is screaming at me to kill them all so that Ferver will return and see it and then be forced to live with the same pain that I am constantly battling.

My fingers grip the hilt hard as I force my knife back into its sheath while Alistair crosses the room and grabs Papa Osteria by the arm. Even though I'm no longer manipulating his fear, he doesn't resist when Alistair yanks him up from the floor and starts hauling him across the room. I pry my fingers off the hilt of my knife and then jerk my chin at Ferver's mother and sister.

"Get up," I order.

With their hands still tied behind their backs, they struggle to their feet.

"Let's go," I say, and jerk my chin towards the doorway.

Mama Osteria looks at me with wide and terrified eyes, but Ferver's sister glares at me now that I'm no longer manipulating her fear. Anger flickers in her green eyes, and she tosses her long blond hair back over her shoulder with a jerky motion. But she and her mother still walk willingly across the kitchen and through the hallway to the small room filled with cleaning supplies.

Alistair is already there with his prisoner, who has now gotten down on his knees inside the closet, while Alistair remains in the hallway outside.

"Get in and get down on your knees," I tell my two prisoners.

The mother quickly hurries inside and does what she is told while keeping her gaze on the floor. The sister, however, stares daggers at me as she does the same. I just stand there in the doorway, watching her get down on her knees between her parents, while more fury roars up inside me. Why is she glaring at me like that? I am the one who is angry. I am the one who has been wronged. They deserve everything they're getting.

"We should just kill them all," I say, not taking my eyes off the glaring sister.

Her parents whimper, but she just clenches her jaw.

Next to me, Alistair raises an eyebrow in silent question.

"If we let them live, they will just ruin everything." Rage and hatred churn inside me as I flex my hand in an effort to block out the memories of my own parents, which are trying to flash before my eyes. "It's what they do. This entire fucking Silver Clan. All they ever do is destroy everything around them."

"*We* destroy things?" the sister suddenly snarls. "You're the one who—"

I shove my magic towards the tiny spark of pain in her chest.

She has been kneeling on a stone floor for the past forty minutes, so I knew that she would at least be feeling a little pain. Latching on to that violet spark, I increase it in a rapid burst.

She screams in pain.

Her parents whip their heads around to stare at her in shock and panic before turning desperate eyes on me. They don't know exactly what I'm doing, but they can see my eyes glowing, so they know that I'm doing *something*.

"Please, stop!" Papa Osteria yells at me.

I increase the strength of my magic again. Even though there is no pleasure this time, since I didn't create the pain from nothing, satisfaction still courses through me as I watch the blond dragon shifter bow forward and scream in pain again.

"Why are you doing this?" her mother cries.

I keep the pain steady, making my victim gasp and bow forward until she is pressing her forehead against the floor. "Because you killed my parents."

Jerking upright, the sister suddenly locks furious green eyes on me. Her blond ponytail swishes through the air from the sharp movement and slaps against her back. Anger crackles across her whole face, pushing out the pain for a moment.

"I haven't killed anyone!" she growls.

"Yes, you have," I reply, my voice hard and merciless. Fury roars inside me. "Your entire clan has."

"My clan? What are you talking about?"

"Jessina killed my parents."

"I'm not Jessina!"

"You're a part of her clan. Which means that you are just as guilty as she is."

"No!" she screams at me, her voice splitting the air like the crack of thunder. "I haven't done anything. Why are you hurting *me*? I've never even seen you before. *I* haven't done anything!"

I stagger back as a sudden realization hits me like a gut punch. Sucking in a sharp breath, I stumble backwards and hit the wall on the other side of the hallway. I feel like I've been kicked in the chest by a horse.

Because suddenly, I don't see a blond dragon shifter glaring back at me with furious green eyes.

I see a silver-haired fae with eyes that are a mix of turquoise and lavender.

My eyes.

Me.

I see *me*.

I see myself, screaming at Draven with anger and outrage in my eyes. Screaming in frustration and hurt and utter desperation that what they're doing isn't fair. That I never enslaved any dragon shifters. That I am being punished for a crime that I didn't even commit.

Bane and Jessina's voices echo inside my skull.

It's your turn to live in poverty. It's your turn to struggle. It's your turn to be slaves.

You need to be punished for what your ancestors did.

You deserve everything you got.

Their voices morph into my own.

This is where he belongs. Cowering on his knees before me. This is where they all belong.

He deserved it. It's high time that the Silver Clan feels what the rest of us have been forced to endure under their rule. This is how it's supposed to be. Them, on their knees, before us. Before me. It's their turn to be afraid. It's their turn to kneel and bow and grovel. It's their turn to feel what it's like to be truly powerless.

I want to slit his mother's throat, just so that he can feel what I felt when Jessina killed my *mother.*

They deserve this.

They deserve everything they're getting.

Bile surges up inside my throat.

Slapping a hand in front of my mouth to stop the vomit, I stare back at the Osteria family with wide eyes. Bane and

Jessina's cruel voices continue echoing inside my mind, saying all the exact same things that I have been thinking for weeks now.

Cold horror washes through me.

I am turning into them.

Oh Goddess above, I am turning into the Icehearts.

"I need air," I gasp out to Alistair.

Without even waiting for an answer, I rush past him and towards the back door. Throwing it open, I burst out into the neat garden full of trimmed bushes and artfully placed flowers. I only make it three steps before my knees buckle.

Crashing down on the grass, I bend over the flower bed in front of me and puke. My stomach heaves as I vomit into the colorful flowers over and over again. Digging my fingers into the soft grass, I grip it hard as I empty the entire contents of my stomach into that flower bed.

Once there is nothing left to throw up, I gasp air back into my lungs. Gripping the grass tighter, I try to keep myself from swaying as the entire world around me seems to tilt.

That cold panic remains inside me like ice, freezing my blood and keeping me trapped there on the grass, while horrifying similarities dawn before my eyes.

Similarities between me and Jessina Iceheart.

When she was young, she had no power because she was enslaved by that group of fae. So when she got free, she relished the feeling of having power over others. Relished the feeling of being the one in control. The one who gives the orders. The one who gets to watch everyone else bow and beg at her feet.

I've done the same. Ever since I escaped the Ice Palace, I have breathed in the intoxicating power I've felt when I have been in control. I've loved every single second of those moments when I've had the power. When I've made people kneel and obey my orders.

And Jessina killed my parents in retaliation for me hurting Bane, her fated mate.

I vowed to do the same. After she hurt Draven and murdered my parents, I vowed to kill everyone she has ever cared about.

She was humiliated and violated by that small group of fae six thousand years ago, so she spent the rest of her life getting revenge on *all* fae. She punished innocents simply because they belonged to the same nation as the ones who hurt her.

I did the same. She killed my parents, so I vowed to wipe out the entire Silver Clan. I almost killed this family today for that exact reason. Even though they are completely innocent of the crime. They are civilians. They don't even know who I am. Let alone that Jessina has killed my parents.

My stomach heaves, and I vomit again. But nothing comes out. Only bile that burns like acid in my throat.

Oh Goddess.

I am more similar to Jessina Iceheart than I want to admit.

Dragging in an unsteady breath, I try to slow my pounding heart. My entire head is spinning. With great effort, I release my death grip on the grass and push myself away from the now ruined flower bed. Sitting back on my ass, I draw my knees up and rest my elbows on them while I rake my fingers through my hair. And then I just breathe.

Fuck. What am I doing?

If I start taking my fury out on innocent civilians, I'm no better than the Icehearts.

There has to be a line.

Goddess above, there has to be a line. There *is* a line. And this is it. *This* is the line that I won't cross.

Orion was right. Only a villain can take down another villain.

And I *will* be a villain to my enemies. I will be utterly merciless and completely ruthless to anyone who stands in my way.

I will get my fucking revenge. All of it. But on the *right* people. Not on innocent civilians. I will not take revenge on people for a crime they haven't committed.

They are not responsible for what the Icehearts have done. Just like I am not responsible for what that small group of entitled fae did six thousand years ago.

Dropping my hands from my hair, I tilt my head back and gaze up at the overcast sky above. Thick dark gray clouds float lazily over the heavens. A couple of birds soar past high above.

I drag in a deep breath.

It disturbs me to my core that I actually understand Jessina and Bane now. I understand the rage, the hatred, the intoxicating feeling of power, and the feral need for revenge. I understand it all.

Because I want it too. The only difference is that now, I will only direct it at the people who deserve it. I won't take out my fury on innocents. I won't torture sisters or slit the throats of mothers just because I'm angry about what someone else has done.

I will happily kill and torture the people who do the Icehearts bidding, because *they* are standing in the way of our freedom.

And I still want revenge. I remember the pain Draven had to endure when the Icehearts whipped his wings. I remember the fear and shock on my parents face when they died on a cold stone floor in pools of their own blood. I remember the crippling regret that still hits me every time I'm reminded that I will never know if my parents loved me.

I don't want justice for that.

I want revenge.

Vicious, merciless revenge.

And I will get it.

I will carve that revenge out of Bane and Jessina's bodies until they have paid for it with their blood. Because they killed my parents. And they hurt Draven. They tortured him and enslaved him for two hundred years. I would kill them for that alone. He is *mine*.

So I will get my revenge on the Icehearts and everyone who

helps them. But I will not cross that final line and punish an entire clan for a crime that only a few of them committed. I am disturbingly similar to Jessina Iceheart in how I react to things. So I need to pull myself back from the edge. I cannot cross that final line. I refuse to become a new Jessina.

I will get fucking everything.

But I will not become *her*.

CHAPTER FORTY-THREE

Dread twists inside me as I open the back door and slip inside. I don't want to face Alistair. He saw everything. He saw me torture an innocent woman for a crime she has not committed. How am I supposed to explain everything that has been going through my head for weeks?

While trying to swallow down that sense of dread, I walk past the now closed door to the cleaning closet and approach the open doorway to the kitchen. But before I reach it, Alistair steps out.

My heart jerks.

"Here," he says, and hands me a glass of water. "I've locked the Osteria family in the closet. By the time Ferver comes back to let them out, it will be too late for him to warn people about us anyway. So I think we should just go meet up with the others."

Taking the glass of water, I stare at him in disbelief. Isn't he going to... I don't know, mention it? What I just did? How terrifyingly similar I am to Jessina Iceheart? Anything?

He doesn't. And there is not a single shred of judgement on his face. He looks at me in exactly the same way as he always does. As if this didn't change his perception of me in the slightest.

Still stunned, I walk over to the kitchen sink and raise the glass of water to my lips. After rinsing my mouth, I drink the rest of the water. It helps soothe some of that acidic taste of bile in my throat.

"They've started taking off," Alistair says, craning his neck to look out the window. "We should hurry."

"Yeah," I reply.

After setting down the glass on the counter, I jog after Alistair towards the front door.

The city outside is in chaos. Ferver apparently followed our orders to tell every soldier he met on the way up to the barracks about the fake invasion as well, because silver dragons explode into view in open squares and atop rooftops all around us. Dragons roar and wings boom through the air as they push off and shoot into the sky.

I drag in a deep breath, still trying to get my wits back after the horrifying realization in the Osteria house and my embarrassing breakdown in the garden. Alistair still says nothing about what just happened. I glance over at him where he is jogging up the street next to me.

"Thank you," I say, my voice so soft that it's barely audible over the screeching dragons that take off into the sky.

Alistair glances at me from the corner of his eye, looking genuinely surprised. "For what?"

"For... not commenting."

Understanding blows across his face, but he just lifts his toned shoulders in a casual shrug and shifts his gaze back to the chaotic street before us. "Yeah, well, I'm not exactly a bastion of morality myself. And everyone needs to find their own limits. Figure out where they draw the line."

Some of the embarrassment that still lingered inside me starts to fade, and a small smile tugs at my lips.

"I don't have a lot of limits myself," Alistair continues while we round the corner and jog up the next street. Then he flicks a sideways glance at me again while a teasing smile curves his lips. "I mean, I got Maximus to poison you, and I stole your clothes, and I almost burned your face off—"

"Huh, I'd forgotten about that."

He chuckles. "And I threatened to snap your skinny little neck for just asking me a question. So there are very few things I wouldn't do. But I don't hurt animals. That's where I draw the line."

"That's why you were so relieved when I pulled Talon out of the way during the last Atonement Trial?"

"Yeah." He rakes his hands through his curly blond hair and tilts his head back a little to heave a deep sigh. "I, uhm... Do you remember I told you that people in our court would hold me down and burn me to prove to the dragon shifters that they were good little fae who were on the dragon shifters' side now?"

My heart twists in pain. "Yes."

"Well, one of the guys who burned me, he had a pet rat." Regret crashes over Alistair's features, and he swallows. "I killed that rat to hurt him. But I felt so sick afterwards that I could barely eat for an entire month." He gives me a serious look. "People usually think that they know their own limits. But often, you don't actually know where you draw the line until you step right up to it. Or even cross it."

His words settle deep inside me, calming that jumble of conflicting emotions.

"So don't beat yourself up over it." His gaze is steady as he looks at me. "You needed to figure out where you draw the line. Now, you have. And that family back there will be fine. They'll recover from this without issue." He grimaces. "As opposed to the rat."

A short laugh, full of relief and gratitude, escapes my chest. Alistair smiles back.

Those final flickers of embarrassment and panic inside me fade away, replaced instead by a steady sense of certainty.

The burning rage and hatred in my soul are still there, thrashing inside me like black waves in a roaring fire storm. I'm still angry. I'm still furious. I still want revenge. I want to watch Jessina's heart break and her soul shatter as I take everything from her.

She took my family from me. She destroyed any chance I had of finding out if my parents actually loved me. She and Bane have tortured and humiliated my mate for centuries. They have kept me and Alistair and Isera and everyone in the Seelie Court trapped and broken and suffering for millennia.

And no matter how much some righteous person might tell me to forgive and forget, I know deep within my furious heart that I will never be able to do it. I want my revenge. And I am going to get it. I will get fucking everything.

But I will not do what they did. I will not punish people for a crime that they have not committed. That is where I draw the line. The only line I draw. Everything else is fair game.

I glance over at Alistair as we continue jogging up the street. The Ice Palace looms above us there on the mountainside, and a host of silver dragons have now begun to take flight from it. The entire city is booming with the flapping of wings while civilians scream and rush up and down the streets to get out of the way before the attack reaches the city.

Alistair just keeps his gaze on his surroundings while I study the side of his face. There is a lot more to this fire wielder than most people know. He feels things more deeply than almost anyone I have ever met. And he understands people and looks out for them in a way that I didn't expect.

It strikes me right there that Alistair always waits to make sure that I don't get left behind. When we were trying to escape the Unseelie Court, he waited to make sure that I followed instead of just taking off between the trees. And in the throne room when everyone hurried back through the portal after we had gotten Draven back, Alistair stayed behind to make sure that I got through it as well. He does a lot of little things like that.

Back in the Seelie Court, I thought I knew what kind of person Alistair was. But I really had no idea.

"You know," I begin. "For someone who keeps insisting that he's not a team player, you're actually an incredibly reliable guy."

His cheeks flush bright red, and his gaze darts to me. Drawing his eyebrows down, he tries and fails to look menacing as he huffs, "I could still snap your skinny little neck."

I grin. "Sure."

While Alistair continues trying to battle the blush on his face, we sprint the final distance up through the chaotic city. All around us, people are yelling and rushing back and forth while dragons explode into view on rooftops. A large silver dragon lands on the defensive walls around the Ice Palace and lets out a bellowing roar. It echoes across the city so loudly that I have to resist the urge to press my hands over my ears.

My skull rings as the dragon roars again. It's followed by roars from hundreds of dragons up ahead as the soldiers in the Silver Clan barracks shift and leap into the sky. Winds slam down over the city from the storm of beating wings.

Hope flickers through me as Alistair and I dart down the next street and towards the library. If our plan worked, and it looks like it might have, all the soldiers who were guarding the library where Lavendera is working have now been sent to defend the city from our fake invasion instead.

I drag in deep breaths, my heart slamming against my ribs, as we round the final corner and skid out onto the open stretch of stone that surrounds the grand library.

And come face to face with Bane and Jessina Iceheart.

My heart jerks as Bane flashes us a smug smile.

Every instinct inside me is screaming at me to attack. Or run. Or both. But I force myself to do neither.

Standing on the flat stone ground just outside the library, the

Icehearts watch us in silence for another few seconds. Jessina is wearing a sparkling silver dress, and her white hair has been pinned up slightly before falling down her back. As usual, Bane's black hair simply ripples down his back like a smooth waterfall. He is wearing fancy royal formal wear as well, but neither of them has their wings out.

"I told you it would work," Bane says.

"You didn't actually do anything, though," Jessina replies as she flicks a glance at him from the corner of her eye.

"I gave the order."

"Mabona's tits," Alistair interrupts, staring at them from across the stone ground. "You even sound like them."

Bane flashes us another smug smile while Jessina just lifts one shoulder in a nonchalant shrug. Staring at them in disbelief, I shake my head.

Mabona's tits, indeed. Nysara sure knows how to cast realistic glamours.

Isera and Orion, who are currently glamoured to look like the Icehearts, remain where they are while Alistair and I close the final distance to them. While the rest of us were scouting out taverns and threatening people, Orion and Isera went off on their own to visit Nysara, Orion's spy here in Frostfell. Thankfully, they managed not to kill each other long enough for Nysara to use her magic to glamour them.

"All the guards left the moment we showed up and commanded them to fly out to defend the city," Orion says in Bane's voice.

"All except one," Isera adds, and annoyance flits across her, or rather Jessina's, face. "He must have been ordered not to let anyone inside."

Following her gaze, I look towards the doors to the white stone library. A single dragon shifter, dressed in silver armor, is standing resolutely in front of the doors. No, not standing. I narrow my eyes as I study his left wrist. He has handcuffed himself to the left door handle.

"We've tried to break the door down," Isera continues.

"And break *him*," Orion adds.

"But we can't get it open, and he isn't budging," she finishes.

Alarm shoots up my spine as I stare between the two of them. "He won't open the door? Even for you, glamoured as the Icehearts?"

"No."

"Shit," I curse. Ice washes through my veins as realization hits. "They must have anticipated this. Of course they wouldn't leave her unprotected. They're way too smart for that. There must be some kind of special code word or passphrase that they use to make sure that only they can get him to open the door." I snap my gaze to Orion. "Can't you find it in his head?"

"I can't read people's minds," he replies. "I can only see bad memories, remember?"

Tension crackles through me as that sudden stress returns with a vengeance. If we can't get Lavendera soon, Draven, Lyra, and Galen are going to be forced to fight the entire might of the Silver Clan. If we wait too long to leave, the Silver Clan is going to realize that no dragon clans are coming and return to the city, and then Draven and the others will be forced to shift in order to buy us time to get out. They will get swarmed.

Panic pulses through me.

I can't let that happen.

"He has a lot of memories of being tortured," Orion continues. "And I mean *a lot*. Too many for me to even sift through." He shifts his gaze to me, holding it with serious eyes. "It's all done by the Icehearts, though. So he has obviously been thoroughly trained to withstand torture. We won't be able to break him in time."

A snarl of rage and panic rips from my chest. I am so fucking tired of being outplayed by the Icehearts! Why do they always have to think five steps ahead?

"We are getting through that door," I declare. That endless rage burns through me as I stalk forward, my furious eyes locked on the guard who is putting Draven's life at risk. "He is opening that fucking door right now."

"Didn't you hear me?" Orion says as he and the others scramble after me. "He has been trained to withstand torture."

"It won't matter," Alistair replies, a knowing smile suddenly sliding across his lips. "I don't call her Soulstealer for nothing."

I come to a halt in front of the stubborn guard, my friends flanking me on both sides. He raises his chin and glares back at us all defiantly. Impatience crackles inside me like bolts of lightning. Every second we waste is another second that brings Draven closer to danger.

Those awful memories of when he was swarmed by dragons in the sky above Rin's floating islands flash through my mind. Memories of dragons who tore at his wings and clamped their jaws through his side. I am not letting that happen again. Draven has protected me for so long. It's time that I start protecting him. I don't care what kind of villain I need to become. I will protect him.

Summoning my magic, I visualize a massive bone white flame of fear before me.

"Open the door," I order the guard.

He just stares back at me, his chin raised stubbornly.

I slam the flame of fear into his chest.

His eyes widen, and a shuddering breath rips from his lungs.

Pleasure floods my entire body as I increase that flame into a wildfire. That wonderful warm and sparkly feeling drowns out the panic and the stress and the anger about yet again being two steps behind the Icehearts. It soothes all of my fears, all of my insecurities, and all of my sorrows.

I keep increasing the strength of my magic until the guard's knees start shaking.

"Open the door," I demand.

His face is white with fear as he stares back at me, but he still doesn't open the door.

More, more, more, my soul urges.

Leaving the wildfire of fear in his chest, I cut off the flow of my magic. Harsh coldness, full of panic and fury and regret, crashes over me. The sudden change is so violent that I almost stumble back a step.

While blinking to clear my head, I summon a black flame of despair and shove it straight into the guard's chest.

That wonderful pleasure floods me again, and I draw in a breath of relief.

Fear alone apparently isn't working. Probably because he has been trained so well in withstanding torture. Part of that training must involve the ability to ignore fear, after all. But one thing he can't protect himself from is hopelessness. It doesn't matter how strong-willed he really is. If I change the entire core of his personality into someone who feels that everything is hopeless, there will be no reason for him to keep resisting.

Increasing the strength of my magic, I shove it down the connection and straight into his chest until that black flame of despair is so massive that he breaks down in hopeless sobs on the ground.

His hand is still handcuffed to the left door handle, so it juts up at an awkward angle, but he doesn't even seem to notice it. All hope, all light, all the defiance and resistance bleed from his eyes as he kneels there on the ground before me and stares up at me, his gaze full of fear and despair.

Power thrums inside me.

I am a fucking god.

With this power, I could lay the world at my feet.

Part of me wants to. Desperately. I have to be careful of that. I refuse to become a new Jessina Iceheart. I don't want to rule the world. I just want freedom. And revenge.

"Open the door," I command.

His head slumps forward in defeat as the endless despair drowns his entire soul and breaks all resistance. There is no protection against my magic. He would rather have died in pain than open this door. He would never have lost hope on his own. But none of that matters in the face of my power. I can simply change him until he becomes who I need him to be. Someone who is overwhelmed by despair and who considers all resistance pointless.

Hopelessness clings to his entire body as I pour my magic into him until I break his will completely. A cry of despair rips from his lungs.

Twisting on his knees, he places his palm against the door and murmurs something under his breath.

A pulse shoots through the air.

I stagger back from the force of it as the shockwave hits me straight in the chest.

It stuns me enough that I lose the grip on my magic.

Cold regret and burning rage rush in to fill the void.

Again, my mind urges me. *Do it again.*

Gritting my teeth, I drag in a controlled breath while forcing myself to ignore the urge. The more I use my power to create emotions from nothing, the more I want to keep using it.

On the ground, the guard lets out a long whimper of despair. "No. No. No. He's going to kill me."

I flick a glance down at him, but before I can put him out of his misery, Isera grabs the side of the door that the guard isn't currently handcuffed to.

Then she yanks it open.

CHAPTER FORTY-FOUR

A deep grinding sound echoes across the stone ground as the door is pulled open. The sound of it makes my hair stand on end. For some reason, it feels like the door to hell was just opened.

But no demons pour across the threshold to attack me. Only rows and rows of books are visible inside the door.

Snapping out of the strange apprehension, I shift my gaze to Isera and Orion. "Ready?"

They nod.

There are two reasons why we needed Nysara to glamour them to look like Bane and Jessina. The first reason was to make sure the guards obeyed. The second reason is to make sure that Lavendera obeys. She would never leave with us voluntarily, but if the Icehearts order her to go with us, she will surely do it.

"I'll keep watch," Alistair says before casting a worried look up at the sky. "But hurry."

Most of the dragons have flown out across the plains now to meet the supposed clans who are attacking. But it won't be long before they figure out that it's all a lie.

After giving him a nod, I dart across the threshold and into the library. Isera and Orion stride in after me, making sure to stick to their Iceheart personas.

Since there are no windows in the library, the ceiling is full of glowing crystals. I flick a glance up at them, expecting them to be faelights. But they're not. They look… older. More organic. They only give off a low golden glow, but since the ceiling is full of them, they emit enough light to see by.

My heart slams against my ribs as I run across the smooth stone floor to check the nearest aisle.

It's empty. Only tall bookcases packed with tomes stare back at me.

I continue towards the next one. And then the next one. And the next.

All of them are empty.

Dread crashes over me as I sprint back across the floor, checking each aisle again.

"What?" Orion calls in Bane's voice from where they are standing in the middle of the open space at the front of the library.

I can barely hear him over the pounding in my ears even though the rest of the library is dead silent. Swallowing down a flash of panic, I finish checking each aisle before I turn panicked eyes towards him.

"She's not here," I say.

Their mouths drop open.

"What?" Orion presses out again. "What do you mean *she's not here?*"

"It's empty. There's no one here. It looks like no one has even been here—"

"Guards are coming!" Alistair bellows into the library.

I snap my gaze towards the door and then drag in an unsteady breath as a sudden realization hits me like a punch to the gut.

This is a trap.

After what happened in the Seelie Court, they knew that we were targeting Lavendera. So they deliberately spread the word among their elite soldiers that she was being kept in here, knowing that we would break in.

Dread pulses through my veins as I stare at the impenetrable stone walls around me.

An isolated building with no windows and only one door that leads out. It's the perfect place for an ambush. And we walked right into it.

"Alistair," I yell. "Get in here." Without waiting for an answer, I whirl around to face Isera and Orion. "Go out there and tell them that we have already escaped down into the city. If Lavendera isn't here, she must be in the castle."

While Alistair skids into the library, Isera and Orion hurry across the polished stone floor before slowing to a more regal walk as they reach the door. Grabbing Alistair's arm, I yank him out of sight right before our fake Icehearts stride out across the threshold.

"They have already escaped," Orion yells in Bane's voice. "They disappeared down into the city. Find them!"

"But sir," a hesitant voice replies from somewhere outside. "Earlier, you told us—"

"Are you disobeying orders, soldier?"

"N-no," he stammers. "Sir."

"Then do as I said."

Boots thud against the ground as the people outside rush to obey the orders. I breathe a sigh of relief and sneak up to the door.

"It's clear," Isera says. "Let's go."

Alistair and I dart out through the door. This high up, I can see out across the city and the plains beyond. Silver dragons are flying out over the grasslands in every direction. It won't be long now before they realize that no one is out there. And once they do, they will fly straight back to the city. That is when Draven, Lyra, and Galen will be forced to shift and shoot up into the sky in their dragon forms right above the city to draw the Silver Clan's attention while we find Lavendera. If that happens, someone is bound to get hurt. So we need to find her first.

"They must be keeping her inside the Ice Palace," I repeat while panic pulses inside me like crackling lightning. "We need to—"

"More soldiers are coming!" Alistair yells.

My heart leaps into my throat as I whip my head around and stare in the direction he is pointing. Ice sinks into my stomach. He's right. An entire hoard of Silver Clan soldiers is sprinting towards us from the direction of the barracks.

"Run!" Isera snaps.

We take off across the stone ground and up the path towards the Ice Palace. I know that Isera and Orion could probably fool this next group as well, but we can't afford to get bogged down here. We need to find Lavendera before Draven is forced to shift in order to buy us time.

My breath rasps through my throat, which still stings from the acidic bile I vomited earlier, as I sprint up the path that has been cut into the mountain. Isera's glittering silver dress streams behind her as she runs in front of me while Orion is bringing up the rear. Alistair and I stay in the middle where we will be least visible.

I have no idea what the soldiers below are thinking of this strange display from their emperor and empress, and I barely dare to turn around to look.

Blood pounds in my ears as I push my legs hard while hurtling up the mountainside. I suck in deep breaths.

"They've stopped at the library," Orion calls from behind. The damn Unseelie King doesn't even have the decency to sound out of breath. "It looks like they're busy securing the building."

"Good," I rasp between heavy breaths.

"A detour like this wasn't part of the plan," Isera says from the front as we crest the hill and the side gate that is set into the high defensive walls becomes visible before us. "We're running out of time. Ryat and the others will be forced to shift in the next twenty minutes or so."

A desperate noise slips past my lips. I don't want to watch my mate battle hoards of dragons practically on his own again.

"Open the gate!" Isera commands.

The dragon shifter who is guarding the side gate leaps to attention. After fumbling with his keys, he shoves the gate open right before we reach it. When I run past him, I flick one glance at his face.

My heart jerks when I realize that it's the same guard who I tricked so many times when I was a prisoner here.

Which means that he recognizes me as well.

His mouth drops open when he sees my face, and he immediately starts reaching for his sword. But I was already moving. While sprinting in through the gate, I slash my dagger across his throat. I watch him gurgle in a breath before crumpling to the ground, blood streaming down from the wound across his throat. I feel absolutely no sense of guilt or regret whatsoever.

For a moment, I was worried that my little breakdown in the Osteria house would have made me revert back into that insecure girl who wrung her hands about everything. So I'm relieved to find that it hasn't. I'm still willing to be a ruthless villain in order to win. I just won't wipe out an entire clan full of people for crimes they haven't committed once we do win.

"Friend of yours?" Orion says from behind as we run across the castle grounds.

"He knew exactly who I was," I reply, my voice hard and unapologetic. "And I'm not taking any chances."

"Look at that. I think I'm rubbing off on you all."

"Focus," Isera growls from the front.

"Then I have another question," Orion continues. "This is a big castle. How are we going to find one little fae in it?"

"We should split up." She casts a glance at us over her shoulder. "Agreed?"

"Agreed," I reply. "But Alistair and I won't be able to make it far once we're indoors. Even if there is chaos inside, there will be guards around the Icehearts' private quarters."

"I'll handle those." She shifts her gaze to Orion. "You're not familiar with the layout of the castle, but I trust you can find the throne room at least?"

"Of course." He gives her a look full of challenge. "I'm a king."

"I'll take the kennels," Alistair says. "That's where they kept her last time we were here. Mabona knows they don't treat her very well, so they might be keeping her locked up there now as well."

"Good point." I drag in another deep breath before I can manage to say, "There's a dungeon underneath the castle too. I was locked up in it at one point, so I know where to find it. I'll check that."

"We don't have much time, though," Orion says, his voice now dead serious.

"I know. Draven and—"

"It's not just that. These glamours that Nysara created are so complex and detailed that it is draining a lot of her magic. I'd say we have less than thirty minutes before it runs out."

Alarm shoots up my spine. Without these glamours, we will never get Lavendera to come with us. Let alone get out of the city without being killed.

"Alright." Isera sweeps her gaze over us. "So we meet back here outside this door in fifteen minutes. No matter what."

We all nod in agreement.

Yanking open one of the side doors, we barrel into the Ice Palace and immediately take off in separate directions.

My heart pounds so loudly that I can't even hear the thudding of my own boots against the ice floor. The entire palace is in chaos. Servants and messengers are running up and down the hallways, barely glancing at the people they meet. I still keep my head down and my hair covering my ears so that they won't realize what I am.

Skidding around the corner, I have to throw out a hand and brace myself against the cool ice wall to stop myself from crashing right into a side table. My pulse thrums as I push off from the wall and take off along the corridor.

There should only be three more corridors between this one and the stairs to the dungeons. The dungeons are situated far below, inside the roots of the mountain, but I should be able to make it down there and back up again before fifteen minutes have passed. Unless there are still guards down there.

My breath saws through my throat as I sprint the final distance to the door that leads down into the dungeons. It's not guarded up here at least. So far so good.

Yanking it open, I start down the stairs with quick steps while shoving my magic out in rapid bursts. I aim at different emotions each time in an effort to estimate how many people are down there. As far as I can tell, there appears to be four people down there. However, I have no idea if they are prisoners or guards. And since my magic doesn't appear to work properly on Lavendera, I can't know for certain if she is down there or not.

Since I don't have time to sneak, I jog down the steps as fast as I can without tripping. My boots thud with each stride, and the sound echoes between the stone walls. The temperature plummets with every step. This deep under the mountain, the air is cool even though it's summer.

"Who's there?" a male voice calls up from the dungeons.

A jolt shoots through me. *Oh, shit.* There is at least one guard down there then. While drawing in short tense breaths, I summon a massive flame of fear as I continue running down the steps. This will only work if I'm fast enough.

I still don't know if it's because it's impossible for the body to handle two flames of the same emotion or if it's because the heart simply cannot handle being hit with that much fear that fast. But every time I have done this, it has worked.

However, if the guard manages to attack before I can hit him again, I'm screwed.

With tension crackling inside me like a storm, I run down the final distance while searching desperately for any sign of the guard who yelled earlier.

Once I reach the final ten steps, a dragon shifter in silver armor suddenly becomes visible on the ground below.

I slam the fear into his chest.

His eyes widen, and he opens his mouth as if to scream.

Panic shoots through me.

Yanking up a second flame of fear, I shove it into his chest.

He gasps. Terror crashes over his features, and the hand that was reaching for his sword instead flies up towards his heart.

Then his eyes roll back in his head and he collapses down on the ground.

"What was that?" another male voice calls from farther down the hallway.

From my last visit to this place, I know that the guards have a room down there where they play cards to pass the time. Apparently, the guy I just killed wasn't alone down here.

I suck in short shallow breaths as I leap over the guard on the floor and skid into the section that houses the cells. Running from one side to the other, I search them all for Lavendera.

"Dude, did you hear me?" the second guard calls. "Was someone coming?"

My pulse thrums in my ears as I cast a panicked look in his direction.

Snapping my gaze back to the iron bars in front, I search the final cells for Lavendera.

She isn't there.

But someone else is.

Shock and confusion hit me like a slap as I reach the final cell and find a stately man in elegant green robes sitting against the rough stone wall inside the iron bars. His turquoise eyes are wide, and he just keeps raking his hands through his blond hair while shaking his head. He is looking in my direction, but it's as if he's staring straight through me.

"No, no, no," he repeats, his voice hoarse, as if he has been screaming.

For a moment, all I can do is to stare at him in disbelief.

Because this is Kander von Graf. Leader of the Green Dragon Clan.

What in Mabona's name is he doing here?

Then I suck in a sharp breath as I remember what happened outside the Green Clan's mountain a few weeks ago. Lavendera showed up with all of those elite soldiers. And Kander refused to open the door. Is this how they punished him for that insubordination?

"Hey, did you hear me?" the second guard calls again. "Is it von Graf again? I swear if he starts screaming again, I'm going to lose my fucking mind."

His voice snaps me out of my stupor, and I whirl back towards the guard I killed. After closing the distance to him in two quick strides, I crouch down and unhook his keys from his belt.

"Do we need to come out and help you?" the guard yells.

I sprint back to Kander's cell and shove the key into the keyhole before grabbing the bar so that I can yank it open.

A hiss rips from my lips as my naked palm meets the iron bars. It immediately cuts off the flow of my magic and almost sends me to my knees. Ripping open the door, I yank my hand away from the iron as fast as possible.

Magic flows back into me, but even that brief contact added to the already building exhaustion inside me. I need to get out of here. Now. If I have to fight two more guards, I might not make it out of here at all.

But if I can rescue the leader of the Green Dragon Clan, he will be in my debt. And that is going to be crucial to winning this war.

"Let's go," I hiss at Kander.

"No, no, no," he just keeps mumbling while staring right through me. "I felt it. I felt it fall. It's all over."

Horror washes through me as I stare at him. The Icehearts must have tortured him extensively to turn him into this blabbering mess. Fear suddenly grips my heart. What if he won't be able to help us anymore? What if they've tortured him so much that his mind has snapped? Then he might not even remember how that partnership between fae and dragon shifters works anymore. Goddess above, we need that information.

"I felt it," he continues mumbling. "It's—"

"Kander!" I snap, dread still gripping my chest.

He starts slightly and then blinks hard. At last, his eyes seem to slide back into focus. His gaze darts from me, to the dead guard, and then to the open cell door. My heart stutters as a burst of hope flickers inside me. Did he recover? Is he back to normal? Please, Mabona, let his mind be intact.

I jump in surprise as he suddenly leaps to his feet and runs towards the open cell door.

"We need to—" I begin.

But he doesn't stop.

He just sprints right out the door and starts hurtling up the steps. A low growl escapes my lips. He could've at least waited for me.

Spinning around, I hurry back into the hallway.

"You!" a male voice screams.

My heart leaps into my throat, and I whip around to find two dragon shifters in silver armor staring at me in shock from the other end of the corridor.

"Mabona's fucking tits," I growl.

They scream as they charge towards me.

Summoning my magic, I shove a massive violet flame of pain into the first guy's chest.

Pleasure floods my body. But so does exhaustion. I've used a lot of powerful magic in a very short time, while also sprinting across the entire city. Twice. And touching iron.

The first guard goes down screaming on the floor as I increase the flame of pain in one sharp yank before cutting it off. His sudden collapse makes his friend slam into him from behind. It almost sends him tumbling down on the floor as well and buys me enough time to whirl around and take off up the steps.

Air rasps through my throat as I drag in desperate breaths while sprinting up the stairs.

Two seconds later, boots start pounding against the stone steps behind me.

A noise of pure desperation rips from my throat. I don't have time or energy to fight this guard right now. Lavendera isn't here. We need to find her and get the hell out of here before Draven and the others are forced to shift and put their lives in danger.

Pounding up the steps, I run with everything I have.

The back of my neck suddenly prickles.

On instinct, I leap into the air above the next step.

A sword whooshes through the air barely a second later. It slams into the stone wall on the other side of the narrow stairs with a metallic clashing sound.

Landing on the step again, I twist with the motion and swing my leg through the air. My boot cracks into the side of the guard's face. He grunts in pain, and his head snaps to the side from the forceful kick. I reach for my magic, aiming for that spark of pain since it will consume less energy than creating one out of nothing.

But before I can shove my magic forward, the guard launches himself at me.

Still off balance from my kick, I topple backwards as he slams into my legs, tackling me down on the steps.

Pain shoots through my spine as my back hits the edges of the steps. Gasping, I try to concentrate enough through the pain to summon my magic again, but the guard has already yanked his sword back.

Ripping out my dagger, I stab it towards his face.

He jerks back, evading the hit, but the move also forces him to abandon his own strike.

While still blinking my eyes into focus, I reach for my magic again and shove it at him right as he uses his grip on my legs to yank me down the stairs. My stomach lurches and my leather armor scrapes against the stone steps as I'm hauled downwards.

A moment later, my magic slams into the spark of pain in his chest.

With a scream, I pour a torrent of magic down it while stabbing my knife at his face again.

He screams in agony as I force his pain into a searing wildfire.

His sword wavers in the air.

And my dagger sinks right into his eye.

Another cry of pure agony tears from his lungs. The sound echoes between the cold stone walls so loudly that my ears hurt.

Ripping the knife out of his eye socket, I kick my knee up hard. He rolls to the side, still screaming in pain while reaching for his bleeding eye. I knee him in the face and then haul the rest of my body out from underneath his with a cry of desperation.

Screams of pain echo between the walls from the guard on the steps as well as the guy on the floor down below, who now has a massive flame of pain stuck in his chest for the rest of his life.

I drag in deep breaths while my vision swims from exhaustion.

Staggering to my feet, I wipe the blood from my dagger and ram it back into its sheath.

The guard throws his other hand out, aiming for my ankle.

I increase the pain in his chest in one massive burst that makes him scream his lungs out.

Then I cut off my magic and hurtle up the steps.

CHAPTER FORTY-FIVE

Throwing the door to the dungeon stairs shut behind me, I sprint down the corridor and towards the side door. My heart slams against my ribs. I don't know how much time has passed since we went inside. The others might have already left at this point. With or without Lavendera.

A messenger jumps out of the way as I skid around the corner. Her blue eyes widen in surprise, but before she can get a closer look at me, I take off down the hall and sprint towards the next intersection.

"Hey!" she calls after me. "Are you—"

I slam right into Jessina Iceheart.

Air explodes from my lungs as I run straight into the two people who just came charging out of the hallway on my right. Dragging in a deep breath, I leap back and snap my gaze between them.

"Watch it," Jessina says, and then casts a sharp look at the gaping messenger. "And get to work!"

With a small shriek of panic, the messenger darts away.

For a moment, my brain is still screaming at me to attack the person in front of me. But I know that it's not actually Jessina.

It's Isera. And more importantly, she has another person with her.

Lavendera Dawnwalker.

"Let's go," Isera says in Jessina's voice.

Without waiting for a reply, she takes off down the corridor with Lavendera next to her. I scramble to catch up and then dart along the glittering ice halls with them. My gaze slides to Lavendera as we run. I have no idea what Isera said to her to trick her into this, but it appears to be working. She is barely even looking at me. All she does is whatever Isera tells her.

Air that tastes of mountains and ice fills my lungs when we burst out through the side door and out onto the castle grounds. Orion, who still looks like Bane, and Alistair jump out of the way to avoid getting mowed down when we sprint out onto the flat stone ground outside.

Surprise and relief flashes across Alistair's face when he sees Lavendera, but he quickly wipes the expression off his features and snaps his mouth shut. We can't risk saying anything that will tip her off to the fact that she is being tricked.

"Let's go," Isera repeats, her own naturally authoritative tone blending with Jessina's voice perfectly.

Lurching into motion, we race back towards the side gate. Isera and Orion lead the charge while Alistair and I bring up the rear. Lavendera stays in the middle, and she continues keeping her mouth shut.

Chaos is spreading rapidly across the palace grounds. Someone has found the guard that I killed, and servants are now running towards the castle to raise the alarm. Everywhere I look, people are yelling and darting across the ground with panic in their eyes. Most of them are probably remembering the human uprising a few months ago, which must have been very frightening for the ordinary civilians who work here.

"Clear the way!" Orion bellows in Bane's voice as we close the distance to the side gate.

The panicked servants who had gathered there leap back at the sound of their emperor's voice and immediately start stammering apologies. As if they are somehow responsible for the guard that I killed or the fact that his corpse is now blocking the way.

We simply leap over it as we run through the open gate and back out onto the sloping mountainside outside the high defensive walls. I suck in a deep breath of relief as we leave the Ice Palace behind and continue down the path that leads down towards the city.

Even though it has been months since I was trapped in this castle with an iron collar around my throat, my entire soul still balks at being back inside those thick ice walls. And it must be even worse for Isera and Alistair, who suffered a lot more than I did in there. I glance over at Alistair as we run towards the first fork in the path. He is clenching his jaw slightly, but apart from that, he shows nothing on his face.

It must have been truly horrible for him to return to the kennels, where he was locked in a cage for weeks. Same with Isera. She ran all the way up to the Icehearts' private wing to find Lavendera. I don't know exactly what the Icehearts put her and Alistair through in there, but it can't have been easy for her to return.

Alistair suddenly sucks in a sharp breath.

I snap my gaze to him.

Alarm flashes in his eyes as he jerks his chin towards the left and then the right. I flick my gaze from side to side while we turn right and sprint down the path that leads directly down into the city rather than towards the Silver Clan barracks and the library.

Ice spreads through my veins.

There, on the horizon in both directions, silver dragons are starting to return to the city.

My heart leaps into my throat. We need to make it to the empty house where Grey has a portal waiting for us before they reach the city. Or Draven, Galen, and Lyra are going to be in the fight of their lives.

"Uhm," Alistair begins in an effort to bring that to Isera and Orion's attention without blowing their cover.

"I see it," Isera confirms.

Running beside her, Orion flicks a glance at her before casting a quick look back at us. His eyes are serious and full of warning. "It won't be long."

I swallow down a flash of dread, because I understand exactly what his warning meant. It won't be long now before Nysara's magic runs out and their glamour disappears. We need to make it to the portal before then.

Before the magic runs out.

Before the silver dragons get too close.

Before Draven and the others have to shift and engage in battle.

Before Lavendera can figure out that this is an abduction and not a mission from the Icehearts.

Blood pounds in my ears as we sprint the final distance down the path and towards the first street ahead.

The silver dragons are getting closer on all sides.

I flick my gaze desperately over the rooftops, praying to Mabona that Draven doesn't shift yet.

Panicked screams echo across the city as the civilian dragon shifters rush back to their homes to take cover. My lungs burn as we hurtle down the street and then take a sharp left before going right. For the first time, Lavendera casts a confused glance behind her. Alistair and I just look back at her, trying to project a calm that I'm sure neither of us feels.

People scramble out of the way as we charge down the next road.

A market square opens up at the other end of it.

I drag in short shallow breaths while trying to block out the exhaustion that courses through me. We're not even halfway to the portal yet. Since we couldn't set it up in a place where any dragon shifter might find it, we had to open it in one of the now empty areas where the humans used to live. Unfortunately, those areas are located farthest from the castle.

Dragon shifters are hurriedly shoving wares down into carts and pushing them into the buildings that line the market as we cross it. They still think a massive attack is incoming, and they're trying to protect their livelihoods from being destroyed in the fighting.

I whip my head from side to side, but from down here, I can no longer see the horizons clearly. My heart hammers in my chest. I have no idea how close the silver dragons are to the city.

"We need to—" Isera begins.

Her glamour drops.

And so does Orion's.

Panic shoots up my spine as the fake Jessina and Bane who used to run at the head of our little group suddenly transform back into Isera and Orion. Jessina's white hair turns black, and her glittering silver dress becomes black fighting leathers. Next to her, Bane's smooth black hair changes to a dark blue color, and a spiky black crown appears on his head. The silver formal wear bleeds into dark blue and black, with only hints of silver decorations.

Lavendera slams to a halt in the middle of the market square.

It's so abrupt that I almost barrel right into her.

Throwing myself sideways, I barely manage to jump out of the way and come to a halt a few steps from her instead. On her other side, Alistair stumbles upright as well.

"No," Lavendera says. Shock laces that one word, and her face is full of disbelief as she stares at Isera and Orion.

They glance down at their own bodies, no doubt confirming that the slight shimmer, which is what people see from the inside of a glamour, is now gone. Then they turn slowly to face Lavendera.

"No!" she repeats. This time, the word rips out of her like a desperate scream.

"We're getting you out," I tell her.

Her gaze snaps to me, and fury burns in her pink and purple eyes. "I don't want to get out! I can't."

"You don't—"

Branches shoot towards me. A gasp rips from my lips, and I throw myself to the side right before they can crash into my chest. Rolling across the cobblestones, I leap to my feet right as fire roars through the air.

"Get away from me!" Lavendera screams.

I stare in shock as trees and branches and roots shoot out from around Lavendera and stab out in all four directions towards all of us in one massive attack. Jumping back, I yank out my knife and slash at the branches that try to ensnare me.

A dragon roars overhead.

Snapping my gaze up, I find four silver dragons speeding across the rooftops. Winds slam down into the market square from their wings as they pass.

A second later, three black dragons explode into view atop the rooftops farther to my left.

Dread crashes over me.

No. No, no, no. This wasn't supposed to happen.

Draven, Lyra, and Galen, now in their dragon forms, let out bellowing roars as they shoot up into the sky. The four silver dragons screech and turn sharply in the air, focusing on them instead.

Wings boom as Draven and the others fly towards them at full speed. Opening their jaws, they breathe massive torrents of fire that shoot straight towards the silver dragons.

I dive forward as another tree slams towards me.

Lavendera, standing in the middle of the open square, shoots attacks at all four of us at the same time. Massive trees and sharp branches and tangling twigs flash through the air with terrifying precision.

Flames roar across the ground as Alistair tries to keep up with her rapid pace and burn the wood to ash before it can reach him. On my other side, Isera is yanking up sheets of ice one after the other to stop the attacks that just keep smacking right through her ice.

Orion leaps back, barely avoiding the branches that aim to trap his ankles, while casting alarmed glances at Lavendera. His eyes, which were glowing in the beginning, are not glowing anymore. Which can only mean one thing. Just like mine, his magic apparently doesn't work on Lavendera.

Dragons roar above us, and ice flames crackle through the air above. I suck in a sharp breath and duck instinctively, but the silver dragons weren't aiming at us. They were aiming at Draven.

Torrents of fire stream through the air, crashing into the ice flames, as Draven and the others block the attack.

Black storm clouds gather in the sky above. Thunder rumbles, joining the booming of wings and roaring of fire and ice, as Draven summons his magic.

I slash desperately at the branches before me as Lavendera intensifies her attacks. Branches shoot towards me like arrows, followed by entire trees. Forced to abandon my attempts with the knife, I instead focus solely on trying to evade the rapid onslaught. Leaping and twisting and ducking, I throw myself back and forth across the cobblestones to escape.

Alistair shoots massive waves of fire at the trees that crash over him while Isera slams up wall after wall of ice to protect herself. Across from me, Orion is leaping and ducking the branches as well.

Lightning cracks through the air above.

I suck in a sharp breath as the boom splits the air loudly enough to rattle the windows around us.

Draven roars and breathes more fire at his attackers while

storm winds howl around him. Thunder and lightning echo between the stone houses as Draven spreads the black storm across half of the city. The dark clouds block out the sunlight, casting the square around us in murky darkness. From inside the buildings around us, people cry out in fear.

Fire roars through the air, incinerating a massive chunk of trees as Alistair loses his patience and throws everything he has at Lavendera. But more trees just keep shooting up from the ground, blocking the flames and then shooting back to attack Alistair. Isera alternates between yanking up walls to protect herself and throwing sharp sheets of ice at the trunks in an effort to cut them down.

Lavendera screams in frustration.

Trees shoot out around her with so much power that I'm forced to throw myself down on the ground to escape them. Rolling over, I narrowly evade a cluster of stabbing branches before I manage to leap to my feet.

My heart pounds as I stare at Lavendera.

She is fighting four people at once, two of whom are the strongest magic users in the entire Seelie Court and one who is the fucking Unseelie King.

And she is still *winning*.

Seeing this display of power now, I realize with shocking clarity how much she was holding back when she was pretending to be a contestant in the Atonement Trials. Even when she was battling the Dryad Queen earlier, she wasn't fighting at full power.

Shock clangs inside me as I gape at her.

What the hell is she?

Where does all of this power come from?

Is it because she actually is half dragon shifter, just as I have been suspecting? Is this what they meant when they were talking about a partnership between fae and dragon shifters that made both races more powerful? A child born from both bloodlines?

Lightning splits the air above.

Ice flames shoot across the rooftops and crash into torrents of real dragon fire as Draven and the others fight in the dark storm clouds above.

A mass of trees shoots towards Isera. I scream a warning, but she has already seen it as well. Slamming up a wall, she throws herself to the side. To my left, Alistair is forced to do the same thing.

Both of them roll across the cobblestones and jump to their feet only a few strides from me.

"This isn't working!" Alistair yells over the snapping branches and roaring fire and booming dragon wings.

I suck in a deep breath. "We need to—"

While still forcing Orion back across the square on the other side, Lavendera starts hammering us with a rapid hail of branches. Alistair yanks up his palms and shoots fire at them while Isera blocks them with ice walls and throws sharp shards between the crashing trees towards Lavendera. Dark storm clouds churn around us.

Gripping my knife tightly, I stare at the desperate battle before me.

I am so fucking useless in fights when I can't use my magic. If only I could—

A sudden idea hits me like a lightning bolt.

Reaching inside me, I pull at the faint spark of pain that still lingers inside me from when my back hit the edge of the stairs in the dungeon. While still leaping and ducking branches, I reach that faint emotion towards Lavendera even though I know that it will be so weak that she won't even feel it.

Anticipation pulses through me when I manage to connect it to her.

I might not be able to manipulate the emotions she already has, since her head is so messed up, but I can apparently attach my own sane emotions to her.

"I can create an opening!" I yell at Alistair and Isera. "Tell me when."

The two of them, who have trained and fought together for weeks both inside and outside the Unseelie Court at this point, just exchange a look and a nod.

"When I shoot two blocks right after each other," Isera says.

I jerk my chin down in a nod as well.

Raising both hands, Alistair begins pouring a massive flood of fire at the trees.

Across the stones, Lavendera grinds her teeth and slams more trees back at us while Isera starts up a barrage of her own. Ice shoots through the air. Sheets and shards and walls smack into the wood.

Dragons roar above us. Crackling ice flames and real fire clash in the skies, drowned out by booming thunder and howling winds and cracks of white lightning.

I flex my fingers on the hilt of my knife while impatience streaks through me.

Isera shoots two round blocks of ice right after each other.

My heart leaps into my throat as I yank up my hand.

"This is going to suck."

I ram the dagger right through my own shoulder.

CHAPTER FORTY-SIX

A scream of agony rips from my lungs as my dagger hits bone and I twist hard, causing pain to shoot through my body.

Across the cobblestones, Lavendera gasps.

She staggers a step back in shock, her magic flickering for a second, as my own magic, which I connected to her chest, forces her to feel half of my sudden pain.

And that second is all Isera needs.

Lavendera barely manages to shove the first block of ice away with a tree branch, but the other slams right into her solar plexus. Air explodes from her lungs, and her eyes widen. Then her body convulses, and she crashes down on the cobblestones.

All the trees and branches that were attacking us vanish in a flash. And so does my magic connection to Lavendera.

I yank the dagger out of my shoulder with a gasp. Pain throbs inside me now that I feel all of the pain myself. Blood wells up from the wound, but I aimed for a spot where I wouldn't sever any important muscles, so I can still move my arm with some effort.

Isera sprints forward, aiming for the now unconscious Lavendera.

"We're not making it to the portal!" Orion calls from across the square as he runs back towards us as well. His eyes are full of command as he shifts them between Alistair and Isera. "Signal to Draven. We're going with the backup plan. We need to get out. Now."

Neither of them argues because we all know that he's right. Lavendera won't stay knocked out forever, and when she wakes up, there will be hell to pay. We only won this fight because I managed to use the element of surprise. It won't work a second time.

Not to mention our other problem.

Dark storm clouds rumble above us, lit up by flashes of lightning and streams of dragon fire. Three black dragons fly through the clouds, maneuvering around each other with expert precision while only two silver dragons remain. But not for long.

The four who arrived first were just the fastest, or the first group to realize that the invading armies were a lie, but the rest are on their way as well. And they will be here soon. We need to get out before that happens.

Orion takes Lavendera's unconscious body from Isera and throws her over his shoulder while Isera instead runs back to where Alistair is standing.

Raising one hand, they start shooting fireballs and blocks of ice straight up into the air in a prearranged pattern. Draven will see that and know what to do.

A deafening roar echoes from above, confirming that Draven has seen the signal. Orion and I hurry towards Isera and Alistair so that we are all clustered together.

Dragon fire shoots through the air as Galen and Lyra force the surviving two silver dragons back. A moment later, Draven in his massive black dragon form shoots out of the clouds and swoops down over the square.

Orion sucks in a panicked breath as Draven opens his claws and scoops up all four of us, along with the unconscious Lavendera, before climbing into the air again. His wings beat hard, sending blasts of wind slamming down into the market square that makes the remaining wagons and booths skid across the ground and crash into the stone walls. People scream inside their houses.

Winds rush between his claws and rip at our hair and clothes as he flies back up into the storm and then lets out a bellowing roar.

Black storm clouds explode around him as he uses his magic to throw them across the entire city to hide us from view. Galen and Lyra come shooting back towards him from either side, heading straight towards each other. My heart jerks when neither of them slows down.

But right before they can crash into each other straight above Draven's back, black smoke whooshes out around them as they shift back into humans. Lyra's wavy brown hair streams above her head as she plummets down with Galen next to her.

The moment they hit Draven's back and grab on to his spikes, he takes off at full speed.

Howling winds and booming thunder help mask the beating of his wings as he speeds through the thick black storm clouds. Somewhere behind us, the two surviving dragons roar in frustration.

My heart slams against my ribs.

This won't work if the rest of the silver dragons have reached the city. If they're too close, like when we were fighting our way out of the Ice Palace all those months ago, we will never be able to escape without at least one of them seeing us. And as soon as one dragon knows where we are, they will sound the alarm and call all the others to them. At which point we will be overwhelmed.

Dragging in panicked breaths, I keep flicking my gaze

between Lavendera and the clouds around us. If she wakes up too early, we're screwed. If the other silver dragons managed to get too close to the city before Draven spread out the storm clouds, we're also screwed.

Blood pounds in my ears and my heart feels like it's going to beat out of my chest.

A jolt shoots through me as a thick forest suddenly becomes visible below.

Draven flexes his claws around us.

My heart leaps into my throat.

Grabbing Lavendera, I pull her to me and wrap my arms firmly around her body while Draven flies down to the very bottom of the thick cloud cover. My shoulder screams in pain from the still bleeding wound in it, but I grit my teeth and hold Lavendera's unconscious body tightly.

Then he shifts.

My stomach lurches, and I have to snap my mouth shut to stop a scream, as we plummet straight down towards the thick canopy below.

A massive dragon can't fly down and land without anyone spotting it. But eight tiny humans can certainly fall through the air and disappear into the trees before anyone can see where we went. Since the skies are full of silver dragons, we can't fly away from Frostfell. We need to hide until Grey realizes that we're not coming and that we went with the backup plan and that he needs to open a portal here instead.

Branches rip at my black fighting leathers as I hit the canopy. But just like we predicted when we chose this exact part of the forest for our backup plan, the dense leaf crowns at the top of these trees break our fall as gently as a tree possibly can.

Pain still pulses through my body as I tumble down between the branches and leaves and then hit the grass below. But I keep my arms around Lavendera the entire way down. We didn't go through all of this trouble just for her to land on her head and die after we escape.

Rolling over on my back, I let Lavendera's body do the same as I release my grip on her and instead drag in a deep breath. Pain pulses through my injured shoulder as well as my back and my entire left side now. But I'm alive.

And so are my friends.

Sitting upright, I whip my gaze from face to face.

Orion brushes leaves from his fancy blue garments and puts the crown, which he was apparently holding in his hand when Draven dropped us, back on his head. Alistair blinks and shakes his head while still sitting on the ground. A few steps away, Isera simply gets to her feet silently. Galen scans the grass for Draven, who rakes a hand through his now messy black hair while getting to his feet, and Lyra simply jumps up from the grass with a wide grin on her mouth.

"*That* is what I call a job well done," she declares with that beaming smile on her face.

"A job well done?" Orion demands. He looks furious. "Do you have any idea just how close we came to losing just now?"

"What do you—"

Lavendera gasps awake. Scrambling to her feet, she snaps her gaze from side to side.

I jump to my feet as well, getting ready for a fight.

But she doesn't start attacking us straight away. Instead, an awful expression of dread and panic washes over her beautiful face.

"No," she breathes, and her voice breaks on the word. Fear pulses in her eyes as she looks around, as if searching for someone. "No. What have you done? They will think I left on my own. They will think I betrayed them. I will never get it now. I will never get it."

I stare, horrified, as something seems to break inside her. Fear and dread and sheer utter desperation crash over her face while tiny panicked noises rip from her throat.

Then her eyes abruptly slide out of focus.

Blinking, I stare at Lavendera as she suddenly begins disassociating the way she often does. My heart beats hard as I watch her just stand there and stare unseeing at a tree a few steps away.

"Uhm," Alistair begins, very eloquently saying what we were all no doubt thinking.

"Malachi's fucking balls," Orion snaps, shattering the sudden silence like an explosion. "You people are insane!" Raising his hand, he stabs it in the direction of the city we just escaped. "We were almost captured five times during this absolute shitshow of a mission!"

"It worked, didn't it?" Draven replies with a scowl.

"Barely," he growls, fury flashing in his black and silver eyes as he instead stabs his finger towards Draven. "But you don't know that, because you didn't see all the traps we walked right into." His gaze snaps to the rest of us. "Malachi's balls, you're supposed to be smart. Do you have any idea how close we came to losing today?"

"But we didn't," Isera retorts, her eyes as hard as his.

"We almost did! And do you know what would've happened if I had been caught impersonating Bane Iceheart?" He flings his arm out and stabs his hand towards the horizon. "That fucking psycho dragon shifter would've made it his mission in life to slaughter every single person inside my court." A snarl rips from his lungs as he rakes his hands through his hair. "I cannot keep risking my court like this."

"Yes, you will," Draven reminds him. "Because you don't have a choice. So if you think our schemes aren't good enough, feel free to actually start contributing more."

"Contributing more?" He shoots Draven an offended glare full of disbelief. "We only pulled off this insane scheme because of me. Because I ordered Nysara to glamour us." Narrowing his eyes, he turns to Isera. "And I will not risk my court like this again until you prove that you are a descendant of the Seelie Queen's second daughter."

A hysterical laugh suddenly rips through the air.

I jump in surprise and whirl towards the source of it. Lavendera, who is now blinking her eyes back into focus, turns towards Isera and Orion while continuing to laugh. It's a strange laugh. It doesn't sound mirthful at all. Instead, it's laced with insanity.

"No," Lavendera begins, while still chuckling like a crazy person. "I can tell you, without a doubt, that Isera is not a descendant of the Seelie Queen's second daughter."

Dread crashes over me. *Fuck.*

Orion's gaze sharpens as he snaps it back to Isera. "So, you did lie, little viper. Our entire bargain is based on a lie."

"No," Isera counters, keeping her chin raised and her expression one of calm composure. "I was telling the truth."

He stabs his hand towards Lavendera. "She just told us you were lying!"

"And you're just taking her word for it? Where is her proof? Can't you see that she is just trying to sow discord? Because she is on the Icehearts' side, for Mabona's sake! Use your head."

Lavendera stops laughing, and her eyes become serious as she looks between the two of them. "Isera is not a descendant of the Seelie Queen's second daughter."

"How can you be so sure of that?" Isera demands. "The dragon shifters claim she died, but her body was never found. So where is your proof? How can you prove that I am not a descendant?"

Pain flickers in Lavendera's eyes. "Because *I* am the Seelie Queen's second daughter."

CHAPTER FORTY-SEVEN

My jaw drops. "What?"

"I always hear the whispers, you know." A faraway look blows across Lavendera's face for a moment as she draws her fingers over the scar that cuts across her cheek and jaw. "From people wondering how I got this scar. I got it in the war."

"What war?" I breathe, my heart now pounding in my chest.

"*The* war." Her gaze sharpens, and she looks from face to face with a serious expression on her beautiful features. "I was there. Six thousand years ago. I fought in the war. I was nineteen when the Icehearts decided to slaughter my entire people for a crime committed by a small group of outcasts."

"I don't understand." I stare at her while shock and disbelief clang inside my skull. "How can you be over six thousand years old? That's six times longer than a fae is supposed to live."

"I know." A laugh slips from her lips until it turns into a sob. Pain and insanity flicker in her eyes. "Trust me, I know."

Dead silence falls over the thick woods for a few seconds as we all just stare at Lavendera. In the distance, dragons roar and beat their wings as they fly back and forth across the city, trying to figure out where we went. But I can barely hear them over the ringing in my ears.

The first person to break the stunned silence is Alistair.

"Mabona's fucking tits." Anger pulses across his face as he flings his arm out and stabs a hand at Lavendera in accusation. "If you're the daughter of the Seelie Queen, then why the hell are you fighting for the Icehearts now?"

Pain and desperation once again shine in her eyes. "Because only they can give me what I want."

"And what is that?" I demand.

"The Soul of Trees," a new voice suddenly says.

We all whirl around, half of us dropping into fight stances, before we find the source of the voice.

The Dryad Queen glides out of the lush green vegetation to my left. Her hair and dress, still made up entirely of vines and leaves and twigs, ripple behind her when she moves. We all watch her, but her brown eyes are entirely focused on Lavendera.

"You said that the only way we would get it back was if they *give* it to us," the Dryad Queen says, ancient power dripping from her voice. "So we did as you said. We backed off. We left you alone so that they would not grow angry and keep it from you out of spite." Fury flashes across her face. "But then I hear from this fae," she nods towards me, "who fell into our lands last year, that the Icehearts are making you fight and kill each other for sport."

"I was—" Lavendera begins.

"You know what would happen if you were to be killed!"

"Of course I do!"

"We made an agreement."

"I know. And I'm trying." A sob full of pain and desperation escapes her lips. "I'm *trying*."

"Your way is not working. It has been six thousand years. If they were going to keep their word and give you the Soul of

Trees in exchange for loyal service, they would have done it already."

"Stop," Draven demands before Lavendera can reply. His voice pulses with authority as he looks between Lavendera and the Dryad Queen. "Explain what the hell is going on here. How can you be over six thousand years old? What agreement did you make? And what is the Soul of Trees?"

The Dryad Queen slides sharp eyes to Draven but doesn't answer. However, she doesn't shut down his questions either, so Lavendera heaves a long sigh.

"It was towards the end of the war," she begins. "I was leading a group of my friends on a mission to take out the Icehearts' information center, but we were ambushed. The Icehearts had been hunting me across the world because of my very rare tree magic, and my friends knew that. So they... traded me to the Icehearts in exchange for their own lives." A harsh laugh rips from her throat. "They survived that day but were then executed along with everyone else when we lost the war."

My heart twists. By Mabona. Her own friends sold her out to the Icehearts?

"After that, I was... tortured." The flat way she says that word makes me think that it was brutal and extensive. "Earlier that year, Bane had stolen the Soul of Trees from the dryads."

The Dryad Queen lets out a low growl while age-old fury burns in her eyes.

"And they used that to fuse me with the Mother Dryad," Lavendera finishes.

We all just stare at her. My head is pounding.

"What does that even mean?" I ask.

"It means that I've had an immortal dryad living inside my head for six thousand years!" she snaps.

I jerk back in shock. "That's why you don't age? Because you have been fused with the... Mother Dryad?" I say the title hesitantly since I don't even understand what it means.

"Yes."

"And that is why we hate the Icehearts," the Dryad Queen adds, her voice cold. "Only the Mother Dryad can create new dryads. But she is trapped inside Lavendera Dawnwalker. And if she is killed, the Mother Dryad dies as well, and then there will be no more dryads. Ever."

"Azaroth's flame," Lyra curses under her breath.

"The Soul of Trees is an artifact," Lavendera begins.

"It is not an *artifact*," the Dryad Queen hisses. "It is the Soul of—"

"It is an artifact," Lavendera interrupts, frustration flashing across her face. "It is a precious and meaningful and invaluable thing for the dryads, but it is a physical item, which means that it is also an artifact."

The Dryad Queen narrows her eyes but doesn't dispute the point.

"It is the only thing that can split me and the Mother Dryad back into two people," Lavendera continues, that desperation bleeding into her voice again. "Bane and Jessina promised that they would give it to me if I served them loyally."

"And you *believed* them?" Isera retorts, her eyes cool.

"I didn't have a choice!" Her chest heaves, and her gaze slides in and out of focus several times. "I have no idea where it is. *We* have no idea where it is. And it's not like I can just search for it freely. I am kept on a very short leash. Always guarded. Always observed. They always know where I am and what I'm doing. So the only way I can get it is if they give it to me. And it's the only thing I want! It's the only thing that will give me freedom."

"But why did they even do that in the first place?" Galen asks, shaking his head at her in confusion. "Why did they want to fuse you with the Mother Dryad?"

"To raise the thorn forest, of course."

Isera, Alistair, and I all jerk back slightly in shock.

"*You* raised the thorn forest?" I ask. I feel like the entire world is tilting around me.

"Yes. When they fused us, it created a massive power surge as our magic combined. That is how the thorn forest around the Seelie Court was created." Agony floods her features. "And that is ultimately why we lost the war."

My heart hammers in my chest. "So if we find this Soul of Trees and use it to split you and the Mother Dryad…?"

"The thorn forest will disappear. It's kept in place by our combined magic, so if we split, there is nothing left to hold it together."

I drag in an unsteady breath as my head spins. I knew that Lavendera would be important. But this… This is beyond anything I could have guessed.

"But don't you see?" Galen begins carefully while still shaking his head at her in disbelief. "*That* is why they will never give you the artefact. If they do, the thorn forest will disappear. They never had any intention of giving it to you."

"What else was I supposed to do?" she yells back at him, her voice almost breaking with desperation. "We have no idea where it is, and I have no chance of finding it on my own since I haven't been able to set one foot outside the Ice Palace without them knowing about it. So it was either do what they want and there is a slim chance that they might actually give it to me. Or actively work against them, which they would hear about within five minutes, and ensure that they never give it to me. And I want it. I want to be free from this!"

My heart twists painfully again at the pure anguish in her voice.

"You think you've had it bad, being forced to do their bidding for two hundred years?" she demands as she locks eyes with Draven. "I've been forced to do it for six *thousand* years! I've lived for six thousand years with another person inside my head."

Insanity flashes in her eyes like bolts of lightning. "Do you have any idea how fucking crowded that is?"

All of her strangeness suddenly makes perfect sense. All of the odd things she says, the way she just completely disassociates from the world, the way she stares unseeing at walls while her mind retreats, the random panic attacks when she screams about how crowded it is.

It's because there is another person inside her head. And not just a person. An immortal dryad who is an entirely different species from her.

Another broken sob rips from Lavendera's chest, and her knees suddenly buckle. Hitting the grass hard, she gasps in panicked breaths. "I just want it to stop. Please, make it stop."

The Dryad Queen's features soften in a way that I have never seen before. Crouching down, she wraps her arms around Lavendera and pulls her close to her chest. "You have been so strong, Daughter of the Dawn."

Tears stream down Lavendera's face while broken sobs continue racking her chest. "I'm so tired."

"I know, child. But I need you to be strong for a little while longer."

I glance around at my friends. They all seem to be thinking the same thing, because they nod. All except Orion, who is staring at Isera with intense eyes. My heart jerks at the reminder of that. Orion now knows that Isera lied, which means that his promise to help us is no longer valid. And that means that we have lost the Unseelie Court.

But we have also gained a lot.

After seeing all my friends nod, I shift my gaze back to Lavendera and the Dryad Queen. "We will help you find the Soul of Trees."

Lavendera just continues crying, her eyes sliding in and out of focus as the Mother Dryad no doubt continues taking over her mind for periods of time. But the Dryad Queen lifts her head and looks up at me.

Her eyes are serious as she gives me a slow nod. "And you have brought Lavendera back to us, and in so doing moved the Mother Dryad out of harm's way, which means that we will honor our agreement. The dryads will go to war."

My heart stutters as both dread and anticipation swirl through my chest.

The dryads are with us. And with Lavendera no longer helping the Icehearts, they have lost their ability to use dragon steel. Which means that Rin Tanaka is now on our side, which in turn means that half of the other dragon clans are as well. We also know how to remove the thorn forest. And what's more, we have someone who was alive six thousand years ago. Lavendera knows everything that happened back then. She knows everything about our culture. She must know how the partnership between fae and dragon shifters worked.

For the first time in weeks, hope washes through my soul like warm summer waves.

This mission was a roaring success. At long last, we might finally have everything we need to take the fight to the Icehearts. We might actually win this war now.

With a smile on my face, I look up to meet my friends' eyes again.

Alarm crackles up my spine.

I scream as an arrow shoots straight towards Draven's neck.

CHAPTER FORTY-EIGHT

A fireball slams into the arrow, incinerating it one single second before it can pierce Draven's neck. But he doesn't even have time to look in Alistair's direction, because another hail of arrows shoots towards us.

I leap back as arrows speed through the air from all sides. Storm winds howl through the trees as Draven summons his magic to sweep them aside while Isera yanks up an ice shield in front of Orion right before an arrow can hit him in the eye.

Panic clangs through me as I yank out my dagger and whip my head from side to side, trying to locate our attackers. My shoulder still screams in pain, and exhaustion rolls through my entire body.

Battle cries echo between the trees.

Then a horde of dragon shifters sprint out from between the trees, swords and bows raised. The leader goes straight for Draven.

When I see her, my mind just... stops.

Diana Artemisia, leader of the Purple Dragon Clan, swings a sword straight at Draven's chest while half of her soldiers fire arrows at us from between the trees and the rest charge forward with blades as well.

Diana who is supposed to be our ally. Diana who is supposed to be all the way back in her homeland right now where she is supposed to be creating the distraction that made the Icehearts fly away from Frostfell.

How did she make it here so quickly? And why the hell is she attacking *us*?

Steel flashes in the corner of my eye.

Throwing myself to the side, I barely manage to evade the sword aimed for my head. Arrows continue pelting us from all sides. Ice, fire, storm winds, and tree magic flash around me as my friends work to block the ranged attacks while at the same time trying to fend off the people with swords while also trying to figure out what the hell is going on.

I yank up my dagger to block another sword strike while twisting myself out of reach of a third one. My heart leaps into my throat as more arrows cut through the air. They hit a shield of ice with wooden snapping sounds as Isera yanks up a wall on my left before they can reach me.

"Diana!" Draven bellows while parrying her strikes with his sword. "What the hell are you doing?"

"I'm sorry," she says, but she doesn't stop. Her sword flashes through the air as she attacks Draven relentlessly. "I don't have a choice."

Draven, who looks to be holding back since he doesn't want to kill someone who is supposed to be our ally, stares at her in shock and confusion while yanking up his blade to block her strike and sending wind magic crashing through the trees to knock the arrows away at the same time.

Understanding hits me like a punch to the gut.

While ducking another sword, I leap back and twist out of the way of another arrow. My head spins and there is a panicked ringing inside my skull. I don't want to be right about this. If I am, we might have just lost the war without even knowing how.

"Lavendera!" I scream. "Cancel all orders."

She doesn't reply.

Whipping my head towards her, I find her still kneeling on the ground, staring at the scene around her with wide eyes. The Dryad Queen is back on her feet, defending Lavendera with vicious fury.

"Lavendera!" I yell again while yanking up my blade to block another sword. Metal clashes against metal. "All the orders you have issued through dragon steel, all the orders that are floating around there in the back of your mind, cancel them!"

Her eyes snap back into focus. Giving her head a hard shake, she leaps back up to her feet and closes her eyes as she no doubt focuses on canceling all her previous orders.

Vines shoot up in front of her as the Dryad Queen protects her from a massive hail of arrows.

"STOP!" Diana screams.

The soldier who was about to slam his sword into my neck freezes mid-swing.

I whirl towards Diana right as she grabs the piece of dragon scale on her armor that protects her forearm. Her green eyes are filled with fury as she yanks off that piece of armor and drops it on the ground. She is still holding her sword, but she pulls out a short knife from her belt as well. I tense up.

Two steps in front of her, Draven flexes his grip on his own sword but makes no move to attack her.

With a scream, she rams the knife down into her forearm and slices a deep cut. Blood wells up from the wound, but she just shoves her knife back in its sheath and digs her fingers into her arm. Then a hiss rips from her lips, and she yanks her hand back.

"Get it out!" she yells, desperation lacing her voice, as she flicks wild eyes between me and Isera. "Get it out!"

I lurch into motion, but Isera is closer. Taking three long steps across the now flattened grass, she grabs Diana by the wrist and reaches into the wound with her other hand. Gritting her teeth, she pulls.

A sickening, wet, snapping sound echoes between the trees.

Then Isera pulls out a piece of dragon steel from Diana's arm.

I feel like I'm going to be sick. This cannot be happening. If this is real, it would mean—

"I tried to tell you," Diana yells at Draven, that desperation still lacing her voice. "Azaroth's flame, I did everything I could to make you understand. I tried to convince you that you couldn't trust me. I told you, God damn it. Right before you left my lands, I told you that I wasn't on your side!"

My entire body turns cold. Dread spreads through my every vein like ice as I stare at Diana while my mind tries desperately to deny what is unfolding before my eyes.

"I tried to warn you!" Diana yells again, her eyes wild as her gaze darts between all of us. "And now, you've walked right into their trap!"

"How long?" Draven begins. Disbelief shines on his whole face as he stares at her. He swallows. "How long have you been wearing dragon steel?"

"Since after I sent my people to kill you outside the Ice Palace. It was my punishment for that." Shaking her head, she looks between us all desperately. "They were playing you from the very beginning. They made it overly obvious that Rin was wearing dragon steel so that you wouldn't suspect that I was too. And now, you've walked right into their trap."

"What trap?"

"Azaroth's flame, we need to get out of here! Now. He was right behind me."

"Diana!" Draven locks commanding eyes on her. "What trap?"

"The archives." Fear blows across her face. "They used you to break the wards on the archives."

"What archives?" I ask, dumbfounded.

Then realization slams into me with such force that I stagger a step back.

"No," I breathe. But it's more of a desperate plea than a refusal.

"They ordered me to tell you that they were looking for the Gold Clan," she says. "And that Lavendera was in charge of it. All so that it would plant the idea in your mind that something important was happening inside a library. Then, when they had everything ready, they spread the word among their elite soldiers that Lavendera was locked in the library while working on something important, so that you would take the bait and break into it."

"No," I repeat, my mind still refusing to believe it.

"She's right," Lavendera says quietly. "After the Icehearts threatened to destroy the Green Clan's archives in order to make them swear allegiance, they managed to ward them. The library with the archives was physically in the Icehearts' possession, but they could no longer get inside. They have been torturing members of the Green Clan for millennia, trying to get them to drop the wards. It has never worked." Her gaze slides to me. "That all changed when they realized what you can do."

My heart jerks. "Me?"

"They had never considered it before. They've always seen emotion magic as a weak type of magic. But after the human rebellion you ignited in Frostfell, they realized that there is a way to break the spirit of someone who refuses to break." She gives me a sad smile. "You simply change their emotions so that there is no spirit left."

Staggering a step back, I drag in an unsteady breath.

"That guard who was handcuffed to the door of the library was a member of the Green Clan and the current guardian of the wards," she continues. "He has never broken under torture. So they used *you* to break him."

My head rings. I feel like my skull has been hit by a giant hammer.

But it makes sense. Goddess above, it all makes sense. The countless memories of being tortured by the Icehearts that Orion could see. The library that looked like no one had been in for ages. The Silver Clan soldiers rushing in to secure the building as soon as the door was open. Kander von Graf in the dungeon rambling about how he felt something fall. Even the door was fucking green, for Mabona's sake.

Alarm suddenly shoots up my spine, and I snap my gaze to Draven. "Kander was in the Ice Palace dungeon. He's here."

"That's what I'm trying to tell you!" Diana yells, and swings an arm out to stab a hand in the direction of the city. "He was right behind me! With the archives on the line, he will do whatever the Icehearts want. And they want him to—"

"Change our memories," I finish for her, dread pulsing inside me like a living breathing thing.

"Oh fuck," Alistair says.

Shock and disbelief and utter fucking rage burn inside me. I can't believe it. I can't believe that they managed to play us this thoroughly. Goddess above, how could I have been so stupid?

We have been such fools. All this time, we've been outmaneuvered. They used us. From the very beginning, they used us. We might have gotten Lavendera. But they got everything else. They lost the battle but won the war. With the Green Clan at their complete mercy, they can change our memories and make it so that we don't even know each other.

I drag in an unsteady breath. How the hell are we supposed to win now? For every step we take forward, they take two more.

Clenching my hand into a fist, I try to breathe through the panic and fury inside me. I am so fucking tired of being outsmarted.

Draven whirls towards Orion. "When will Grey realize that

we've had to change to the backup plan and open a portal here instead?"

The Unseelie King slides his gaze to Draven and opens his mouth.

A dragon roars above us.

I gasp as ice flames slam down straight towards us through the canopy.

Fire surges up from right next to me.

Throwing my arms over my head, I curl up in a ball to protect myself from the insane heat that crashes over me as a massive dome of fire shoots up right above us. The ice flames from the silver dragons above slam into Alistair's fire dome with a sharp hissing sound that makes steam explode through the air.

The Dryad Queen screams as the fire burns through the entire canopy above us.

Then the ice flames stop, and Alistair collapses down on one knee. His entire body sways and his eyes slide in and out of focus. Using that much raw power that quickly, and after all the battles we have already been fighting, must have depleted most of his energy.

With no leaves and branches blocking the way, I can now see the mass of silver dragons that hover in the air above us.

"Get down!" Draven bellows.

I throw myself down flat on the ground right before black smoke explodes across the grass. My heart jerks as Draven in his dragon form appears above us. His legs crush the grass only mere strides away from where we were standing. With a roar that rattles my very bones, he leaps into the sky and beats his massive wings while breathing fire at the dragons above.

"Stay down!" Galen yells while lightning cracks across the sky as Draven summons his magic.

More black smoke explodes above us as Galen and Lyra shift one after the other and leap into the sky as well. Winds slam down over us from their beating wings as they fly up to help Draven.

The rest of us leap back to our feet. Through the now missing canopy, I can see a mass of silver dragons speeding across the fields and heading straight towards us.

All around us, the Purple Clan looks to Diana. She hesitates.

"Help them!" I scream at her.

"We need to get out of here," Isera snaps over the booming wings and roaring fire from above as she turns to Orion. "When is—"

I react on instinct.

One moment, I'm standing on the grass.

The next thing I know, I'm tackling Isera out of the way as something green shoots through the air.

"Kander!" Diana yells at the leader of the Green Clan, who has suddenly appeared from the trees.

Isera crashes down on the grass from my unexpected shove but whirls towards me right as Kander's attack hits me.

The force of it is enough to throw me backwards.

I hit the ground hard and roll several times before I manage to push myself up to my knees again. My fingers are gripping the hilt of my knife hard. I glance down at it. But I appear to have made it without accidentally stabbing myself.

"Selena," a shocked voice says from a few strides away.

Looking up, I'm met by a pair of stunned blue and silver eyes.

I glance over my shoulder before turning back to meet her gaze again. My brows furrow in confusion.

"Who's Selena?"

BONUS SCENE

Do you want to know what Isera and Orion were up to when they were on their own? Scan the QR code to download the exclusive bonus scene.

Made in the USA
Coppell, TX
27 October 2025